GLENCOE

ECHOES IN TIME - BOOK TWO

By M MacKinnon

Printed in the United States of America
Paperback ISBN: 978-1-959096-71-9
Ebook ISBN: 978-1-959096-72-6

Library of Congress Control Number: 2023933311

DartFrog Plus
A division of DartFrog Books
4697 Main Street
Manchester Center, VT 05255

To Margaret Hastie – started as a landlady, became a lifetime friend. Thanks for your infinite kindness, inspiration, and support on this journey.

OTHER BOOKS BY M MACKINNON

The Highland Spirits Series
The Comyn's Curse
The Piper's Warning
The Healer's Legacy

The Echoes in Time Series
Drumossie

CONTENTS

PRONUNCIATION OF GAELIC NAMES

Faolán - Fill-an
Siònaid - Show-na
Seumas - Shay-mus
Domhnall - Dom-nall
Ailis - A-lis
Caomhainn - Koo-vin
Marsailli - Mar-saw-ly

GLOSSARY

SCOTS AND SCOTTISH-GAELIC EXPRESSIONS

Bairn - **n.** child
Bampot - **n.** a foolish, obnoxious person
Bonnie - **adj.** pretty, handsome
Braw - **adj.** brave, excellent
Canny - **adj.** careful, clever
Canty - **adj.** excited
Close - **n.** alley between buildings
Coo - **n.** cow
Croft - **n.** a small farm field and cottage
Dinnae fash - don't worry
Dobber - **n.** jerk, fool
Dreich - **adj.** dull or gloomy, used to describe the weather
Eejit - **n.** idiot
Fash - **v.** trouble
Gowk - **n.** fool
Greeting - **v.** crying
Haud yer wheest! - Shut your mouth!

Ken/kent - **v.** know/knew

Leannan - (Gaelic) **n.** sweetheart

Mangit - **adj.** crazed, confused

Maw - **n.** popular card game in seventeenth-century Scotland

Mince - **n.** mess

Mo gràdh - (Gaelic) **n.** my darling

Plaid - **n.** a crisscross or checked garment (Tartan is a specific type of plaid.)

Rig - **n.** a strip of land used for tenant farming in seventeenth-century Scottish Highlands

Roy - **adj.** red (Robert MacGregor was called Rob Roy because of his red hair.)

Skelp - **v.** slap

Sleekit – **adj.** sly, crafty, sneaky

Sot - **n.** A foolish or contemptible person

Wanton - **n.** a sexually unrestrained woman

Whingeing **v.** whining

PROLOGUE

FEBRUARY 13, 1692

The snow came faster, pelting everything in its path with a fury that seemed sentient. Icy flakes clung to her eyelashes, melted, dripped into bleary eyes, and froze there. The cold was a living thing, reaching into her soul and sucking each breath away. Was it a wolf she heard, or only the relentless wind, howling in triumph?

She was staring at death; she knew it. She could not last much longer in this wild maelstrom of wind and snow. She had already lost sensation in her hands and feet, and her mind was wandering into forbidden territory. It conjured up a roaring fire, raucous drunken voices, a cacophony of laughter, song, and camaraderie, and threw the images at her as a taunt. Only hours ago, but how quickly time twisted joy into horror.

A figure came to her out of the storm, and she whimpered in relief. Cloaked in light, beloved face shining with the promise he had given, the future he had drawn for them. His lips parted into the smile she adored, and he held out his hand...

She wrenched her tattered mind away from the image, knowing it for the lie it was. He would not come. Why should he? The smile had been a mask, hiding the treachery behind warm brown eyes.

"I love ye," those beautiful lips had said. "I will come back t' get ye, I promise. Jist wait a little longer."

Just wait a little longer.

Bitterness flooded her mind, colder than the stinging ice that beat at her frozen body. Wait a little longer. Until the fire dies to embers, until the ale is gone, until the hall is quiet but for the snoring of satiated men and the whisper of mice stealing the last crumbs of food from beneath the table.

Wait. Until shadows rise up and the night awakens to the swish of dirks pulled from scabbards and the retort of muskets fired close at hand. Until the gurgle from ruined throats and the sighs of dying men break the silence. Just wait.

The women were spared—or so she had believed at first. But that was another lie—their fate was much the crueler one. She and the others were pulled from their beds and led to the open front door. Clad only in their nightclothes, they were thrust into the heart of the blizzard.

Before the door closed, she turned and looked for him. Searched the hard faces of the men who had spent the week as honored guests. Just last night those faces had smiled, those hands now holding dirks and swords and muskets had waved tankards and chanted Highland songs with their unsuspecting hosts.

A figure stumbled into the doorway and stood, swaying. She stared in horror at the hand that had held and caressed her just a day before. Now that hand held a dirk, from which blood ran and dripped onto the snow. She whimpered and turned away into the storm, defeated. The betrayal was complete.

The terrified women had made little progress through the vicious storm—her fault. Her weak leg slowed them down, as it always did, although none complained. They were used to her weakness, and too kind to move on without her.

The chief's wife had succumbed first to the vicious elements. Blue lips without even the strength to move, limbs that refused to hold a once-sturdy body, she folded into the snow and was just...gone. Another sat down against a rock and crossed her arms in defiance. "Come back and get me," the woman said, although they knew it meant good-bye.

She and the youngest had struggled along together, until a turn of the head told her she was alone in the alien landscape of snow and ice. She turned back to search, but her last companion was lost, melted into the white landscape as if she had never been.

She could no longer feel her feet, and looked down to see that her shoes were missing. When had that happened? She limped on, heedless of her movements. Snow fell from frozen hair and covered the shoulders of her thin gown. The wind battered at a numb body, forcing her to her knees.

"Rest," it sang, "you have done enough." She rolled onto her side and then to her back, and stared into the abyss of white that swirled above and around her.

How beautiful it was! She could no longer feel the cold, so perhaps the storm was abating. It would be good to rest for a moment. Her eyes closed.

Words found their way into her mind.

"What is your desire?" a voice whispered.

She ignored the words, drifting on the edge of awareness.

"What is your desire?" the voice said again, more insistent. A stab of annoyance—must she answer for it to leave her alone? She reached for the words she needed and found them. Buried in the frozen depths of her mind, cold as the snow that covered her with its white mantle.

She forced her lips open, pushed the words out into the storm. "Revenge."

There was silence for a moment.

"That is not the right answer," the voice said. It was tinged with disappointment. "If you pursue this path, the outcome may not be worth the cost."

"I care not," she managed.

"You will become a revenant," the voice said.

She felt herself drifting. "A rev-enant?" she managed.

The words swirled and ebbed in the howling wind. "cursed to exist...but one purpose...vengeance."

"That is—all I want," she whispered.

"Granted." The voice sighed in her mind. "You will have your wish."

Snow swirled and settled around her, but she could no longer feel its cold embrace. Her thoughts drifted, broke into icy shards, and vanished. The wind wailed and surged, sculpting mounds of white in the stark landscape.

When the blizzard finally blew itself out, the morning sun glistened on the sea of white that covered everything in its frigid beauty. Nothing moved; nothing disturbed the silence in the glen.

CHAPTER ONE

ARGYLL, SCOTLAND - 1676

FAOLÁN

"Faolán Edward Dughall Campbell!"

Faolán froze, his wooden sword held above his head. His mother's voice resounded through the hall and drowned out the sound of his sister's wailing. It was followed immediately by the woman herself, as she sailed through the doorway and grabbed her son by the hair.

"How many times do I need t' tell ye not to battle yer sister, ye wee scamp! If ye hurt her, I'll hae yer heid on a plate!" She yanked his head back and forth for emphasis. Tears sprang into Faolán's eyes, but he blinked them away angrily. He was a man, even if he was only ten years old. He would never let the women in his family see him cry. His wretched six-year-old sister was doing enough crying for both of them.

Little Doirin dropped the stick she was using as a sword onto the floor. She stopped crying and looked back and forth between her mother and brother as she assessed her options. Her blue eyes lit and the wailing resumed, increasing in volume.

"I wasnae hurting her, Mam! She was havin' fun till my sword hit her elbow—it wasnae even hard. She's fakin'!"

His mother shook him once more and then released his hair. Her voice lowered to a gentler tone, and she crouched down in front of him, capturing his glassy eyes with her own.

"I ken that, lad." She spared a sidewise glare at her daughter, and the tears stopped like magic. "I'm just saying, ye're bigger and stronger than she is, and a wooden sword is still a weapon. Ye hae t'go easy, ye ken?"

"But she was a fuckin' MacDonald!"

Faolán's brown eyes widened as his words reached his ears, too late. Now he was in for it. Morag Campbell abhorred cursing more than anything, and she didn't take prisoners. He closed his eyes and prepared for doom.

He heard an intake of breath, then a choking sound, which resolved itself into a wheeze. He braced himself, but the blow didn't come. After a while, he squinted one eye open to see his mother, red-faced and gasping for air.

His mouth fell open. Was she *laughing*?

"Mam?"

She straightened to her feet and schooled her face. "Stand up, lad."

Faolán scrambled to his feet and waited for the inevitable. His mother sighed, but her hand stayed put.

"Well," she said slowly, "I certainly understand why ye were so eager to defeat her, then. But dinnae ye think she's a bit wee to be a soldier?"

"Never too young t'be a soldier, aye?"

Faolán turned as his father strode into the room. *Ahh, salvation.* Dughall Campbell understood—he had been a real soldier until he'd hurt his back. And Da hated the MacDonalds too.

Morag Campbell rounded on her husband. "Ye take this wee fool and see if ye can knock some sense into him—ye're the one put these ideas into his heid. And hae a thought to his language too. Don't think I dinnae ken where that came from!"

Faolán wilted. Mam ruled the house, and her word was law. She'd check with Da later too. When this was all sorted, he'd be lucky to get by with a skelping.

Morag turned and pinned her daughter with a gimlet gaze. "And dinnae ye think I'll be feelin' sorry for *you*, either, lass! Ladies dinnae fight!" She sighed again. "Let's go get ye cleaned up."

She grabbed little Doirin by the hand and hauled her out of the room. As the door closed behind them, a small voice rose in a whine, "But he *always* makes me be th' fucking MacDonald!"—followed by the crack of a hand and a renewed bout of wailing, real this time.

Faolán kept his head bent. For a long moment, there was almost complete silence in the room—the kind of quiet that is somehow louder than a hundred people all screaming at once. Then his father put a hand on his shoulder.

"C'mon, lad. Let's sit down. Ye're old enough to hae a man-to-man discussion about soldierin' wi' your Da, aye?"

Faolán's eyes widened to the size of dinner plates as he trailed after his father. *Man-to-man?* Warmth spread through him. His little frame straightened and his shoulders went back. *Man-to-man.*

Dughall led the way to a bench, pushed his son onto the rough wooden seat none too gently, and sat down beside him.

"Now, why were ye whackin' at your sister wi' your wee sword?"

"Well, I hae t' practice for when I join th' army, ye ken?" Faolán gave his father an earnest gaze. "An' she's th' only one who'll do it—if I give her my share o' sweets. I dinnae mean t' hurt her, really!"

His father patted his shoulder. "I ken that, lad. But ye hae quite a few years before ye need to worry about practicin' swordplay. And it'll be the time when ye're old enough t' ken that real soldierin' isnae about dislikin' your enemy."

He gave his son a long stare. "A soldier doesnae go to war because he doesnae like someone, lad. He goes t' keep the peace. It's verra different."

Faolán looked confused. "But—ye hate the MacDonalds, dinnae ye?"

Dughall Campbell took a deep breath. "Well, I cannae say I favor th' clan, lad, but I dinnae *hate* them. 'At's a verra strong word, hate is, and ye'd best understand it b'fore ye use it. There's a big difference between hatin' a man and hatin' what he stands for. Do ye ken that?"

"N—no." The boy squirmed in his seat. "It isnae the same thing?"

His father sighed. "Nae, lad, not at all. "Th' MacDonalds and the Campbells have been fightin' for hundreds o' years, so long that we oft times forget why. The simplest way t' unnerstand it is, our two clans hae different ideas about what's best for Scotland an' who should be king, aye?"

Faolán's eyes clouded. "Weel, but everyone already kens that. The king is Charles, aye?"

"Aye, but the problem isnae with King Charles th' man, lad." His father's brow creased. "The problem is that th' MacDonalds want t' *be* the king. They think they should rule Scotland, like their ancestors did once't long ago."

"The MacDonalds ruled Scotland?" Faolán asked, shock mirrored in his wide brown eyes.

"Weel, not all o' Scotland. But hunnerds o' years ago they ruled th' Western Isles, and they niver got over losin' 'em."

Faolán was entranced. "But why d' th' Campbells and th' MacDonalds allus fight each ither? Did th' Campbells want to rule th' Western Isles too?"

"Nae. Th' Campbells have always stood for th' king, lad. We dinnae think we're the lords o' th' land--we ken who he is--and we'll fight anyone who wants t' take the crown away from th' rightful king. Ye ken?"

"I—I ken." Faolán nodded his head. "So that's why we hate—er, dinnae like—th' MacDonalds, aye?"

"That's part o' it. There's a lot more, like religion

and culture, but that can wait till ye're older. Th' point is, each MacDonald is a man wi' rights and thoughts o' his own, just like each Campbell. So, I dinnae want ye sayin' ye hate all the MacDonalds just because o' the name."

He fixed his son with a meaningful stare. "And I dinnae want ye usin' yer wee sister to practice war-craft, aye?"

Faolán gave his father a stubborn look, then sighed, and nodded. "Aye. I willnae."

"And I dinnae want t' hear ye cursin', ye ken? 'Cause your mam'll skelp the hides off o' us both, and just like th' army, part o' bein' a man is keepin' the peace. Now, go find your sister and apologize. And steer clear o' your mother for a wee while if ye're canny."

CHAPTER TWO
ISLAY, SCOTLAND - AUGUST 1684

SIÒNAID

It isnae th' big things. It isnae a death, or a witch's curse, or even a monster under your bed. 'Tis a small, unimportant thing like a tiny hole in th' thatch, or an ember fallin' out o' the hearth...or th' sharp sting of a bee that has meandered across th' path you've taken a hundred times b'fore.

Siònaid knew the exact moment, the exact *second*, when her life changed forever. She had awakened to a tiny ray of sunlight coming through a new hole in the thatch. The rain that had plagued the island for a week now was gone, swept out to sea, and the birds were celebrating a new morning.

She could hear the sounds of her two older brothers arguing as they did every morning. The smell of new thatch mingled with the subtle, woodsy scent of heather and the smoke from the cook fire as her mother stirred the porridge. Such an ordinary day.

A sudden joy gripped her at the easing of the weather. Beitris was waiting; the horse would be eager to get out of the stable after being cooped up for so long. If she were lucky, Siònaid might be able to sneak out for a run before anyone noticed. She dressed in haste and tiptoed to the doorway of the room.

There was no one left in the sleeping chamber besides her—the boys were probably already wolfing down the porridge as if no one ever fed them, which would keep her mother busy as well. She threw on her gown and peeked into the outer room. The backs of two heads reassured her—but where was Mam? Probably bent over the cook pot. She took a deep breath and ran for the door.

"Siònaid! Where d'ye think ye're going, ye wee scamp?" Her mother's voice flowed out of the house as if it had a will of its own. Siònaid laughed and kept going. Mam couldn't catch her; at twelve years old she was the fastest runner on the island, faster even than the boys. There'd be a skelping later, of course, but right now that didn't matter. Beitris was waiting.

This was her secret pleasure, a chance to get away from family and obligations and be one with her beloved island. Together she and Beitris had navigated these paths until they could make the trip in their sleep. Siònaid was a MacDonald of Islay, descended from the Lords of the Isles, and the mountains were inscribed on her soul.

At the highest point on the trail, she stopped her horse and sat still for a moment, face upturned toward the morning sun. Down and off to her left the sea sparkled like gems, reflected light bathing the cottages in warmth.

She wished Da could stop working long enough to enjoy the sun and the warm summer air. It was he who had given Beitris to her and taught her to ride. He'd given her the freedom to enjoy her childhood, to run with the wind despite her mother's misgivings. She'd love him forever for such a gift.

Had Mam ever been young? It didn't seem so. She worked from dawn to dark, keeping the home fire going, cooking, cleaning the fish, going to the market, chasing her three unruly children. She seemed always to be tired, always cross. Surely she had never felt what her daughter was feeling at this moment.

Siònaid shook her head. "It willnae happen t' me," she told Beitris. "I willnae get marrit and have t' work my fingers t' th' bone. Ye jist wait and see."

Beitris snorted and shook her head. Siònaid laughed and gave her mount a pat.

"Believe or nae, I'll show ye."

She turned back to the path and pointed the horse's head toward home. Beinn Bheigier, the tallest mountain on Islay, loomed against the horizon on her left and cloaked the pathway in shadow. Siònaid saluted the mountain, grateful for its staunch presence.

Something buzzed near her ear, and she batted it away. Beitris let out a high-pitched whinny of surprise and pain and reared, throwing her rider out of the saddle.

Land and sky changed places and Siònaid was flying, turning end over end in a glorious dance that defied gravity. A strange euphoria, a feeling that she was one with the elements, ended with a crushing blow against the unforgiving earth and an excruciating lance of pain, followed by merciful darkness.

She awoke in her bed, gasping at the agony that burned its way up her left leg when she moved. Tears sprang to her eyes, and through them Siònaid saw her mother sitting beside the bed, head bowed and eyes closed.

"Mam?" A weak voice sighed in her ear, a tiny trembling whisper that she recognized in surprise as her own. Lilias MacDonald's head jerked up and a look of fright crossed her face, replaced quickly by that fierce protectiveness that only a mother can summon.

"Ye're awake! Oh, my darlin'. I am sae glad." Her mother's face wore a smile that was somehow more frightening than the tears—a fixed, rictus grin that was too wide and too frozen to be real.

"Tell me." Siònaid forced the words through stiff lips. She had to know--needed to know—so she could deny whatever the truth was that would cause that smile.

"Ye've had an accident." The words came slowly, as if dragged from her mother's mouth. "It was bad, darling. Verra bad."

Siònaid waited.

"Ye've been—sleepin'—for a week. The doctor was afraid ye might niver come back to us." Her mother's breath hitched and she swiped a hand across her eyes.

A *week*? Siònaid let her mind circle around the words. That was ridiculous. Just a few minutes ago she had been riding Beitris on the mountain path, enjoying the rare perfect weather in the Highlands. Her mind reached for some sense, shied away from it, came back and approached the memory on little cat feet.

The mountains. A buzzing in her ear, a sudden squeal from Beitris...she was flying through the air, and then—nothing.

"Wha' happened? Is Beitris aright?" Sudden fear for the horse gripped her. Was this what her mother was afraid to tell her?

"She's fine." Lilias' gaze was directed over Siònaid's shoulder, her voice bitter. "Th' damn horse is fine. Ye—"

Time stood still. Siònaid knew in that moment that this was the scene she would remember forever. The fear and regret in her mother's eyes, the clutch of a cold hand on her heart. The knowledge that she would never be the same.

"Is there somethin'—wrong—wi' *me*, then?" It was the hardest thing she had ever done in all her twelve years on this earth, forcing those words out into the air and giving them life. She wanted to reach out, grab them back, and stuff them away deep, never to be heard. That way they could never be answered.

Lilias MacDonald let out a shuddering sigh and met her daughter's eyes for the first time. A tear worked its way out of the corner of a bleary blue eye.

"Ye broke your leg when ye fell, darlin'. Th' healer set it as best he could, but he said the damage was verra great. 'Twas good that ye were asleep; th' pain would hae been hard t'bear. Ye may—ye may not—"

"May not?" Siònaid held her mother's eyes. "May not—?"

"Ye may not hae use o' the leg." The words dropped into the quiet room and spread out to fill the space, bringing with them a growing panic. Not have use of her leg? What did that mean? Not run as fast? Not dance as well? Not—walk at all? Suddenly a red anger welled up and drowned her thoughts.

"Just tell me!" she shouted. "What cannae I do nae more? Stand? Walk?" She gripped the edges of the coverlet and pulled herself into a sitting position, ignoring the stab of pain in her left leg.

"Am I—a cripple?"

CHAPTER THREE
INVERNESS, SCOTLAND - PRESENT DAY

*It is a curious thing, watching a
strong man fall to pieces.*
—Jodi Picoult

The stranger was quite lovely. She leaned across the table to talk to her companion, laughing at something the other woman said. Blue eyes, perfect teeth. What he could see of her figure was stunning. He'd never seen her before, which meant she was probably a tourist, in on one of the buses that thronged Inverness even in winter. Which also meant he'd never see her again. She was just what he needed tonight, enough perfection to satisfy any man.

Daniel was going to be that man, he decided. He stood up, and the walls of MacAlpine's Pub tilted. He shook his head and grabbed for the edge of the bar, but the room continued to shimmer like the Highland mist when it met the morning sunlight.

He looked for the woman, but now there were two of her. The twins wavered and became one again. The woman continued to talk to her friend as if she hadn't noticed. She split, danced away from herself, and became three.

Well, three were too many, even for him. A wave of nausea washed over him, and Daniel pushed himself away from the bar rail. Time to leave. He edged his way down the bar, concentrating his attention on the wooden door that led outside and away from the stifling atmosphere of the crowded pub. Only a few more feet; he could do this.

Somehow a chair leg became entangled with his foot and he stumbled and fell to one knee. A hand grasped him under the arm and pulled him up.

"Ach, laddie! Ye're fair bladdered tonight, aye?"

Daniel shook off the arm and lunged for the door. He hung onto the handle for what seemed a very long time, but managed eventually to shove his way out into the frosty Highland air. The change in temperature did not help his situation—he stumbled a few feet, bent over, and lost the contents of his stomach onto the sidewalk.

Keep moving; get away from the smell—c'mon, you're an expert at this!

An expert. Through the fog of alcohol, Daniel could hear the derision in his mind's voice. When your own brain labeled you a loser, how much further could you sink?

He swiped a hand across his mouth and forced himself to walk a few more steps, until the stench of vomit diminished to a more tolerable level. The snarky voice in his head congratulated him for his achievement, so to celebrate the victory he leaned against the stone wall of the building next to the pub and let himself slide down to sit on the sidewalk. *Just till my head stops spinning—just a minute.*

"Look at that! What is this city coming to, letting vagrants camp out on the street like that?" Daniel looked up to see two middle-aged women glaring at him. They caught his glance and turned away in disgust, before hastening their steps to get away as quickly as possible.

"I'm not a vagrant," he mumbled under his breath. Then he looked down at himself. His shirt had splotches of something that had likely resided in his stomach not too long ago, one pant leg was torn where it had caught the table leg, and his jacket and tie were missing altogether. *Wonder where those went?* he thought in mild surprise. He shook his head and leaned back against the wall. *Just a minute.*

When he opened his eyes again, a fog had settled over the silent street, obscuring the roadway and the now darkened pub. It was as if he floated in a formless world, devoid of touch, sight, or sound. In a sudden panic, he pressed his back against the wall behind him and felt the reassuring sharp edges of stone.

Through the fog he could see the faint outline of a street lamp at the corner, its small beam of light fighting to be recognized in this amorphous atmosphere. *You're not helping,* he told the lamp. *You're only making it worse.*

Two things found their way into his numbed mind. He was freezing, and he was sobering up. Damn it.

What time was it? How long had he been sitting here? He pulled his knees up and huddled into himself. He had to get up, go home. He had work tomorrow. Still, he sat, mesmerized by the surreal beauty of this alien environment. It felt strangely good to be so totally alone. Solitude was his natural state, anyway—his choice.

He had to stop this, though—get his act together. He wasn't an alcoholic, really he wasn't, although he had a sneaking suspicion he might be headed down that path. A sudden self-loathing flooded him. Living a lie was exhausting, and lying to himself worse. He had a job, a decent one, and even though he hadn't really earned it and didn't like it all that much, he couldn't afford to lose it.

He did what he had to do to stay under the radar. His family accepted him as the black sheep, some- one with no ambition who cared more for women and socializing than actual work, and he was happy to nurture that image. They didn't trust him with anything important, anyhow, letting him go his own way as much as possible. But tonight's little outing proved that things were getting worse.

He closed his eyes again and leaned his head back against the wall.

Just another minute.

"Are ye a'right?"

His heart jumped and his eyes snapped open. A woman floated in front of him. Daniel took a deep breath to slow his racing heartbeat and studied her curiously. Okay, she wasn't actually floating; it was merely an effect of the fog. She was young and quite pretty, if you liked the waif look.

Her black hair was long and hung loose around the shoulders of her white gown, and luminous grey eyes peered at him from a pale face. Except for the hair, she blended into the fog as if she'd been conjured from it.

"D'ye need help, sir?"

Her voice was soft, the words formal, and the accent one he'd never heard before. He struggled to answer, but all that came out was a croak. The woman cocked her head and studied him as if waiting for some sign of intelligence. She seemed prepared to wait as long as it took.

Daniel thought about trying to stand up, but before he could translate the thought into action the woman knelt beside him. She regarded him with that level grey gaze, and waited. One slim hand stretched forward and then was pulled quickly back.

He managed to find his vocal cords. "N-no. I'm fine."

A soft, musical laugh told him how ridiculous she thought that was, and the woman shook her head.

"I dinnae think so," she said. "Ye seem poorly, and ye're nae dressed for th' weather."

Daniel took another look at her. "Are you?" he asked. "I mean—why are you wearing that, outside?" His eyes flicked over the white gown. "Do you usually run around Inverness in your nightgown?"

The woman looked down at her dress with surprise. "Oh. No, I dinnae think so." She looked bemused, as if she had just noticed what she was wearing. Then she turned those amazing grey eyes on him again. "This is—Inverness? I dinnae think I hae been here b'fore."

29

Daniel forgot the cold, and the fact that he was sitting on the sidewalk in front of a dark pub in the middle of the night next to a woman dressed in her night clothes. His world narrowed to a tiny corridor where he and the girl simply stared at each other.

"Hmm," he said finally. "So—where are you from?"

An odd look passed over her face. She flinched and looked away into the fog for a long moment, as if she were concentrating on something. When she turned back to him, her eyes were damp. "'Tis nae important."

So, she didn't want him to know. Was she in some sort of trouble? Had she run away from an abusive husband? No, she was too young to be married, surely. His imagination spiked. A criminal? Or, had she maybe escaped from an institution? New Craig's was just over the bridge.

He gave himself a mental slap. Who was he to be passing judgement on someone? Here he was, ten feet away from the remains of his own night of insanity and still wearing the evidence, and he was wondering what was wrong with *her*? He snorted at his own arrogance, then focused on the woman and gentled his voice, just in case.

"My name's Daniel."

"Ahh." She nodded.

Daniel waited, but nothing more came. So, she didn't want him to know that, either. Suddenly the dark, foggy night and the lack of humanity on the street didn't seem so comforting. He pressed his back into the rough stone wall of the pub.

The woman's mouth turned up in a sweet smile that lit up her face, and she rose gracefully. Something else struggled to the surface and froze Daniel in place. From his position on the ground, he stared at her feet and felt a cold finger run up his spine. In the middle of winter, this woman was standing on the street with no shoes. He closed his eyes to dispel the image, but when he opened them, the feet were still there, still bare.

Without thinking, he reached out and placed his finger against one small foot. He jerked it back so fast he would have fallen over backwards in shock had the wall not been there. The foot was a block of ice. *How could anyone be oblivious to such cold?*

He hauled himself to his feet somehow and backed away, suddenly feeling the need to put some distance between himself and this odd person. He struggled to find words, thought of something clever, and lost it again in the fog swirling in his brain.

"Umm," he managed after a moment. He turned and scanned the street to see if anyone else had noticed the strange woman, but the two seemed to be alone on the sidewalk. He turned back, and gaped.

No, not two of them. He was the only one on the street—the woman was gone.

Daniel leaned against the wall and allowed himself to slide down to the pavement again. He probably shouldn't be attempting such strenuous activity as standing yet. His brain was assuring him that he wasn't ready. You shouldn't move about much while you were hallucinating.

That was new too. He had never seen visions before, especially not like that one. So now his forays into alcohol were conjuring fairies. He giggled, pleased with himself. At least he'd made her pretty.

He leaned his head back against the wall and let his eyes close, and there she was. Her image was so crystal clear in his mind that he snapped his eyes open again. Nothing. Daniel sighed, in mingled relief and regret. She wasn't real, and yet he could see her in his memory, every detail imprinted on his brain. He gave it up as a bad job and allowed himself to drift away.

The cold woke him again. A few minutes—hours? Who knew? He made the effort to work his way to his feet and regretted it immediately. Nausea rose into the back of his throat, but there was nothing left in his stomach, so after a minute, it receded. He leaned over, gripped his knees, and waited for the sickness to go away.

A thought swam into his head. There had been something wrong with his fairy's feet—besides the lack of footwear. One foot was turned inward in an unnatural position, as if she had been put together wrong. No, more as if her leg had been broken and set badly. Strange, in this day and age.

Would his mind add such an incongruous detail to a hallucination? Another wave of nausea swamped his senses. Yes, it might do, if this wasn't a hallucination at all. *If it was real.*

Daniel swallowed the bile in his throat. Why did he feel as if he'd seen those feet before? No, that was ridiculous, because he had never met this sprite in his life. She wasn't someone it would be easy to forget.

He closed his eyes again and willed the image to go away. One thing was certain—he was going to stop drinking. This shite had to stop.

CHAPTER FOUR
INVERNESS, SCOTLAND
- PRESENT DAY

*You and I are the remains of an unfulfilled
legacy, heirs to a kingdom of stolen
identities and ragged confusion.*
—Susan Abulhawa

A girl in a thin white gown stood in the
shadows. She wore no coat, and the gown
was damp. Black hair straggled around
her shoulders and down her back. She seemed
unaware of her attire or the temperature on this,
the coldest night of winter in the Highlands. Her
attention was focused on a man across the street.

She watched the drunken man struggle to his feet,
saw him stare at the place she had stood only minutes before, then spin around, nearly losing his balance. He shook his head, repeated the process, and
then began to trudge up the dark street, swinging his
head from side to side as if in search of something.

The girl knew what he was looking for. *Me. He's look-ing for me.*

She shrank back into the shadows and he passed by without seeing her. The man was not her busi-ness, although she still felt the pull that had drawn her to stand in front of him, to talk to him, to gaze into his confused brown eyes. An overwhelming ten-derness had swept through her, along with a desire to smooth that dark hair away from his brow and comfort him. Her hand had come up of its own voli-tion and she had reached out...

His eyes had met hers, and she had felt a jolt of recognition before she jerked her hand away. She did not know him! What was she thinking, to approach a stranger like this?

So—*where are you from?* His words had delivered a shaft of fear that pinned her in place and stole her breath.

Where are you from? Such a simple question, and yet so difficult, because she had no answer. All she could remember was the numbing cold that had surrounded her, filled her body and her mind, and stolen her memory.

"My name's Daniel," the man had said, and the fear inside her had deepened as he waited for a response she could not give. A nice name. She wished she had one to give in return, but the truth was she had nothing. Her mind was a blank—no, an abyss, a dark void with strange images swirling close enough that she could just glimpse them and then darting away. She didn't *know*. Her name, her home, how she came to be standing in her nightdress in the middle of the road in...Inverness, he had said.

She shook her head and watched the man called Daniel vanish into the darkness, then looked down to study her gown. There were smudges where she had knelt beside the stranger, but otherwise the garment was as clean as if she had just donned it. Clean and wet. In fact, she was damp from head to feet. *Bare feet.*

Where are my shoes? She gaped at the white feet, turned her ankle to study the sole. No cuts or bruises, just some dirt from the path. They didn't hurt, either. In fact, now that she thought about it, she felt no sensation at all. Not pain, not an ache, just...nothing.

She held out an arm, saw hands that were slim and pale where the wrists emerged from the night-dress. She pulled a sleeve up to the elbow, wiggled her fingers. She could feel the air surge around and between them, but it wasn't cold or warm. It just *was.*

Odd. Something nudged the edge of her con-sciousness. She had seen the drunkard, watched him disgorge the contents of his stomach before he slid down the wall and fell asleep. Watched people walk past him, giving him a wide berth as if he carried plague. Some of them laughed or sneered, shivering as they pulled their warm cloaks closer about them-selves before moving on about their business.

Their warm cloaks. That was it. They were dressed for cold weather. The girl looked at the street, at the icicles that hung like knives from the eaves of the buildings, and down again at her arm that had no gooseflesh. She felt a different kind of chill go through her. Not from outside—this was a slithering, damp iciness that came from deep within. She knew

35

that feeling; she had felt it recently, but she could not remember where or why.

Cold inside—not outside. Shouldn't she be feeling the effects of temperature that would cause warmly dressed people to shiver like that?

"Ye're nae dressed for th' weather," she had told the man, and he countered with "Are you?" The drink he had obviously enjoyed might account for some obliviousness to cold, but he *had* been shivering. And what about her? She should be freezing, yet here she was standing on the street in bare feet and a thin gown...and she felt nothing at all.

There were other odd things. For the first time she took note of her surroundings. Brick and stone buildings that rose into the sky, windows with shiny panes. They stared back at her and glinted with malevolent black eyes. Glass—it was called glass. But how did she know that? Did they have such things where she came from?

There were strange lights that seemed fixed in the sky. She limped over to the nearest light and found that it was in fact suspended from the trunk of a tree. No, not a tree—the material was hard and smooth, akin to the iron kettles used for cooking. The candles were odd as well, unblinking as if someone had frozen the flame in time, and encased it in more glass. She shook her head in bewilderment. None of it seemed familiar.

Her gaze traveled upward, and she gasped. She hadn't noticed before, but not a single roof was thatched. She knew without searching for a memory that houses should be roofed of thatch, and their walls made of peat. Here the roofs were covered with flat plates, pieces overlapping each other like the feathers of a bird, and there was no thatch to be seen. Even in the darkness, this was truly a city of wonders.

She did not know this place, Inverness. How did she come to be here? And where had she come from? Why couldn't she remember? Her memory was like a swirling wall of clouds that gathered before a winter storm, opening for a moment and then coming together to return the world to darkness.

With no destination in mind, she pushed herself off the wall and immediately stumbled. A look downward confirmed it. She had felt the dragging of her left foot along the dirt pathway without noting it, as if it were a part of her innermost existence, something that needed no reminder. She tried walking, her bare feet making silent footfalls on the wet slushy pathway. Her progress was unsteady because one foot turned in slightly, causing an awkward, stumbling gait. *She was lame.*

Had she always been this way? She didn't think so, though she had no reason for the thought. A hollow feeling, not quite a memory but a painful jolt of recognition. Taunts and jeers, sidelong glances and stares of mixed annoyance and pity when she couldn't keep up. Then the memory was gone as quickly as it had come, but the emotion it invoked persisted. Whatever happened had scarred her life and changed her forever. She couldn't grasp the reality, but it hurt all the same.

She walked along the path, following the direction the drunken man had taken. She had no wish to see him again—*liar*, her mind jeered. Well, it was reasonable, she argued back. He was the only thing that was real in this place.

He had spoken to her, acknowledged her, made her feel that she was real. He had asked her name and expected her to give him one. She held onto that, pushed it into her heart where it would be safe. Of course, she had a name! It would come to her if she just gave it time. Perhaps when daylight came she would find someone who could tell her how to get home to the people who knew her name.

Home. A laugh, devoid of humor, escaped into the wintry air. And how would she tell anyone where that was?

With a crack she could almost hear, the wall of clouds parted, and a memory slammed into her brain with a ferocity that sent her stumbling. She leaned against the nearest building and grabbed her head with both hands. Images surged through her mind like waves in a Hebridean storm. She paused to reflect on that. So, she knew about storms, about the sea.

The image dissipated, gave way to another. A croft. Faces set with hatred, angry voices casting insults, arms that reached and hands that pinched as they hauled her from her bed. Gunshots. Snow, bitter wind, cold like nothing she'd ever known.

More images flowed into her mind. A woman's face, cold and white, already covered with a thin sheen of snow. A voice, calm and even, offering her something—whispering words she could not understand. Something about vengeance.

Vengeance. Another image filled her head—a man. Dark hair loose and hanging over his shoulders, shirt untucked and bloody as if he had just been in a fight. Brown eyes huge with horror, hands gripping a knife that dripped with blood.

She cried out in pain and anguish, and the memories receded. Bits and pieces swam through her brain, none making sense. The man had to be hidden somewhere inside the chaos, and he was important; of that much she was sure.

The memories were there, hiding just out of sight. She leaned against the rough stone wall of the building, closed her eyes, and concentrated on breathing. In and out, the raspy breaths softening and smoothing out. The terror of the images began to fade, and with them the fear.

She stood up. She was alive. *Hold on to that.* No matter how empty her mind was at the moment, she had a past, a life, a name. She'd been someone's daughter, maybe someone's sister. She was real. The relief brought by that thought was a balm.

Perhaps the release of fear and anxiety was the catalyst, but the darkness began to thin and images took shape as more memories appeared behind her eyes. They were vague and misty, as if she were watching from a great distance, but she clung to them like a drowning soul who has found a spar of wood in a roiling sea. The images swelled and grew and surrounded her, and she held them close as they continued to unfold.

A place. Mountains reared against the sky, impossibly huge. She could hear the ripple of water nearby.

A river? A path, winding through gorse and heather. Clouds, hanging so low that the mountain tops were lost in their mist.

The rain of memories stopped like the slamming of a door. The girl looked around at the alien world in which she found herself and felt the fear rise again. An internal chill swelled and filled her body with foreboding. She sensed there were no memories here.

How had she come to be in this place, Inverness? Why could she not remember? What had happened to steal her memory? She felt a panic begin to build. What was wrong with her? She looked down again at her damp nightdress and reached for the thought, turned it over in her mind.

She could not feel the winter's harsh breath or the sidewalk under her feet. She had no idea what had possessed her to kneel in front of a drunken stranger, or why she had run away from him as if from the devil himself.

The last thing she remembered was bitter cold, numbing air. Why? It made no sense. Had there been an accident of some sort? There had been a voice, whispering that she would have her wish. What wish? She should have died in that storm, like the others.

Others?

And the chill was back, bringing with it a panic that spread through her body and wrapped its icy fingers around her heart.

She should have died.

CHAPTER FIVE
INVERNESS, SCOTLAND
- PRESENT DAY

*What he feared the most was that all
this hiding had made it impossible
for him to ever be found again.*
—John Corey Whaley

D aniel shook his head and regretted it immediately. This was the worst part of his forays into drunkenness—the sobering up. It all made so much sense, sitting in the pub. Just one drink to dull the pain, another to smooth the edges of his decision, and maybe just a last one or two to put a sheen on the evening. Didn't everybody do that once in a while when life became difficult?

Shite, who was he fooling? He was making excuses for giving up, and even he didn't believe them anymore. And it wasn't once in a while now. It had become a vicious cycle of attempted escape and nausea and recrimination.

But tonight had been worse than usual. First of all, he might be losing it a little lately, if he was honest with himself, but he didn't usually get this drunk. Most evenings ended with a nice buzz and a slightly guttered walk home—if he was lucky, a one-night stand with a pretty stranger. Not an embarrassing communion with a brick wall and a momentary conversation with one of Hamlet's weird sisters.

If she was real, who was she—that woman? Daniel stopped short in the dark street. More important, why was he still thinking about her? He seldom remembered women, out of sight, out of mind. He hadn't even gotten her name before she'd left, and he'd likely never see her again. So why did he care?

His memory conjured up the image of the waif-like girl with a musical lilt in her voice. He could have lost himself in the beauty of that voice. Hearing must be the last sense to hang on when you're blootered, because his sight had certainly let him down.

I mean, och aye, what was she wearing? He remembered something about a nightgown; he'd asked about that; he was pretty sure. Some white, flowy thing. Maybe she was a holdover from the sixties, or some bohemian artist type. Or a gypsy. The long, unkempt black hair, the bare feet, aye, that must be it. *Bonnie though, if she cleaned up...*

Now he wished he'd been more with-it. He remembered luminous grey eyes, a pale face, and not much else. Except for that voice. What had she said? Some comment about the weather, about him not being dressed for it.

He looked down at himself, at the puke-stained shirt and filthy pants, and cursed under his breath. He scrabbled for his hand sanitizer and gave it up as a lost cause. It was in his coat pocket, and he'd left the damn coat in the pub. Suddenly the cold night air assailed him and he began to shiver. Well, there was no hope for it, he'd have to wait till morning to retrieve the coat. Maybe he'd find his tie too.

Daniel pushed himself off the pub wall and stood, swaying. Tomorrow was still a workday, and he'd better show up on time if he wanted to avoid the usual recriminations from the boss.

It was a shite job...no, if he were honest it was a good one and he was lucky to have it. It might even have been tolerable if the boss was anyone other than his uncle.

Ranald MacArthur was a stickler but a fair man, to everyone but his nephew. He singled Daniel out and didn't mind yelling or even hitting him in front of the other workers, and then the man wondered why the employees under Daniel were less than eager to listen to their boss.

He shivered again, but this time the cold had nothing to do with it. His uncle's unfair treatment, annoying as it was, didn't disguise the fact that it was his own fault. He should be able to stand up for himself, but he was afraid.

Afraid of people. Afraid of talking in front of groups, of failure if he tried. Afraid of fear. Mostly, he was afraid of what happened to his body when he was forced to face the thing he was afraid of.

The thing had a name. After the first time, when his throat tightened and the room closed in from the sides until he felt as if he were trapped in a coffin, he'd looked it up. Punched in his symptoms —sweating, dizziness, nausea, racing heart—and the result had come right up. He didn't need to see a doctor to know. Panic disorder.

He had something called panic disorder—the fear of having a panic attack. Even the definition sounded stupid and unfair. Fear of having a panic attack could result in an attack? How was that even allowed? It sounded like medical gibberish.

There were lots of other fun things that liked to hang around with a panic disorder. He'd always been neat and tidy, maybe a little too focused on germs and the need for cleanliness, but he'd have to admit the last few years had seen a subtle slide into obsession.

And of course, that had a name too, obsessive-compulsive disorder. That explained his affinity for gloves and sanitizer, his avoidance of handshakes. He couldn't prove he had OCD, but all the signs were there. *It's on the Internet, so it must be true*, chanted the mocking voice in his head.

He'd skipped the rest of the medical stuff and scrolled to the treatment for panic disorder. Therapy with a qualified professional. Prescribed medications. Well, that screwed it; his uncle had no use for disability of any kind. He'd call him mental, probably hit him some more in front of the very people he was afraid of.

Maybe if Father were still alive. No, *get serious*. His father had written him off ages ago, practically handed him to Uncle Ranald to deal with, and now that Father was gone, his uncle was all he had. It hadn't seemed like much of a change at the time; the two men were brothers anyway, cut from the same rough cloth.

Daniel had a vague recollection of a different kind of father, a cheerful man who piggy-backed his young son, took him fishing, and rough-housed with him and his older brothers, who always had time to indulge his baby daughter Sophie. A man whose soul had disappeared the night his beloved wife died, leaving a cold, unfeeling shell and a house empty of love.

His mind wandered back to those early days, and the familiar bleak depression crawled in and swamped his senses. Daniel had been five when his mother died, and if it hadn't been for his older sister Iseabail, he might not have survived the loss. Izzy had stepped in, tried so hard to take Mam's place, and he adored her for it.

Daniel let a smile cross his features as he remembered following her around like a puppy, grateful for her smile and any kind word. If he'd had a tail, he'd have wagged it for Izzy.

After a time, the memories of his mother had faded and blurred, and he was left to face the new incarnation of the man who called himself Father. The young Daniel was grateful that the target of his father's grief and anger was his older brother Ewan instead of him. It was so much better to be ignored than blamed.

The family had fragmented, unable to cope with the abandonment of both parents. Ewan left as soon as he turned eighteen, and a year later Iseabail married and moved away. Josh left, and then Adam, until only he and Sophie were left. With only the two rattling around in the old house, it became impossible to avoid Father's scathing eye, and Daniel discovered a new companion—fear.

Had this been when it started? Or had it been when Father sent him to Uncle Ranald? It didn't much matter, the problem was *now*. His uncle didn't believe in phobias, or any mental weakness for that matter. There was no way he could risk this getting out, so he just had to do his best to hide the symptoms and avoid situations that might bring on an attack.

Medication was out. But there was one thing that never let him down, and it didn't need a prescription or a visit to the shrink. Alcohol took the edge off his fear, made him feel stronger, smarter. The occasional visit to the pub could only help, aye? He knew he was lying to himself again, but this was *his* life, and if he let it go down the tube, it was his business. He'd study this thing and figure out how to control it on his own, best he could.

And how's that been working for you, lad? Daniel shook his head again, but he had never been able to fool the voice in his head. *Alcohol's your answer? Ach, what an eejit!* He pushed the voice back where it belonged and forced his feet to move. He could barely feel his toes now, and the shivering was intensifying.

Something moved in the close next to the pub, and Daniel glanced into the darkened recess without interest. Three men stood together; their heads were bent in apparent conversation. None of his business. Just before he turned his head back to the road, one of the men grunted and swayed back and away from the others. Another of his companions reached out and put his arm around the man, pulling him into a close embrace.

A threesome. Ach, disgusting. Well, what do I expect, this time of night? Daniel hurried to get past the opening to the close and its activities, his thoughts returning to his own self-pity and his current situation. Things were getting worse at work, and he had the uneasy feeling that he and his uncle were headed for an explosion.

He wondered why Uncle Ranald had agreed to take him on. What had his father said to convince his brother that fostering his youngest son was a viable idea? Dour and taciturn, his uncle didn't suffer fools. He existed for the company and had no patience for anything that got in the way of its success, like wayward nephews.

The only person Ranald MacArthur respected was his son, Callum, the golden child. And who could blame him?

Daniel idolized his cousin too, although he had no illusions that he could ever follow in his footsteps. Callum was a nicer version of his uncle—just as driven and focused, but kind and patient. More than once he'd stepped in to cover for his cousin, earning him Daniel's eternal gratitude and loyalty. They were an odd couple, to be sure, but somehow, mostly thanks to Callum's efforts, they'd ended up as friends.

In the close off High Street, the three men stood still as if in deep thought. Then the one holding onto his companion let go, and the man sagged and fell to the ground. The two watched him impassively for a moment before one bent down and wiped his knife clean on the man's shirt.

"That lad," said the other. "He was lookin' this way; d'you think 'e saw?" he said, in a low voice.

"Dunno. I guess we'll have t' watch him just 'n case. If 'e talks, we'll be the last thing 'e sees, aye?"

They gave the man on the ground another look, and then turned and stole into the night, following the path taken by Daniel MacArthur. They caught up easily and shadowed their quarry as he made his way down the darkened city streets. They noted the address of the house he entered and watched until a light went on in a second-floor window.

The two men retraced their steps and reentered the close. Nothing moved; the man lay where he had fallen. One of his erstwhile companions stooped to put a finger against the throat of the still figure, then looked up at his companion and shook his head. The other nodded, and together they dragged the body to the bin at the farthest end of the narrow alley and hoisted it in. Without a backward look, the killers stole quietly out of the close and were lost in the darkness.

CHAPTER SIX
KILLIECRANKIE, SCOTTISH HIGHLANDS - 27 JULY, 1689

ANDREW

I t was the waiting that was hardest.

Fighting was easy, he was sure—a man had but to follow the commander's orders and let instinct take over. His father had told him with pride that the Highlanders' battle plan, perfected through centuries of war between clans, was a mindless, screaming bedlam that never failed to strike horror and fear into any enemy foolish enough to challenge the wild, barbarian men of the north.

And today he was one of those men. Today he would stand beside his father and stare into the eyes of the bastards who had dared to drive out his king. He would send them running back to that pretender, William of Orange—what kind of man would allow himself to be named after a fruit, anyway—and show him that James VII was the rightful king of Scotland, that the 'Glorious Revolution,' as William's lackeys called it, had failed.

Andrew MacDonald wandered through the crowd of soldiers gathered on the slopes above the Pass of Killiecrankie. There was a general air of excitement, as if every man knew that the time was upon them. Sometime today, they would be face-to-face with William's soldiers.

High up on the slope were Viscount Dundee's sharpshooters, hidden and ready for their orders. Even further up, at the highest point above the pass, Blair Castle loomed over the valley like a giant grey gargoyle. Blair was the goal of both sides. Seizing the castle from the Dukes of Atholl would give the winner command of the routes north and south, and the Jacobites had gotten here first. But they had still to repel the enemy, and Andrew was scared to his boots about that part.

Nearby was an old building, a storehouse of some kind, perhaps. Andrew stood against the stone wall of the structure and stared down into the pass through which the government troops would have to come. He felt by turns exhilarated and nauseous, his stomach a churning mess of anxiety, anticipation, and fear.

"Halò!" Andrew turned to see a lad about his own age grinning at him. The young man stood arms akimbo, looking as if he hadn't a care in the world. A wild mop of curly, bright red hair sprouted from under a cap, making him look like a mountain sprite.

"H-halò."

The young man bounded over to Andrew. "It's abit t' happen. We're goin' t' rout them howling' scabbies and send 'em back to London crying fer their mithers, aye?"

He stuck out a hand. "I'm Rob. Surname MacGregor, but most call me Roy, 'cause o' th' hair." He pulled at the tangled mass of curls and rolled his eyes.

"Andrew. Andrew MacDonald." His hand was grabbed and pumped up and down vigorously by the lad called Rob Roy. A surge of excitement seemed to translate from the other into his own body, erasing the nausea and anxiety like magic.

"My da's here," Rob told him. "He's been trainin' me, and now that I'm eighteen," he puffed out his chest "he says I'm a man, and I'm ready."

"My da's here too," Andrew told him. "I'm nineteen, bit this is my first battle. I dinnae want t'come, bit"

"Dinnae want t'come!" Rob MacGregor stared at him with uncomprehending blue eyes. "Why th' hell not?"

Why th' hell not? Andrew thought for a moment. He wasn't sure, really. All his life he'd wanted to be a soldier, a warrior like his father, but when the moment finally arrived, he had hesitated. Reality wasn't like imagination. Reality was killing, blood, and death.

He hadn't told his father about his fears. He'd dressed and followed like a dutiful son, but his insides were curled into a ball that took residence somewhere near his gut and wouldn't go away. He teetered between excitement and raw panic, and at times it seemed as if the panic was winning.

But now, caught in the honest gaze of this young man, he felt a change. The knot of fear that had taken root untangled itself and fell away, leaving only the anticipation of victory in its wake. He grabbed Rob MacGregor's hand again with both of his.

"Dunno. Must'a been mangit for a minute, ye ken?" He grinned at his new friend. "Let's show th' bastards, aye?"

A call went up from across the slope, and suddenly the chaos disappeared as if it had never been. Hard-faced men lined up and faced the mouth of the pass. The two youths wiped the smiles from their own faces, saluted each other, and blended into the ranks to find their fathers.

At first he saw nothing. Then, like a colony of red ants, the government force began to make its way up the narrow pass, moving like an inexorable tide.

So many! Andrew felt his mouth go dry. He gripped his targe until his knuckles whitened, and sneaked a glance at the man standing at his side, his narrowed eyes lit with anticipation. He remembered the same look in the eyes of Rob Roy, and his heart sank.

A hand clasped his shoulder, and his father spoke softly. "Ye'll be fine, lad," Domhnall MacDonald said. "'Twas like this for me, too, my first battle. I hae faith in ye."

Andrew felt the strength in his father's grip, felt the faith and the pride run down and through him. Da wouldn't lie to him; if he said it would be fine, then it would be.

Another command rang out, and he recognized the strong voice of John Graham of Claverhouse, the Viscount of Dundee. The Viscount was a legend; to his Highlanders he embodied the strength and passion of the Jacobite army. To a man, they knew that with 'Bonnie Dundee' as their leader, they could not lose.

The sharpshooters high on the slopes opened fire. Government soldiers, trapped between the steep hillside on one side and the fierce River Garry on the other, had little chance to return fire at the Jacobites who were protected by the stone building between the armies. They retreated out of range and waited.

And waited. Andrew was a bit disappointed. Was that all? The sharpshooters had done all the work, and now the sun was low in the summer sky and night would soon be falling, leaving little time for the pitted action his friend Rob had talked about. Why were they all just *sitting* here?

His father read his expression and grinned at him. "Just hold on, lad," he said softly. "Dundee's waitin'. Wouldnae do to have the sun in our eyes, aye? It'll be soon."

Chlanna nan con thigibh a' so 's gheibh sibh feòil!

The scream rang out over the valley. *Sons of the hounds, come here and get flesh!*—the Cameron war cry.

As one, the clansmen who had muskets lifted them and fired toward the pass. They threw the spent guns aside and reached for their swords as they ran toward the enemy.

Bàs no Beatha! The Clan Maclean war cry, *Death or Victory!*

Ard Choille! High Wood, Clan MacGregor's call.

Other screams rose, until a cacophony of sound filled the air and reverberated off the high slopes.

Dh'aindeoin có theireadh e! Domhnall MacDonald's voice rose in the scream that was their clan's war cry. *Gainsay, who dares!* echoed the voices around him, and suddenly Andrew was on his feet and running down the hillside toward the British troops, his shrieks joining the others in a horrifying aggregate of demonic sound.

The men stripped off their plaids as they ran, discarding the heavy garments in the interest of speed. As they neared the government line, they formed a wedge and piled into the front lines of shocked soldiers, mowing them down as they stood trying to affix their bayonets with shaking hands.

A few government soldiers rallied and stood firm, but they were swatted aside like flies by the maniacal Highlanders. The Jacobites retreated back up the hill, leaving the enemy to collect its dead and wonder what had just happened.

Twice more William's army was subjected to the phenomenon that would later be known to history as the Highland Charge, and by the time night fell, it was over. The Jacobites had won, but at great cost; they had lost Bonnie Dundee, dead of a bullet to the heart.

As Andrew MacDonald headed back to Glencoe with his father, conflicting emotions swirled in his mind. Relief. Satisfaction. Wonder. Pride. And under it all ran the uneasy feeling that something in him had changed. This was just the beginning, in this lust for victory he could lose his soul.

When he had run with the others down that hill, he'd given up his humanity and become an animal; no, that was not right. An animal killed to survive. Men killed their own kind simply because another told them to do so.

Something in the depths of his being stirred and uncoiled. Andrew fought a rising nausea and knew a fear that eclipsed the one he'd had before the battle. He felt soiled and ashamed to be human.

He was worse than an animal. In that mad rush down the hill, something precious had been lost and something else gained. When he'd thrust his sword through the first red-coated body in his way, seen the fear in the soldier's eyes, and then watched them go blank, a new understanding dawned. Andrew realized that he'd taken his first human life, and *he'd enjoyed it.*

CHAPTER SEVEN
GLEN COE, SCOTLAND – SEPTEMBER 1689

SIÒNAID

Siònaid was surprised to discover that, as she put miles between herself and Islay, the cloud of depression that had suffocated her for the past six years began to lift, until it broke free entirely upon sight of the glen that was to be her home.

Glencoe was the most beautiful place she had ever seen. The mountains that rose like majestic sentinels on either side reminded her of Beinn Bheigier back home, and for a moment she was gripped with homesickness that turned like a knife in her chest.

But here there were so many more mountains, standing together on one end as if trying to guard the river that flowed from somewhere out of sight behind them to fall into the valley as a majestic waterfall. The river must have begun in a high place, for it rushed by in a turbulent lashing of waves, as if eager to get through the valley and away to the sea.

Siònaid shook herself out of her fantasy. It was lucky she didn't have to cross that river to get to her new home. She couldn't see it yet, but Da had told her that Glencoe village was on the northwest end of the valley, near the river where it met a huge loch. So that meant it was on this side of the river.

She stole a look at her father and noticed he was biting his lip again. He'd been doing that for much of the journey here, refusing to look her in the eye and talking more than usual about mundane things. Not like Da at all. Was he nervous? Maybe regretting sending her this far away? Would he miss her?

There was a time, not too long ago, when she would have been happy to turn right around and head back to Islay, if only he'd said the words. But now there was something new bubbling up inside her, something delicious and hopeful.

"Da?"

"Um, are ye aright, lass? Th' leg isnae gie'n ye too much trouble?"

"'Tis fine, Da. I've been ridin' for on four years noo, and as long as someone helps me t' get doon, it doesnae hardly hurt at all."

It was the truth, for the most part. Riding a horse was the only time her leg didn't hurt. The pain that came when she walked went away and she was twelve years old again, riding Beitris along the forest paths in the shadow of her beloved mountains. She could forget she was lame, forget the pain and the embarrassment. She could fly.

It had been so hard to get her parents to allow her to ride again. Her father had wanted to put Beitris down, as if it were all the horse's fault. Only her mother's frantic begging that he might hurt his daughter more, that she might relapse into that terrifying state of hopeless apathy again, gave him pause. Instead, he sold her beloved horse a week after the accident and refused to discuss the animal with his daughter.

The weeks spent in bed after awakening were a black hole in her memory. Once she had thought she might fall into that hole, had wanted to. But it was true what they said, that time heals all wounds. The edges of the hole had contracted bit by bit, until the blackness existed only in her nightmares.

Her father cleared his throat, and Siònaid mustered a bright smile.

"Isnae 't bonnie?" She indicated the view in front of them. "How much more to Glencoe?"

"Just a wee bit more." Cormac MacDonald shaded his eyes and looked down into the glen. "It's slow goin' fer th' horses on this path doon intae th' glen, bit then we'll pick up speed. Domhnall expects us fer supper, sae we should gie started, aye, lass?"

"Tell me o' them now, Da." *Tell me why you're shippin' me off t' people I dinnae ken.* All he had told her was she was going to stay with his friend Domhnall MacDonald, to help with his son. He'd refused to say more, and knowing her father, she hadn't asked.

Islay had let her down. Everything there was a

59

reminder that she would never be the same, that she could not run, or skip, or dance. The real pain came from the sidelong looks, quickly hidden, and the whispered words that people thought she couldn't hear. So *sad...pitiful...th' bairn used t' be sae graceful.*

She embraced the chance to start again, away from those she had known all her life. People who thought they were being kind when they avoided looking at her or turned lest their eyes give them away. They couldn't know that their pity hurt so much more. She almost appreciated the few who made fun of her—at least they were honest.

She shook herself out of the memories and made an effort to listen.

"Weel, they're good folk, ye ken. Glencoe be all MacDonalds and Maclains, not like Islay 'at's bin most took over by th' Campbells." A curse under his breath was quickly suppressed.

Siònaid hid a smile. No matter how hard he tried, her father couldn't stifle the natural antipathy that MacDonalds felt for anyone named Campbell.

"Da, how did ye meet Uncle Domhnall?"

"Weel," her father sent her a sheepish grin. "I was a bit o' a rough lad in my youth, spent some time at th' tavern, an' such." Siònaid's stifled snort brought her father's head up sharply, and he glared.

"No more than any o' the lads, dinnae ye ferget yer respect. I'm a MacDonald, after all. An' it was all b'fore yer mam." He grinned, and Siònaid caught a glimpse of the unruly lad he must have been, before marriage and children and the hardship of life as an island fisherman stole away the glint in his eye. She leaned over and clasped his rough hand in her own. Cormac cleared his throat and looked straight ahead.

"Enyway, one night after drinkin', me an' some other lads came on some coos 'at had broken awa' from th' herd an' we thought 'twas only fair t' share amongst ourselves. Lads that are a bit tipset dinnae make good decisions, ye ken?"

He turned to Siònaid. She bit her lip, schooled her face, and kept silent, though it took all she had. Her father gave her a suspicious look, grunted, and continued.

"Well, th' coos belonged t' Duncan Campbell. He brought some o' his men to git 'em back, an' there was a fair brawl. One o' the bastarts—erm—lads—had his dirk at m' throat, and Domhnall come along an' kicked him 'n the b—" Cormac stopped, choked, and turned red.

"Sorry, lass. Got lost in the rememberin'. Anyhow, I dinnae ken him then. He was jist a MacDonald helpin' another MacDonald. But I owe him my life, an' I'll ne'er ferget it."

"So," said Siònaid, "I'm t' help these Glencoe MacDonalds? Doin' what, stealin' cattle?"

Her father gave another glare under bushy eyebrows.

"Ye're nae too auld for a skelpin', ye ken?"

She laughed. "Sorry."

Her father sniffed and shrugged. "Aye, Th' MacDonalds o' Glencoe have a bad name, I willnae lie about 'at. But Domhnall isnae a scoondrel like some o' that lot. He's a good crofter, works the rig an' minds his business. Nae time fer coos."

He went on with his story. "Ye ken wee Seumas is the one you'll be helpin' with. He's only nine. A sickly lad, so he cannae work the rig, and, weel, ye can read." He said it with a mixture of pride and awe. "He's a canny lad, an' Domhnall thought ye could teach him, gie him somethin' t' do."

Siònaid felt a surge of excitement. She could do that. Share her gift with another. Teach someone else what she had taught herself on an island where most didn't bother with reading and writing. Such things were not needed for fishing or harvesting peat. And who had the time?

A cripple had the time. The day a neighbor brought a child's book of letters left by a traveler and offered it to Siònaid had been the beginning of something magical. She'd held the small volume and gazed in wonder at the pictures that accompanied the letters, and for the first time since the accident felt a stirring inside her, a curiosity about something beyond herself.

She devoured the book and asked for more. Without her noticing, the depression and self-pity lifted and to her surprise, at the end of two years, she could read and write. But there had been no one with whom to share the joy she found in literacy, until now.

The excitement swelled inside her. She couldn't wait to get to Glencoe, where people didn't know her as the poor lame girl. Here she would be the girl who could read. Here, she could breathe.

The village came into view, and Siònaid allowed her horse to slow while she took in her first glimpse of Glencoe. A cluster of small croft cottages with cheerful gardens and well-tended thatched roofs dotted the landscape. Smoke rose from chimneys and spiraled into the clear air of the glen, and the laughter of children could be heard over the rush of water from the river Coe. Smells from the cook fires blended with the smoke rising lazily into the air—stew, porridge, black pudding.

Alone on the other side of the path stood a single croft house, larger than the rest. Cormac MacDonald's eyes followed her gaze.

"'At's the hoose o' Alexander Maclain, the chief," he said, "so his cottage is a wee bit bigger than t'others. Here's yers." He indicated the cottage next to them and tied off his horse in front.

Mine, Siònaid thought. *My new home; my new life.*

Her father lifted Siònaid off her mount. With the first step forward, her lame leg twisted and the familiar pain surged through her. The fantasy she had built dissipated and reality rushed back to taunt her. Tears sprang unbidden to her eyes.

Her father held her arm, worry clouding his face. "Are ye aright, lass?"

She shrugged off the hand and squared her shoulders. This was a new place, a new beginning. She mustered a smile.

"I'm fine, Da. Please let me walk alone. Please?"

He nodded and thrust his hand into his pocket. "Aye, *mo leannan*." He eyed his daughter for a long moment, and then a smile spread over his rugged features.

"I ken how ye feel, but know this—ye're my daughter, and ye'll never walk alone. Shall we go meet yer new cousins, m' lady?"

CHAPTER EIGHT
INVERNESS, SCOTLAND - PRESENT DAY

Strange...how you can be living your dreams
and your nightmares at the very same time.
—Ransom Riggs

The night began its retreat in the face of another bleak winter dawn. In the growing light, the girl could see small drifts of dirty snow lining the edge of the path. Ominous grey clouds hung low in the sky and obscured the mountains in the distance. A new day had arrived in Inverness, and now things that had been covered by the darkness were becoming clear.

It seemed to her that it had been winter forever. She could feel the wind and snow pushing against her tired body. She *had* felt it, hadn't she? The biting sting of the icy pellets as they battered at her face and body, the pain of her bare feet when she stepped on a sharp stone. Yes, she had definitely felt all that. So why could she feel nothing now?

She looked down at her feet. Dirty, covered with scratches and dried blood. They ought to hurt, but there was no pain. She placed one foot on a pile of snow. Nothing. She could feel the pressure of her foot touching the snow, but there was no sensation to accompany the touch. No cold, nor warmth, just—nothing.

She walked to the edge of the strange path and bent to touch the grey surface. It was hard, and wide as well. Wider than any path she'd seen before, and there were no hoof prints to mark the passage of horses.

In fact, she had yet to see a single horse in Inverness. There had been none tied up outside the buildings, no riders amongst the few people she had seen last night.

I ken what horses be. Bit where hae I seen them b'fore? The thoughts spun and teased, but produced nothing out of her ravaged memory.

The dawn air was torn apart by a wail that tumbled her backwards into one of several large barrels that stood alongside the path. A monster, its white eyes blazing, roared past the place where she had knelt but a second before. In its wake, the wind blew her hair into her eyes, and by the time she had pushed it out of the way and disentangled herself from the barrel, the creature was gone.

She scrambled to her feet on the smaller pathway beside the grey path as another monster raced by, and this time she saw red eyes glaring at her in mockery as it vanished into the morning haze.

Eyes in the back of its head, how could such a

thing exist? She stared at the darkness into which the creature had gone without a trace. Shock evolved into something else, a delicious feeling of relief that bubbled up from within, and she began to laugh. Now she understood what was happening here.

It was a dream. All of this—the strange lights, the lack of thatch on the rooftops, the smooth grey path, even the drunken man on the street. All of it had been conjured by her too vivid imagination. She gave herself a mental slap for being so foolish and then stopped.

Was the blizzard a part of the dream? Oh Lord, it had to be! The biting cold, the feeling that she might die, the voice in her mind...the strange man holding a bloody knife. None of it was real. As soon as she woke up, she would be back where she belonged, her memory restored.

She wanted to pinch herself to be sure, but something held her back. There was a part of her that craved adventure, and that part needed to see how far this dream could go before the inevitable awakening.

She picked herself up and studied the path with new awareness. Another monster roared past, but now she was unafraid of its red eyes and horrible shriek. Dream creatures couldn't hurt her.

She realized that the things were similar, but at the same time very different from each other. Most were a bit taller than a horse, but much wider. They rolled on black cart wheels, but their movement, despite the speed, was much more graceful than the wooden wheels of a cart.

As if to challenge her new sanguinity, a new monster lumbered into sight. It was huge, clad in some sort of grey armor, with a humped back and grinning mouth *in its back*. As the girl watched, it slowed at the edge of the path and stopped with a shriek. Men dressed in strange yellow clothing jumped off its neck and ran to gather two of the large barrels in their arms.

The men emptied the containers into the monster's maw, and then threw them to the side of the path before jumping back onto the creature's neck and moving with it to the next set of barrels. As it passed, the girl heard crunching from within, and a fetid odor assailed her nostrils. She shuddered at the thought of the teeth that could make such noise, in a mouth that produced the smell of rot and decay.

Then she burst out laughing. This dream was becoming truly ridiculous now. She watched for a while before continuing on her way. More people were out now, all of them walking on this smaller pathway. None of them paid heed to the monsters racing so close to them; it seemed as if the beasts were confined to their own path. She turned her attention to the people and their odd manner of dress.

All of them wore warm cloaks, and many had strange woolen helmets over their heads in riotous, mismatched colors. Everyone here must live in poverty because the legs protruding from beneath their cloaks were encased in ill-fitting trews that clung to them as if the wearers wore clothing long outgrown.

Her eyes widened as a young woman in a bright purple waistcoat walked by. The woman's legs were bare from the hem of the short cloak to below her knee. She wore black boots that shone in the weak morning light and reflected it somehow. *Indecent.*

"Mam!" a small voice called out. "Look at that lady! She's dressed for bed! Is she a ghost?"

A woman pulled the curious child around and hustled her away, but the strident little voice had attracted attention, and more people stopped to stare.

The girl looked down at her white gown. Even soiled and damp, at least it covered her body. In this dream world of impossible animals and nonsensical clothing, she seemed to be the only one who maintained any sort of propriety. She stared back in defiance, and the people averted their eyes and hurried ahead.

The pathway became a wide cobbled road where the monsters seemed unable to go. A great number of people were lined up outside a large manor on the corner, waiting eagerly for something.

The house's walls were made almost entirely of glass, and there was a curiously arched yellow crown shaped like the letter M above the lintel. As she watched, someone came to the door and opened it. Immediately the guests entered in a rush, as if possessed by a great need. Perhaps they were penitents, and this was their lord's home. It must be a very wealthy family indeed, to invoke reverence from so many.

Could it be home to Inverness's king? She looked above the crown, and read the name emblazoned upon it in huge letters—*McDonald's*. She ran the name over her tongue, and then said it out loud. The name resonated. It meant something to her; could she be related to the king? She looked down at her bedraggled gown and bare feet and a giggle escaped her lips, causing a passerby to turn and stare.

She ducked into the shadow of a doorway and studied the palace with the curious crown. *McDonald.* Well, she needed a name; perhaps this one would do for now. Yes, it suited. She could borrow it for a time, as long as the king did not find out.

She left the cobbled path and found herself once again on a smaller one, with monsters roaring by as before. A portrait next to a red door caught her attention, and she stopped to stare at it in mingled relief and amazement.

There! Kilted men, properly gowned women cloaked in warm arasaids. They looked familiar, well-fed, and happy. A shiver of recognition ran through her in looking at them. One of them wore his woolen bonnet at a jaunty angle, and a ruffled shirt protruded over the belt that secured his plaid.

A wave of homesickness took her breath. Time to wake up. She closed her eyes, pulled her sleeve up, and gave her arm a hard pinch. When she opened her eyes, she found herself standing on the same road as before. Monsters roared by; people chattered as they moved back and forth on the small pathway.

Someone jostled her and she was pushed into the doorway next to the portrait. At the same time, the door opened suddenly. She pitched forward and would have fallen, had it not been for a pair of strong arms that gripped hers and helped her regain her balance.

"Ach, lassie! I ken we're popular, but I never saw someone in such a hurry to see us that she'd fall at our feet!"

The girl looked at her rescuer, then around at the people in the small room. A stout woman in a warm woolen tartan gown smiled and nodded to her from a small couch in the corner, her red curls bouncing.

Another woman looked up from a small table. Tiny, dressed in a serviceable brown gown, she had brown hair and brown eyes that never blinked as she studied the newcomer. She looked for all the world like a small brown wren.

The man who had caught her stepped back. He straightened the plaid over his shoulder and hooked his thumbs into the belt that held it in place. Tall and broad-shouldered, she recognized him from the portrait outside.

"Are ye a'right, lass? Ye must be fair t' freezin'. Where's yer cloak?"

The accented words swept over the girl like the warmth of a peat fire. She gazed into concerned blue eyes and felt peace.

These people were hers; she felt kin to them, though they were strangers to her. They seemed so kind, perhaps they could send her home. Maybe they knew her; surely they could help.

The wren in the brown gown stood and rounded the desk. She clasped the girl's hands in hers and looked her up and down.

"Are you here to join up, then?" she asked. "You'd be perfect. I've no idea why you're not dressed for the weather, but we can fix that. We're glad to have you anyway." She pulled her new recruit over to the other woman.

"I'm Mary Duncan, and this is Betty MacBain.

Betty is our historian and researcher. The lad there who rescued you is my husband, Henry. He sets up all our events and runs the website. I'm the costume designer and the secretary. There are others, of course; you'll meet them later. We all wear more than one hat, and naturally we all have to work regular jobs because this is a labor of love, not a way to get rich. We'll have to get you fitted, but." She caught the stout woman's eye and burst into a peal of laughter.

"Ach, there I go again. First you should probably tell us your name, aye?" She stopped for breath and looked expectantly at the young girl standing before her.

What was wrong with the woman's words? They chased themselves around in the girl's brain. Whatever could a *designer* be, and what did *website* mean? Fear set its claws into her heart, chasing away the comfortable feeling of a moment before. A loud wail sounded outside on the path, as something roared by.

The girl looked at Mary Duncan. She opened her mouth and forced the words out in a whisper.

"My name's McDonald. I—dinnae hae a given name."

Mary looked startled, and then burst into laughter. "You'll be perfect, lass! You've got the speech down already, and MacDonald's a fine name indeed. We'll have to find you a performance name to go with it though. She studied the girl with the huge grey eyes.

"You look like Eve in the garden of Eden, you do. Doesn't she, Betty? All wide-eyed and innocent, newly created by God. What do you think?" She turned back to her guest. "Does Eve suit?"

The girl murmured the name. "Eve. Eve McDonald." She looked up and a tremulous smile broke out on her face. "Aye, it'll do." She curtseyed. "Thank ye."

Mary crowed in delight. "Ach, she's perfect!"

Eve looked from one to the other. "I'm still in th' dream, aye?"

Silence fell on the group. They traded glances, and a curious expression came over Betty MacBain's face. She heaved herself up off the couch and came over to stand in front of their guest, eyes narrowed.

"A dream?" she asked. "I guess what we do is something like creating a dream. Didn't you read the poster outside? Isn't that why you came?"

Eve fastened onto some of the words. "Creatin' a dream?"

"We're re-enactors," Mary Duncan took back the reins. "We do weddings, and school functions, and we'll even set up an ambush if you like." She dipped into a curtsey.

"Meet the Highland Players," she chirped. "Hire us, and we'll bring the past alive."

CHAPTER NINE

INVERNESS, SCOTLAND
- PRESENT DAY

*If I maintain my silence about my
secret it is my prisoner...if I let it slip
from my tongue, I am ITS prisoner.*
—Arthur Schopenhauer

Funny how the weather knew just how to match your mood. Daniel groaned and glared out the window at the grey Scottish winter morning, clouds scudding across the dark sky and rain pounding the pane as if in mockery of the war going on in his head. You'd think he'd be better at this, what with all the drinking he'd been doing recently.

Practice makes perfect. Ach—not when it came to hangovers, apparently. Wasn't there a saying about mixing your alcohol? He made a mental note to stop drinking beer and then whisky—or was it whisky and then beer?

And hadn't there been another saying—his own, in fact—that *I'm never drinking again*, or something to that effect? Right, that one. Only a few hours ago, if memory served.

An irritating voice in his head kept trying to interrupt the sounds of pitched battle, saying, *Perhaps you should listen to yourself this time, lad.* It just made his head hurt more, so he squelched it and closed his eyes.

The woman in the ridiculous nightdress swam into his mind, silencing the clamor and bringing a strange peace. Nothing about the encounter had faded with a new day. On the contrary, the image of his fairy was engraved on the screen of his mind with such clarity, it was as if she stood before him right now.

He kept his eyes closed and gave his attention to the image. Her grey eyes matched the weather outside his window, but rather than the angry roiling of rain-soaked clouds, they were a translucent light grey that radiated calm. He hadn't focused last night on how beautiful those eyes were. He'd been too intent on studying her bizarre costume and her lack of warm attire to notice.

But now those eyes captured his memory and held it, and he felt himself sinking into them. His headache receded into a dull throbbing that suggested he might just live after all, so he gave himself over to the memory of grey, no, almost silver eyes, and let his mind drift for a few minutes more.

The questions that whirled constantly below the surface worked their way to the top again. Who was she? Where had she come from, and where had she gone? Was she all right? He sat up suddenly, gasped, and grabbed his head again. The pounding faded, and the query resumed. Why had she been dressed so inappropriately...and why had she not seemed to care?

Having once again received no helpful answers to the barrage of questions running amok in his head, Daniel gave it up as a bad job and forced himself to sit up on the edge of his bed. He fumbled for his phone on the nightstand and winced at the time.

Already an hour late for work; he'd be hearing it for sure. He looked at his pillow with longing, but it didn't seem so inviting anymore. He glared at it, heaved a sigh, and reached for his phone on the nightstand. No help for it—he had to go. He punched in a button on the phone and listened while it dialed his cousin's number.

Callum MacArthur's voice came over the phone—light and mocking. "Another bad night, cousin? I peeked into your office and was so surprised to see you weren't there."

Daniel registered the sarcasm and bit back a retort. He closed his eyes and took a deep breath.

"Where should I go?"

Without further question, Callum lowered his voice and said, "Go to the site. Father's here this morning, and he's already been asking for you. I'll tell him you're there."

"Shite." Daniel clicked out of the call and stumbled into the bathroom for a quick shower. Thank God for Callum. He could put up with any amount of teasing if it came with the support his cousin always gave.

Half an hour later he pulled his ancient Vauxhall into the makeshift car park and stashed it between a delivery truck and a concrete mixer. He fished a clipboard out of his briefcase, locked the car, and ambled onto the work site, hoping he looked like someone who'd been there for at least two hours.

The blow came from nowhere, spinning him around to face his assailant.

"Uncle!"

"Who do you think you're fooling, you eejit?" Ranald MacArthur's hand raised for another punch and Daniel cringed away. "You think I don't know when Callum's covering for you?" He leaned forward and sniffed. "Shite, you smell like a tavern, and your eyes are as red as stoplights. When are you going to get it together and do something productive?"

"I'm all caught up, sir. The file's on your desk." It was, because Callum had told him yesterday he'd put it there.

"Good. Then you'll be ready to present at the board meeting next week." His uncle gave him a disgusted glare and stalked off.

The drive back to the office was accompanied by a growing sense of doom. He could feel sweat gathering under his armpits, and his hands trembled on the wheel. He sat in the garage while chills ran up and down his back and his heart pounded, a sure sign that an attack was imminent. Gripping the wheel, he focused on his breathing—long, deep inhale, hold it at the top, long exhale, repeat.

He was always mildly surprised when something so simple worked. After a time, his heart rate returned to normal, his face cooled, and only an echo of fear remained to remind him that the real problem lay ahead. The board meeting.

He was expected to speak, to give a report, in front of people. It was impossible. The last time this had happened he had stood like a deer caught in the headlamps until the whispering from his audience became unbearable, then he'd run out of the room just in time to make it to the toilets and throw up.

His uncle hadn't spoken to him for weeks. He'd backed off the presentations though, and for a while, things had improved. Daniel didn't mind doing the necessary research, and on paper, his reports were solid. The one Callum had placed on Ranald MacArthur's desk really was Daniel's work, but he'd stalled in delivering it because the prospect of another session in front of the board loomed like a storm cloud.

The senior MacArthur thought the problem was laziness. *You're just unprepared*, he'd said more than once, *Why else would you refuse to deliver a simple report?* Uncle Ranald was convinced his nephew didn't want to do the work given him because he'd rather hang out in the pubs and pick up women. Daniel couldn't argue with the reasoning, and he couldn't tell his uncle the truth.

Sometimes he wished he could just be sacked like ordinary employees; it had to be better than this. He suspected his uncle got a perverse pleasure out of his failures, so he could vent his frustrations by using his nephew as a punching bag. If Daniel had a shred of self-confidence left, he would have quit long ago. What kept him from cutting and running was the knowledge that it was all his own fault.

Maybe he could tell Callum about his situation. He knew his cousin was bewildered by his behavior, but he was too loyal to say anything. Yes, he'd tell him soon; when he'd learned how to handle his condition and defeated it. He would cure himself, somehow, and no one would ever need to know why he avoided crowds, why he never had a lasting relationship, why he resorted so often to alcohol to solve his problems.

He made it up to the third-floor offices of MacArthur Construction without running into anyone. As he walked through the reception area, he noticed the three secretaries gathered around the water cooler, gossiping about something. They gave him a distracted glance as he walked by, and then returned to their discussion.

"He didn't call her?"

"No, they were supposed to meet at the Castle Tavern for drinks, but she said he never showed. Bastard. She waited all night, and he never once texted or answered her calls."

"Ach, shame. Liam texted me that he didn't show up at the site this morning, either. Maybe he quit."

"I thought this one was a keeper, though. She has the worst luck, aye?"

The voices receded as Daniel made his way to his tiny office at the end of the hall. For a minute, he'd thought he was the bastard they were talking about. Had he promised to meet someone last night? Wouldn't be the first time, and he'd been in no condition to remember.

But he never made plans for a round two with any woman, and anyway the secretaries had seen him come in, so it couldn't be him they were talking about. See? He was a bastard, but not that kind of bastard. At least he didn't give them hope that there could be something more. He wondered vaguely who the jilted friend was, and decided he didn't care. He had enough problems of his own.

He wiped down his desk, straightened his calendar, and added a pencil to those already lined up in a neat row. The next hour was spent going over his copy of the report he was supposed to present tomorrow. He stood in front of the mirror and practiced until he decided he sounded reasonably decent. Maybe he could pull this off after all. There was a first time for everything.

He was pulled out of his self-congratulation by a loud clapping and turned to see Callum grinning at him from the doorway.

"Jesus! Don't you ever knock?" Daniel felt his face heating.

"I did. Some eejit was talking too loud to hear, I guess."

"Shut up. Um...how did I sound?" He hated the pleading note he heard in his own voice. Callum gave him a sharp look.

"Passable. So, you couldn't get out of it this time, eh?" Daniel didn't miss the look of concern on his cousin's face.

"When did I ever have a chance to get my own opinion in? I was lucky to get by with just one punch. And thanks for texting me that the boss left for the site, ye wee gowk."

"Wasn't my turn to watch him," Callum shrugged.

"Was there something you needed?" Daniel said in an icy tone.

"Just wondered—weren't you at MacAlpine's last night?"

"Aye, for a while. Why?"

"Cops pulled a body out of a bin in the close this morning."

Daniel's eyes widened, and his heart stood still. "A man or a woman?"

"Don't know. Heard it on the way in. But you be careful, aye? Doesn't do to be stumbling home in the dark these days, ye ken?" Callum turned to leave, shaking his head. "This used to be such a quiet city. Ach!"

Daniel was left staring at the door of his office. A feeling of dread spread from his stomach and wrapped itself around his heart like a fist.

Cops pulled a body out of a bin in the close this morning.

A vision of a woman with silver-grey eyes swam out of his mind. Eyes luminous like moonlight and shining with life. A pale face quirked in a mocking smile as she made fun of him.

Daniel made his way back to his chair and sank into it. The report he was supposed to be practicing sat in front of him, but all thoughts of board meetings and angry uncles had fled with Callum's news. He pulled his laptop over and entered a query in the search bar.

A brief notice came up; the same thing Callum had told him. A body had been found early this morning in a rubbish bin at the end of the close next to MacAlpine's Pub. Nothing else, just the statement that the police were investigating. Daniel closed the laptop and stared at it.

No. It couldn't be his fairy. It just couldn't.

CHAPTER TEN
INVERNESS, SCOTLAND - PRESENT DAY

So, you have to keep it together, kid...
you can't let them see this. You
can't let these cracks show.
—Tahereh Mafi

allum MacArthur stood in the center of the darkened construction site and studied the nearly finished office building. The structure gaped, a huge zombie with unblinking black holes for eyes, as if it were mocking him somehow. Scaffolding clung to one side like a giant spider. He felt a shiver run down his spine.

What was wrong with him, making a building into a living creature? A malevolent one, at that. He had never been given to fantasy, and he wasn't about to start now. Callum shook off the feeling and studied the construction with a workman's eye.

Most of the three-story edifice was finished now. The walls and slabs were poured. The scaffolding was due to come down as soon as the windows were placed and then the cosmetic work done to imitate the age of the surrounding structures. Everything was coming along as it should.

Callum prided himself on his attention to detail, had always been able to spot the joint that didn't meet precisely where it should, the almost undetectable tilt in a bearing wall, or the tiny leak from a cracked water pipe. It was part of what had made him the youngest vice president in the long history of MacArthur Construction.

The structure stood tall and proud in the dimming light of dusk, proclaiming sovereignty over the older buildings on the street. Its new skin of concrete, pristine and flawless, shone in the growing darkness as if to deny any attempt to cast it into shadow.

Here he was again, giving life to an inanimate object. Callum shivered again. Time to get off this damn work site and out of his own head. Without a backward look, he turned his back on the nearly finished structure and strode away.

He pulled his Land Rover out onto Millburn Road, empty at this time of day, and drove back into town past Morrisons and the Eastgate Shopping Centre without paying attention to the familiar landmarks. He needed sleep, but that wasn't going to happen anytime soon. He skirted the tourist area and drove along the river until he passed the Grieg Street Bridge and parked on Castle Road.

He knew what was bothering him. It was stored safely away in a corner of his brain that allowed no access to anyone but himself. At rare moments like this when it reared its reptilian head, what he really wanted was a drink.

Callum knew just whom to call for that.

He pulled his cell phone out of his pocket and dialed the familiar number. Daniel was probably already ensconced in a corner of one of his favorite pubs, but maybe he could catch him before he was totally blootered and share a pint or two.

No one picked up, and after a few rings, the call went to voicemail. Callum ignored the invitation to leave a message after the beep and clicked off. It wasn't unlike his cousin to ignore calls when he was drinking. He'd just have to check out the usual haunts if he wanted to find him, and he wasn't all that sure he really wanted to anymore.

What the hell was wrong with Daniel, anyway? He was smart, good-looking—any number of women would attest to that, in the same breath that they cursed him out—and he had a good job which he seemed bent on throwing away. He gave out all the signs of a pleasure-loving playboy. Someone happy enough just to flit through life, from bar to bar and woman to woman.

But he wasn't happy. Callum knew Daniel better than anybody, even his own family, and he could see the signs of desperation in his cousin as if they were written in blood on his forehead. Daniel was on a downward path of self-destruction, and he had put up a wall that was harder to breach than the concrete of the new building on Millburn.

Callum sighed, locked the car, and walked the short distance to the high street. MacAlpine's was less crowded than usual, perhaps because of the body that had been found in the close next door, but still the bar was lined with locals bent on chasing away the day's woes and tourists taking selfies of themselves in the oldest tavern in Inverness.

Daniel wasn't there. He wasn't in The Keg or Bar One either. Callum debated whether it was worth walking to the Castle Tavern, and decided he no longer needed that pint. His cousin would have to solve his own problems. He walked back to his car, put it in gear, and began to drive.

The streets of Inverness emptied early on weeknights, especially during the winter. An odd sense of foreboding invaded his mind as he drove through the darkness toward—what? He looked up suddenly, startled to find he was pulling into the garage under his office building, with no recollection of the journey.

And Daniel's the one with the problem? Callum sighed to himself, but climbed out and took the stairs to the third floor. There was always work waiting for him, and he wasn't in the mood to go home to his empty apartment. He walked through the dark reception area and down the hall toward his office and stopped.

There was a light under the door of Daniel's office. Callum pursed his lips. The wee git had forgotten to turn off the lights again. Da would have a fit if he saw that when he came in tomorrow. He walked to the door and opened it, reaching for the switch.

Daniel sat at his desk; hands fisted in his hair. He looked up, and Callum reeled back at the sight of his cousin's face.

He looked haunted. The circles under his eyes had darkened and his face was the color of the papers strewn over the desktop. He attempted a smile, a rictus grimace that reminded Callum of the Joker in the Batman movies. He brought up a shaking hand, let it fall again, and put his face back in his hands.

"Daniel? Good God, lad, what's the matter?"

Daniel's shoulders slumped. From between his fingers, muffled words found their way into the room.

"I can't do it, Cal. I know this stuff from front to back, but I can't do it."

"Why not?" Callum moved forward to stand in front of the desk. "I heard some of it yesterday when you were practicing. You have your shite together—you were great!"

Daniel made a warding gesture, and raised his eyes to look at his cousin.

"I know. I know all that, but I can't do it!"

Callum tried for levity. "Can't do what, you numpty? Just give the report the way you did in here, for Christ's sake."

Daniel stood up. "I can't. There will be people there. The whole board will be there."

"Weel, noo, and isn't that what a board meeting is? What the hell am I missing here?" Callum ran his hand through his hair in frustration.

"I—I have—a thing."

Callum restrained the urge to jump over the desk and throttle his cousin.

"You—have a thing. Well, that explains it then." The sarcasm dripped off his tongue and was lost in the despair written on his cousin's face.

Daniel sat back in the chair. "Aye. A thing. I panic when I have to face people. I freeze and start sweating and my heart feels as if it's going to jump out of my chest."

"You mean, like stage fright?" Callum asked. "That's pretty normal when you're the center of attention, isn't it?"

"No! I mean, like I think I'm going to die. I can't breathe and I get dizzy and sometimes I pass out. It has a name." He put his hands back over his face. "I have panic disorder."

Callum stared at him in shock. Then he pulled a chair out from the small table in the corner and sat down in front of the desk.

"Why didn't you tell me this before?"

Daniel shook his head. "I don't know. You've taken on so many of my problems already, and what can you do anyway? Telling you won't make it go away."

Callum studied his cousin's drawn face. Then he pulled the open laptop around to face himself and typed in a few keywords. He read for a long time. Then he looked up from the computer.

"That's why you ran out of the room the last time? When Da asked you to report on the electrical subcontract?"

"Aye. I just made it to the toilets before I threw up. And that was just one committee. This time he wants me to stand in front of the whole board and do a formal report! I can't!" The last came out as a wail.

"Are you sure about this? Do you have a diagnosis?"

"No. I looked it up. But I know that's what it is. There's medication for it and therapy."

"So? Have you done any of that?"

Daniel laughed, a dry bark devoid of humor. "Aye, right, and have Uncle find out? He hates me enough already. I'll take care of it myself, thank you."

Callum reflected. Part of what Daniel said was right; Ranald MacArthur would find out. He always did. And he wouldn't accept it.

"He doesn't hate you, Dan. He just doesn't get you. Neither do I, really—wait! Is that why you've been drinking so much?"

Daniel shrugged. "I haven't—"

Callum gave him a whack on the shoulder. "Don't lie. Not to yourself and not to me." He went back to the computer screen. "It says here you avoid situations that might cause you to panic."

"Check."

"You might avoid large open spaces, or enclosed spaces." He looked up. "Doesn't that cover just about everything?"

"Aye." Daniel's face was tight. "Just about everything."

"Do you know when this started?" Callum bent his head to the computer and tapped the keys. "It says here that there might have been a trigger of some sort." He looked up. "Makes sense—I don't remember you being such a git when we were younger." He ducked Daniel's swipe and returned to the laptop.

"I dinnae ken about a trigger, but I remember the first time it happened," Daniel said. "I was in the bus station, coming home from uni for Christmas. People were rushing around to get to wherever they were going, and all of a sudden, the walls started coming in on me and I couldn't breathe. I thought I was having a heart attack and I couldn't get anybody to listen to me and then I passed out." He shuddered at the memory. "And I think it's getting worse. I've started hallucinating."

"What?"

Daniel studied his cousin for a long moment, took a deep breath, and told him about the strange woman in the nightgown. To his mingled relief and annoyance, Callum didn't seem terribly impressed by the story.

"You were drunk, Dan. You probably ran into a homeless person and decided she was an angel or something."

"I never said she was an angel!" Daniel clenched his teeth. "She was wearing a nightgown in the middle of winter, and she had bare feet."

"A-hum."

"And then she disappeared!"

Callum put his hands up in defense. "A'right, lad. She was a homeless, sleep-walking, hippy angel. I get it. And I'm sure the fact you were steaming drunk had nothing to do with it."

"Shut. Up. I knew I shouldn't have told you."

Callum held up one hand in apology. "Sorry. Seriously, Daniel, I'm glad you told me about this, though I'm a bit scunnered you didn't do it sooner. I'll help as much as I can, but let's start with the drinking. Stop hanging out in the pubs, or take me with you when you go, aye?"

"I've given up drinking."

"As of when, two nights ago?"

Daniel shrugged. "Have to start sometime. I can do it. It's not like I'm an alcoholic."

Callum gave him his best side-eye. "Right. Let's go with that."

On Millburn Road, the MacArthur work site stood silent and empty, except for the low moan of the winter wind that blew through the empty windows of the concrete building. The wind drowned out the soft sound of a scurrying night creature near the bins at the edge of the site, and muffled the creak of a tiny crack as it appeared high on a bearing wall.

CHAPTER ELEVEN

PERTH, SCOTLAND - 1690

FAOLÁN

The door swung open to hit the wall with a bang and Eòin Arthur swept into the room like a thunder gust, waving his arms. Nobody moved; they were used to it.

"Did ye hear?"

Not a single head raised from the table where five soldiers were engrossed in a heated game of Maw.

"Are ye plannin' t' take all night, then?" Faolán Campbell asked in a deceptively pleasant voice.

"Ye ken I need only win one more trick, aye?" Hector Burns said. "I want t' savor th' moment."

"Ye ken that'll be hard t'do, since I'm abit t' spoil it," Archie Campbell drawled, as he threw out his trump card.

"Ach, ye dung heid bastard!" Hector moaned, and the rest of the table burst into laughter.

"Cannae ye hear me?" said Eòin. "I hae news!"

Faolán said, without looking up, "Ye always have news, Eòin. What is't this time?" Someone snickered.

"We're movin'!"

Every head snapped up. "Movin'? Where to? Why? Where'd ye hear that?" Hector demanded; the game forgotten.

Having captured the attention of his comrades, Eòin took his time. He shuffled his feet, looked at the ceiling, and waited until Isaac MacConnechy stood, made a show of cracking his knuckles, and strode over to stand a foot away from Eòin, towering over him.

"Fort William!"

"What? Who said?" Isaac stared at him.

"Ye ken I hae my ways," Eòin said.

Archie stood as well and advanced on Eòin, stopping next to Isaac. They were the two largest men in the company, standing well over six feet to Eòin's five ten, but the smaller man stood his ground.

"Ye mean ye put yer gob agin' th' door and listened t' yer superiors, ye wee rattie," Isaac said, but there was no heat in his voice. "Did ye hear anything else whilst usin' yer ways?"

Eòin grinned. His chin jutted in defiance, but there was a sparkle in his eyes.

"Aye, I did." He leaned forward and lowered his voice to a whisper. "Ye ken how Cap likes his whisky, aye?"

"Who doesn't ken 'at?" Isaac snorted. "He's a drunk and a bankrupt too. 'At's all ye got?" He whacked Eòin on the shoulder. "What's 'at have t' do wi' us movin'?"

Eòin rubbed his shoulder and glared at his comrade. "Ye ken where Fort William be, aye? Well, I jist happened t' be th' body t' serve the captain and Sergeant Arthur last night." He puffed out his chest. "They hardly kent I was there. Ye ken I can be verrrra quiet when I need t'be. A'most invisible, like."

He ignored the resulting snorts and continued. "After a few drams, he was right canty and let it slip abit movin' t' Fort William. Said he's ready t' take th' bastarts on." He stopped and waited a beat. "An' he told th' lieutenant 'at th' orders came doon from th' Master himself."

Archie rubbed his chin. "Take th' bastarts on? Weel, that is interestin', innit?" he said, almost to himself. "Cap's excited about somethin' other than drinkin' and gamblin'. Canty about fightin' someun' other than his own troops. Hmm. Wonder who they are, these bastarts?"

Eòin's eyes grew huge. "Ye dinnae ken who Captain Campbell hates most in this world? Where ye been?"

Faolán crossed one leg over the other and leaned back in his chair. "Th' MacDonalds," he said. "He really hates th' MacDonalds."

Hector shrugged. "Who doesnae?"

Eòin took back the reins of conversation. "No, ye dinnae git it. Cap hates the Glencoe MacDonalds more'n most. Remember after Killiecrankie?"

"Wasnae there," said Isaac. "What about it?"

"On th' way back from th' battle," Eòin said, "th' MacDonalds passed through lands belongin' t' one Captain Robert Campbell," he gave a dramatic pause, "aye, th' same bastart we love so much, an' like

MacDonalds allus do, they decided to have some fun and do some raidin'." He put his hands on his hips and assumed a lofty look. "Dinnae you lads pay attention?"

"Nothing t' do wi' me," Isaac said defensively. "I'm nae from those parts."

"Well, take my word for it," Eòin said. "When he's stinkin', Cap'n goes on abit the MacDonalds and what lawless bastarts they be, an' how he's goin' t' pay them back. Gets all riled up and starts spittin' and growlin' like a dog."

"Where's Cap'n's land, then?" Hector asked.

"Funny ye should ask," said Eòin. " It's verra near Fort William. And what else d'ye ken is verra near Fort William?" He stopped and stared his audience down.

Now he had the attention of everyone in the room.

"Glencoe, 'at's what," he announced.

Silence fell as each man took in the words. In his head, Faolán heard his father's voice from long ago. *The point is, each MacDonald is a man with rights and thoughts o' his own, just like each Campbell. So, I dinnae want ye saying ye hate all the MacDonalds just because o' the name.*

He had tried to bide by his father's wisdom as he grew into manhood. He'd met many men named MacDonald and tried to see past the name, see the man inside. And for the most part, it had worked. He'd even met some he could call friends.

But these weren't ordinary MacDonalds. The MacDonalds and Maclains of Glencoe were the worst of the lot. They were by and large a despicable bunch, known for being cattle raiders and thieves. It was hard to hear his father's voice of reason when the subject was the MacDonalds of Glencoe.

And every soldier in his regiment felt the same way. The men of Robert Campbell's three companies were all Campbells themselves or septs of Clan Campbell, and all had stories to tell of mayhem that could be attributed to the MacDonalds of Glencoe.

They also knew that their captain was a drunkard and a debtor whose lands had been frittered away through his own mismanagement. It was a last-ditch attempt to support his family that had led him to become an officer in the Earl of Argyll's Regiment of Foot, and nothing the men in his command had seen or heard provided evidence that he had mended his ways.

It would be natural for Robert Campbell to look for a convenient scapegoat rather than face his own failings, and even more natural for that scapegoat to be the clan who had made a mockery of him following the Jacobites' surprising victory at Killiecrankie.

Faolán thought about that. Victory is fleeting, and things had not gone so well for the Jacobites after Killiecrankie. The MacDonalds and other Jacobite clans had been incensed when their precious James had suffered a final defeat in July, sending him scampering into exile.

Like other Highland clans, the MacDonalds were defiant in their refusal to accept William as their monarch and proved their pettiness by increasing the frequency and violence of raids on clans loyal to the government. Faolán allowed himself a chuckle at the likely reaction from his captain at such audacity.

The orders had come from the Master, Eòin had said. The laugh died in his mouth. It really wasn't funny. The Master was Sir John Dalrymple, first Earl of Stair, and just last year the earl had been named Secretary of State for Scotland. He was a man who had the ear of King William himself.

But why would such a man want to bother with the likes of a small clan like the MacDonalds of Glencoe? It didn't make sense. They were a small branch of Clan MacDonald—ostracized even by others of their own clan for their stubborn pride and unlawful behavior. But they weren't alone in their defiance of the new king.

Few of the Highland clans were playing nice; they were staunch Jacobites and not about to submit to anyone other than James willingly. This whole enterprise was fraught with danger.

Was William looking to make an example of one of the more recalcitrant clans? The Glencoe lot would certainly fit that bill.

Faolán was proud to be a soldier in His Majesty's army, the greatest fighting force in the world. All Highlanders weren't like the MacDonalds; the Campbells had always stood proudly with the government, and Argyll's regiment was made up almost entirely of men named Campbell like himself, fiercely loyal to King William. Men taught to obey orders without question.

Captain Robert Campbell never deigned to explain his thinking to his men, of course. It would have been inappropriate and they seldom caught sight of the man. Orders were relayed by Sergeant Arthur, who was as impenetrable as a wall. But still, it would be nice to know.

Faolán wondered if his fellow soldiers felt the way he did. Things were heating up, with no sign of cessation in the hostilities between supporters of the new king and those fiercely loyal to James Stuart. The companies sent by William to keep peace in the Highlands had to tread very carefully.

A chill crawled up Faolán's spine. The stars were aligning in a way sure to bring chaos. It didn't help that the commander of the Argyll Regiment of Foot was an inebriate with an agenda. And now they were moving to Fort William, right under the shadow of the MacDonalds of Glencoe. What could possibly go wrong?

CHAPTER TWELVE
GLENCOE, SCOTLAND - 1690

SIÒNAID

"Seumas, pay attention, ye wee scamp!"

Siònaid rubbed a hand over her forehead. Another headache was building, and as usual, she could lay it at the feet of young Seumas MacDonald, her unwilling pupil. Sometimes working with him was like digging stones out of her horse's hooves. Difficult, and just as unpleasant.

A look of utmost anguish crossed the lad's face, one honed by twelve years of practice as the baby of the family, abetted by a natural cleverness that was entirely wasted in this crofter's cottage. Siònaid sighed and waited.

"But cou-sinn! Why d' ye make me learn auld stories abit people dead and gone? Why do I need t'ken all that? His Majesty doesnae need me to read t' him!"

Siònaid looked at the lad and mustered her strength. This was akin to marching through a swamp, with sucking mud underfoot and biting midges poised to eat her alive.

The truth was, Seumas was right. There was little enough sense in teaching the lad to read and write, really. He would consider himself lucky to make it to adulthood. Thin and frail, he caught every childhood illness and took twice as long as others to recover. His lungs were weak, each winter possibly his last.

It was the reason her charge did not work the rig with the others in the glen, the reason she was here. She was to teach him reading and writing to fill his endless hours, to stave off the self-pity that he had every right to feel. When he balked at learning letters, her heart broke, and she had to remind herself that she was all he had, that his irritation was earned and must be handled with patience.

It was natural that Seumas showed little interest in learning letters. His father Domhnall could not read. Siònaid had no idea if Andrew was literate; certainly, there were no books in the croft before she came.

Although some in Glencoe could read, most could not. The villagers absorbed their history through stories told around the fire at night, not from books. Still, it was her job to teach Seumas, and teach him she would.

As his reading skills improved, she began searching for reading material for him. She'd been lucky to find a traveling peddler on a trip to Ballachulish. Luckier still that the man had a pile of well-worn books in his wagon, which included treasures like the writings of Chaucer, Shakespeare, Virgil's *Aeneid*, and the poetry of William Dunbar. She found children's books like Aesop's Fables and a treasury of Bible stories for children.

At first, she'd thought the book written for children by a Scottish historian only three years ago was the epitome of good fortune. That is, she thought so until she attempted to teach its contents to young Seumas MacDonald.

"It's not auld stories, it's history. And when ye refer to his Majesty the king, I ken ye mean King James, aye?" She pinned the boy with a glare. "And I ken ye be canny that James is at present hiding." She caught the look of outrage on her young charge's face and amended her sentence. "I mean, *holding court*, in Ireland? Or perhaps France?"

Red-faced, Seumas puffed his skinny chest out and stretched his little frame to its full height.

"There be no other king of Scotland!" he said, with utmost dignity. "If ye're a real MacDonald, ye should ken 'at. Sides, I'm gonnae join th' army an' fight fer th' king, I tauld ye. I dinnae hae t' ken letters t' fight. Andrew doesnae read books, an' he was at Killiecrankie."

"But that is exactly why ye need t' know the history o' your country," Siònaid said carefully. "If ye just mean to follow orders without thinking of the reasons for your being there, ye dinnae need t' know much." She stopped and relaxed her expression. "But if ye wish t' be a leader and *give* the orders, ye need to ken *why* ye're telling your men t' rush down the hill toward other men."

She paused, and then delivered her master stroke. "Ye'll be rushing toward other men who ken their own history."

She forestalled Seumas' next argument by holding up her hand.

"And ye're too canny to be a follower. Ye'll be a leader; men will follow *you*." She watched the light come into the lad's blue eyes, and tried to keep the sadness from showing on her face. It took so little to please him. He had the heart of a warrior, encased in a body that seemed destined to betray him.

Life was so cruel, sometimes. She remembered her own self-pity when, at the same age, she'd been told that she might never walk again, that she would never ride a horse, or dance. And here she was, walking, riding, albeit more slowly and with far less grace than others. Dancing might not be in the cards, but there was no one to dance with here in Glencoe, anyway. She no longer pitied herself for her misfortune; it was useless to pine for what could never be.

She looked again at the eager young face in front of her. He was possessed of a creative, intuitive mind and an indomitable spirit, and she was going to do whatever she could to nurture those traits. Maybe he could beat the odds. Maybe he would make it to manhood, after all. And if so, if she had anything to do with it, Seumas MacDonald was going to make a difference in this world.

"Now, stop tryin' t' distract me." She waved a finger at him and assumed her best tutor face. "We were learning about Charles II, aye?"

Seumas rolled his eyes. "Aye. The Merry Monarch. Ye *tolt* me this already, cousin, an' he isnae king any more, anyway. Can we talk about archery, pleeease?"

"Are ye torturin' your cousin again, ye wee rattie?" a deep voice sounded from the doorway. Siònaid looked up and smiled at Seumas' brother Andrew.

"He is. He's making me an auld woman before my time," she said. "I can almost feel my hair turnin' grey."

Andrew sat down across from the two and regarded Siònaid with his calm blue eyes. So like his brother's, those eyes. In fact, although Seumas had a mop of blonde hair and Andrew's was jet black like her own, the two brothers looked remarkably alike, if you disregarded Andrew's handsome face, and tall, muscular body and ...*stop it, lass, no need to go there.*

It was hard not to, though. Andrew was the most handsome man she had ever seen, although it could be allowed that the pickings were small. Glencoe had plenty of men, but a great many of them were rough, uncouth louts. Not the kind to inspire a fluttering heart.

Siònaid had heard tell of the reputation attributed to the Glencoe MacDonalds. Bullies and reprobates, stubborn as oxen. Easy to anger and impossible to placate, especially when drinking. They were all cattle thieves and belligerent warmongers.

She had assumed the stories to be true, since they came by way of her own family and acquaintances on Isla, and those were MacDonalds too. Surely they wouldn't sully their own name without cause.

But rumors and stories could be wrong, at the least, exaggerated by time and distance. Or maybe her adopted uncle and his family were different. In the year since she had arrived at Domhnall's house and kissed her father good-bye, she had met only a handful of men, and Andrew did not fit the general picture at all.

Far from being a boisterous bully, he was quiet and reasonable. He was gentle with everyone, especially his younger brother, which would have been enough to win her heart even without the looks.

Andrew didn't drink, and he abhorred violence. He'd told her about Killiecrankie, about his reluctance to go. Uncle Domhnall insisted, though, and it would be unfilial to refuse.

He believed in the Jacobite cause; he had told her once when they were alone. He thought that James was the rightful king. Killiecrankie was an outstanding victory, and he should have been proud to be a part of it. But then he'd shared a secret, and sworn her not to tell another person.

The bloodlust he'd felt as he rushed down the hill toward the British troops had frightened him to his bones, he told her, and the fear was rooted deep in his soul.

"I kent I wanted to kill them," he'd told Siònaid. "But I wasnae in control, wasnae *me*. I was an animal, a creature without a brain, an' it scared the hell out 'a me. I ken men have t' fight for whit they believe, and I was proud o' Da an' the ither men, but I wasnae proud o' myself. I cannae shake th' fear o' what I b'came when I was there, an' I hope I dinnae have t' go agin."

He had looked at her, blue eyes bleak and clouded, and whispered, "I've niver told anyone about this. D'ye think I'm a monster?"

No, she did not. She thought him a man of courage, one who was afraid, yet faced his demons and stayed the course. His honesty was refreshing, and his willingness to tell her about his fears a kind of courage in itself.

Now Siònaid looked away from Seumas' brother, away from those compelling eyes. There was danger here, and it didn't come from outside. It had nothing to do with history or battles or whether the king should be named James or Charles. It came from inside her own heart.

Siònaid sensed that it would be very easy to fall in love with this man.

CHAPTER THIRTEEN

INVERNESS, SCOTLAND
- PRESENT DAY

Fear is a clever, treacherous adversary.
It has no decency, respects no law or
convention, shows no mercy.
—Yann Martel

ou can do this.

Daniel stood at the podium in the company boardroom and looked out at his audience. Nine men and two women, the movers and shakers of MacArthur Construction, Ltd. sat, hands poised over the keyboards of their laptops...waiting.

The meeting had been moved to the evening in order to accommodate the schedules of some of the senior board members. Daniel's eyes flickered to the darkened windows, where shadows recoiled from the lights in the room and swirled like ghosts. He forced himself to look away from the windows and out into his audience.

The silence grew and lengthened. People began to look up from their keyboards and regard him with expectant looks. Those who were new to the board looked around at their colleagues in mild confusion and growing interest. The older members seemed resigned; they'd seen it all before.

Daniel had eyes for only one. Like an animal at bay, he stared at his uncle in desperation. Ranald MacArthur sat like as if carved from stone, brows knitted over narrowed steel-blue eyes. He leaned over the table like a predatory cat, ready to pounce on his victim and tear it to shreds if it moved.

No problem there. Daniel's hands had glued themselves to the edges of the podium. He couldn't have moved if all the demons of hell were gathered to swallow him whole.

Someone leaned over and whispered to a colleague, and was answered by a short laugh, quickly hushed. More whispers. The sound grew and expanded and filled the room like the hissing of so many snakes.

"What's he doing?"

"Why is he just standing there? Isn't he going to say something?"

"What a numpty. Wasting our time when we have other things to do."

A throat cleared. Daniel forced his head to move just enough to see Callum. His cousin's eyes locked on his and he nodded his head vigorously. His mouth formed the words: *You can do it. Just like you practiced. You know this stuff. Come on, Dan. Keep your eyes on me. Please.*

Daniel forced his dry lips apart. "G-g-ood m-or-ning. I'm here to-to-" He stopped, cleared his throat and began again. "I'm here to—"

To his horror, the people were squeezing forward as the walls of the room moved in upon them. They pressed toward him, reaching for him; someone had him by the throat and he could no longer see Callum. His heart beat a frenzied rhythm that called *Get out! You have to get out!*

"I-I'm sorry." Daniel pried his fingers off the edges of the podium and stumbled away, making for the side door out of the boardroom.

In the hallway he bent double, clutching his chest as his heart gradually slowed its frenetic pace and his throat opened just enough to allow for a wheeze. His vision cleared and the sweat dried on his skin. He stood and leaned against the wall, eyes closed.

A hard fist sent him reeling away from the wall, to land on his back in the middle of the hallway. Uncle Ranald stood over him, fists clenched for another blow.

"What the fuck!" Fury laced the words that hissed between his uncle's stiff lips. "I gave you a week! Do ye ken how embarrassing it is to watch you stutter around up there?"

Daniel scrambled to his feet. "It's not—"

"Shut up!" The words were a roar. "That was your last chance! If you had any idea how much ridicule I'm subjected to because of you, you'd crawl out of here on your belly!"

"I'm-I'm sorry—"

"Sorry? If you were sorry you wouldn't let Callum do your job for you! All you had to do was read what he'd prepared, but you couldn't even be bothered to do that." Douglas MacArthur curled his lip.

Something broke. Daniel straightened his spine and faced his uncle, face white and lips bared. "It wasn't Callum! That was my report!"

His uncle raised his hand again, and shoved it into his pocket as the boardroom door opened. The two stood in tense silence while the members emerged, only too aware of the curious glances directed their way. When the hallway was clear, Douglas spoke again, his words laced with venom.

"From now on, Callum will be taking over your position since he does your work for you anyway. It was only for your father that I put up with you this long, anyway. You can go hang out in one of your favorite taverns, or do whatever it is you do instead of working—you're out!" His steps echoed down the hall as he turned the corner toward the lifts.

Daniel stood alone in the empty hallway. *Well, this is what you wanted, aye?* the voice mocked him. *You hated this job, anyway. Now you can get on with it.*

Get on with what, though? Unemployment? An empty life, devoid of purpose or meaning?

"It's not what I wanted!" he shouted down the hall. The words bounced off the walls and echoed in the empty space.

Part of that was true. This wasn't what he'd wanted. He liked the construction business, the knowledge that he was a part of creating something that would stand for years. Man's triumph over gravity and time. He liked being a part of it, more than he'd realized. And now it was gone.

Self-pity swamped him as the voices in the board-room swirled through his head. *Just standing there; what a numpty; wasting our time...*

Daniel hunched his shoulders and leaned against the wall. Acid rose in his stomach. Well, they'd be sorry now that the court jester was gone. He'd been the barometer against which they could measure their own success. The eejit who'd ridden the nepotism train and still managed to fall off.

Who got sacked by their own family, anyway? Daniel shoved himself off the wall and walked to the lifts. His uncle's ringing condemnation sounded in his ears. *You can go hang out in one of your favorite taverns, or do whatever it is you do instead of working.* Right, then. No sense standing around here, when there was good whisky waiting to take the edge off his misery.

He left his car in the garage and walked the few blocks to MacAlpine's, grateful for the cold wind that whirled around him and forced his concentration away from today's debacle. As he'd hoped, the pub had only a few locals on a weeknight. Regulars, like him.

His favorite table in the corner was empty as usual. Too far from the bar for most patrons, it allowed him to see everything in the pub without rubbing too close to any people. Once he had a dram or two inside him, it didn't matter so much. Liquid courage was the ticket to a night of simple-minded enjoyment. He usually didn't remember much of it the next day, which was an added bonus.

He'd barely lifted the first dram to his lips when the door at the front of the pub banged open to admit an odd group of people. Dressed in seventeenth-century clothing, they hailed the barman as they took a large round table across the room from Daniel and began a loud and boisterous discussion in old Scots.

He sighed and put the whisky down, untasted. The Highland Players. There were many like them, people who couldn't get their heads out of the past and felt that they owed it to society to remind everyone that once Scotland had been a wild, untamed place where barbarians roamed around in kilts and spoke Gaelic. Apparently while they waved tankards and gave out bulletins.

Surprisingly, Callum was a member. Once he'd tried to recruit Daniel to the cause, telling him that their country's history was the gateway to the future and would help him visualize the possibilities in architecture and construction here and now. It had washed over Daniel like so much white noise, and Callum had wisely given up after the first try.

He had nothing against re-enactors, they just seemed to expend a hell of a lot of energy on something that was dead and gone. He stared at his untouched whisky and forgot about them as he sank back into his well of depression.

"Ach, noo, and who's the new beauty?" A raucous male voice barked from across the room, and Daniel looked up to see three young men standing next to the Players' table. Locals, he thought. They looked vaguely familiar, but he couldn't place them. They'd obviously been in the pub longer than he had, judging by the swaying and slurring. The speaker leaned forward and reached his hand across the table.

One of the women—a tiny thing in a brown gown--stood and slapped the hand away. She glared at the men and put her hands on her hips.

"You leave her alone, Fergus Maclain! Go back to your ale and let others enjoy themselves. You hear?"

"Ahh, c'mon, we dinnae mean nothin'. S'not often we see such a pr'tty lass. We jist wanna make her acquaintensh. Right, lads?" His companions giggled and nodded at their leader. Apparently Fergus was the brainy one.

The single male at the table sighed and stood as well. "If you lads aren't planning to leave, I guess we will. Ladies?" The entire group stood and made to leave, but they found their way barred.

"Ach, why don' you let the lady speak for 'erself?" Fergus whinged. He swayed on his feet.

Daniel took the opportunity to focus on the woman in question as she stood to go with the others and froze in astonishment. She was the woman in the nightgown, the one he'd met right outside this pub a week ago. His fairy.

She wasn't wearing a nightgown now. She had on a long tartan skirt and shawl over a white blouse. Her feet were no longer bare; now they were encased in brown boots. Her black hair had been combed and tied up with a green ribbon, and she had a brown woolen cloak over her arm. But it was the same girl; he was sure of it. She was pretty, more than pretty actually, now that she no longer looked like a wet kitten.

The man named Fergus reached again for the girl's arm, and suddenly Daniel was on his feet and sprinting across the room to stand in front of the surprised group of men.

"Get out." His voice was low, but steady. "They asked you nicely, aye?"

"Who's talkin' t'you?" One of the men jutted out his chin. "This isnae your business."

"Aye, it is now. I'll tell you one more time. Leave these people alone." Out of the corner of his eye, Daniel saw Fergus raise his fist and blocked it with his arm. "You have to be better and faster than that," he told the group.

The drunken men exchanged glances, and suddenly they all came at Daniel with fists flying. One caught him on the shoulder, but that was the only punch they got in. Everything he'd always wanted to do when his uncle hit him flashed through his mind, and he forgot the group behind him as his body took over. He kicked one in the shin and threw another over his shoulder. Another was spun around and sent sprawling into a table.

It ended as quickly as it had begun. Fergus Maclain pulled his friends to their feet and they all took off, banging the door of the pub behind them.

Daniel leaned over with his hands on his knees, his breath coming in gasps, and watched them go. Then he turned to the group of Highland Players.

"Thank you, lad," said the older man. "They weren't thinking to take 'no' for an answer, I'm afraid." He held out his hand. "I'm Henry Duncan. This is Betty. And this is my wife, Mary." He indicated the tiny woman in the brown dress.

Mary Duncan stepped forward and put a tiny

hand in his. "Thank you. Nobody bothers us usually," she said. "I can see we're going to have to keep an eye on our new lass, she's much too pretty," she added with a laugh that sounded like the tinkling of bells.

"This is our newest recruit, Eve McDonald," she said to Daniel. He followed her pointing finger and turned to face the girl.

His fairy did have a name, after all. Expressionless, she stared back at him with those huge grey eyes, and something flipped over inside his chest. A word swam out of his brain.

Danger.

CHAPTER FOURTEEN

INVERNESS, SCOTLAND
- PRESENT DAY

Deep within, there is something profoundly
known. A quiet truth that is not a version
of something, but an original knowing.
—T.F. Hodge

"Well, that was unpleasant." Mary Duncan sniffed as the Highland Players emerged onto the High Street. "I didn't expect something like that to happen at MacAlpine's."

"It's pretty unusual," her husband agreed. "First time we've had any problems there. It's a hangout for music lovers, not drunken shite bags, but those lads are known troublemakers.. Not bad, just stupid when they're bladdered, which is most of the time. I for one won't be put off my favorite haunt because of them."

Mary sniffed again. "I suppose you're right. It is a tavern, after all, so where there's alcohol, there can always be trouble. I'm not letting those eejits drive us out of our favorite pub either, no worries about that."

Betty fastened the button on her woolen cloak. "It seems we weren't the target of their interest, anyway. They were only interested in the lass." She turned to look at the girl in question.

"Are ye all right, Evie?" She placed an ample arm around their newest member and gave her a squeeze.

Eve bent her head to stare at the sidewalk. She traced a circle on the pavement with one foot, as if it was the most interesting activity in the world.

Mary and Betty exchanged a glance, and Mary shook her head. "It's all right, lass. Those lads were just drunk. I don't think they meant anything by it, and thanks to your young man in the corner, they were sent packing with a few bruises to remind them how to behave in front of a pretty girl."

Betty grinned. "You found yourself quite a champion in there. Did ye see his moves? Like a ninja, he was." She laughed at the memory of the fury on their hero's face, his flying fists and feet.

Eve's head came up. "What's a ninja?"

The Players exchanged glances again. "Don't mind about it," Henry said. "Here's your cloak."

Eve took the proffered garment, fastened it around her shoulders, and directed her eyes toward the sidewalk again.

"It's understandable," Henry continued. "They were frightening, weren't they?" He paused and gave a forced chuckle.

A weighted silence fell on the group. Eve could feel their curiosity, knew they were all looking at her, but she had nothing to tell them. They didn't know why she was so ignorant of words that were likely common to them, and something told her to hide the secret of her lost memory as long as she could. If she bided her time, it would all come back. It had to.

The memories were there, hiding just out of sight. No matter how empty her mind was now, she had a past, a life, a name. She'd been someone's daughter, maybe someone's sister. She stared into the kind faces of the Highland Players and felt a surge of hope. They meant well; they would help. And meanwhile, she was Eve McDonald from...somewhere.

She would have to listen, to learn the words and customs of this place, Inverness. The Highland Players had taken her in, made her one of their own. She felt safe with them. But she couldn't tell them. Not about her blank mind, not about the cold she felt inside. Not yet.

Unbidden, her thoughts strayed to the man who had bested the drunks in the pub. He'd been so different from those ruffians with the groping hands. She shuddered. The man called Fergus had come so close she could smell his fetid breath, see the leer on his ruddy face, and the broken blood vessels in his bleary blue eyes. He'd reached out a hand, grabbed for her wrist...

Something about the—*ninja*, they had called him—with his brown eyes like dark velvet, made her feel that she might be safe with him too. That he could protect her, that if he promised to do so, she could trust in that promise.

I will come back to get you, I promise. Just wait a little longer.

The words filtered up from somewhere inside her, swirling like snowflakes. Where had they come from? What did they mean?

The man had fought for her, a stranger. He'd stood up for her, protected her from those horrible men. She allowed herself a smile at the memory of Fergus and his friends as they faced their adversary in the pub.

They had stumbled out of the pub, almost falling over each other in their hurry to be gone. The evening ruined, Mary had shepherded the Players out soon after.

Now Eve looked at her new group of friends; could she really call them that? She wondered what to tell them. How could she make them understand, when she had no idea herself what was happening to her?

Mary Duncan responded instinctively to the fear in Eve's eyes and reached out to clasp her arm in sympathy. The girl jumped as if she'd been burned and pulled her arm away.

Mary exchanged a look with the other Players. "Let's go to the office," she said. "The lass needs something to warm her up. Is that all right?"

Eve nodded wordlessly and allowed herself to be drawn down the street. After a hundred feet, she stopped.

"I'm sorry. I dinnae mean t' be rude." Tears shone in her eyes. "I-I jist dinnae ken"

"It's all right, lass. No worries," Mary patted her arm. "Take your time."

"Wh--wha' happened t' that man? Th' one 'at tried t' help?"

The other three looked at her. "Well, I guess he's still in the pub," Henry said. "Maybe I should go see if he's all right, aye?"

"Aye," said Mary. "We'll take her on."

Henry turned and jogged back to MacAlpine's. The women continued on until they reached the red office door with the portrait in front. Eve felt herself relaxing as she had the first time she'd seen it, the day she'd literally fallen into their arms and become one of the Highland Players.

Was it only two days ago? Oddly, now they seemed the only real thing in her life. These people had accepted her without question, given her food, lodging, and the kind of clothing that grounded her. They made her feel that everything would make sense if she only stayed with them and waited. They knew there was something different about her, but they asked no questions.

For herself, Eve was careful not to talk about the things that bothered her. What were the lights that lit the path at night and had no flame? Why was the path made of that hard grey substance? What were the monsters that raced along it and bellowed their anger at people?

Asking such questions would draw attention. It was obvious that the other people in Inverness took these odd things in stride and had no fear of them. She'd just have to wait and watch and the answers would come.

What bothered her most was her reaction to the temperature. Her attire had been woefully lacking for this harsh weather; she should have been freezing, but she was not. Nor could she feel the sensation of cold by touching. She wondered if she would be burned if she put her hand in the fire. Best not to try it until she knew more.

Eve had given this much thought, as she allowed Mary Duncan and Betty MacBain to replace her ruined nightgown with new garments that matched theirs, but all the thinking did was bring on headaches.

As for the new clothing, it was odd too. The stitching was a thing of wonder, but the material itself thin and flimsy. There were not enough layers; she had been scandalized to discover at least one less undergarment than was appropriate. Even so, the garments were much better than the nightgown. Or they would have been, had she been able to feel the warmth.

Why could she feel nothing?

Eve had given up the thought that this was a dream. It had been difficult to lose the comfort of this construct, but the truth could no longer be avoided. A dream would never last this long, and it was filled with things her imagination could not possibly have created.

Betty fumbled in her pocket bag for the key, and the three women crowded into the small office space. Mary went straight to a table at the back and put on the tea.

"Remember, ladies," she said over her shoulder, "we have a wedding faire tomorrow. Eve, it'll be your first taste of the past, aye?"

"Aye." She was becoming used to parroting the word 'aye' to answer the questions she could not understand. She'd find out in due time what a 'wedding faire' was; there was no sense worrying about it now.

"You'll meet more of the Players," Betty said. "And if you're lucky, you'll meet our leader. He sometimes comes to the events. He's a bit of a mystery, is our Baltair."

"Henry's no th' leader?" Eve asked in surprise.

"Lord, no," Mary Duncan said, as she brought over a tray with three cups of tea and handed it out. "Watch it, lass! Let it cool a minute, or you'll burn yourself."

If only. Eve waited until the two women sipped their tea and sampled hers. She could taste it, but as to temperature, she could feel nothing.

The door swung open to allow two men entrance. Henry slammed it shut as quickly as he could, but several papers on the desk flew into the air and landed on the wooden floor. Mary looked up in annoyance, and then smiled at the newcomer.

"Ladies," said Henry, "meet Daniel, our savior from the pub. He was nursing his wounds all alone, so I brought him along for a proper thanks."

The man called Daniel shuffled forward. He gave a cursory nod to the older women, and then his eyes searched for and found Eve. Her own eyes widened in shock.

She knew this man! He was the drunk from her first night in Inverness, the rude man who had made fun of her while he could hardly stand on his own two feet. He was the first person she'd seen here, and even in their short interaction, he had left an impression she could not define.

His eyes were not glazed from alcohol this evening. They were warm and somehow familiar, as if she knew those eyes like she knew her own reflection. Something inside her uncurled and spread out. It crept through and wrapped itself around her heart, bringing simultaneous warmth and searing cold.

An image flashed into her mind and was gone. In its wake came the sure knowledge that she knew this man, that his existence meant life and death to her. She felt peace and inexplicable joy, laced with a bitter hatred that hung over her like a black cloak.

Eve stepped back in near panic and trod on Betty MacBain's foot. The older woman yelped and the illusion was dispelled instantly.

Henry's new friend stood as if rooted and continued to stare at Eve. He opened his mouth and closed it again.

The three older historians exchanged glances but said nothing. In the next second, the silence was shattered when the door to the office opened again to admit another young man.

Heedless of the tension in the room, the newcomer marched forward and clasped Daniel's hand in his own.

"Dan!" said Callum MacArthur. "You decided to join up after all, aye? Good for you, lad."

He turned to Eve and grinned. "I must say, Henry, I thought you were lying when you said you had a new recruit and that she was a rare beauty, so I thought I'd better check her out myself."

He spun suddenly and regarded Daniel with narrowed eyes. "Wait! Is that why *you're* here?"

Daniel remained silent. He didn't move, nor did he take his eyes off Eve.

"Weel, noo," Callum said, his accent suddenly thick. "'Tis interestin'. I ken I'd better put in a wee bit more time here." He clapped his cousin on the shoulder, perhaps a little harder than necessary.

"Let the games begin!"

CHAPTER FIFTEEN
INVERNESS, SCOTLAND
- PRESENT DAY

*The enemy is anybody who's going to get
you killed, no matter which side he is on.*
—Joseph Heller

"Come back to work."

The voice was rough, harsh, but there was an odd quaver in it that Daniel had never heard before. He stared at his phone's display to make sure it was his uncle speaking.

"What?"

"Not to the office. I can't trust you here yet. I'm giving you a chance to earn back your place."

"Why?"

The voice rose, became agitated. "What do you mean, why? I'm giving you a chance, you numpty! Take it before I change my mind."

Daniel sighed. That sounded more like the man he knew.

"What's the job?"

"Did you hear about the body found in a close last week?"

"Aye," Daniel said. "Callum told me." *I was probably right next door when it happened, drunk out of my mind and looking for a one-night stand.* He thought about how much fun it would be to tell his uncle that, but decided it wouldn't be worth the consequences.

"The dead man was our project manager on the Millburn site," Douglas Campbell said. "He was stabbed and his body thrown into the rubbish bin. The police are investigating, but so far they have nothing."

An image danced at the back of Daniel's mind, a memory of something he couldn't quite place, and then it was gone.

"Anyway, I need you to take his place."

"Me? On the site?"

"Do you want it or no?" Exasperation coated the voice.

Daniel closed his eyes. He wasn't going to let his uncle know, but this was perfect. No board meetings, no interactions with pompous arses who judged you for your words, not your actions. He could do this. It would get him out from under his uncle's gimlet gaze and away from the constant comparisons to his perfect cousin Callum. He opened his eyes and dredged up a nonchalant tone.

"Sure. I'll do it. When do you want me there?"

"Right now. See Big Angus, the foreman. He'll give you the background." The phone clicked off.

Daniel stared at the black screen for a moment, and a slow smile spread over his face. To be sure, the job was a demotion. He'd been an executive, and now he was just a manager. He probably should've asked what the pay would be, but anything was better than no pay at all, and he'd be away from the stifling environment of the office. A win-win, for sure.

He extracted his car from the garage, made his way to the construction site on Millburn Road, and parked in the lot next to the trailer where his office would be. No one was around so he waded through the mud and sauntered in, unable to suppress the grin on his face.

The smile died at sight and smell of his new workspace. Dust bunnies glared at him from the corner and hunched under the metal desk. The prints from hundreds of work boots ran together in meandering paths across the floor, obscuring the sickly green and white linoleum that was chipped down to the wooden base floor in more than a few places. His shoes squelched on something sticky.

Charts and safety posters hung in various angles on the walls, but at least they covered some of the damage that had been done to the cheap grey paneling over the years. How old was this trailer, anyway? He conjured the image of his small but pristine office back at headquarters, and bet his uncle had never set foot in the work site trailers. Maybe he just didn't care, as long as the job got done.

Papers were strewn about the desk, the floor, even on top of an ancient microwave that clung to the shelf on a battered cabinet in the corner. Many of the papers sported coffee rings or unidentifiable stains, and the air was redolent with the odor of stale food, dust, and something that smelled suspiciously like wet dog. Above the mess, he detected a faint odor of marijuana.

Daniel's face blanched. He was expected to work in this?

He took a deep breath, regretted it instantly, and exhaled. It was what it was, and this situation could be attributed to none other than his own self. Best to get on with it.

But before he searched out Big Angus, his OCD was demanding action. Wonder of wonders, there was a box of gloves in the corner cabinet. Suppressing a shudder, he began to collect the papers strewn about the floor, and stacked them all into a cardboard box he'd found upside down in the corner. Most were probably junk, but they'd have to be gone through to make sure.

A metal nameplate on the edge of the desk read 'Kevin Chisolm, Project Manager.' That went into a rubbish bag along with the outdated schedule that hung askew from one push pin on the wall, and a dirty coffee mug containing an inch of coffee with a skin of mold on its surface. The mug proclaimed "Rule #1: The construction manager is always right. Rule #2: If the construction manager is ever wrong, see rule #1."

Ha, ha. Kevin, you're a comedian. Then Daniel remembered that Kevin Chisolm had met a grisly end in the close next to MacAlpine's Pub. *Sorry, mate.* A wave of nausea rose into his throat, bringing with it a new sense of guilt. *I might've been right next to you, and I couldn't help. I was drunk, again.* The thought was like a slap, and suddenly Daniel remembered what his memory had almost captured this morning.

There had been three men standing in the close that night, heads close together as if sharing a secret. He'd thought they were up to some rather perverted shenanigans and distanced himself quickly. But what if it was something else? If they had seen something, wouldn't they report it? A sudden chill slithered up Daniel's spine. Or maybe had they *done* something.

He shook off the feeling and went to find a bucket and mop. For the next hour, he worked to remove the grime from his new office, sure that his workers would appreciate the extra effort on their behalf.

The door opened and a bear stumped into the trailer. It removed its hood and resolved into a man, albeit the largest man Daniel had ever seen. His face was covered by a bristling black beard and mustache counterbalanced by a bushy pair of eyebrows and eyes as black as cinders. Brown canvas pants were tucked into a pair of mud-spattered work boots, and a red buffalo-plaid flannel shirt peeked out from under the black fleece-lined parka. A fresh set of muddy footprints trailed across the floor behind the newcomer.

The man looked around the clean office, and his eyes widened. Then he turned to Daniel.

"I'm Angus Graham, yer foreman," he boomed. "Lads call me Big Angus. Been here the longest, so I know the most. Whatever ye need, I'm yer man." He held out a paw.

"Good to meet you," Daniel said. He held out his gloved hand and watched it disappear into that of the other man. "I'm the new PM, and Unc--er, Mr. MacArthur--told me you're the man to see."

Graham narrowed his eyes and gave Daniel the once-over. He looked from his new manager to the sparkling office, shook his head, and made a clucking sound with his tongue. "The boss sure knows how to pick 'em," he said.

Daniel tamped down his irritation. Was there something wrong with a little cleanliness on the job site? He looked into Big Angus' challenging black eyes, and more of the enthusiasm he'd felt earlier drained away. This wasn't going to be quite the picnic he'd imagined, but he'd be damned if he was going to let this big oaf squash him like an unwelcome bug at that picnic. He might be the new guy here, but he was still the boss on this site.

He shifted his weight so that his feet were planted a half-meter apart, crossed his arms, and held the man's eyes with his own.

"I'll take you up on that, Mr. Graham," he said formally. "How about we get started right now?" He gestured to the chair he'd placed before the now clear desk, and turned without looking back to take his seat behind it.

Big Angus stared for a minute, then grunted, and took the chair across from Daniel. "At least ye dinnae waste any time," he said.

Did the voice hold a grudging note of respect? *Probably wishful thinking.*

"I haven't had time to go through the reports yet," Daniel began, sending a disgusted look at the box of papers. "But I think you could best get me up to speed by giving me a bit of background on the job itself, where we are and such, and maybe some roadblocks I might encounter right away."

Big Angus gave him a sharp glance. "Not a bad place t' start, lad, and roadblocks is a good word. There be a lot of 'em, more'n I've seen on other jobs."

"Like what?" Daniel was intrigued by the tone in the big man's voice.

"Like yer crew itself," Graham grunted. "There's some of 'em bear watchin'. Somethin's not up to the mark there."

"Did Mr. Chisolm say something?"

"Er—no." Big Angus looked around as if someone might be listening, and lowered his head over the desk. "An' that's what I find some-ut odd."

"Why?" Daniel felt suddenly as if he should be whispering. The atmosphere in the trailer had taken a menacing turn. Was Graham having him on? Why would he share something like this, so soon after they met?

"I dinnae ken." Big Angus' accent had thickened. "Allus I can say is, some-ut was goin' on, and the boss never said anythin'. If he'd known, he shoulda told me, and if he didn't know..."

He shook his head and looked at Daniel as if startled to find him there. The big man stood and backed toward the door.

"Don't pay me no mind," he said, one huge hand on the handle. "Get yerself a roster and get t' know the crew. Then we'll talk." He opened the door and slammed it shut behind him.

Daniel listened to the thump of Angus' boots on the wooden steps. He sat for a while in the silent trailer, wondering what had just happened. Questions rose and swirled in his brain.

Was Big Angus trying to tell him something? Warn him about something? It was clear that he had some misgivings about Kevin Chisolm, the previous manager. What did Graham think was happening on the job site? And why share, even for a moment, with someone he obviously thought was useless? *The boss sure knows how to pick 'em.*

Still, it hadn't been scorn he'd seen in those black eyes. He knew the look; he saw it in the mirror every morning. It was fear. Such an emotion might be expected in himself, but it was something he'd never imagine seeing in someone like Big Angus.

Did it have anything to do with Chisolm's death? Murder was rare in Inverness. Coincidences were rare anywhere.

Daniel peeled off his gloves and put on a fresh pair. He gave the box of papers a look of hatred and then pulled it over. He wasn't going to get anywhere until he went through that lot, got to know the workings of the site, and the men on this job. He needed to find out as much as he could about Kevin Chisolm, and he was going to get to the bottom of Big Angus.

He looked at the mess in the box and shoved it away again. *Later.*

He sighed. Why had he ever thought this would be easy? He felt like a rabbit, hiding in the brush while the hunter drew ever closer. This seemed like a war and he was a soldier without any weapons.

Never mind, for the first time in his life he thought he might want to win this one. He wasn't sure why, but he suspected his life might depend on it.

That, at least, was something to be going on with.

CHAPTER SIXTEEN

GLENCOE, SCOTLAND - OCTOBER 1691

SIÒNAID

"Cousin! Are ye listenin'?"

Siònaid turned her head and met the anxious gaze of young Seumas.

"Aye, course I am," she said. "William o' Orange--"

"Nae, ye're not. We passed 'at part awreddy! Ye dinnae want tae learn this mince any mor'n I do. 'Cause ye ken 'at..." He paused for effect. "James. Stuart. is. our. king." The lad's look was a triumph of smug superiority.

Siònaid sighed, then smiled in spite of her resolve. He never gave up. Seumas was a true Glencoe MacDonald--stubborn to a fault and unwilling to accept the history that was being written now, no matter how often she spoon-fed it to him.

Stubborn, but not weak-minded. Though resistant at first, he had taken to learning letters as if born with the drive to read, applying the sounds of the old language to paper with remarkable affinity. Siònaid had long exhausted the small supply of books she'd brought to the glen as well as most of those gleaned from the peddler in Ballachulish.

Soon she would have to rely on memory and old stories told around the fire of an evening, which brought its own problems. It was one thing to know letters, but one must have something to write about. And the politics hurled around the croft by men well into their cups were anything but balanced. Seumas was just a product of his environment, and that environment was sternly Jacobite.

"Seumas, it is 1691. William is th' king. James has been in exile in France for months, ye ken 'at. He isnae comin' back, no matter how much ye wish it. If ye're t' be a man, ye have t' accept it and move on."

The lad knitted his brows and tossed his head. "But it isnae fair!"

Siònaid could not help the laugh that bubbled its way to the surface. Seumas was recalcitrant when it came to studying, but he was always honest.

"D'ye think th' kings come t' be because tis fair?" she asked. "Havenae ye learnt that politics an' war are what change th' face o' th' world? Nae jist here in Scotland, but everywhere!" She patted his hand. "*Fair* hasnae anythin' t' do with it, lad."

"Then I'll learn politics, an' I'll change all 'at." Seumas nodded his head vigorously. "Cousin, whit does a politicker do?"

Siònaid made a supreme effort to school her expression. "*Politician*, an' he works wi' th' king tae make decisions 'at will help his people." *And many times, himself,* she thought, but that truth could wait till he was older.

"Wi' th' king?" Seumas' eyes were saucers. "Then 'at's whit I'll do. I'll be a politician. I'll help th' king, an' then he willnae hafta hide in France." He sat up and straightened his small spine.

"Whit do I hafta study?"

Two hours later, Siònaid sat watching Seumas and pondered the change in her young pupil. Having a goal in life, even a lofty and unattainable one, certainly made a difference. It had been nothing short of astounding, his eyes alight and hands gesturing as he asked questions and debated like a seasoned scholar.

Her heart swelled with pride, and then fell. He was so intelligent, might indeed have made a good politician given the means, and the years. But that was just what he did not have. Fate was against young Seumas, and he was living on borrowed time.

She gave herself a mental slap. *Why the melancholy? Years ago, people thought you'd never walk again, but look at you now.* Doctors could be wrong; she was proof of that. She straightened her left leg as far as it would go and tried not to wince. A little pain and a limp were not too great a price to pay for the joy of walking on her own.

What could it hurt to let him dream? And who was she to think she was wise to the vagaries of fate? He'd made it to the age of twelve despite the odds; perhaps he might yet outgrow the weakness in his heart that caused so many illnesses and oft left him gasping for air. Surely there was always hope.

She summoned a bright smile and looked at Seumas.

"What d'ye say to a wee walk? It'll be dark soon, but it doesnae do t' be cooped up here too long, aye? Yer brain'll turn t' mush."

She winked at her pupil. "An' politicians shouldnae have brains o' mush."

The two walked in companionable silence down the dirt path toward the river and the village proper, Seumas careful to keep his pace slow to match his teacher's awkward gait. It was early October, and leaves on the trees high up on the slopes were a glorious medley of color, red-gold of oak mingling with the yellow and orange of birch and rowan in a counterpoint to the dark green of pine.

The sun dropped below the mountains and the two watched the dusk settle over the valley and fold down to cover the hillside in a soft purple cloak. As always, the majesty of Glencoe took Siònaid's breath away.

A scream rent the quiet air of the glen. Siònaid's heart lurched and her head snapped to the left. Without conscious thought, the instinct passed down through ages to mothers and caregivers had her arm flinging out to protect Seumas. Leaves rustled in the shrubbery near a clump of boulders in the far distance, accompanied by grunts and curses. Another scream split the air. A black-cloaked figure emerged and turned back to face the shrubbery, where nothing now moved.

The path along the floor of the glen was in full view in every direction, surrounded only by low grasses and small shrubs. Siònaid felt suddenly like a small mammal with nowhere to hide from the approaching hawk.

With a massive effort she shook off her fear, grabbed Seumas's hand, and turned him around. She stumbled and regained her balance. At a limping run, she pulled her charge back toward the way they had come, not stopping until they reached the door of the cottage and were safely inside.

Siònaid leaned back against the door and tried to slow her heart. What had just happened? It was a blur of sound and images in her memory--screams, grunts, a man dressed all in black. Turning so slowly, turning, had he spotted them, frozen there on the path? Seen a helpless woman and a child?

He had to have, silhouetted as they were against the fading light. The man had not meant well, that much was obvious. He could have caught up to them, so why had he not?

A sharp pain brought her out of her memories. Seumas. She looked down and saw that his little fingers were locked onto her hand and his nails had cut into her skin, drawing blood. She knelt to face him, and saw a pasty face anchored by eyes that stared straight ahead, right through her. He was shaking so hard she could hear his teeth chattering through pursed lips.

"Seumas!" No sign that he had heard her. She placed the back of her hand against his forehead-- damp, hot. What was wrong with him? This was more than fear; he seemed not to know she was there. The lad couldn't have come down with a fever and chills so suddenly, could he? She held his shoulders and brought him around to face her. "Seumas!"

His eyes found hers and his mouth opened.

"I saw—" He choked out the words. "I saw—" The next second he had bent double and thrown up all over the front of her gown. His eyes rolled back in his head and he collapsed against her, unconscious.

Siònaid looked about for help, but the house, usually crowded now that the crops were in, was eerily silent. She carried Seumas to his pallet in the corner of the cottage and laid him down. His body still shook, but at least the tortured, gasping breaths had ceased. She changed her gown quickly and returned to sit beside him, stroking his hair helplessly.

After a few moments, Seumas opened his eyes and sat up, but the fear was still evident in his anxious blue eyes. He reached for her and clung like a limpet while the sobs rose and fell and tears soaked into her dress. Long after he was quiet, she held him and rocked him like a baby, love and worry for this young lad filling every part of her being.

And she wondered. It had been a frightening experience, surely, but Seumas was not a fearful child by nature. His reaction seemed more than fear, almost like *grief*. Something else was wrong.

Of course, he had seen the blacked cloaked figure too. This was probably her fault, for giving in to her panic and frightening him. She chastised herself for her lapse in judgement and hugged the lad closer.

Seumas pushed away and stood up. He straightened his frail body, trying to make himself as tall as he could.

"Cousin, ye dinnae need t' squash a man, aye?" He gave her a lofty look and turned away. "Bit, thanks," he muttered, and stalked away, but not before she captured the look in his eyes.

Haunted. She thought back to the words he had gasped.

"I saw—"

What had he seen, that she had not?

CHAPTER SEVENTEEN

HIGHLANDS, SCOTLAND
- 15 DECEMBER, 1691

FAOLÁN

They crouched in the shelter of the pines, waiting. Excitement was like a living thing, dancing and swirling around the men of the Earl of Argyll's regiment, whispering into their ears and wooing them with promises of danger and turmoil, real fighting after so much waiting.

MacDonalds. They were going to take the fight to a pack of heathen MacDonalds.

"Are ye sure th' bastarts are comin' this way?" Archie Campbell whispered. "What if they're goin' roon by th' other side?"

"Haud yer wheesht! D'ye nivver shut it?" Hector Burns bit out the words. "Christ, it's freezin'!" He blew on his fingers in a vain attempt to warm them.

"They're comin,'" Faolán said. "Eoin's th' best scout we have, ye ken that. Bein' a nosy wee bugger comes in handy."

"Bit why is Cap'n Campbell here?" The whisper came from Faolán's right. He turned to see Isaac MacConnechy looking off into the trees behind them, and followed the other man's gaze. His eyes narrowed.

What *was* Captain Robert Campbell doing out here? Sure, he hated the MacDonalds more than any of them, but their commander never lowered himself to accompany his men on scouting missions. In fact, hidden as they were by the shrubbery and the gloom of Glencoe's pine forest, it didn't seem as if Cap'n even knew they were here. Was he on a mission of his own?

Maybe this was a chance to find out something about the reason they'd been posted to this out-of-the-way place. Over the year since their move, the men had grown tired of all the secrecy, the blind obedience without any return.

Like the others, Faolán had no problem with following orders, and he was itching to know why they'd been posted to Fort William for the last year, keeping an eye on clans like the MacDonalds of Glencoe. It couldn't be to spar with a few of the wee skellum likely just looking for trouble; that just made no sense at all.

"MacDonalds of Glencoe are plannin' something," their captain had informed them. "Ye're to keep an eye on 'em fer th' crown, an' report back eny suspicious behavior."

Those were their orders? Everything the MacDonalds did was suspicious, the bastarts, but nothing the regiment had seen or heard in the last year indicated that it was any different than usual. They were crofters. They went out each day and worked the small rigs next to each cottage, went in to supper, and went to bed. Likely got drunk somewhere in there, as well.

They were also thieves, a right bunch of petty criminals thoroughly disliked by others in the glen. Occasionally a group of them would make a foray in search of cattle that had strayed from their herd and gleefully make off with their 'find,' and they had no problem with fighting the rightful owners as long as the groups were fairly even.

They were good fighters, especially when they'd had a whisky or two for courage, and usually managed to seize the cattle without much of a fight. None of it endeared the MacDonalds of Glencoe to their neighbors, and their reputation had grown.

All of this was duly reported back to Captain Campbell. In the year they'd been here, the reports were made and received with monotonous regularity, and nothing had come of the information. "Keep a watch, men," was the response. Captain seemed content to hole up in his quarters, drinking and playing at cards with his sergeant. Sometimes he didn't even bother to look up from his game.

Faolán was pretty sure Captain Campbell didn't care a whit whether they watched the MacDonalds or danced a caleigh with them. He rarely talked with his men and seemed impatient that they would even bother to report what they'd learned. There was never anything consequential that would explain their presence here.

And that was the problem. The army wouldn't waste good men on nonsense like this. There had to be a bigger picture, and this was their chance to find out what it might be. It was a huge risk he would be taking, but perhaps worth it if there was a chance of understanding what was going on. It beat waiting for a bunch of MacDonalds to wander by.

Faolán made a decision. Today *he* was going to be the nosy wee bugger. He tapped Isaac on the shoulder and tilted his head toward the place in the trees where they'd glimpsed the captain.

His friend nodded and the two crept silently away from the rest of their company, taking a circuitous route that ultimately brought them round to the other side of the copse of trees. They made no noise, their footsteps silent on the carpet of pine needles. A year of creeping around stalking MacDonalds had given them the ability to move like ghosts.

They stopped beneath the shelter of a huge pine. If they came any closer they'd be detected, and the tingling up his spine told Faolán that would be a very bad thing. If caught, he and MacConnechy, and perhaps the entire company, might face anything from dishonorable discharge to confinement and hard labor. Worst case, if they stumbled upon something they shouldn't, it could mean death.

Faolán looked at MacConnechy. Of all the men in his company, Isaac was the one he trusted the most for his loyalty and discretion. A stubborn look passed over the other youth's face, and he nodded. Faolán gave him a grim smile. For better or worse, the decision had been made. They craned their heads forward, looking for any sign of the captain.

"'Tis a go." The words rose into the quiet air of the forest. Not Captain Campbell's voice; this was another man.

"Are ye sure...willnae..?"

Faolán knew that voice all too well. The nasal whine of their less than esteemed captain, Robert Campbell of Glencoe, rose out of the bushes not twenty feet beyond where his two men crouched.

"I ken th' man well. Contrary t' th' end. Ye ken... nigh four months... He'll be wantin' tae send a message...willnae sign till th' last."

"The king wants...example..." Campbell's petulant voice rose again. "Maclain...that bastard..."

"Shhh!" the other hissed, and the voices were hushed suddenly. Faolán and Isaac froze where they crouched in the shadow. The bushes ahead of them parted and Captain Campbell stepped out of the cover. Without looking, he strode off through the dark pines toward the west, rustling branches as he went. Silence fell upon the copse of trees once more.

Isaac stirred, but Faolán put his hand on his arm.

"Nae. Hold," he whispered.

They waited for five minutes, and then the bushes parted again and a man stepped out onto the path. Tall and lean, he was dressed from head to toe in black, so that standing still he blended into the tree trunks as if part of the forest. If they hadn't known he was there, they could have walked right into him in the gloom.

This man was much younger than the captain, seeming nearer to Faolán's own twenty-four years. Perhaps it was the clothing or the furtive movements, but he exuded an air of darkness, a sense of menace that made the hair on the back of Faolán's neck stand up. What was this man doing in the woods, meeting with a captain of the Earl of Argyll's regiment in obvious secrecy?

The man stood stock still, as if he sensed he was being watched, while Faolán and Isaac tried to keep their very breathing as silent as possible. Faolán's legs were beginning to ache from the crouching, and he could feel the cold seeping into his joints, but there was no way he could move without being heard. So, he tried to take his mind off the growing discomfort by ruminating over what he had heard.

The words tumbled from his memory. *Willnae sign. King...example. Glencoe.*

Sign. A proclamation had been issued in Edinburgh last August, offering a pardon to all Highland clans if they signed an oath of allegiance to King William before the end of the year. Was that what this was about?

Everyone knew it was going to be a problem getting the Jacobites to sign the oath. The honor of the Highlanders had been touched, and no man wanted to be the first to renounce his loyalty unless James was to give them permission to do so. William was firmly ensconced on the throne and not going anywhere, but rumors of French fleets on the sea kept hope alive in Highlander hearts that James Stuart was returning to take back his country.

Now it was December, and only a handful of clans had signed the oath. Other rumors swirled through the ranks, whispers of dire consequences if the deadline passed without the required signatures by the clan chiefs. Consequences that would be meted out by the government army.

Whatever this clandestine meeting was about, Faolán had a sinking sensation in the pit of his stomach that told him the year of waiting was coming to an end, and that he like as not wasn't going to enjoy what was coming. *Be careful what ye wish for. Ye might just get it.*

Faolán and Isaac jerked as a shout rose in the distance, and suddenly the air was alive with war cries and curses. Branches cracked and bushes swished as the men of the Earl of Argyll's regiment sprang into action. The MacDonalds had arrived.

Faolán turned his head and peered back into the gloom, but he saw nothing. The man in black was gone.

CHAPTER EIGHTEEN
INVERNESS, SCOTLAND - PRESENT DAY

Do I wait for the future? Or is the
future now? Or is the past now? Or
is now whatever I want it to be?
—Nicole Schubert

"There. You look just perfect, as if you stepped out of the pages of a history book." Mary stepped back and ran a practiced eye over Eve. "It was a braw day when you walked," she gave her musical laugh, "I mean, when you *fell* into our lives."

Eve looked down at the garment she was wearing. It had elements of a style she seemed to recognize, although she couldn't say why. Like the clothing on the poster, the dress called to her, as if something was knocking on the locked door of her mind, clamoring to get out.

The pattern of the dress was a wondrous tartan whose colors were bright and cheerful—deep red and forest green blending with a rich brown the color of newly turned earth. Perhaps these Players were of the nobility, as she'd seen nothing else so fine in Inverness.

"Now, for your hair." Betty approached with some sort of weapon brandished in her hand. It seemed to consist of a long barrel of silver, and had a black tail that trailed to the floor and ended in a growth with two lethal-looking spikes, like the fangs of an adder.

"Your hair is so lovely; once we curl it around your face, you'll be the prettiest lass at the faire. Just sit here near the outlet."

Eve backed away in horror. "Ach, noo, I cannae! I'm no wedded!" She heard herself and stood stock still. This *was* improper, but how did she know? Was it a memory? She closed her eyes and concentrated, working at the door in her mind, but it stayed fast. The feeling of wrongness receded. Still, it had seemed so real. It had to mean something.

Mary cocked her head. "You seem to know quite a lot about style in old Highland dress, lass. I know what you mean, but that rule went out in the early part of the eighteenth century. We generally wear clothing from the time of the '45 for our events."

She looked at Eve's pale face and wide grey eyes. "Put the curling iron away, Betty. We won't need it."

"It's all right, lass," she continued. "Let's just put it in a snood, aye?" She produced a length of ribbon and handed it to their new member.

Eve took the ribbon gratefully. She passed it through her hair and tied it in a bow at the top of her head without thinking, as if her hands knew what to do. She gave Mary a sweet, tremulous smile and turned to face Betty, who winked and shrugged.

"No worries, lass, we all have a say in what we wear, as long as it fits the general historical picture. Mary's the expert in costume, if she says you look perfect, you do. Are we ready, then? Come on, Henry and the others will be waiting."

They left the office and proceeded along the walking path, called a *pavement*, Eve remembered. The larger path was called a *street*. Her vocabulary was increasing, but so were the images in her mind. And the problem was, the images and the reality didn't match.

She remembered pathways, but not like these. They were dirt, kept free of growth by the constant trample of horses' hooves. The edges in her hazy memories were grass, but here there was something hard that lifted the road to the pavement. It had a name, too, *kerb*.

Eve congratulated herself on remembering that one. Every word she learned gave her a greater feeling of accomplishment; every smile from Mary or Betty lifted her confidence. Now she knew that the huge beasts that screamed down the road were not monsters. They were not alive at all, and rather than eating human beings, they were controlled by them. Somehow they did it all without horses, but understanding that miracle could wait for another day.

She knew that Mary and Betty were curious about her lack of knowledge, but they said nothing, and she thought she might just love them for it. She had intercepted more than one sidelong glance when she fumbled with language or asked a question about something she should have known, but they were kind and explained without question. There was still a knot of fear curled in her gut, but it seemed to be shrinking. Or at least it was asleep for the moment.

It awoke with a howl as the group stopped next to a large carriage that stood beside the pavement, its door open to reveal the innards inside. Eve reeled back when she realized she was expected to get *inside* the thing. All her newfound confidence evaporated, and she backed away whimpering.

"Hush, child," Mary murmured in her ear. "It's all right. Look." She climbed into the carriage, sat in an empty chair, and fastened something across her body.

Betty pushed Eve from behind. "This is one of the vans we travel in to events. "Climb in; we have others to pick up, and we can't be late or we'll lose our table."

Eve allowed herself to be pushed into a chair between the two women. *Van*, Betty had called it. Another new word. There was a chair next to Henry in the front, and in addition to the three in which the women sat, there were three more behind. The material in which she sat was called *leather*. It had been dyed a drab grey that blended into the walls and floor so that the whole thing resembled a cave.

Henry turned from his place in the front and waved.

"Welcome, lass. Your first event. You're in for a treat."

Eve watched as Betty fastened a belt across her

ample girth, and looked to see that there was one for her as well.

"Buckle your seatbelt, lass. It's the law."

She fumbled with the odd ribbed material until Mary reached over and fastened it into a hole next to the seat. Her heart lurched at the feeling of restraint, and she gripped the side of the chair until her knuckles turned white.

Dinnae fash! she told herself. *These people mean ye nae harm. If they be no afraid, it must be a'right. Jest follow an' watch—Ach!*

Eve screwed her eyes shut as, with a loud roar, the van lurched and began to move away from the kerb and into the roadway. She reached for the strap of her seatbelt and clutched it with both hands. After a while, when nothing untoward happened, she opened her eyes and dared to look out the window, watching in fascination as the buildings of Inverness flashed by.

No one else seemed fazed at all by this miracle, so she studied Mary and Betty and schooled her face into a look she hoped matched theirs. Boredom. Indifference. Normalcy. It took everything she had.

The van continued to wind its way through the streets of Inverness. Eventually it stopped and the door slid open again. Betty got out and pushed a button on the top of her chair, and Eve watched as the back folded forward. Betty remained standing on the pavement and gestured to someone to get in.

A man stepped into the van and ducked to squeeze past the middle seats.

"No! Take my seat, lad," Mary said. "Those back seats are so cramped, and there's no leg room. It's good to be short sometimes, aye?" The man smiled his gratitude and took the seat next to Eve as Mary made her way into one of the rear seats.

"Ahem."

Eve turned to the man who had spoken..

"Hullo. Didn't we meet last week, at the office?" he said. "It's nice to see you again. I'm Callum MacArthur, remember?"

She smiled. "Och, aye, I mind." She bobbed her head. "I am Eve."

The man winked. "Oh, I remember."

Out on the pavement, Betty eyed the remaining man with sympathy.

"I wish I could give you my seat," she said, "but as you can see, there's no way I'd fit back there. Eve, maybe you—" she eyed the white knuckles on hands still fastened to the strap of the seatbelt, and shook her head. "I guess it's you, lad."

She waited for the man to climb into the van, but he stood rooted to the pavement.

"Is there a problem?" Mary called from the back seat. "It's cramped back here, but you're young and agile, you can fit. And I don't bite, I assure you. You'll need to get a move on though, we don't want to be late."

Still there was no movement from the man on the pavement. The van's occupants turned to see what was holding them up, and Eve felt her heart hitch.

It was the drunk from her first night, the man who had saved her in the pub and later come with Henry to the Players' office. Daniel. She couldn't remember anything else about the encounter; she'd been too busy staring.

It seemed that every time she saw this man he was in a different state of distress. This time, his eyes were fastened on the rear of the van, his face pale. Sweat had broken out on his brow, and his hands were clenched at his sides.

Callum assessed him and said quickly, "Daniel, why don't you ride in the front?" He gestured to the chair next to Henry, which held three large crates.

"I'm sure we can move those boxes to the back, aye?"

"Ach," said Betty. "We should have thought of that ahead of time. What a pack of numptys we are!" She opened the front passenger door and hefted the objects out, passing them to Mary in the rear.

She smiled at the man standing on the pavement. "There you go, lad. All yours. We usually just have the three of us, the others meet us there." She hoisted herself back into the van and took her seat next to Eve.

The man on the pavement took a deep shuddering breath and climbed into the front, keeping his eyes forward.

Callum was watching his friend. Eve looked back and forth between the two, sensing the tension in the posture of the man in the front seat. As she watched, he took a deep breath and relaxed. The color came back to his face and he smiled as he turned to answer something Henry had asked.

Maybe this *van* thing was as new to him as it was to her. But no, somehow that did not make sense. She had been afraid; yes, it had taken all she had to climb into the thing. But the reaction of the man called Daniel was something else.

She thought about how he had stood rigid on the pavement, the naked fear in his eyes. The way he gasped for breath, the sweat. For a moment she had thought he was going to faint.

There was no sign of distress now, but she hadn't imagined it. Maybe this strange feeling had something to do with the connection she had felt to this man, right from the beginning. Perhaps it was why she had dared to approach him on the street, to speak with a total stranger. Whatever the cause, the odd sensation of tenderness and repulsion she felt was real. Maybe it was the reason she had run away from him. The reason she could not look away now.

She reached into the pudding she had for a brain these days and groped for a memory, something that might explain what she had seen. Nothing came. But she *had* seen something like this, somewhere.

As if he felt her eyes upon him, the man called Daniel turned and looked at her. A slow smile spread over his handsome face, and his liquid brown eyes crinkled at the edges.

Eve could not feel it, but she knew in the deepest part of her that she was blushing. She forced her eyes away and turned to her left, to find another pair of eyes fastened on hers. These were clear blue and innocent.

"Are you all right, lass?" Callum asked and smiled. A beautiful smile, just for her.

Eve summoned a wan smile and gave a jerky nod. She turned to Betty, on her right, and let out the breath she'd been holding.

"So, whit happens at a wedding faire?" she heard her voice chirp.

CHAPTER NINETEEN

NÈAMH HOUSE, SCOTLAND
– PRESENT DAY

*Your memory is a monster; you forget—it
doesn't. It keeps things for you, or hides
things from you, and summons them to
your recall with will of its own. You think
you have a memory, but it has you."*
—John Irving

The place called Wedding Faire was breathtaking. A great house dominated the landscape of stately pines, with a rolling lawn that stretched down to meet a huge body of water. The lawn was broken by a spiral pattern of tilled earth, interspersed with artfully placed shrubbery and patches of ivy.

"Nèamh House is known for its garden, lass," Mary said. "Doesnae look like much noo, bit in summer it'll be a riot o' color."

Eve looked at the tiny Player at her side. The woman's accent had thickened considerably, as had the speech of the others upon arriving here. Now she was much easier to understand than she had been back in Inverness.

"Nèamh House?" she asked Mary. "Heaven? I kent ye called it Wedding Faire."

Mary laughed. "Nae, lass. Nèamh House is th' name o' this place, an' ye're right, it means Heaven in th' Gaelic. A wedding faire is...weel, ye'll ken well enough what 'tis when ye see it." She paused and cocked her head. "Ye speak the auld tongue, do ye?"

Did she? The word felt right, as if it belonged on her tongue. *Nèamh* . She had been able to pick out a few words on the buildings in Inverness; were they Gaelic? Was that her language?

It wasn't the language spoken by the Highland Players, or by any of the other people she'd heard since arriving in Inverness, and yet she understood it as if she'd been raised speaking the 'auld tongue.'

Mary gave her an appraising look, but said nothing.

"Come lass, there's others ye need t' meet," she announced, and shepherded Eve over to the path that led to the grand house.

"The lads look braw, aye?" Betty's voice came from behind them. "They do us proud, they do."

Up ahead, Callum and Daniel stood on either side of the path, swords held aloft and almost touching in the middle as people streamed under the arch they'd made.

Eve's gaze went back and forth between the two men. Braw, indeed. And yet so different. They were cousins, Callum had told her in the van, but she never would have guessed it. His dark hair was short and neatly combed, a glossy crown that seemed to reflect the sunlight, setting off blue eyes that sparkled as he caught her gaze. A verra handsome man, was Callum MacArthur, and he seemed well aware of the fact.

If Callum was the sun, Daniel was the moon. Or rather, the moon on a cloudy night. A rainy, windy cloudy night. It wasn't that his hair was dark like Callum's; rather he bore an untidy mop of light brown streaked with gold and a hint of red. The untamed look was likely caused by his tendency to run a hand through it frequently, as if trying to find something to keep that appendage busy. If the idea was to put his hair in place, he was failing miserably at it, but for some reason the thought made Eve smile.

No, it wasn't his looks. The darkness came from his demeanor—and his eyes. Daniel's eyes were unreadable depths of brown that seemed to pull her into them. Eyes with secrets, eyes that shared nothing. Compelling, dangerous eyes. Eve shivered. Now she was just getting fanciful. His dour expression likely meant he was a loner, that was all.

As they passed under the human arch, she heard a chuckle and turned her head in time to catch a wink from Callum. She blushed and turned away, a mistake. Now she was staring straight into Daniel's velvet brown eyes. She felt herself sinking into them as before, and for the life of her, she couldn't look away.

Another shiver went through her. What was it with this reaction? Daniel rolled his eyes and grimaced, and the spell was broken. His expression said he'd rather be anywhere else, doing anything else, and Eve realized why it seemed so familiar. He was out of place here, just as she was. And why did the thought warm her? She gave him a reassuring smile and was rewarded with a curt nod.

Mary patted her arm and gave her a nudge, and she realized she had stopped under the arch of swords and was holding up the line of people waiting to pass through. She allowed herself to be pushed up the pathway that led to the huge front door of the estate.

At the last moment, she turned around. Two sets of eyes, one blue and one brown, were watching her. Callum's expression was one of pure male admiration, where Daniel's eyes gave nothing away. Callum winked at her again before turning back to his task. Daniel frowned and directed his gaze to the sidewalk at his feet.

Was he angry with her? She'd done nothing to deserve his contempt; they'd barely exchanged ten words during the trip to Nèamh House. A feeling of disappointment was chased by one of annoyance, and she settled her face in an answering frown just in case he looked up again. Two could play at that game. They were strangers, and it looked as if they'd remain strangers.

"Are ye ready, Evie?" Mary's voice came from far away. The woman shook her head. "Ye near tripped o'er th' door step, with yer woolgatherin.'" She linked her arm with Eve's and together they entered the huge, double doors that marked the entrance to Nèamh House.

The inside of the house was even more beautiful than the outside, if that were possible. Eve found herself staring at the high mullioned windows, an immense fireplace that took up most of one wall, and the huge fixture of lights suspended high above. The floor was covered wall-to-wall by a plaid pattern of dark red and forest green.

"Th' Clan Cameron tartan," Mary told her. "Nèamh House is owned by an American. His kin made a fortune in real estate or some such, an' he needed somewhere t' spend it so he came here searchin' fer his roots, and decided to stay. Verra proud of his heritage, he is—makes donations t' the National Trust, so we're happy t'have him."

Eve let the words flow over and around her. As usual, she could make no sense of most of Mary's information, but she tucked it away to go over later.

Betty came up beside them, and they left the great room and passed through several more. Eve gave up trying to take it all in, as the two Players were nearly dragging her along, seeming eager to get somewhere. But then, she'd found in the past days that the Highland Players were always in a hurry, always making plans or calling people on something she'd learned was a *mobile phone*. They'd offered her one, but she'd backed away as if it might burn her. She was not about to be touching something that held people captive inside it and signaled its needs with a monotonous ringing tone.

"The faire is set up beyond the patio," Mary said, and they passed into an area open to the sky, where people were gathered, eating and drinking. *Patio.* She tucked it away. A man dressed in a tartan garment like the pattern on the floor in the great room stood off by himself. He held a bag with sticks of some kind jutting from it, and as Eve watched, he placed the end of one stick between his lips and took a deep breath. Sound poured out from the bag, a harsh, shrieking call like a thousand sea birds.

Eve's world stood still. A piper! He was a piper. Pictures formed in her mind and images rose up to engulf her. In her memory, a man dressed in a plaid stood on the hillside near a village with small houses roofed in thatch—yes, it was called *thatch*—and played his pipes in the dusk of a summer's evening. Men straggled home from their work on small plots of farmland, lured by the smell of stew and baked bread, and women called out to small children in the language Mary had called Gaelic.

"Evie! What's wrong?" A voice sounded next to her ear, and the image dissipated. She was back in the crowd of oddly dressed people at Nèamh House, tears streaming down her cheeks as the piper played on.

Mary and Betty guided her over to a chair and gently pushed her into it. Betty stood in front, her substantial form acting as a shield against curious eyes, and Mary pulled over another chair and sat facing the girl. She took Eve's hands in her own and dropped them immediately.

"Your hands are like ice, lass! Are you poorly?" The thick accent was gone, and concern marked her expression. Eve pushed her hands under the apron of her dress and looked up. A tremulous smile lit her pale face.

"He's a piper," she said, her voice filled with wonder. "A piper."

The two women looked at each other.

"Well, aye, that he is, lass," Betty said. She nodded her head vigorously. "Isn't he, Mary? A piper. An' a good one too." The two women exchanged glances and Betty shrugged her shoulders.

Eve's smile widened. "I remembered." The words came out in the softest of whispers.

Mary straightened and the two Highland Players pulled Eve from her chair. Betty put a substantial arm around her.

Callum and Daniel emerged onto the patio.

"Brian and John relieved us," Callum said, flexing his arm. "Good thing; thought my arm was going to fall off."

"What's on with her?" Daniel's voice was sharp as he looked at Eve.

"Nothing, lad," Betty said. "She was startled by the bagpipes, is all."

Callum snorted. "Bagpipes can be startling, for sure," he said, "but I've never known them to make someone so happy. He walked to where Eve stood with Betty and patted her arm. "You should smile more, lass, it suits you."

Daniel's morose expression deepened.

Mary took charge again. "Let's get this thing started, aye?" With a last look at Eve, she turned and led the group from the patio and through another door into a bright, sunlit room filled with tables.

Eve's eyes widened at sight of a wondrous gown that hung in the center of the room. Pure white, with lace and beads bedecking the bodice, it swept into a skirt of frothy material that seemed to float of its own accord.

There was a table that held jewelry, another that displayed pictures of great estates like Nèamh

House, and still another with arrangements of flowers in every color imaginable.

"Ahh, the Caledonian Bakers are here." Betty's voice was reverent. "Best wedding cakes in the Highlands; hope they brought samples."

"Focus, Betty," Mary said. She led them to a table behind which stood a larger poster like the one outside the Highland Players office in Inverness. On the table were displayed swords and dirks, mugs and glasses, all etched with the Players' name. Three men and a woman stood behind the table, and Eve was pleased to see that one of the men was Henry Duncan.

"Well met, lass," he said. "I'd like ye t' meet some of our other Players. The lassie here is Ailis Brodie, a cousin of Betty's. This is Bennet MacGillivray," he indicated the younger man on his right, "an' this lad is wee Caomhainn. Lads, meet Eve MacDonald."

Eve blinked at Wee Caomhainn. He was the biggest man she'd ever seen, towering over even Henry. He grinned at her and made a bow.

"At yer service, lass," he said. "Ye ken our Henry is a funny one, aye?"

The other man looked at Callum and Daniel. "Guid t' see ye here," he said to Callum, "and who's the new lad?"

"My cousin—I mean mah coosin," Callum said. "Hae tae gie intae character, aye? His name's Daniel."

Daniel bobbed his head but said nothing.

Callum smirked at Daniel. "Doesnae say much, our Daniel. Ur Evie's no sae new, though," he went on, "She has th' talk doon awreddy." He grinned at Eve. "How'm ah doin'?"

Before Eve could figure out what Callum was talking about, a silence fell on the group. She turned to see that another man had appeared behind the table. Tall, slim as a reed, the newcomer wore his long, straight white hair tied in a queue. Unlike the others, whose tartans were varied and colorful, his jacket and kilt were a solid black, set off by a white shirt. Black eyes in a pale face, it was almost as if he had no color at all.

Such an odd man, Eve thought. His hair suggested he was elderly, but his unlined face and ramrod straight back told a different story. He could have been any age at all.

"Eve, Daniel, this is the founder and leader of Highland Players," Mary said, her voice soft, almost reverent. "Baltair, meet our newest recruits."

"I'm pleased to have you join us."

Eve froze. Paralyzed, she stared at the leader of the Highland Players, into eyes black as pitch. The soft voice flowed into Eve's ears like music. It swirled in her mind and grew, then ebbed until it became a whisper that only she could hear.

She had heard that voice before, somewhere in the past she had lost. The words swam into her memory from an impossible distance. *"What is your desire?"* And her answer. *"Revenge."*

The black eyes never left hers.

"Are you ready?" Baltair whispered.

CHAPTER TWENTY

NÈAMH HOUSE, SCOTLAND - PRESENT DAY

*Love, like everything else in life, should be
a discovery, an adventure, and like most
adventures, you don't know you're having
one until you're right in the middle of it.*
—E.A. Bucchianeri

aniel watched the color leach from Eve's face. Truth was, he had been watching her and trying not to be caught at it since he'd gotten into that cursed van back in Inverness. He pushed the thought away; right now, such a little detail was of no importance. There was something wrong with Eve McDonald.

No one else seemed to have noticed, except for that creepy leader of this Godforsaken band of misfits. Baltair, wasn't it? Not a proper Scottish name at all—it sounded mystical, like a wizard from Harry Potter. Maybe the lass was afraid of ghosts, because that guy sure looked like one, with his white face and black getup. Pretentious git.

Daniel looked around the group. The rest of them were going on about the damned wedding faire, for God's sake, while the lass was falling apart right in front of them. An instinct he hadn't known he possessed took over and his brain shifted into automatic. He reached out, took her hand, and pulled her from the group in front of the table, out of the room, and away from the house.

Beyond a tiny squeak she made no sound, but at least she allowed herself to be drawn away. Daniel slowed when he realized she was stumbling, her lame leg impeding her progress, but she didn't seem to notice and so he didn't stop until they'd reached the car park where the van sat. Unlocked, thank God. He opened the front passenger door and waited for her to climb in.

Eve stood as if in a trance. Did she even know he was there? He sighed and bent over, put his right arm around her back and his left behind her knees, and picked her up. He lifted her into the seat and closed the door carefully behind her. Then he rounded the van, opened the driver's door, and climbed into the seat.

She was still sitting motionless, looking straight ahead out the windscreen. Her silvery eyes were vacant, the pupils dilated and fixed. Chills raced up and down his arms and he flexed his fingers. They were tingling. His eyes narrowed, and he reached over to place his hand on hers.

The chill was coming from her.

His fairy was freezing, and she didn't even seem to notice. Aye, it was winter, but the cold that had held the Highlands in its grip for the past three weeks was subsiding. Down coats were giving way to lighter jackets; temperatures were running from seven to thirteen degrees most days. Spring was coming.

He remembered the first time he'd seen her, standing in her nightdress on the street outside the pub. It was understandable that her foot was frozen to his touch then; it had been one of the coldest nights of the year, and her feet were bare. But now? She was properly clothed in her woolen dress and warm boots. She shouldn't be so cold—was she ill?

"What's wrong?" he asked. She didn't answer, didn't move.

"Eve! Are you poorly?" He prodded her arm, and finally she turned her head slowly and looked at him. A shudder wracked her thin form, and she began to shake.

Daniel twisted his head, then reached behind into the middle seats, and snagged a car blanket from the floor. He wrapped it around Eve, pulled her into his arms, and hugged her.

"I'm nae cold," she mumbled into the blanket.

"Eh?"

She pulled away to look into his face. "'Tis nae what ye think."

He kept his voice light. "Coulda fooled me, lass. You're shaking."

"It-it isnae from cold."

"Then what is it? What happened in there?"

Eve was quiet for a long time. She searched Daniel's

face, and what she found there seemed to settle her. The shaking subsided and a wan smile appeared.

"I dinnae ken," she said, her voice the barest of whispers. The grey eyes remained locked on his, and the smile grew wider. It was like the sun coming out from behind the clouds after a storm, Daniel thought. Beautiful beyond reckoning.

"I dinnae ken," she repeated, "bit I'm rememberin'."

Confusion drew his brows together. "Remembering? You forgot something?"

"Aye. Somethin'." She laughed, a musical tinkle that echoed inside the van.

Daniel didn't know what was so funny, but it didn't matter as long as it produced that laughter, that smile. He decided he'd do just about anything to keep that smile on her face.

"You do look pretty when you smile," he said. Then he thought about her words. "But what is it you've forgotten that makes you so happy to remember?"

Eve stiffened and drew back further. She stared into his eyes and he felt as if she was reading his soul, judging it. Finally, she relaxed on a long breath.

"Somethin' means—everythin'," she said, and waited for his response.

Daniel stared at her. She wasn't joking; he could see that, but what on earth did she mean?

"I have nae memories. I cannae mind where I come from, who are m' family; I must hae a family, but I dinnae ken mine."

Daniel gaped at her. "You mean, you have amnesia?" he asked at length.

Tears appeared in the grey eyes. "I dinnae ken

what 'at is. I ken only that I woke up standin' on th' path, er, street, lookin' at ye."

A small smile reappeared, and she leaned forward as if preparing to share a secret.

"Ye were fair blooter'd," she whispered.

Daniel winced. "Aye, I remember. Not my finest hour."

Eve's lips quirked. "Ye smelled somethin' fierce an' yer eyes were runnin' an' yer clothes were stained wi'—"

"I said I remember!" Daniel put up his hand to stop her. "I was there," he grimaced, "sort of."

His stomach turned over at the recollection of that night.. For someone with no memory, why did she have to remember *that* so clearly?

He decided it might be best to treat it as a joke. "As I recall, you weren't in such great shape yourself. You were barefoot, your hair was a mess, and you were dressed in nothing but a nightgown." He caught a look at her stricken face and wanted to call the words back. "I'm sorry, lass, I was just teasing."

"But tha's it," she said softly. "I dinnae ken why I was there. I dinnae ken where I was! I dinnae remember anythin'!" Her voice rose. "I dinnae ken Inverness, or why I was in a nightgoon, or who I am."

She paused, gathered herself together, and let her breath out slowly.

"Daniel..."

"Yes, lass?"

"Wha's this thing—em-nees-a?"

"Amnesia. It's a condition where you have memory loss. It can be caused by a head injury, like an accident, or an emotional shock, or drugs."

"What er drugs?"

Daniel registered that odd question. Who in this day and age didn't know what drugs were? Was she making this up? No, whatever her problem, her fear and anxiety were real.

"Never mind. I'll explain later. Anyway, amnesia can also be caused by a high fever, or brain damage from alcohol, or—"

"Do ye hae em-nesia, then?"

Daniel choked, then narrowed his eyes. Was she having him on? She looked back at him, her own eyes round and innocent. No, damn it, she wasn't. She was asking him honestly, based on what she had seen that night. *And let that be a lesson, lad. Out of the mouths of babes.*

His mind returned to something else she had said.

"You don't know who you are?"

She looked down and twisted her fingers together. "Nae."

"Then how do you know your name? Did someone tell you?"

"Mary Duncan gae it t' me. She said I reminded 'er o' somebody name o' Eve."

She brightened. "So mebbe I am named Eve. Do ye think 'at's possible?"

If he lived to be a hundred, Daniel would never disparage any idea that brought such a look of hope to her face. If she thought she might be named Eve, then Eve she was. Besides, it wasn't hard to believe that Mary Duncan might know more than met the eye.

In fact, he wouldn't be surprised to hear that Mary and her whole crazy lot were practicing magic out of that wee office of theirs. That bastard Baltair wasn't the only strange one in the group.

"Did Mary also tell you your name was MacDonald?"

Eve grinned at him. "Nae. I picked 'at name myself. It was on th' castle."

Daniel gave her a confused look. "The castle? Inverness castle?" His face cleared. "Oh, you mean on the statue of Flora MacDonald out front?"

Eve shook her head. "Nae on a statue. On th' castle. 'Tis written next t' th' golden croon. I think th' king' o' Inverness lives there."

Daniel shook his head to clear it. What in hell was she talking about? The king of Inverness? A golden crown? Then it hit him, and he sucked in his breath to keep from bursting into laughter.

"Did the crown look like this?" He drew the hamburger chain's distinctive logo in the air with his finger.

Eve nodded, beaming. "'At's it! I kent I was verra clever to pick th' name."

Daniel wanted, more than anything he'd ever wanted in his life, to fold this adorable person into his arms and never let go. How brave she was. Not knowing who or where she might be, she still found happiness in a world that must be so frightening to her.

She'd already endeared herself to the Highland Players, to him, and he suspected to Callum as well. And that was a problem that would have to be faced later. Because he wasn't giving her up, no matter where she came from or what her name was.

And yet, there was something wrong with her story. He felt himself drifting down from the cloud she'd put him on.

What kind of amnesia caused a person to forget things like McDonalds? To not know what drugs were? In his copious online studies on panic disorder, he'd come across nothing that would cause a complete and total loss of memory like that. Of course, he was far from being a doctor, so perhaps it was possible.

"Daniel? Are ye listenin'?" Eve's voice sounded worried. "I said, d'ye ken th' king'll mind if I borrow his name?"

And that did it. Daniel pulled her into his arms and held her close.

"No, lass, I don't think King McDonald will mind at all. I think he'd be honored. You did w"

Footsteps sounded outside the van. Daniel realized that he was still holding onto Eve, and pushed her back into her seat as the driver's door was flung open.

"Well, here you are," Callum said. "They need everyone to work, and you two disappeared all of a sudden so I offered to come out and see if everything was all right," He ignored Daniel and looked across to Eve. "And so, I'm asking—is everything all right?"

"Everything is fine," Daniel said. "She was"

"I was asking Eve," Callum said. His voice was tight and his blue eyes shot sparks.

Eve looked between the two men and her smile faded. For that alone Daniel wanted to punch his cousin in the mouth.

"She was cold," he said. "I remembered there was a blanket out here in the van, so we came to get it." He leveled his gaze at his cousin, but Callum refused to look at him. Instead, he raised his head and spoke to the sky.

"Ahh, I see. She was *cold*, so instead of leaving her in a warm building while you went out to get a blanket, you dragged her out into the *cold* with you to sit in a *cold* van. Makes all kinds of sense."

Daniel shrugged. "Seemed like a good idea at the time." He pushed the driver's door further open, forcing Callum to move aside or be hit, and climbed down. He planted his feet and glared at his cousin.

"Didn't you say everyone was needed to work?" he said. "I guess we'd better be getting back then, aye? Eve, bring the blanket with you." He clapped his hand on Callum's shoulder.

"Time tae gie intae character, och aye?" Daniel smirked at his cousin. "Thenk ye fur yer kindness, coosin, in comin' tae rescue us from th' heavy wither. Aye, Evie?"

There was no answer. Both men turned to stare into the van. They were alone in the car park; Eve was gone.

CHAPTER TWENTY-ONE
GLENCOE, SCOTLAND –
20 DECEMBER, 1691

ANDREW

hat an eejit!

Andrew MacDonald bent his head and shuttered his eyes to hide the contempt he felt for his clan's laird.

"Aye, I'll sign, but I'll nae gie th' bastarts an easy time o' it!" Alexander Maclain's voice filled the cottage, his outrage apparent for all to see and hear.

"I'm off t' Inverlochy t' sell my soul t' the devil, bit I willnae do it till th' end o' the month. It's only fair tae make the gover'mint bastarts sweat a wee bit, aye?"

Amidst the cheers that greeted this announcement, Andrew's reaction might have been noted for its absence of felicity. That is, it would have been had most of the men not been so far into their cups that they could barely stand.

As it was, no one saw the scowl that darkened Andrew's face as Maclain struggled to his feet and raised his cup, sloshing much of its contents into the straw as he strove to remain erect.

Amongst these men Maclain's word was golden, but Andrew knew he wasn't alone in his disdain for the laird's bloviating. The chief of the Glencoe MacDonalds had been sounding off since August, when the royal proclamation came out offering pardon to all Highland clans if they signed an oath of allegiance to William by the end of the year.

At first Maclain had adamantly refused even to consider such a betrayal to James, the rightful king, and he hadn't been the only one. The clans had been slow to accept William's offer, many outright refusing to make the journey to Inverary to sign the document. Alexander and his men had gone even further, stepping up their raids on any cattle whose owners looked the other way.

In truth, the cattle were an excuse to avoid wholesale slaughter between warring clans, and everyone knew it. Men were too valuable to their families and farms to risk being killed in battle, so any slight—and there were many—could be avenged by stealing a man's cattle instead of meeting him with a dirk.

But Maclain had gone too far. By taunting the crown on the terms of the pardon, he was risking the lives of his entire clan. Andrew watched the chief strut drunkenly about the room. These men, those around this table who inflated their laird's ego and looked the other way, they were the problem. They were going to get everyone killed, if someone didn't intervene.

Andrew cast his mind back to the conversation he'd had with his father two months ago.

"Mebbe if I keep away, my displeasure will be noticed when my voice is no longer heard," Domhnall had told his son.

"Th' king has bin more than generoos t' us. He's offered t' pardon th' clans fur what happened at Killiecrankie e'en when so many gover'mint troops were killed."

He sighed. "It dinnae help 'at some o' th' lads celebrated the victory by leavin' a path o' destruction through th' lands of a certain Cap'n Robert Campbell o' His Majesty's Royal Forces." He paused and then added under his breath, "the wee bastard—may he rot in hell."

Andrew watched his father closely. Domhnall MacDonald was a canny man; he had never let himself get too bothered by his clan's less than savory exploits before, although he'd refused to partake in cattle thievery long ago. A furrow appeared between the younger MacDonald's blue eyes. He'd never noticed before, but his father looked...old.

"Is there somethin' more, Da?"

Domhnall wiped a hand over his brow. "Dinnae ken. Jist, Campbell's at Fort William noo, too close fir comfort. I'm worrit 'at th' king has some other plan, an' we'll no get by sae easy."

"Wha' kin I do?" Andrew asked him.

"Keep yer eyes an' ears open. Go t' th' gatherin's an' tell me whit ye hear. We'll talk it o'er."

Andrew nodded. "Ye think our laird will do somethin' stoopit?

"Nae, no stoopit, more like reckless. Alexander's a proud man. Sometimes his pride makes him stooborn, an' when he's drunk, it's worse." He reached over and patted his son's knee.

"I dinnae ken," he said, "but I have a bad feelin'. No matter what happens, we must protect th' family. You, wee Seumas, an' Siònaid. Her faither trusted 'er t' my care, an' I willnae let him doon."

Now Andrew sat at the table in Alexander Maclain's cottage and let the chaos around him fade away.

Da's wrong, he thought. It was reckless if those other eejits ran off raging with drink. It was deadly if the clan's chief gave in to his hatred and led his men to disaster. Maclain held every life in Glencoe in his hands—those same hands that right now were waving in the air like those of a lunatic.

Andrew picked up his cup and pretended to drink. Across the table, Maclain went on ranting about the *gover'mint*, and the pardon, and what he'd like to do to William if he ever saw him in person, while the other old coots hooted and hollered their praise.

More often than ever these days his thoughts went to Killiecrankie, his first battle. His first kill. Three years ago now, but he still woke up some nights sweating, his heart racing. He hadn't told Da about the nightmares...or about the slithering feeling in his gut, the *satisfaction*. The desire to do it all again. And Domhnall MacDonald, only too glad to be home on the rig and away from battle, had never asked.

Maybe he should have.

He felt something dark and familiar rise in his gut. It been happening more and more frequently, a black need that begged for release, a desire to feel that elation that came from watching the light go out of a man's eyes.

Until last October, he'd kept it subdued, pushed into the darkest corner of his soul. Then had come the incident in November. It wasn't his fault what had happened that day, but it had changed everything.

Suddenly, he felt nauseous. He put a hand on his forehead, but it was cool to the touch. He wasn't sick. Did *sickened* count?

Andrew had gone faithfully to the gatherings at his laird's house. He'd kept his eyes and his ears open, and he'd reported back some of the things he'd heard to his father. But even Da didn't know everything.

He told himself he'd made the right choice, but the truth was there had never been a choice. Whatever happened, he had done what he had to do, there was no going back now. At least his family would be safe.

His thoughts turned to them. *Seumas.* Something was bothering his little brother; his natural exuberance was gone and he slunk around the cottage like a shadow. He no longer followed Andrew around, dogging his footsteps. Now Seumas spent all his time with his head buried in his books, or clinging to Siònaid.

His heart warmed at the thought of Siònaid. He conjured up her image. Tiny thing, she was; Seumas was going to catch up to her in height soon, if she didn't watch out. Graceful in spite of her limp, quite pretty, with that long black hair and those huge grey eyes.

She had a lilting island accent, too, that made him seek her out just to ask questions and listen to her answer them. If it hadn't been for the farming, and for other things, he might have joined Seumas in his lessons.

Other things.

"Ah ken aam shupposed tae gang tae Inverary, but if I hae tae sign th' damn thin' I want tae do it in front o' a solger, nae a damn gover'mint arse!" Alexander Maclain's voice slurred across the table.

The smile slid off Andrew's face. He stood up and made his way to the door and out. No one saw him go. No one ever did; he was getting good at this.

As he made his way down the path to his own cottage, the weather seemed to pick up his mood. It was snowing again, flakes that were more ice than snow. Pellets stung his face and his boots crunched on the whitening path. The snow was already deep enough that had he not known where it was, he could've walked right off the path and onto the rig in the dark.

Winter in Glencoe. The cottages huddled into themselves, as if afraid to get too close to each other. Flickers of light in the small windows were the only indication of human habitation. The rigs were empty now in winter; all the crops salted and stored away inside the cottages, making them even more crowded. He hoped everyone was asleep and blessed the darkness that would shadow his face and hide his thoughts.

Siònaid.

Would she forgive him? Would any of them forgive him? He'd let himself slip that one time, bared his soul to Siònaid, and told her about his inner demons. But she didn't know all of it. She'd thought he was noble.

It didn't matter. If things turned out right, none of them would ever know, and if it all went to hell, it didn't matter anyway.

CHAPTER TWENTY-TWO
GLENCOE, SCOTLAND - 1
FEBRUARY, 1692

SIÒNAID

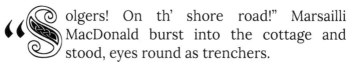"olgers! On th' shore road!" Marsailli MacDonald burst into the cottage and stood, eyes round as trenchers.

Siònaid stilled her foot and looked up from the spinning wheel, glad for anything that would rescue her from the boredom of watching the wheel go around endlessly while producing something that was supposed to look like wool, but resembled more an endless snake that had eaten something bad and deposited it in lumps along its length.

"Solgers?" she asked. "From where? An' close th' door, will ye? You're lettin' in th' weather."

Marsailli ignored her. She drew her breath in and let it out dramatically. Siònaid sighed. She bit off the end of the wool, studied it for a minute, and consigned it to the basket as a lost cause. Then she turned on the stool and prepared to give her full attention to the young girl who stood in the open doorway with excitement flashing from her blue eyes.

At fourteen, Marsailli was the youngest woman in the croft and possibly the most tiresome; she meant well, but was a born gossip and not above adding a bit of exaggeration to her stories to make life just a wee bit more interesting. The solgers were as like to be villagers coming home from a morning of fishing as anything else.

"Comin' from Ballachulish," Marsailli told her. "Hunnerds of 'em, Robby said."

"Ahh," Siònaid said, drawing out the word as far as it would go. "Robby said."

Marsailli's blush bled into her red hair. She frowned, stomped one foot, and put her hands on her hips.

"Aye, Robby saw 'em with 'is ain eyes!"

"Robby saw hunnerds o' solgers comin' up th' shore road from Ballachulish?"

Marsailli nodded her head vigorously. "Aye. Robby said—oof!"

She was pushed to the side as the open doorway admitted Andrew, followed by Marsailli's father John and her brother Ciaran. Within seconds, the croft was filled with the bodies of large men.

There was an urgency about them, a sense of purpose that Siònaid had never seen before. They paid no attention to the women but went to their pallets and extracted muskets and swords from hidden recesses.

Siònaid grabbed Andrew's arm as he passed by and swung him to face her.

"What's going on? Are there really solgers comin'?"

Andrew took both of her hands in his. "Aye. there are. We dinnae think they mean harm, but we're nae takin' chances, aye?" He captured her eyes with his own. "Ye dinnae need tae fash yerself. I'll ne'er let anythin' happen tae ye."

He made as if to release her hands, but she clutched his and held him in place.

"Who are they?"

Andrew sighed and set his musket against the wall.

"Gover'mint."

Siònaid's breath caught in her throat. "King's men?"

"Aye. About a hunnerd. John's taken twenty men t' wait at th' end a th' glen tae see why they're visitin' us in th' middle o' winter. Da's with him. He told us t' hide our weapons outside in th' hay an' thatch in case o' need." He gave her a smile that didn't quite reach his eyes. "Doesnae hurt tae be prepared, aye?"

He made to leave, but Siònaid held him back.

"John Maclain's there? Th' chief's son?"

Andrew blew out a breath. "Aye. Th' solgers 're wearin' red coats an' grey breeks. That means it's Argyll's reg'ment, so that's good."

"Why's it good?" Siònaid pressed. "Who's Argyll?"

Andrew's lip twisted. "Archibald Campbell, the tenth Earl of Argyll. It's his captain who'll be leadin' th' men."

"But why's it good?"

"Th' captain is one Robert Campbell. A right bastart, t' be true, but by way o' being a kinsman t' our chief."

"Our chief?" Siònaid asked. "Alastair Maclain? How on earth is a Campbell kin t' a MacDonald?"

"Not sure m'self," Andrew said. "Somethin' wi' his mother, an' one o' her husbands bein' a MacDonald, an' the chief's wife is her granddaughter, so the captain is kin by marriage. Not pure blood, o' course, an' Robert Campbell surely hates th' MacDonalds o' Glencoe, but th' tie shuid keep us safe.

"An' that's enough—I have t' go, *leannan*." He picked up his musket and ran out the door to join the others.

The croft was eerily silent in the wake of the men's departure, but not for long.

"Ye see?" Marsailli said. "Robby wus right."

"Aye." Siònaid said, her voice soft and distant. "Robby wus surely right."

But her mind was not on Marsailli or the triumph in her young voice. She was remembering Andrew's last word before he left the croft.

Leannan. Darling.

Despite the anxiety over the unusual visit by government soldiers and what that might mean, Siònaid felt a warm feeling make its way through her body. *Sweetheart.* He'd called her *sweetheart.* She tucked the word away to be revisited and pondered later, but she couldn't help the smile that she knew must be spreading over her face.

A small hand tugged on her gown, and Siònaid looked down to see Seumas' worried face upturned to hers.

"Is 'e gone?" he said.

Siònaid's smile disappeared, and she knelt to look into the boy's anxious blue eyes. She'd forgotten he was there, sitting in the corner with his books as usual. These past weeks the lad had made himself almost invisible unless the two of them were alone in the croft.

Seumas was no longer the exuberant student she'd known since becoming a member of this family. Was he ill? He'd seemed to be getting better, but the memory of that attack was never far from her mind. He said little, and refused to go outside unless she made him. Even then he rarely ventured far from the croft and never without her.

The fear in his eyes, the way he'd gone rigid, and then collapsed into her arms, haunted her. It hadn't happened again, but something had broken inside young Seumas on that day back in October.

She pushed the soldiers and Andrew into the back of her mind and concentrated on her young charge. Did it have something to do with the black-cloaked figure they'd seen near the woods that afternoon? The scream that had sent her into a limping run, dragging him along behind her? Was this all her doing?

Siònaid pulled him into her arms and hugged him tightly. Time to deal with it—the guilt that rose up to choke her whenever she looked at Seumas. There was something very wrong with him, and it had nothing to do with frailty or illness.

She stroked his hair. It had to be faced—this might very well be her fault—for reacting in panic that day and frightening him so badly. The experience had caused him to have some sort of attack from which he hadn't recovered. He'd become timid and fearful because of her overreaction to a barely glimpsed figure and a scream.

But...her hand stilled on Seumas' head. *Had* it been an overreaction? News had come two days later; the body of a young man from a croft at the other end of the glen, discovered near the edge of the mountain not far from Glencoe. He'd been stabbed, and his body thrown into the bushes.

What passed for law in the village had found nothing to explain the killing. There was a great amount of posturing and threatening the unknown killer with heinous acts of retribution if found, but the lad had been a known troublemaker, and it was assumed he'd met his end through his own fault. The men had honored his passing by getting drunk and singing songs in his memory. Glencoe justice.

But *someone* had killed him. Her worry for Seumas threatened to close her throat, and she fought the tears that rose into her eyes at his fearful expression. She'd discussed it with Andrew and Uncle Dom, but they were as much at a loss as she about the source of Seumas' distress.

She'd told Andrew of the black-coated figure and the scream that had sent them running for the croft that day, but he'd assured her that there could be no connection to the death of the young man from up-glen. The body hadn't been found anywhere near Glencoe, he said; there was no way she could have heard anything from the village path. He patted her hand and told her that too much reading was making her imagination run wild.

Siònaid had smiled and agreed that was likely the case. But the part of her that would not let her lie to herself knew he was wrong. She had seen and heard something, and so had Seumas.

She hadn't told anyone about the lad's strange reaction. She wasn't sure why, but she sensed that Seumas wouldn't want her to; he never mentioned it and somehow it seemed intensely personal, an experience shared by the two of them alone.

A memory teased its way to the surface of her mind, something Seumas had said. She prodded it, and slowly it opened itself to her recollection.

Is 'e gone? he had said.

The croft had been full of men, but Seumas MacDonald had said *he*, not *they*. As if he was afraid of someone in his own cottage. A person he saw every day.

She held him tighter and tried to dispel the dread that gripped her mind.

I saw—he had said back then. She knew he must have seen the same thing she did, a black-cloaked figure in the far distance. But what if it wasn't the some*thing*, but some*one*? And what if it was someone he knew?

CHAPTER TWENTY-THREE

NÈAMH HOUSE, SCOTTISH HIGHLANDS - PRESENT DAY

*I will hurt you for this. A day will come
when you think yourself safe and happy, and
suddenly your joy will turn to ashes in your
mouth, and you'll know the debt is paid.*
—George R.R. Martin

"I am not your enemy."

Down below, the faint sound of bagpipes could be heard from the patio of Nèamh House. The late winter sun reflected off the waters of the firth, and motors could be heard as faire goers arrived and left.

But here, high on the hillside and deep within the shelter of the pine forest, the mist refused to lift even though the day was near its peak. Wispy tendrils wrapped around the trunks like wraiths and reached grey fingers into the clearing where Eve stood facing Baltair, hands fisted at her side.

"Are ye my friend?" she countered. "I dinnae ken a friend would snatch me awa' an' spirit me deep intae th' forest against my will, aye?"

Baltair gave her a level look, devoid of expression. "I never said I was your friend, lass."

"Then what are ye? Why did ye bring me here? And how?" She should have been frightened; there was something about this man that exuded power and mystery, but all she felt was irritation and curiosity.

"What do you remember?" he asked.

"Dae ye always answer a question wi' a question, sir?" Eve was trying her best to sound as if she were the one in charge here, but she suspected Baltair wasn't fooled in the least.

"Do you always avoid answering the first one?" There was humor in his tone, but nothing about this scene was funny. She felt like a mouse being toyed with by a very large cat—a cat that knew exactly what it was doing and when to pounce.

She sighed. "All right. I dinnae remember anythin'. Nae, that's nae true—I remember ye. I remember hearin' yer voice, just a while ago an' once before."

His lips creased into a smile that transformed his face into something otherworldly, a palette of incomparable beauty and almost ethereal magnificence. Then it was gone, replaced again by the pale, unlined, and expressionless visage she had seen behind the table at the wedding faire.

Baltair shook his head. "And that is really all you remember?"

Eve thought about the question. Slowly, more images crawled out of the murk and danced before her eyes. Yes, she did remember more. She remembered thatched roofs and farmland, huge mountains, and a fast-running river. The smell of peat and cook fires. Horses.

And a man with brown eyes, a man who held a bloody dagger and caused her heart to flip and her chest to constrict with—what? Anger? Hatred? Surely not...love?

She folded that memory and pushed it into a dark corner of her mind. No, she would not be telling anyone about that one. Not Daniel or Callum, and certainly not the man who stood before her, his black eyes fixed on hers. Not until she understood what it meant.

But there were things she *could* ask Baltair. Things she had to ask.

"Do ye ken where I came from?"

"Aye." He said nothing more. So, he wasn't going to tell. This just wasn't at all fun. She tried again.

"Do ye ken who I am?" Her heart was racing; she could feel it thumping like a war drum in her chest.

"Aye. I ken who you were."

What odd phrasing—who she *was*?

"Do ye ken why—" Eve felt suddenly dizzy. Baltair stared at her, waiting. She took a deep breath and let it out, opened her mouth, and the words tumbled out in a rush.

"I cannae feel anythin'. I dinnae feel cold when I ken "tis cold. I dinnae feel warm when I sit near th' hearth. If I stub my foot, ur cut my hand, I dinnae feel it. There is nae bruise, nae bluid." She stumbled to a halt, her breathing harsh and labored, as if she had been running.

"Do-do ye ken why that is?"

Baltair held her gaze. "Aye."

Anger surged through Eve, bringing tears of helpless fury. She wanted to hit the man, standing there so smug and sure, to pummel him until he howled for mercy and agreed to tell her what she needed to know. She wanted to wipe that self-satisfied smirk off his arrogant face. How could he be so disinterested, when she had just bared her soul, shared her innermost fear with him?

She planted her feet and clenched her fists. "Why do ye keep saying *aye*? Ye pulled me up here, awa' from my friends, fer a reason. What d' ye want?"

A shadow passed over Baltair's face. He continued to stare at Eve for a long moment, and then he sighed.

"It is not what I want, lass," he said, his voice gentle. "It is what *you* want."

"I dinnae understand!" Now the tears came, born of frustration and impotence. She squatted down on the forest floor, put her hands over her face, and sobbed. All the fear, the uncertainty, the strangeness of her situation came together and released themselves in those tears.

Baltair made no move to console her. He stood still and watched as she cried herself out. After a few moments, Eve's sobs dwindled into whimpers, then faded away altogether. She sat for a while with her face in her hands, listening to the sounds of the forest, and then stood and brushed the pine needles off her skirt.

Without another look, she turned and walked down the hillside, toward Nèamh House, toward

Mary Duncan and Betty MacBain, toward Henry and Callum—toward Daniel. Baltair did not stop her.

As she walked, Eve thought about the strange man she'd left behind. Who was he? What did he want from her? Because he certainly wanted something, else why spirit her away like that?

Was he a wizard? A ghost? No, maybe an angel? Was she dead, and was this heaven?

Eve stopped short and thought about that. Maybe when you died you went to a different place, a magical place. Maybe God took away all your memories and you had to start over to make new ones. Perhaps that was why she couldn't feel anything; God didn't want her to suffer from the cold or the heat.

She began walking again. No, that didn't make sense. This couldn't be heaven. It was Scotland; she had seen the signs, in two languages. *Scotland. Alba.*

And whatever God might want mattered little because she *was* suffering. The not knowing was killing her.

Besides, she *did* have memories, and more were coming every day. She remembered a blizzard, the feel of the ice on her face. She saw the brown-eyed man as clearly as if he stood before her now, and she knew he was real. She felt the hatred, the betrayal. Knew that if she saw him again, she would kill him for what he had done.

Kill? Was she willing to kill for this memory? She leaned over and emptied the contents of her stomach into a pine bush. The wind was increasing, swirling the leaves and needles and rustling in her ear, but inside her mind, words began to form.

The rustle became Baltair's voice; it whispered in her head as it had twice before. *What do you want? You will have your wish.* And this time there were new words. *You will be a revenant, cursed...*

Was she cursed? If this was not heaven, could it be hell? Eve turned to look back up the mountain path, where nothing moved except the branches of the trees. Was Baltair, then, not an angel but the devil?

No. Eve forced her breathing to slow, waited until her heartbeat slowed, and her thoughts stopped stabbing at her like a thousand tiny knives. No matter how infuriating the man was, she sensed no evil in him. He was frustrating, to be sure, but what had he done to her, after all?

He had brought her to a beautiful mountain clearing and asked her questions. Granted, he hadn't answered hers, but there had been no threats, no demands; he had not forced her to do anything. All the fury came from her.

Perhaps it wasn't his fault. What if Baltair couldn't tell her what she wanted so desperately to know? Maybe he had been trying to help her to find the answers within herself. And she had reacted like a child who has been denied the treat she wants, whinging and greeting like a baby.

It is not what I want, lass. It is what you want. He had looked so sad when he said those words, so disappointed.

Eve pivoted on the mountain path and started upward again. The wind had picked up and the bushes were quivering as if to say, *Hurry up! Go!*

The walk back to the clearing seemed to take much

longer than the journey down, but she'd been pro-pelled by anger then and likely hadn't noticed. Walking uphill was harder too. After a while, she sat down on a tree stump. Had it been there before? And she rested for a few minutes before going on. The path mean-dered through the forest, as if it had nowhere to go and all the time in the world to get there.

Finally, she stopped and turned in a circle. She could hear the bagpipes behind and below, and through a break in the trees, she could see the sun glistening off the water of the firth, far away. Everything was as it had been before. But the clearing and Baltair were gone. She was alone on the mountain.

Eve began to retrace her steps down to Nèamh House, her mind numb. She picked up her pace and hurried as fast as she could go without tripping; almost racing toward the only normalcy she now knew. She needed Betty's arm around her, Mary's soft words of encouragement. A face appeared in her mind, and she quickened her step. She needed to see Daniel.

The path ended at a meadow behind the car park, and Eve felt relief bubble up and threaten to spill out at the familiar sight of the Highland Players' van. People were arriving and leaving, but Daniel and Callum were gone, so she bypassed the park and walked up the paved path again.

Two men dressed in Highland attire held their swords aloft as she approached. She hadn't met these two yet, but they must be part of the Highland Players. She nodded to them and proceeded through the great room of Nèamh House, out onto the patio, and into the room where the wedding faire was in full swing.

A group of people was clustered around the Players' table, gesturing and talking. She heard Callum's voice, rough and agitated, and Mary's soothing tones. The man named Bennet was arguing with the other man, she'd forgotten his name, Wee something...and behind the table, watching it all and saying nothing, was Baltair.

"She couldn't have gone far! Dan and I were right there!"

"Settle down, lad, Henry and Daniel are out looking for her. It's impossible to get lost here."

"Maybe she wandered into one of the rooms in the house and fell asleep."

"Ailis is talking to the manager. We'll check everything; calm down."

"Hmmm." Baltair put his hand up, and like magic, the noise died to nothing.

"Here she is," he said, his tone calm. "Glad you're back, lass. You caused a right ruckus."

Eve gaped at him. In the next second, she was rushed by Mary and Betty and squeezed like a dish rag.

"You gave us such a fright," Betty said. "Don't do that again; my heart can't stand it!"

"Somebody go and find Henry an' Daniel and tell them Eve's been found," Mary ordered. "Evie, come stand behind the table and take Wee Caomhainn's place. All you have to do is give the guests a pamphlet, aye?"

Before Eve could comply, Daniel rushed into the room. Heedless of the watching Players, he took her by the arms and looked deep into her eyes.

"Don't ever do that again, you hear?" he said, his voice rough. "I'm tired of losing you."

Eve couldn't answer. The breath seemed to have left her body, and she felt as if she were suspended in the air. The people in the room receded into the distance; all she could see were Daniel's eyes. Velvet brown eyes filled with dread, like the ones in her memory. The eyes of a man who had once pledged his eternal love—a wild-haired man who held a dirk dripping with the blood of her family.

Words rushed into her mind with the freezing wind of a blizzard.

If you pursue this path, the outcome may not be worth the cost...

you will become a revenant...

cursed to exist for but one purpose...vengeance.

Granted. You will have your wish.

Eve wrenched her eyes away from Daniel's and turned to look at the man who stood behind the table.

Baltair's eyes held all the sadness in the world. Slowly, he nodded.

CHAPTER TWENTY-FOUR
MILBURN ROAD, INVERNESS, SCOTLAND - PRESENT DAY

Owning our story can be hard but not nearly as difficult as spending our lives running from it.
—Brené Brown

D aniel glared at the box of papers on his desk. He heaved a sigh and put on a pair of plastic gloves. Might as well get this done. He pulled the box over and began to remove the wrinkled, sometimes stained documents one by one, holding each gingerly, and then assigning it to a pile according to its subject matter.

Material orders, architectural drawings, construction diagrams, change orders, invoices, all went into the growing heaps on the desk. The work was monotonous, almost rhythmic. He stacked by rote, allowing his mind to wander while his hands did the work.

In the background, he could hear the rain drumming on the roof of the trailer. Early spring in the Highlands—wet, muddy, and cold. The weather matched his current mood perfectly. His thoughts meandered, stalled, and inevitably returned to that day two weeks ago at Nèamh House, to the look on Eve's face.

What was wrong with his fairy? Why was she avoiding him? His brows drew in. Did it have anything to do with that Baltair person? Daniel knew he hadn't imagined that look, how her expression had changed from delight to confusion in a matter of seconds. He'd caught the exchange with Baltair when her head turned away from him. The nod from that bastard, like a secret communication.

The man knew something. His face was always expressionless, but there had been something in those black eyes that gave him away. For just an instant they had held—what? Melancholy, sorrow?

And in the next second, Eve had thrust Daniel away. She'd directed her gaze to the floor and refused to meet his eyes. For the rest of the faire, she passed out pamphlets with a smile that never reached her eyes, and on the way home in the van, she answered direct questions like a robot, saying nothing unless forced to do so. Since he was afraid of what he might hear, he'd asked no questions at all.

He hadn't seen her since. She didn't have a mobile, which was both irritating and incomprehensible, so he couldn't call or text. He'd stopped in at the Highland Players office once or twice, but she hadn't been there and he didn't want to give himself away by asking for her.

Those eerie people probably knew more than they were saying too. He felt even more like an outsider than usual, but this time it rankled. They had been kind, especially that Mary Duncan, and Henry had clapped him on the shoulder and told him not to worry; they'd take care of the lass.

They'd take care of the lass. Not him. As if Eve needed to be protected from something or someone. As if they were all united in some secret plot to leave him out.

He knew he was being childish and fanciful. They had welcomed him in as one of their own just a few weeks ago, given him a costume, drilled him on the old speech patterns. But that bloody Baltair bastard was their leader, and Daniel knew he hadn't been wrong about that look. He might be damaged, but he wasn't an eejit.

Something broke into his brooding, and he directed his attention to the paper in his hand. It was a simple change order for labor to add additional electrical outlets to the primary office space. Nothing special. He looked more carefully at the document and realized what it was that had distracted him.

It was thicker than the others because it wasn't one paper but two. Another page was stuck to the back of the one he was holding. He inserted his thumbnail between the papers and carefully peeled them apart, curling his lip in disgust.

It didn't bear thinking about what kind of substance had acted as the glue here. It wasn't being unkind to say his predecessor had been a slob; it could have been jelly or sugar from a glazed doughnut, or any of a hundred things he didn't want to think about. Was one pair of gloves enough for this job?

The writing on the second paper was almost obliterated with coffee stains. At first glance, it looked like an order for rebar, simple and straightforward. But there was something wrong with the requested size. It was a far smaller thickness than the project design would call for. Had it been meant for another job? Daniel picked up his mobile and punched in a number.

"What's up, boss?" Big Angus lumbered into the trailer, peeled off his raincoat, and plunked his bulky frame down in the metal chair. Daniel averted his eyes from the muddy boot prints that trailed from the door to the chair, and passed the materials order over to his foreman.

"Rebar." Angus shrugged. "What about it?"

Daniel waited. Big Angus watched him for a minute, then shrugged again, and looked at the paper in his hand. He studied it, made as if to hand it back, then stopped, and looked at it once more.

"Cannae be for this site," he said. "Rebar's too thin t' hold up a building this size. Mebbe got mixed in by mistake."

"Was Mr. Chisolm in charge of more than one job?" Daniel kept his voice even.

Angus looked down at the signature above *Project Manager*.

"No," he said. "Company policy. You'd know that better'n me, aye?"

The two men stared at each other in silence. The rain continued to ping on the metal roof of the trailer, but Daniel didn't notice. He was remembering a dark close, three men huddled too closely together.

Callum's words: "*Cops pulled a body out of a bin in the close this morning.*" And his uncle: "*The dead man was our project manager on the Millburn site...stabbed and thrown into the rubbish bin.*"

The back of Daniel's neck prickled. What had Kevin Chisolm been involved in?

He stood suddenly and stripped off the gloves. "Let's go see the crew, shall we?" he said to Big Angus.

He took off his dress shoes and stacked them neatly side by side in the tray he'd bought for the purpose. He knew Graham was watching him, and he was pretty sure what the big man was thinking.

So what? Daniel shrugged. He snagged his work boots from the tray and sat down in the chair he'd placed by the door. The project manager should dress neatly, even if everyone else on the site looked like something dragged in by a wildcat. It sent a message, elevated the job.

You're such an arse, the derisive voice in his head said. *You do it because you can't help it. And the only message you're sending is that you're a pretentious bampot.*

"Shut up," he muttered. "You're no help."

"I didn't say anythin'," Angus said.

Daniel looked up to see an aggrieved look on his foreman's face.

"Sorry, wasn't talking to you," he assured him. He finished tying the laces on his boots and grabbed his parka from the hook above the tray. "Let's get on with it."

A crew of laborers was working to remove the scaffolding at the north end of the building.

"We should start wi' Rob Erskine," Big Angus said. "He's got th' ear o' the lads—it's why they elected him steward." Daniel nodded, and Angus pulled up his radio. A moment later, a middle-aged man in jeans and hooded rain jacket appeared at the edge of the scaffold and waved down to his foreman.

Angus stuffed the radio back into his belt and cupped his hands around his mouth. "We need ye fer a minute, Rob!" The man nodded and scrambled down the scaffolding ladder. He loped across the muddy site and stood before them, grinning.

"Thanks, I needed a wee break; some of those numpty's'll give you a headache if you let 'em."

Daniel knew Robert Erskine as a no-nonsense man whose cheerful, devil-may-care demeanor belied a keen intelligence. Erskine loved the hands-on aspect of the construction business and seemed to have no ambition beyond what he was doing now. He was honest and reasonable, and when the laborers chose him to be their steward, he accepted the position with gratitude and pledged to be worthy of their trust. So far he'd proven them right in their choice.

Now he waited patiently, hands clasped behind his back.

"We wanted t' get yer opinion on somethin'," Angus began. "We came across somethin' odd in the records, an'." He broke off and sent a side glance at his project manager.

"To begin with," Daniel said, watching the steward's eyes as he spoke, "how well did you know Kevin Chisolm?"

Erskine's brows drew together. "Chisolm? Not well, really. Never worked with him before this job." He studied his boots for a long moment, before looking up and focusing on Daniel once more.

"It was an awful thing, what happened to him," he said quietly. "Nobody should be killed like that and then thrown away like rubbish."

Daniel cleared his throat. " Aye. Do you know if he was working on another job besides this one?"

Erskine looked bewildered. "No! I mean, that's the rule, isn't it?"

Neither Angus nor Daniel answered.

"He kept himself to himself, didn't socialize much with the crew," Erskine said. He paused. "A couple of the lads hung around with him after hours; I saw them leaving together a few times. They might be able to tell you more about him."

Daniel's eyes caught a flicker of movement, and he looked up to see two of the laborers peering down at them. When they saw him watching, they turned and walked quickly across the plank to the other side of the scaffolding.

Daniel returned his attention to the steward. "Might those lads have been Allan and Dunbar?"

A look of respect crossed Robert Erskine's honest face. "That's the ones!" Then his expression darkened. "They're not in trouble, are they?"

Big Angus held up his hand. "No, nuthin' like 'at," he said. "The boss here would like t' talk with 'em, s'all."

Erskine looked relieved. "I'll get them," he said, and loped back toward the scaffolding.

"Send 'em t' th' trailer!" Angus called after him. He turned to his manager, squinting through the raindrops that dripped from his hood. "'At's right, aye?"

Daniel thought of the mud that was about to be tracked across the floor of his office.

"I suppose it's as good a place as any," he said, and led the way back through the puddles.

As they passed by the center of the office building, neither man heard a tiny popping sound that was masked by the rain, as the crack in the bearing wall worked its way upward.

Minutes later, the door of the trailer was pushed open and two laborers stepped inside, dripping mud from their boots. They squelched over and slid into the metal chairs Daniel had placed in front of the desk. Big Angus had moved a chair to the back of the room, apparently trying to blend in with the wall. *About as inconspicuous as an elephant*, Daniel thought.

Frank Allan and Gil Dunbar looked at him with wary eyes. Their glances darted to each other and then back to him.

Daniel forced a smile.

"Thanks for coming in so quickly," he said. He took a breath and exhaled.

"I understand you were friends of Mr. Chisolm, and I wanted to tell you how sorry I am about what happened."

The men glanced at each other again.

"Thanks, Mr. MacArthur," Gil Dunbar said. "Yeah, it's sad about Mr. Chisolm. But I don't know what you mean about we was friends." He looked at Allan again. "I wasn't friends with him. He was my boss. I ain't friends with nobody; I just do my work and go home." He looked at the other man. "Was you friends with Mr. Chisolm, Frank?"

"Nope," said Allan. "Hardly knew 'im."

"Was it Mr. Erskine said we was friends?" Dunbar asked. His lips parted in a smile that reminded Daniel of a crocodile he'd seen in the Edinburgh Zoo when he was a wee lad.

"Mr. Erskine thinks everybody is friends, ye know?" He waved his hand in the air. "Good man, 'at Mr. Erskine."

They were lying. With the sixth sense he'd developed by searching his own motives for everything, he knew it. *But why?* There was something here, if he could just catch it by the tail.

He waved his hand in the air. "He is a good man," he said, plastering an affable smile on his face. "Funny, he thought you were friends, aye?"

The men pushed back their chairs and began to stand.

"Just one question, before you go," Daniel said, still smiling. The two laborers sat back down, slowly.

"Did Mr. Chisolm work at another job?"

The two men looked genuinely puzzled.

"I don't think so," said Dunbar, after a minute. "He never said." He stopped, stood up, and gave Daniel another smile. "If that's all, we have to get back to work. Got a pint waitin' after, aye?" He made for the door, followed closely by Allan.

Big Angus rose and seated himself in the chair vacated by Frank Dunbar.

"They're lyin'," he said. "Wonder why?"

Daniel shook his head. "We'll have to keep looking." He looked at his watch. "Time to call it quits. Tomorrow I want you to ask around, will you? But be careful."

Big Angus stood and lumbered to the door. He turned with his hand on the knob.

"You too, boss," he said. "You were the one askin' th' questions, mind. You be careful." And he was gone, stumping down the steps and away into the rain.

Daniel sat for a long while, staring across the room at nothing. He thought of Angus' words, and his thoughts traveled again to a dark close on the High Street. A shiver went through him. *You be careful.*

There was a knock on the metal door, and he started in surprise. It was late; everyone should be gone. Besides, no one knocked here, they just stomped in as if they owned the place. He stood and walked around the desk. At the last minute, he picked up a paperweight and hefted it in his right hand. *You be careful.*

He opened the door and stood, transfixed. The paperweight dropped to the floor.

On the bottom step stood Eve McDonald. She was coatless, wearing jeans and a faded red tee shirt with "Manchester United" emblazoned across the front, and she was dripping wet.

She stared at him; her grey eyes were wide.

"Do ye—do ye know me?" she asked, in a trembling voice. "Have ye met me before?"

CHAPTER TWENTY-FIVE
MILBURN ROAD, INVERNESS, SCOTLAND - PRESENT DAY

Maybe love at first sight isn't what we think it is. Maybe it's recognizing a soul we loved in a past life and falling in love with them again.
—Kamand Kojouri

D aniel looked both ways, but the lot was empty. He grabbed Eve's hand and pulled her into the trailer, locking the door behind them. With his free hand, he reached for his parka and placed it around her shoulders.

"I dinnae need that." Her voice was so low he barely caught the words.

"You'll catch a cold," he insisted, and herded her over to the desk. He rolled his padded chair around to the front, pushed her into it, and pulled over one of the metal chairs for himself.

Alarm bells were going off in his head. What the hell was happening here? He hardly knew this girl; they weren't in a relationship—he didn't *do* relationships! He needed to stop whatever was going on with himself right now, get her and her damned hypnotizing grey eyes out of his office and out of his life so he could go home and discuss all this with a bottle of whisky.

Daniel wrenched himself out of his head and struggled for something innocuous. The weather? The latest stock reports? The fact that his guest had arrived on his doorstep dripping wet and without a coat?

He considered that. "Why don't you have a coat?"

There. That was the tone he wanted. He sounded calm, didn't he? In charge of his emotions, able to handle this? Inside, his heart jittered and his inner voice was crooning, *She's here! She came to you!*

"I dinnae need it," Eve's voice broke into the bedlam in his mind. "I dinnae need it, I dinnae need it, I dinnae neeed it!" The litany broke on a sob and she buried her face in her hands.

Daniel sat back, shocked by her vehemence. What was she talking about? She didn't need what?

He watched her for a minute, afraid to do or say anything. He was such a dafty, incapable of handling the important things because his heart was telling him that this might be the most important thing in his life, and the voice inside his head was shouting, *Don't you dare screw this up!*

He didn't know what to say; his brain had evacuated his body and his mind was blank. So, he stopped trying to think, reached over, and pulled her into his arms.

Miraculously, it seemed the right thing to do. Her sobs gradually subsided and her breathing evened out. She didn't move out of his grasp, just lay with her head against his racing heart.

"I cannae feel th' cold," she said at last, not moving. "I cannae feel cold, nor heat, nor th' rain, an' I dinnae ken why I'm this way."

She pushed back and away from him and captured his eyes with hers, begging him to understand.

He didn't. Daniel had no earthly idea what she was talking about. He only knew he would be perfectly happy if he were to die here, looking into those eyes. But the little bit of sense he had left told him that this—what they were doing right now—was what she needed.

"Tell me," he said simply.

She searched his face, nodded on a hiccup, and sat back in the chair; her hands were clasped on her lap.

"I told ye I have nae memories," she began. "That was true, then."

Daniel said nothing, waiting.

"I'm rememberin'." She paused. "Or at least I'm seein' things. I ken they must be memories, coz they're so different from Inverness."

"Different? How?"

"Houses built o' peat. Roofs made o' thatch. An' I feel as if I ken them, nae like th' houses here."

Daniel's eyes widened. "Eve, there are no houses like that anymore. Well, there are a few, but they're very old and there are none around here. Houses aren't built that way anymore."

His eyes lit and he grinned at her. "But it's a clue. Maybe you're from the Western Isles. There are a few thatched houses left there."

His brow furrowed. "But still, even in the most

remote parts, most houses are built from stone or wood today, and the roofs are very like those in Inverness. Shouldn't those be a part of your memories?"

Eve shook her head. "I dinnae remember anythin' like that."

"I'm in the construction business," he said. "We're working on an office building." He watched the confusion shadow her face and gestured toward the door of the trailer. "The building outside—have you never seen anything like it?"

"Nae." She shook her head. "I dinnae think so." Frustration colored her tone. "I dinnae ken so many things." She took a deep shuddering breath.

"But I ken both the auld language and the one people here speak; Mary says 'tis called English. I can read it an' write it, too, bit I dinnae ken how."

Her voice rose. "It frightens me. I dinnae ken what's happenin' to me, an' it frightens me so much, Daniel!" She buried her face against his chest again and fisted the front of his shirt in her small hands.

He was silent, remembering the King of Inverness who lived in a fast-food restaurant on the High Street. Daniel wasn't a doctor, but he would've bet that wasn't an assumption anyone with amnesia would ever make. There was no logic to it, and she knew it. Her fear hung thick in the room.

Something about her distress steadied him. Yes, he was confused about her situation, but no more so than she. She wasn't playing him for a fool—Lord knew he could handle that all by himself—Eve genuinely did not understand what was happening with her body and her mind.

There was so much she didn't know. Yet she knew about thatch and houses made of peat, and she spoke English with a strange accent like that used by the Highland Players when they were performing as people of the past.

Another thought slithered into his mind like a snake, cold and dispassionate, and the calm evaporated like a Highland mist.

Was she...insane? It would explain so much. A chill slid through him. He was alone with this person, and she had his shirt in a death grip. He looked at the door, only twenty feet across the room, and wondered if he should just cut and run. Then he looked at the slip of a girl before him, still wet from the rain and begging him with those eyes, and felt shame course through him. Could he be any more of an arse?

"Are ye a'right?" she asked him.

"I'm fine." He averted his head and looked at the calendar on the wall.

"Are ye sure?"

He swung his head back to her. "I said I'm fine!" He watched her lip quiver and cursed himself. "I mean it, Eve. I'm okay." He took one cold hand in his and forced a smile. "We were talking about you, not me."

She said nothing, but those grey eyes remained locked on his, as though she were studying his soul. He felt naked, vulnerable. As if she could see right through him and read his carefully guarded secrets.

Whatever she saw on his face, it wasn't good. Her

lips tightened and her eyes glistened. He'd frightened her again, damn it.

What now? Was this where he was supposed to say something comforting? Oh God, he was pure shite at this! He felt as if he were walking on ice, that any false step might plunge him into oblivion.

The silence lengthened, punctuated with small, hitching breaths that were definitely hers, because he didn't think he was breathing anymore. He desperately needed a drink.

Daniel made an effort and pulled himself together. "Um," he ventured, "you said you're remembering. Isn't that good?"

"Aye...nae," she said. She looked away from him.

He took her hand and gave it a tentative squeeze. "Is there something else?"

A moment that seemed like an eternity passed, and then she turned to face him again. That silver gaze met his and she stared into his eyes again as if searching for something.

"I asked ye if ye kent me. I dinnae remember, but I feel as if ye're there. Ye're a part o' my memories."

A thrill like an electric charge raced through him at her words. She remembered him? Forget the fact that such a thing was impossible; she thought it was so, and that was enough. He felt suddenly light, weightless. The sloppy grin that had somehow found its way onto his face widened.

"Well, I've never lived in a thatched house, so it can't have been me," he said, keeping his tone light.

Wrong. A stricken look passed over her face, and she looked down at hands that had become white at the knuckles.

"Ye think I'm mad, dinnae ye?" She raised her head and stared at him.

Daniel winced. He let himself sink into those luminous eyes again and sighed.

Hell, what does it matter? Maybe she is, so what?

He reached for her other hand and held them both in his own.

"No, Eve, I don't think you're mad. I don't understand what's going on here either, but I think you're as sane as I am."

Well... began the derisive voice in his mind, *...about that...*

"Shut up!" he told it. Eve jumped and pulled her hands from his. "Sorry, lass, I wasn't talking to you."

She blinked, looked around the trailer, and returned her gaze to his. A slow smile stole across her face.

"Hmmm, I dinnae ken if ye're th' one t' talk to about this," Eve said. She nodded to herself. "Maybe we're both mad, then."

She patted his hand and the smile widened.

"I feel much better noo."

Daniel gaped. She was making fun of him! A moment ago, she'd been sobbing in his arms, pouring out her fears to him, a stranger, and now she was joking with him. He knew she was afraid, but she was fighting. It hit him again that Eve McDonald was quite possibly the bravest person he'd ever met, and suddenly his world lightened.

She wasn't crazy, not at all. She had come to him— Daniel MacArthur— not Callum or that damned

Baltair and his crew of misfits. She had given her trust to *him*, and he was damned if he was going to betray that faith.

I should tell her about the panic attacks. It's only fair. She wouldn't judge—would she?

Without warning, the anxiety swooped in like a raptor and clamped its claws into his chest. Drops of sweat beaded his forehead and he could feel his heart jump into overdrive. His vision clouded and nausea rose into his throat.

It had never happened this fast! He tried to calm himself, get control, but it was too late. His throat closed and he couldn't breathe. His heart was about to stop; this time he was going to die! He squeezed his eyes shut and waited.

"Daniel."

He forced his lids open and focused on the concerned grey eyes in front of him. Pools of silver, deep and soothing. He felt himself sinking into their depths, floating. A musical voice filtered through the pain in his mind, and he latched onto it like a drowning man.

"'Tis a'right, lad," the voice soothed. "Ye'll be fine. Look at me an' breathe. 'At's it...jist breathe. Guid lad."

He followed the sound, gave a jerky nod, and reached into his mind for his breathing exercises. Slowly, so slowly, the nausea receded, his heartbeat returned to a normal pace, and the band around his chest loosened. Without conscious thought, he reached into his shirt pocket for his handkerchief and wiped the sweat from his face. Then, with great care, he sat back in his chair and gave Eve his attention, waiting to see the look of scorn he knew would be there.

She wasn't looking at him. She wasn't looking at anything. Her face was lit from within, eyes huge and round. It was if she were staring into her own mind, seeing something only she could see.

"Seumas," she murmured.

Daniel frowned. "Who's Seumas?"

She didn't answer. It was as if she couldn't hear him.

"Seumas," she said again, her words the merest whisper. "'Tis a'right, lad. 'Tis a'right. Jist breathe."

CHAPTER TWENTY-SIX

GLENCOE, SCOTLAND - 1 FEBRUARY, 1692

FAOLÁN

hit th' hell ur we doin' here?" Isaac MacConnechy whispered to Faolán.

"I hae no idea. Marching right intae Glencoe in full uniform? We're just askin' for trouble."

Faolán looked up to where their captain stood at the head of his troops, then turned his head slightly and scanned the rows of men standing at attention behind them. In normal times, the sight of one hundred and twenty government soldiers in the red and grey of Argyll's regiment would have filled him with pride. He was making a difference, doing his king's work. Scotland was safe because of soldiers like these in the Earl of Argyll's Regiment of Foot.

So, what was bothering him now? When had pride become trepidation? What was causing the sinking feeling in his gut? Because there was something off about this mission, and he wasn't the only one who felt it. Faolán wasn't given to fancy, but since the announcement that they'd be going to Glencoe, a crawling sensation of *wrongness* had set in, and it had intensified the closer they got to Glencoe and Glencoe village.

It was no secret that Captain Robert Campbell hated the Glencoe MacDonalds to his core. So why was he leading his men on an expedition right into the home of his bitterest enemy, swords and muskets shining in the weak winter sunlight? Was it all just a show of strength? Captain Campbell did enjoy posturing, but this all seemed unnecessary and dangerous.

And what about the timing? All but one of the Highland Jacobite clans had signed the king's oath of allegiance by December 31 as ordered, and even though Maclain of Glencoe had been three days late in signing, his oath had been accepted along with the others. The promised reprisals for refusal to submit were rendered useless by his signature. William was firmly in charge of the Highlands, and peace was at hand. Now the army was needed only to assure that peace.

Except...Argyll's regiment was made up mostly of Campbells, and Glencoe was all MacDonalds and Maclains. It was incumbent upon the army to keep order in the Highlands, of course, but there were other regiments, other men less inclined to bring out the worst in each other. Choosing Campbells to face off against MacDonalds was a terrible idea, unless there was more to this than they were being told.

Faolán exchanged a glance with MacConnechy. Since that day back near the end of December, when they had seen Captain Campbell meeting with a man in a black cloak in the secrecy of the pine forest, they'd kept their eyes and ears open.

It would have been grand if they had Eòin and his stealth at hand, but Faolán and Isaac had decided to keep what they had seen to themselves. If Eòin knew, so would everyone else in the company. He was the best at ferreting out information, to be sure, but the wee man simply couldn't keep anything to himself.

Faolán's attention was arrested by the sight of twenty clansmen, dressed in the hunting tartans of MacDonald and Maclain, walking slowly up the road from the direction of the village. Their leader was a man of middle years, and he carried himself with pride. He led his small force to the foot of the glen and stopped, arms crossed over his chest.

"Who's 'at?" came a whisper at Faolán's back. He turned to see Hector Burns leaning forward. "Cannae be th' chief, aye? This lad's too yoong."

Faolán shrugged. "Most like his son. Seems t' have some authority," he answered without turning his head. "But do ye notice? He seems nervy, like he kens th' Cap'n."

"More like he smells somethin' bad," MacConnechy said, his voice dry. "We have that look more often than no."

A titter began and was immediately controlled. Faolán understood; despite the joking, every man was on high alert and ready for the unexpected. Anything could happen here, in this situation. They were led by a captain who followed his own agenda and shared nothing with his men, facing a foe—for the Glencoe MacDonalds could be called nothing else—on their own land. And preparing to ask that foe to put them up for two weeks! It seemed the height of stupidity.

Suddenly, Captain Campbell strode forward and clasped the younger man's hand in his.

"John! It's a braw day t' see ye, cousin, despite the weather!"

The voice that carried back to his men was robust and cheerful, and by the relaxing of the Glencoe man's shoulders, a relief to him as well.

Cousin? Then the two did know each other. How were a Campbell and a MacDonald related? Not to mention, how was Captain Robert Campbell related to this particular MacDonald?

The captain put his arm around the shoulder of the Glencoe man and turned to face his troops.

"Men," he boomed, "I'd like ye t' meet John Maclain. He's th' oldest son o' Alexander, whose wife is by way o' bein' kin t' my mother, so we're cousins."

Did no one else see the insincerity in the smile plastered across their captain's face? Faolán wondered. His gaze travelled back and forth between the two men. *Do they not see the expression of discomfort on John Maclain's?*

His thoughts were interrupted by his captain's voice again, pitched to carry to the last row of his men.

"I've tauld my cousin here that it's our luck t' run intae his lot today, when our backs are pushed agin' th' wall." He tightened his grip on Maclain's shoulder and pulled him close.

"It's our burden, t' be sure," he went on, "but poor soldiers like us have t' obey orders, aye? We've been out to red up some things Invergarry way, but the weather being chancy, the Colonel called a halt."

"But..." John Maclain tried, but Campbell ignored him.

"Invergarry havin' such a throng there, Colonel would have none of it, an' ordered it t' be Glencoe an' nowhere else."

He turned back to Maclain with another genial smile, wider if possible than the last one.

"So, it's t'be only a fortnight at most, then we'll be on our way. Must say again, I'm fair glad it's you. If you must have soldiers quartered on you, better that it be some'un ye know, aye?"

Maclain's shoulders slumped.

"Ye're welcome," he said, his voice flat. He looked out over the sea of red and grey. "Ye an' yer lads. It's nae much Glencoe has t' offer, bit it's yours."

"Never doubted it for a minute," Robert Campbell assured him. He called to his two officers, and introduced them. "These two are my mother's kin, so it's like t' be a family reunion, aye?"

As the lines of soldiers marched behind their captain and his 'family' toward the village that bore the glen's name, Faolán ruminated on the scene they had just witnessed.

None of it made sense. The captain had indeed

told them they'd be going to Invergarry as part of a mission to collect taxes from each Highland clan, but then, instead of going north, he'd turned them south toward Glencoe, one of the least accessible valleys he'd ever seen.

This glen on the river Coe was like a sword-cut through the wildest of the Highland hills. As they neared Glencoe village itself, Faolán noted that there were few entries on the sides of the mountains, making the glen a natural barrier to outside interference.

The mountains were a natural defense for the MacDonalds of Glencoe, giving them protection from outside enemies. It would be difficult for anyone to creep up upon the village undetected.

Faolán felt a chill on the back of his neck. Aye, it would be difficult for someone who came from outside. But what about *inside*? This mountain arrangement also meant escape from the glen would be challenging should danger come from within. Until now that had been inconceivable, as all the residents were from the same clan, fiercely protective and always suspicious of outsiders.

He thought back to the look on the face of John Maclain, the chief's son. Maclain had not been pleased to see his 'cousin'; the constraint had been obvious in his stiff stance and anxious expression. Regardless of some old link through marriage, the kinship between Captain Campbell and the Maclains of Glencoe was as false as the promise of fair weather in February.

Everything he knew about his captain returned to the proven fact that the man hated the Glencoe MacDonalds with a fervor bordering on mania. When he was in his cups, his fuming passion could be heard throughout the barracks; it didn't take the sneaking of Eòin Arthur to attest to that. It was said that blood is thicker than water, but those who espoused that notion had never met Captain Robert Campbell.

The first crofts of the village of Glencoe came into view. Men and women stood outside their cottages, with curious faces turned toward the unexpected visitors. Children peeked from behind their mothers' skirts.

As they watched their chief's son and his guests approach, Faolán could see puzzled interest, but not fear, on the faces of the people of Glencoe. Ordinary people, Scottish people. They were prepared to open their homes to one hundred and twenty fellow countrymen, simply upon request. Not as MacDonalds or Campbells, but as Highlanders bound by a code of honor as old as the mountains themselves. It should have brought a sense of relief.

Suddenly, his eyes locked with those of one of the villagers—a woman—and all other thoughts fled his mind. She was small in stature, almost waif-like, and her long black hair blew about her pale face with a life of its own. But what caught and held his attention were her eyes, a shimmering grey like the surface of a loch, wide and mysterious.

"H-hmmm." Hector Burns voice came from far away. Faolán jerked and regained his footing in the march. As he passed beyond the place where the woman stood, he turned his head to look behind.

She was still watching him.

CHAPTER TWENTY-SEVEN

GLENCOE, SCOTLAND – 2 FEBRUARY, 1692

SIÒNAID

iònaid MacDonald pulled the hood of her ara-said up over her head and stepped outside the croft. The weather was worsening, keeping everyone indoors, but she blessed the cold wind that clutched at her dress and threatened to wrest the door out of her hands.

She took a deep breath and pulled the heavy door shut with both hands. Whatever the weather had in mind, it was better than the stifling atmosphere inside the croft. Moving amongst all these strangers, she could feel the tension creeping in, threatening to overwhelm her.

So many men! So many...Campbells. She looked toward the chief's house, from which the sounds of revelry had poured into the night air until the wee hours of the morning. The croft was silent now; smoke drifted upwards from its hearth fire as if seeking an escape from the snores of drunken men.

Behind her, the door opened and closed again with a thud.

"Why are ye about so early, an' in such mischancy weather?" Andrew asked, as he joined Siònaid in the doorway. "Surely ye isnae worrit about yon government men." He inclined his head toward the chief's croft, and then back toward their own cottage.

"Weel, I cannae say I like bein' amongst so many solgers," Siònaid admitted. "Though th' guests in our own house seemed mannerlie enough," she conceded. "There's just such a lot of 'em t' take care of, an' for two weeks!"

"Why is it up t' ye t' take care of 'em?" Andrew asked.

"'Cause they're *men.*"

He laughed. "Ach! I'm a man, an' when have ye ever taken care o' me?"

Siònaid gave his arm a swat. "Ye ken what I mean. They're guests. They eat sae much, an' they're sae big, and there's sae many o' them."

She sighed. "An' it's cold out, so I cannae oft'n get away from it. I cannae breathe for the smellin' o' men's sweat." She looked up into Andrew's handsome face. "They're no like you."

"I dinnae sweat?" he asked, his voice puzzled.

"Aye, o' course ye do, it's just..." she paused, then finished in a rush.

"It's just they're *Campbells.*"

Andrew burst out laughing. "Ahh," he said, "they sweat 'cause they're Campbells."

"Stoppit," Siònaid said, her voice cross. "'Tis not about that."

They began to walk along the path side by side, Andrew slowing his pace to accommodate her lame leg. A long moment passed in which nothing was said.

Then Siònaid ventured, "They're sae close, all th' time. They whisper t' each other when they ken I'm right there." She stopped and weighed her next words.

"Seumas is afraid o' them."

Andrew shrugged. "Aye, I've noticed. But ye ken, wee Seumas is afraid o' sae many things these days."

"Can ye talk t' him?" Siònaid said. "Brother t' brother?"

Andrew's face darkened. "He willnae talk t' me. Havenae ye noticed? The wee lad's been skulkin' about, an' he's avoidin' me more'n most."

Siònaid thought about that. Was it true? Seumas certainly was skulking, but was he *avoiding* others? Not her—the opposite was true there—but his own brother?

Now, with the descent on their village by all these men named Campbell, she was afraid for him. She didn't think the men would do something to a child—they were Highlanders like their hosts, and thus the recipients of Glencoe's hospitality. They were trained soldiers, not hooligans.

It wasn't what the men might do that had kept her awake last night. Nor was it the noise emanating from the chief's croft, or the snores that made their own cottage sound like a herd of stampeding cattle.

It was the fear that Seumas might have another attack like the one back in October. Worse, that *he* was afraid it might happen again. Since yesterday she'd kept him by her side, tried to show him that their new guests were not to be feared. She'd plastered a false smile on her face and made an effort to speak with them as she helped with the cooking and serving, but everywhere she went, she was only too aware of the little hand that clutched her skirt, of the stiffness in Seumas' body and the paleness of his face.

Seumas knew his history, and it was her fault. He was only too aware that his precious James had been routed by William of Orange, and that government soldiers like these men were the reason for it. To him they must have seemed like the very same men who had sent his king fleeing in disgrace.

Worst of all, she couldn't tell Andrew about her fears. Her decision not to share what had happened to Seumas seemed foolish now. It left her alone, as if she were stranded on an island populated by wolves that surrounded her and dripped saliva as they waited for her to make a move.

Maybe Andrew could have helped, if she'd told him. But the way he'd dismissed her story about the man in the black cloak still rankled. He'd decided that the scream she'd heard that day was in her imagination—that the cut-off yelp of pain she could still hear in her mind had never happened.

She shivered, and Andrew turned toward her.

"Sorry, lass, ye were sae lost in your thoughts, I dinnae want t' disturb ye. We should turn about and get back, or too many Campbells willnae be th' problem; it'll be too few toes."

Siònaid nodded. More people were emerging from cottages now, braving the vile weather. Perhaps they too hoped to escape the stifling crush of human bodies in their homes. Whatever the reason, the path was filling with villagers and their guests.

Far down the path, Alexander Maclain's door opened and the chief himself emerged, looking none the worse for his night of drinking.

"Andrew, m' lad!" he bellowed. "Come t' see me fer a minute, aye?"

Siònaid thought she caught an odd look on Andrew's face, a lowering of his eyebrows and pinching of lips. It flitted across his features and was gone, replaced by his usual affable expression.

"Looks like I'm bein' called t' duty," he said. "Get on home wi' ye, lass, before ye freeze. Aye?" And he was off, loping toward the place where the chief and two of his sons stood watching the unaccustomed winter traffic. The four men retreated into the house and closed the door against the weather.

Siònaid had nearly reached home when she heard heavy footsteps close behind her. She turned to face three men in rumpled uniforms of red and grey, and took in bleary eyes and day-old stubble. Not the soldiers billeted with her own family; these men were strangers.

The men smiled, grins meant for each other and not for her. An uneasy feeling began to build, and she turned to find that the nearest villager was several feet away and walking the other way. The uncomfortable feeling grew stronger.

Siònaid knew she could never outrun these men, not with her leg impeding her, but her own doorway was only a few yards down the path and a call would surely bring someone. She squared her shoulders and attempted to stand as tall as she could, hoping that it was just her imagination sending these shudders through her body. She forced a smile and reminded herself that these men were guests.

"Aw, such a pretty smile. I think she likes ye, Burt." A short, rather heavyset man spoke in a Lowlands accent, and there was no mistaking the sneer in his words.

"Really, Hal? She's more yer size, dinnae ye think?" The other two shared a laugh. "Yer in luck; this 'un looks like she cannae run away from ye, like most women do!" The man called Burt pointed at Siònaid's left foot.

She shrank back as the man they'd called Hal moved closer and reached out. All right, this had gone far enough. She took a deep breath and prepared to give him a scream he wouldn't soon forget.

Suddenly an arm came from behind Hal and spun the man around. The newcomer shoved him hard enough that he stumbled backward, arms spinning in a vain attempt to regain his balance, and landed on his backside in the pathway.

"H-hey!" Hal sputtered in shock and outrage. "Wha' th' hell" He looked for his comrades, but they had gone still, the laughter wiped from their faces.

Siònaid's rescuer ignored them. "Allow me t' apologize for the behavior of these louts," he said, in a pleasant voice. "They probably forgot t' quit drinkin' last night, but that's no excuse t' act like animals, aye?"

Hal scrambled to his feet and joined his silent companions. The three exchanged glances and backed away, leaving Siònaid and the soldier facing each other on the path.

Siònaid felt as if her limbs had turned to jelly, and she knew her eyes must be frozen in a look of stupefied surprise. She forced her mouth open, but no sound came out.

What is wrong with me? Where are my manners? One hand went of its own volition to her cheek and came away warm.

Again, the man came to her rescue. "My name is Faolán," he said. "Faolán Campbell. May I walk ye t' yer door?"

"S-Siònaid MacDonald," she said, in a voice that cracked as if from long disuse. "I-I remember ye, from yest'day."

Faolán smiled, and those warm brown eyes she remembered from the day before crinkled at the corners. Up close they were chocolate, or perhaps newly turned earth in spring. She wanted to wrap herself in their velvety depths, and felt the blush deepen.

"Aye," he said. "Ye watched us come in t' th' glen. I remember ye too." He smiled again, and she was lost.

Siònaid floated through the rest of the day. It seemed as if she'd never stumbled in her life, never fallen. She was a dancer, weightless, buoyed by a pair of liquid brown eyes that crinkled at the corners. She bantered with the guests, teased Seumas through his lessons, gave extra care to the food and drink she served.

As she lay in her bed that night, her thoughts returned again and again to the few words they had exchanged, the way he had smiled.

He likes me, her mind sang. *He likes me.* And she held tight to the kernel of her new secret.

There is sich a thing as love at first sight. An' I think I'm in love...wi' a Campbell.

CHAPTER TWENTY-EIGHT

INVERNESS, SCOTLAND - PRESENT DAY

*It seems to me that the rain is falling through
my heart and causing it to crumble into ruins.*
—Gustave Flaubert

ow you've done it.

Daniel sat hunched over with his head bent, elbows pressing into his thighs, and his hands dangling between his knees. The rain beat a relentless tattoo on the metal roof of the trailer, echoing the drumming inside his skull.

He'd fucked it up again. Let someone see his weakness, his inability to control himself.

Not just someone. In a few short weeks, Eve MacDonald had become a person who mattered, one who made him *feel* for the first time in a very long time. She had aroused a protective instinct in him that he hadn't even known was there, made him care about someone other than his own miserable self.

Shite, he'd been fooling himself that she cared

about him. All that rubbish about her lost memory, and not being able to feel the cold, and—what was it—oh aye, thatched houses. She'd cried on his shoulder, damn it! Was any of it even real?

Eve had looked right through him and called him by another man's name. Who the hell was Seumas? An old boyfriend? Didn't much matter; whatever had happened between them, the guy couldn't be as much of a git as he was.

He felt a hand on his knee and looked up, startled out of his wallowing. A pair of luminous grey eyes stared into his with concern.

"Daniel?" Eve said. "Are ye a'right now?"

"Who's Seumas?" The words came out with more force than he'd intended. Eve flinched and pulled her hand away. She took a breath and let it out slowly. The silence deepened.

"A young lad."

A surge of relief washed through him. Daniel reached for her hand and captured it in his own.

"How young?"

Confusion crossed her features, and then the grey eyes crinkled a tiny bit at the corners. Was she *smiling*? He intensified his glare.

"I dinnae ken. Verra small, I think." Eve gave a frustrated sigh. "I dinnae remember much. But..." she hesitated.

"What?" *Calm down*, he told himself. *Barking at her doesn't help.*

"I kent he was in distress." She met his eyes again. "Like ye."

Now it was Daniel's turn to wince at the words. He

squared his shoulders and pushed down the mortification that threatened to swamp him. There was no time for embarrassment—no going back.

"How? Tell me exactly what you remembered."

It was as if the sun had come out and bathed her face in light. Eve leaned forward and bobbed her head. She screwed her eyes shut and tightened her face in concentration.

"I remember he was shakin', and sweatin'. He said he couldnae breathe. He gagged, an' then he retched an' fell unconscious."

Daniel stared at her. He wanted to run, get away from this person whose voice reached into his soul and pulled his secrets out for all to see. It was horrible and wonderful.

She *understood*. She knew what had just happened to him because she had seen it before. Whoever this Seumas was, there was no doubt he'd suffered a panic attack.

A *young lad*. Sympathy flooded Daniel's mind. He hadn't begun having attacks until he was in university, and he remembered thinking then that he was dying. He couldn't imagine what that experience would do to a young child.

Eve's voice broke in. "Daniel, there's more."

He forced himself away from the memory of those symptoms and concentrated on the woman in front of him. Her eyes shone and her face was flushed with excitement out of all proportion to the situation.

He'd never seen anything so beautiful.

"What is it?"

"Seumas lived in a cottage wi' a thatched roof."

Thatched roofs again. Eve was very still, watching him. Daniel knew, without understanding why, that his reaction in these next seconds would make all the difference. Was he willing to trust her or not? He took a deep breath, let it out, and forced his expression into a semblance of nonchalance.

"Well, that's that, then. I guess this Seumas lad is a part of your buried memories, aye?"

She sat back against the office chair, relief obvious on her beautiful face.

"Thank ye."

Daniel made a supreme effort to keep himself from pulling her into his arms again because he knew if he did he'd never let her go. He heaved himself out of the metal chair and put some distance between them.

"Shouldn't we get you home? You need to get out of those wet clothes, and it's getting late." There, that sounded normal and reasonable—right? Without thinking about it, he snagged an elastic band from his carefully organized tray of office supplies and handed it to her. "Here, put your hair up, at least."

Eve stared at the band, then took it and threaded her long wet hair through, working at it until she had a messy bun perched on top of her head. She walked to the door and turned to wait for him.

Daniel fetched his umbrella from its stand, and together they walked out of the trailer and across the lot to where his Vauxhall sat, looking for all the world as if it were sulking at being the only car left on the site.

No, not the only car. Daniel caught the glint of glass in the dim light from the streetlamp on Millburn and squinted to see through the rain. The bonnet of another vehicle protruded from around the edge of the scaffolding across the site. The car seemed to be empty.

Curious—who would still be here, long after hours? Maybe a couple of the men had carpooled to a local tavern to slosh off the day's labor.

Daniel helped Eve into the passenger seat, then rounded the car, and got in on the driver's side.

The one thing his car had going for it was the heater. Within moments, warm air was circulating through the interior and he could feel his fingers thawing. Eve didn't seem to notice; she leaned back into the seat and stared out the windscreen at the driving rain.

They sat in silence, each lost in his own thoughts.

"Um, you're staying with Henry and Mary, aye?" Daniel ventured after a moment.

"Aye," Eve said. Her face broke into a smile. "They've been verra kind."

"Do you know the address?" he asked, and was immediately sorry. Her smile fled, replaced by a look of confusion.

"Add-ress?" She ran the word over her tongue. "I dinnae ken."

He sighed. "The number on the house."

She brightened at that. "Och, aye! 'Tis twelve."

Daniel waited, but nothing more was forthcoming. "Ahh. And the street?"

Eve frowned. "I dinnae ken—oh, ye mean th' name on th' wee board at th' beginnin' o' th' road?"

Daniel gawked at her. He would never get used to this. He jerked his head in a nod, and she gave him that smile again, the one he'd trade his life for. He forced breath back into his lungs.

"Aye. That."

She screwed up her face for a second, then grinned again. "Roseberry. 'Tis no far from th' office." She cocked her head at him. "Twelve Roseberry, in Inverness." She sat back in her seat again with a smug little smile and folded her hands in her lap as if she had accomplished a feat of major significance. "Does 'at help?"

He punched Roseberry into the GPS. Yes, it was near the business office of the Highland Players, just a short walk from the city centre.

But something struck Daniel. He'd been too shocked at seeing her outside his trailer at the construction site to think about it at the time, but now the question loomed in his mind.

How in hell had she walked from Roseberry Place to the Millburn site at least three miles away, in the pouring rain, *without a coat*? It wasn't much of a challenge for a fit walker on a good day, but Eve had done it in the rain, on a twisted leg. Seemed impossible, but here she was.

He peered at his passenger, at the jeans, trainers, and red tee shirt still damp from the rain, the black hair that had come loose from its bun and was straggling down her neck. She looked like any other young woman from Inverness, and yet not at all.

Somehow the jeans and trainers didn't suit Eve. She looked much more at home in the Highland Players costume, or in the white nightgown she'd been wearing when he first met her.

An old soul, he'd heard it said of some people. Children who acted older than their years, who seemed to have a deeper understanding of the world around them than one might expect.

Mary Duncan was like that, he thought. Maybe it was why she never seemed to react to the odd eccentricities evidenced by her houseguest. Eve had been absorbed by the Duncans and by the rest of the Highland Players too, without a ripple. They all just seemed to *get* her.

He started the car and they pulled out of the dark park and onto Millburn Road, headed toward the city centre. Daniel glanced in the rearview to see a single car some distance behind, the only other vehicle on the road. Everyone else seemed to be sensible enough to stay inside.

Eve said nothing, and Daniel was grateful. She was too much of a distraction at normal times, let alone on a rainy night with glistening wet roads to navigate.

He turned onto Culduthel Road and slowed to make the sharp turn onto View Street, the huge bulk of Inverness Castle looming out of the mist to the right. The Vauxhall crept down the narrow road behind the hotels that fronted the Ness River. The wipers beat a monotonous rhythm as they swished over the windscreen, creating an almost hypnotic effect.

Daniel wondered at the creeping feeling in his gut as he neared the Duncans' home. The weather? It rained a lot in Scotland, and normally he wasn't bothered by the mist and fog. This was his hometown;

he knew most of its streets well and could navigate without thinking about it. So, what was it?

He glanced at his passenger. Eve still hadn't said a word; her hands gripped the armrest and her knuckles were white in the misty glow from the streetlights. She was frightened. He must be absorbing her fear, that was all it was.

The sign for Roseberry Place came into view and Daniel turned in with relief. Number Twelve was at the end of the street—a semi-detached row home constructed of grey stone, two dormers adorning an otherwise blank facade. It was hard to see in the darkness, but he could just make out that the wooden door was red, like the Players' office door.

He turned off the engine and went round the back of the car, holding the umbrella in one hand, intending to help Eve out on the passenger side. As he passed the rear of the car, he felt a sharp twinge in his side and stumbled against the boot of the Vauxhall. The umbrella fell and rolled away into the grass beside the drive.

At the noise, Eve turned her head back toward him and a sweet smile spread over her face, making Daniel go weak in the knees again. Her eyes widened and the smile morphed into something else in the rain that poured down the car window, but he had no time to process it.

The weakness grew. Blood was pounding in his head and the twinge in his side had become a hot, sharp pain that had him gasping for breath.

Now the pain was radiating from somewhere in his lower back and threatening to consume his entire world. He slipped and landed on his back on the pavement behind the car, blinking into the relentless rain as it poured into his eyes. He turned his head and was surprised to see a vague figure in a black mackintosh, standing only feet away.

Why isn't he helping? Daniel wondered, but the thought skittered away into the darkness, leaving the image of a hand clutching something that glinted in the weak light from the lamp at the end of the drive. In the next second, the figure was gone. Perhaps it had never been.

From a great distance, Daniel heard a woman screaming. As his thoughts faded and his mind closed down, he saw that the puddle next to him was turning red, the color of the Duncans' door.

CHAPTER TWENTY-NINE
INVERNESS, SCOTLAND
- PRESENT DAY

*Just like any and everything else, things
are never what they seem. People change,
or maybe they simply revert back to
everything they're supposed to be."*
—R.H. Sin

The screaming went on and on, a wail of almost inhuman anguish that tore the night into shards. Lights flickered in the windows of houses on Roseberry Place. The door of Number Twelve flew open, and the shocked faces of Mary and Henry Duncan appeared on the doorstep.

A car stood in the drive, the passenger door opened wide to the rain, and near the back of the car stood Eve McDonald, hands clutching her face as she stared down at something behind the car. The screams dwindled to a soft keening, like the sound of an animal in distress.

"Eve! Evie, what's wrong?" Mary called as she raced out, heedless of the rain. She rounded the car and stopped short.

"Oh my God! Daniel!" She dropped to her knees beside the still form on the wet drive. "Henry, call for an ambulance!"

Henry raced back into the house for his mobile and returned moments later with a blanket. He knelt beside his wife.

"Let's get him out of the rain."

"No!" Mary put her hand on his arm. "We mustn't move him until we find out what happened, aye?" She spotted the open umbrella on the grass next to the drive, and held it above the two while Henry spread the blanket over Daniel. A siren wailed in the distance. "It's the best we can do. They're coming."

She left Henry to keep the umbrella over Daniel and straightened to face her houseguest. Eve stood with her hands over her face and rocked back and forth, whimpering.

"Lass?"

There was no reaction. She waited a moment, but it was as if Eve didn't know she was there. Mary put her arms around the girl.

"Evie, it'll be all right. He'll be all right." She rocked with Eve and repeated the words over and over again, until the whimpering faded and the rhythmic rocking slowed.

An ambulance screeched to a halt at the foot of the drive. Two men in the green uniforms of emergency personnel leapt out and carried a stretcher over to Henry and Daniel.

They handed the blanket back to Henry and took over the situation with practiced efficiency. Daniel's airways were checked, an oxygen mask placed over his mouth and nose, and an IV drip started in seconds. One of the paramedics spoke into his radio, and the other looked up with narrowed eyes as he applied pressure to an area on Daniel's side.

"This man's been stabbed," he said sharply. "We've called the police."

"We're taking her inside," Mary said. "The police can talk to us there." She matched the man's stare until he looked away. "And please make sure to keep us informed about our friend Daniel, aye?"

For a moment, the paramedic looked as if he might salute. Instead, he gave a terse nod and went back to his task, and within minutes the ambulance moved off, siren wailing.

Henry and Mary helped an unresisting Eve into the house and led her to the couch, where she immediately curled up and closed her eyes. Mary fetched a dry blanket from the hall closet and placed it over her.

A black cat in the corner of the living room raised its head, yawned, and stretched. It wandered over and sniffed at Eve, then jumped onto the couch and burrowed its way under the blanket.

"Aye, Biscuit, your lass is feeling poorly," Henry said, "so we'll leave her to you." He patted the smaller lump under the blanket and grinned.

"Cats know when something's wrong, don't they?" Mary said, "and those two have a bond. I've never seen Biscuit give a human the time of day before, but she seems to sense that our Evie is different."

Despite their expectation, the knock on the door had Mary clutching at her heart and reaching for Henry. He patted her hand and gave her an encouraging smile.

"Ach, lass, did you commit a crime I don't know about? You're as jumpy as the cat!" He snorted and went to the door to admit the two policemen who stood on the doorstep.

"Hullo. I'm Inspector Mackenzie, and this is Sergeant Murray," the older of the two officers said. "May we have a word?"

"How is Daniel?" Mary demanded.

"I'm sorry, ma'am, we have no word on his condition." He looked at Mary Duncan's set face and cleared his throat. "We'll let you know as soon as we're informed, aye?"

Mackenzie's eyes went to the girl on the couch, and he raised his eyebrows. Mary put a finger to her lips and led the two men into the kitchen.

"She's had a nasty shock," Henry explained. "She was with Daniel when it happened."

The officer frowned. "You know we'll have to speak with her."

Henry sighed. "I understand, but can you give her a few minutes? Poor lass is traumatized."

Mackenzie nodded. His partner took out his notebook and a pen.

Mary spoke up. "Would you like some tea?" Without waiting for an answer, she went to the cabinet and took out four mugs and a tin of loose tea. She poured water into the electric kettle and pushed the button, added tea leaves to a diffuser and fetched the teapot from its place on the counter, working in slow motion as if this was a royal tea party and everything must be done just right.

As she worked, she watched the detectives waiting impatiently in the sitting room. When everything was placed on a tray, Mary took it over to the table, where she poured the tea with great care and handed each man a mug. Finally, she seated herself, folded her hands around her own mug, and looked up with a smug smile.

"Now," said Inspector Mackenzie, "can we begin?"

"Of course," said Mary. "Please do."

"How well do you know the victim, Mr. MacArthur?"

"He's a member of our group, The Highland Players," Henry said.

"Ahh, and what does this group play?" Mackenzie asked. Mary's face darkened.

Henry caught her eye and widened his eyes slightly. He turned to the officers and straightened his back.

"We teach history through reenacting our country's past," he said. "We dress in period costume and present at wedding planning events, give demonstrations of sword fighting, and—" he stopped as the detectives exchanged glances.

"And we'll set up an ambush if you need one!" Mary said, her voice tart.

Sergeant Murray dropped his pen. "You ambush people?" he said. "Seriously?"

His partner cleared his throat.

"Eh. Well. And Mr. MacArthur is a member of your group, you said."

"He joined us just a few weeks ago," Henry said. "His cousin brought him in."

And the young lady on the couch?" Mackenzie asked. "Is she in your group too?"

Mary smiled. "Our Eve? She is indeed. She's a natural, that one."

"And she lives here?"

"Aye. Daniel—Mr. MacArthur—he'd called us to say he was bringing her home."

"From where, do you know?"

"I don't know. Is it important?" Henry spoke up. "We really don't know that much about Daniel. As I said, he hasn't been with us long." He caught another look between the two policemen and put his hand up. "But he's a good lad."

"Hmm." Mackenzie's voice was noncommittal. "Do you know where he works?"

"Oh, aye. Wait a minute." Henry left the table and returned a few minutes later with his laptop. "Our members fill out an information form when they join; it's right here." He tapped the keys and brought up a form, passing the laptop over to the officer. "That's Daniel's information."

Mary and Henry watched as Mackenzie scanned the document on the screen. "MacArthur Construction. Big company." He froze, then exchanged yet another look with his partner.

The younger man frowned, then his eyes widened. "Isn't that where?"

His senior officer interrupted. "MacArthur. Is he related to the owner, possibly?" At the Duncans' perplexed looks, he nodded to his subordinate and waited for Murray to jot down the question in his notebook. "Never mind; we can find out later."

Mackenzie turned back to the Duncans. "Now, can you tell us exactly what happened here tonight?"

Mary spoke up, her voice firm. "That's just it; we don't *know* what happened. We were waiting for Eve to come home, and then we heard screaming," she paused. "We went outside, and it was Evie. She was standing at the back of the car, so I ran to her, and that was when I saw...I saw Daniel on the ground. So, I went to him."

"Did you touch the body?" Mackenzie's voice was a whiplash.

Mary winced at *the body*, then straightened her spine. "Of course not!" Ice dripped from her voice. "We held an umbrella over him, and my husband went in and got a blanket. We covered him with it, that's all. We didn't touch him. Then the ambulance arrived, and the emergency personnel took over and took him to the hospital.

"They said—they said he'd been stabbed." She shuddered, then turned her sharp eyes on the officers. "Instead of asking us questions, shouldn't you be finding out how he is? Protecting him?"

Mackenzie's put a hand up. "I promise you, we'll let you know as soon as we hear from the hospital. Don't worry; because he was attacked, we have men guarding him."

Mary's look was bleak. "Attacked.., of course." She reached for Henry's hand. "Poor Daniel, who would do such a thing?"

"Sir, ma'am, we really do need to speak with the young lady now."

Henry nodded. "Aye. We'd like to be there, though; is that all right?"

"Aye, it'll be okay," said Mackenzie. "As long as no one interrupts." He shot a look at Mary.

There was a barely audible *humph*. Henry cleared his throat and led the way into the living room. Mary raced around him to stand in front of the couch, and straightened herself to her full five feet one inch. She fixed each of the policemen with a fierce look, then turned her back on them.

"Eve?" she said softly. "Evie, are you awake?" Mary gave the girl's shoulder a gentle shake.

With an earsplitting howl, a black ball of fury erupted from the blanket and shot across the room to disappear up the stairs, leaving various levels of shock in its wake.

"Ach!" Sergeant Murray was rubbing his hand, where a long angry scratch had appeared in the animal's wake. "What was that?"

Henry sighed. "That was Biscuit. Our cat. You won't be wanting to ask *her* any questions, I expect?"

"Never seen a guard cat before," Murray muttered. He accepted a handkerchief from Mackenzie and wrapped it around his hand.

A groggy Eve had struggled to a sitting position on the couch. She looked warily from Mary and Henry to the two officers arrayed in front of her.

Mackenzie pulled up the ottoman and sat down, making himself eye level with Eve. The others took chairs nearby, except for Mary who sat down on the couch at Eve's feet, where she could maintain eye contact with the detective.

"Hello, Miss—MacDonald, is it?" the policeman began. "I'm Inspector Mackenzie. I understand you were with Mr. Daniel MacArthur this evening. Do you mind if I ask you a few questions?"

Eve turned an expressionless face toward Mackenzie.

"Daniel?" she asked. A look of confusion crossed her face. "Is somethin' wrong wi' Daniel?"

The two police officers exchanged looks.

"You don't remember?" Mackenzie's voice was soft.

Mary took Eve's hands in hers and looked into her eyes. They were clouded, like a winter sky before a storm. Mary put her hand on the girl's forehead and gasped.

"She's freezing! I think she's in shock. You should stop—"

"I'm weel, thank ye." Eve said. "Bit, why are these men here?"

Now it was Mary's turn to exchange a look with Henry. Something was wrong with their girl; she seemed somehow... *elsewhere*. As if she was only present in the room in body, her spirit gone.

Mary turned to Mackenzie. "I don't think it's a good idea for you to ask questions tonight," she told him. This time her eyes beseeched him to understand. "I think Eve's caught a fever from being out in the rain."

The detective's eyes narrowed. "A fever? Didn't you just say she was freezing?"

Henry stepped in. "Officer, please..."

"I'm sorry." Mackenzie faced them all, and

then spoke directly to Eve. "You see, I need some answers, now, and Miss MacDonald is the only witness to the attack."

"A-ttack?" Eve said, as if from a great distance.

"Yes, Miss. Attack." Mackenzie stared into her eyes. "Your friend Mr. MacArthur was attacked tonight. He was stabbed."

"Stabbed." Her voice was no more than a whisper. "Stabbed. Aye, they were stabbed. All of 'em. Killed. Blood...sae much blood! 'Twas drippin' doon...*he* did 't." Her voice rose to a shriek. "HE DID 'T!"

The four people in the living room of Number Twelve Roseberry Place sat, unable to look away from those crazed grey eyes.

Mary held her hand tightly. "Evie..."

"Why ur ye callin' me 'at?" she said. "'At's no my name. My name is Siònaid."

Mary Duncan walked into the kitchen, retrieved her mobile from its stand on the counter, and tapped a number. The call was answered on the first ring.

"You'd better come. She's remembered it all."

CHAPTER THIRTY

INVERNESS, SCOTLAND
- PRESENT DAY

I am crying over the loss of something
I never had...mourning something that
never was – my dashed hopes, dashed
dreams, and my soured expectations."
—E.L. James

The truck's back-up beeper seemed to go on forever. How big was the construction site that a vehicle needed to reverse that far? He was going to have a word with Big Angus; that kind of incessant noise was completely unnecessary. They'd probably be cited if it didn't stop soon. What a headache.

His head really did hurt, now that he thought about it. Not to mention the cables he seemed to have gotten himself tangled in. He didn't remember any cables lying around on site—could he have tripped over them and hit his head?

Daniel opened his eyes and immediately closed them again against the brightness in the room. His head pounded, and a throbbing pain emanated from his lower back. The beeping continued, its monotonous tone drilling through his brain.

"Dan."

He forced his eyes open again and squinted against the glare. Callum's drawn face peered down at him. His cousin looked haggard; black circles underlined his bloodshot blue eyes and his hair stood out at all angles, as if he'd forgotten to comb it. Something was very wrong if Callum looked like this.

"What the hell happened to you?" Daniel asked. He struggled to sit up and gasped as a red wave of pain engulfed him. Callum grasped him by the shoulders and forced him back onto the bed.

"Stay still, you numpty!" His voice was ragged. "You just had surgery."

"Surgery?" Daniel fought through the fog in his mind. "For what?"

Callum took a breath to speak and was shoved aside violently.

"You got yourself stabbed, you eejit!" His uncle loomed over him. Ranald MacArthur's voice was ragged, tinged with something Daniel couldn't identify.

"You just can't stay out of trouble, can you?"

Stabbed? Daniel closed his eyes and tried to process the information. He'd been stabbed. Someone had stabbed him. It didn't compute. Maybe if he just lay still, this would all go away.

He heard voices, arguing about something.

His uncle, "Are you sure he's going to be all right?"

Callum, "The doctor said he'll be fine; you heard him. He's lucky; the knife missed everything vital."

A new voice, "Sir, don't worry. He's on some very strong pain medication, so he's just sleepy. Don't be too concerned about that."

Concerned. That was the word. His uncle sounded concerned, and that didn't make sense either so Daniel let himself drift. The bright room dimmed, the voices became whispers, and then everything faded into a void of grey shadows. *Like Eve's eyes. That's nice...*He smiled and let go.

When he awoke again, two things became immediately clear. There was pain—a lot of it—and the two men sitting by his bed now weren't Uncle Ranald and Callum.

Daniel studied his visitors. The older man had faded blue eyes and hair just beginning to turn silver at the temples. The younger one had thick red hair, a rather pathetic excuse for a mustache, and a long red scratch on his right hand.

His visitors wore plain clothes, not uniforms, but there was something about them that shouted *cop*. He'd had a few run-ins with the local constabulary, to be sure, but these lads were a step above. His senses began to tingle. He decided it might be best to let them do the talking.

"Hello, Mr. MacArthur," the older man said in an even voice. "I'm very sorry about what happened to you."

Daniel waited.

"I'm Inspector Mackenzie," the officer said, "and this is Sergeant Murray. We're from the CID." At Daniel's blank look, he added, "the Criminal Investigation Department."

He sounds tired, Daniel thought, *as if he says the same words a hundred times a day.*

"We're looking into what happened last night, sir, and we'd like to ask you a few questions if we may. Are you up to it?"

Daniel found his voice. "How's Eve?" he demanded. "Is she okay?"

"The young lady who was with you last night?" Mackenzie nodded to Murray, and the sergeant consulted his notebook. "Miss MacDonald," he offered.

Mackenzie took back the conversation. "She is... shocked," he said. "She's with Mr. and Mrs. Duncan." He held up a hand at the look on Daniel's face. "Physically, she's fine."

The two detectives watched while Daniel processed this.

Physically, she's fine.

He tried to focus on the two detectives and groped for something to say.

"What happened to your hand?"

"Nothing much." Murray pulled his hand back and glared at it. "Had a run-in with a cat."

Mackenzie cleared his throat.

"Are you related to the owner of MacArthur Construction?"

"My uncle."

"Ahh. Do you know of anyone who would want to harm you, sir?"

"No."

"Anyone who owes you money, for instance? Or someone you owe money to?"

"No."

"Do you recall anyone you've come in contact with who might have a grudge against you? Someone you may have offended in some way?"

Daniel felt the nausea rise in his throat. *Any number of people, officer. Half the women in Inverness. The board members...my family.* He swallowed.

"No." Catching the look on Mackenzie's face, he added, "I don't think so."

Daniel stretched and regretted it, nearly crying out from the pain in his lower back. His face paled as the reality sunk in. Someone had tried to kill him.

He shook his head. "No," he said. "I'm a project manager on a construction site. Haven't been there long, so I don't know the men well yet. I'll admit that sometimes people don't like being told what to do by a newbie." He paused. "I can be annoying."

His brow furrowed. "But being annoyed wouldn't make someone want to *kill* me." He looked at Mackenzie. "Aye?"

"You'd be surprised," Murray broke in. Mackenzie sent him a look and he coughed.

The senior officer began again. "Your job site is the office building on Millburn, correct?"

"Yes."

The two detectives exchanged glances again, then Mackenzie resumed. "Have you noticed anyone on the site who shouldn't be there?"

"No. I spend a lot of time in the office, though. Big Angus might know more about that; he's my foreman."

Murray looked up from his notebook. "Big Angus? Angus Graham? Looks like a bear?"

Daniel could feel the pain building again. He took shallow breaths and tried to concentrate. Something floated up from the well of agony.

"Wait. You know him?"

Murray glanced at his superior and cleared his throat.

"Well, you see sir, we've been to that particular site before. Recently."

The two detectives watched Daniel for a reaction. He stared back in confusion, and then it found its way through the fog in his brain.

Oh, shite. Kevin Chisolm.

Something very cold slithered along Daniel's spine. Kevin Chisolm, the foreman who had been killed—*stabbed*—only weeks ago. Dumped into a bin right outside the pub where Daniel was getting himself pished.

He shuddered at the memory. He'd been leaning against a wall only yards away from a murder scene, drunk out of his mind and helpless. He hadn't taken it seriously before, but now the significance of that night swamped him.

Three men. Three men standing together in the close. He'd seen them, seen the murderers.

Did they see me?

His body began to shake, intensifying the pain in his back. Mackenzie looked at his face and reached for the button at the side of Daniel's bed. A minute later a nurse swept in.

"Gentlemen, the patient needs to rest. Please come back later, aye?"

The detectives backed away, and the nurse handed Daniel a plastic cup of water and two tiny white pills. He clutched at the cup, and with a shaking hand downed the medication and lay back with his eyes closed, wondering if the pills would take effect before he threw them up. He should tell the detectives about the three men. He should...tell...

The beeping softened, the darkness floated in, and the room drifted away.

New voices, at least three, pecked at the cloud he was floating on. Daniel kept his eyes closed, grateful for the momentary cessation of pain, as the voices swirled around and over him. Despite his resolve, words began to filter through the mess.

"Poor lad...don't understand...happening in this city!"

"Baltair says...shh, careful!...he doesn't..."

"Those bobbies shouldn't..." a giggle, then "Biscuit fixed him, aye?...Sionaid...shh!"

The Highland Players. Daniel opened his eyes. Arrayed around his bed were Mary and Henry Duncan, Betty MacBain, and Ailis Brodie. Wee Caomhainn was leaning his huge frame against the only part of the wall not covered by hospital equipment, arms crossed on his chest, and a look of uneasiness on his face. His eyes roved around the room as if gauging the chances of a doctor swooping in and doing something medical to him.

Daniel pulled his gaze away from the big man and focused on the others. He had never seen them in their regular clothes before, and the difference was disconcerting. It occurred to him for the first time that there was nothing 'regular' about this lot, and it wasn't only the propensity to wear ancient clothing and speak in old Scots. Seeing them in jeans and jumpers should have been reassuring, but the opposite was true. It was just...weird.

"Daniel!" Mary crowed, and swooped down to give him a kiss on his forehead. "We were so worried. Don't ever do something like that again!"

"Well..." his voice came out as a croak. Betty handed him a cup of water and he drank it gratefully. He cleared his throat and tried again. "It wasn't actually my idea, you know."

He took another gulp of water and grabbed Mary's hand. "How is Eve? The police were here."

Mary gave an unladylike snort. "Oh, them? Aye, they came to us too. I have decided," she straightened her back and raised her nose in the air, "that I do not much like conversations with the coppers."

Daniel choked and spit a mouthful of water onto his blanket. *Coppers*? Had she really said that?

"Anyway, they didn't get anything out of us," Mary went on, unperturbed. "And Biscuit taught that young one a lesson."

"But what about E—er—who's Biscuit?" Daniel asked, feeling more and more as if he had gone down a rabbit hole and hadn't landed yet.

"She's our cat," Henry put in. "Doesn't much like people. Definitely doesn't like policemen."

"Ahh," Daniel murmured, "that explains the scratch. Good for Biscuit." He felt himself gaining strength, as if these people had some kind of healing magic.

"But you know," he added, in an apologetic tone, "those *coppers* are just doing their job. I mean, somebody stabbed me. I'm guessing it's not an everyday thing in Inverness. I don't think they send out detectives from the Criminal Investigation Department for random muggings, aye?"

"Humph," said Mary. She patted his arm again. "Did they give you the third degree?"

Daniel was ready this time; the water stayed down.

"Never mind that." He grabbed Mary's hand again. "Is Eve all right? Did the police bother her? Why isn't she here?"

"Ssssh, lad, slow down." Mary held his hand tightly. "She's all right. But . . ." She turned her head to look at the others.

Betty hefted her bulk out of the other chair in the room. "Aye, let's go and give the lad some rest. He's had a tough day." She signaled to Wee Caomhainn and he sprang off the wall and headed for the door. Betty herded Ailis out and into the hall.

Henry lagged behind and locked eyes for a moment with his wife. Then he too was gone, leaving only Mary by Daniel's bedside.

Something was wrong. The anxiety in the room was palpable, and he knew all about anxiety. His throat tightened as he faced the tiny woman, and sweat broke out on his brow.

"What?" he forced out between stiff lips. "Just tell me. Something's wrong with Eve, isn't it?"

Mary took a breath and exhaled slowly.

"There's nothing wrong with Eve, lad. It's just that, well, she's had a great shock, seeing you bleeding on the ground, and she's not herself."

"Is she coming? Mary, I need to see her! I need to see for myself that she's okay."

"Daniel, I think you need to prepare yourself. When I said she's not herself, I meant that. Literally."

He stared at her, bewildered. What the hell was she talking about? Why could these people never talk in a straight line?

A sense of urgency gripped him and he tried to sit up. The pain roared through his back and stole his breath, and he collapsed back onto the bed.

"I—have to—go—to h-her," he gasped, through gritted teeth. "Help me!"

Mary pushed the button by his bed. "Daniel, you're in no condition to get up, and you don't need to. She's all right; have I ever lied to you?"

"Then, what do you mean, she's not herself?" he demanded. "*Literally*?" The pain and anxiety merged into sarcasm. "Like, is she somebody else?"

Mary sighed. "Yes, lad. She's somebody else."

CHAPTER THIRTY-ONE
GLENCOE, SCOTLAND –
3 FEBRUARY, 1692

FAOLÁN

The weather today was horrible, as wet and gloomy as it had been the first day they'd arrived in Glencoe—was it only three days ago?—and it was taking its toll. Boredom was fully entrenched in the soldiers of the Earl of Argyll's Regiment of Foot. They sulked about, staying indoors to play cards with their hosts, or sleeping off hangovers from the night before. Except for one.

Faolán Campbell paced up and down the glen road, trying to look as if he had any business doing so. His spirits, which had begun on a high, were slowly sinking into the mud beside the road.

What was he thinking? Why would she come out on a day like today? He glared at the cottage where he'd been billeted along with Isaac, Eòin, Hector, and Archie. Why did it have to be so far from hers?

He was used to living with his mates; they'd been together for two years and were more like brothers than fellow soldiers. Despite the constant bickering, he knew that any one of them would lay down his life for the others without a second thought. They shared everything, knew every detail of each other's lives. Different as they all were, each could sense a change in mood in one of their number, and pounce on it.

Oh, and they'd pounced, all right. Thanks to that wee rattie Eòin, who had as usual been in the wrong place at the right time, everyone in the croft knew all about the altercation he'd had two days ago with those drunkards. Hector had gone so far as to christen him the "Hero of Glencoe."

I'm nae hero, he grumbled under his breath. *I dinnae do anythin' any other man wouldnae do 'n th' same situation. For anyone.*

His inner voice was laughing. *Aye, laddie, ye jist keep tellin' yerself that.* And much as he wanted to tell it to shut up, he knew it never lied. He'd done it because of those brilliant grey eyes.

His own eyes traveled down the road to a certain cottage, and as if willed by sheer desperation, the door opened. She stepped out and began to walk toward him.

Siònaid. A MacDonald, and if his heart wasn't lying, the love of his life. How had this happened?

Faolán thought back to his childhood, fighting his sister with a wooden sword for the honor of defeating the MacDonalds. The heavens certainly had a sense of humor, because in the end, he was the one who had been defeated. Losing had never felt so good.

He sauntered along the road toward Siònaid, trying to preserve at least some part of his dignity as a soldier in the British army, but the smile on her face as she turned to greet him told him it was useless. She knew.

"Guid morn, Miss MacDonald. What brings ye out on such a dreich day?"

Her smile was a lantern in the grim morning. "It's a bit crowded inside these days, sir. All these solgers, an' they're all sae hungry! Does th' gover'mint nae gie ye enough tae eat?"

Faolán pulled himself out of his study of her amazing silver eyes and tried to recollect what she'd just said. Something about eating?

She watched him struggle for a while, and the look in her eyes had him weak in the knees. The proximity of her body was doing odd things to him. Here they were, standing in the mud on a cold day in February, and yet he felt as warm as if he were sitting by the fire in his cottage. It was time to change the subject, but to what? They had absolutely nothing in common. He knew nothing about her.

"Why are ye here?" she said, jarring him out of his reverie. It was an echo of his own question about the purpose of their visit to Glencoe, and it had been bothering him since they'd arrived. But how to tell her that without giving out military information?

He thought for a minute, and made a decision. He would never lie to this woman. Ever.

"Would ye believe me if I said I had nae idea?" he asked.

"Aye, I would." The words were strong, and the assurance in them almost sent him over the edge.

"Truly?" He relaxed. "Ye cannae for a minute ken how th' army works. Th' superiors gab amongst themselves, an' sometimes they tell us lesser folk what they're thinkin'. Only sometimes. This *bas*—" He broke off, appalled.

Siònaid giggled in delight. "Go on. This *bas*—what does he do?"

Faolán gawked at her. He knew his face had turned a delicate shade of pink; he could feel the heat without touching it.

"Um, our *captain* doesnae tell us anythin'." He paused, formed his next words without thinking. "Here we are, stuck wi' a rabble o' MacDonalds," he registered a second too late what he had just said and put his hands up in supplication. "I'm sorry, I dinnae mean *you*! I meant th' *other* MacDonalds...no, I mean..." Faolán sputtered to a stop.

Siònaid stared at him for a minute, and then burst out in a musical laugh.

"I dinnae think it could gie any better than th' *bas captain*, but ye did it." Her laughter rolled over him like a soft breeze.

"Ye-ye're no mad?" Faolán asked, when he found his tongue.

"Why shou'd I be mad?" she asked him. "Efter all, I'm no one o' that rabble o' MacDonalds—I'm from Islay." She gave an exaggerated curtsy.

She straightened and faced him, her face serious.

"Faolán, I was raised wi' Campbells aboot, an' many o' them were mean an' cruel t' anyone named MacDonald. I dinnae like them."

She put her hands on her hips and gazed straight into his eyes. "But 'at was some o' them. Nae all."

She looked at the ground, and when she spoke again her voice trembled.

"I like ye."

"Wha'?"

"I said, I like ye. I like ye jist fine."

Faolán could barely hear her words for the pounding in his ears. He felt as if he might float right up over the glen and into the mountains. She liked him? She liked him!

Reality intruded like a splash of cold water.

This can't be! I dinnae e'en know her! How can she say she likes me? Is she—a wanton?

He stepped back, and something on his face must have told her exactly what he was thinking. Her own face flushed, and she stomped one foot. The silver eyes flashed.

"I dinnae mean 'at! She turned and limped away, muttering. "Men ar' such *sots*."

Shame washed over Faolán. He reached out for her arm, thought better of it, and ran to catch up. He planted himself in front of her.

"I'm sorry! I'm an eejit. F'rgive me?"

"Humph." Siònaid didn't look at him, but she stopped walking.

"Ye're right," he said. "Men are sots. An' army men are th' worst. We dinnae—dinnae see many women, only th' sort in bars when we gie a night off."

"An' efter all, I'm a MacDonald, so I must be one o' that sort." Her angry eyes found his and she stared at him, brow furrowed. Then she sighed.

"'Tis my own fault. I misspoke. Ye've kent Glencoe is a wee bit isolated, aye? I dinnae ken many folks I can talk tae abit th' world. I thought—I thought—oh, nivver mind—I need t' get home." She pushed past him and began walking again.

"Yer house is 'at way."

"Wha'?" She blinked and turned around. "Oh. Aye, 'tis." She didn't move, just stared at him in mortification. The silence lengthened.

"I-I like ye too...jist fine." Faolán knew his face must be aflame, but he couldn't help himself.

"I said I like ye, Siònaid MacDonald." It was out. He'd said it and there was no going back.

She nodded. The cloud cover disappeared and the sun came out. The air warmed until it was the rarest of spring days. In the next second, the clouds were back and the harsh Highland winter descended again on Glencoe village, but it didn't matter.

He joined her and they began to walk, past her croft and on down the glen road that led out of the village. Time stood still.

She told him of her home in Islay, of her beloved mountains so like the ones in Glencoe, of her brothers, and her horse Beitris. She talked about her books and her reason for leaving the island to come to Glencoe.

"Seumas is such a braw lad," she said. "He's like a sponge, soakin' up words on paper like a true scholar."

Faolán watched her face light up when she

discussed her pupil. She was amazing, and he'd found her here, of all places.

"I'd love t' meet wee Seumas," he told her.

"Nae, ye wouldnae. Seumas hates folk named Campbell." She grinned at him. "I've been workin' on 'at, but sae far, it hasnae taken root."

"Well, it has t' soon, 'cause this Campbell isnae goin' away."

He realized what he'd just said and stopped. He turned to face Siònaid and she returned his gaze, eyes clouded with the knowing.

It couldn't be. He wasn't here to stay, and of course she knew it. In less than two weeks, he'd be marching on to hell knew where, and she'd be left behind here in Glencoe. A weight descended on his heart.

"We'll figure 't out, *mo ghràdh*," he said softly, and put a hand on her arm. "We'll make 't work, 'cause—"

A hand came from nowhere and wrenched his off Siònaid's arm. He was spun around to face a snarling countenance and an arm uplifted to strike.

"What th' hell d' ye think yer doin'!" the man hissed at him. "Keep yer fuckin' hands off her!"

"Andrew!" Siònaid gasped. She placed herself between the two men. "He's nae doin' anythin' wrong. He's my friend!"

"He's a fuckin' Campbell, and he'd better no touch ye again!" Andrew MacDonald grabbed her wrist and dragged her away toward their croft.

Faolán rubbed his arm. *Who was that arse? Her brother?* He watched as the two reached Siònaid's cottage and disappeared inside. Then he turned and made his way slowly back to his own lodging.

He's a fuckin' Campbell...He'd better no touch ye again, the other lad had said.

Faolán squared his shoulders. *Weel, we'll jist see about that.*

Suddenly he stopped, his hand outstretched to open the door, as something slid into his mind. He'd never met that lad, Andrew, but he was suddenly sure of one thing.

He'd heard that voice before...somewhere.

CHAPTER THIRTY-TWO

GLENCOE, SCOTLAND, 3 FEBRUARY, 1692

SIÒNAID

hat were ye thinkin', lass?" Andrew's furious voice resounded through the crowded cottage. Heads turned at the prospect of something interesting, and all stopped what they were doing to listen.

"Andrew!" Siònaid pulled on his sleeve. "Stop 't!"

He looked over his shoulder at his eager audience and glared. Siònaid smiled brilliantly at their guests before walking deliberately into the sleeping chamber, with Andrew right on her heels.

"How could ye?" he lowered his voice to a whisper. "What if some'un had seen ye out there?"

"What if?" Her voice was a challenge. "Was I doin' somethin' wrong?"

"Ye were talkin' an' laughin' wi' a *man*, a *Campbell*," Andrew said. He ran his hands through his hair in frustration. "He had his hand on ye!"

Siònaid watched him in fascination. She'd never seen Andrew behave this way, ever. He was so even-tempered and soft-spoken. Granted, she'd never been with a man who had his *hand* on her before, either. But he was making it sound as if she'd been caught with her skirts above her head, rolling around in the stable.

She suspected it wasn't that she had been talking to a man, but that the man had been surnamed Campbell. She straightened to her full height and glared back at Andrew.

"Do ye think that little o' me?" she demanded.

He huffed out a breath and turned his back on her. When he turned around again, his breathing was closer to normal.

"I worry about ye," he said softly. "I dinnae ken what 'twas like back home on yer island, bit here..."

"There're people named Campbell on Islay, Andrew. People. Wi' two eyes, nae two heads. They look like us, 'cause they *are* like us." She took a breath to steady herself, then put a hand on his arm. He flinched and shook it off.

"They're Scots," Siònaid said. "They may no want th' same king, but they love Scotland, jist like we do."

"I dinnae care!" Andrew grabbed at his hair again. "D'ye ken what a man in th' army is like?"

"Some'un who fights fer his country?" she asked.

"Some'un who lives 'n a barracks wi' other solgers," Andrew countered. "Who doesnae see women fer weeks on end. Who doesnae ken women like ye."

"An' wha' kind o' woman is a woman like me?" she challenged him. He sucked in his breath.

Faolán said th' same abit solgers, Siònaid thought. She felt a warmth swelling in her heart at thought of his name. *But Andrew's wrong. Nae all the men in th' army ar' like that.*

"Never min'," Andrew said. "Ye dinnae have to unnerstand."

He put his hands on her shoulders and waited for her to meet his worried blue eyes.

"I dinnae want ye t' see 'at man again," he said. "Promise me."

Siònaid stood very still and gazed back at him.

"I cannae," she said. "He's my friend." She felt him stiffen and his fingers dug into her shoulders, but she forced the next words out.

"I'm a groon woman, an' I'll do wha' I think is right. Please, try t' unnerstand."

Andrew opened his mouth, but no words came out. He took his hands off her shoulders, shoved them into his pockets, and strode out of the room without another word.

A small hand found its way into hers, and she turned to find young Seumas at her side. How long had he been there?

"Be caref'll," he said.

Something in his voice had her kneeling to study his face. It was pale and drawn, the way he looked when he was coming down with something. She felt his forehead, cool.

"Wha' s wrong, *leannan*?" she said softly. "Are ye worrit about me?"

He nodded, and tears welled in his blue eyes, eyes so like his brother Andrew's.

"He likes ye," Seumas said. "Dinnae ye ken 'at?" He looked at her with eyes far older than his years. "He's allus liked ye."

"I like him too," she said.

"Not like 'at," Seumas countered. His face turned fierce, little brows drawn together. "Ye like 'at solger. 'At *Campbell.*"

Siònaid felt the blood rushing to her face. "How did ye ken about 'at?" she asked in a voice that cracked. "Have ye been followin' me?"

"Aye," he said. He nodded his head and the blond curls flopped up and down. "Ye're nae verra observ'nt."

Siònaid felt her legs go weak. She sat down on the floor and reached for both of Seumas' hands. He kept his eyes fastened on hers, and something flickered in them. He let out a breath, and his small body began to tremble.

"Hmm—when did ye see him?"

"When he fooght those other solgers fer ye. I kent he was verra braw t' dae 'at." His face wore a look of reluctant approval. "I dinnae ken a Campbell could be brave like 'at."

Siònaid smothered a smile.

Seumas fisted his small hands in hers. "But..."

"But what?" She watched him for a moment. "Are ye afraid fer me?"

He nodded again.

"Seumas, ye needn't be. Ye saw him pr'tect me. He's my friend. His name's Faolán, an' I need ye t' believe me. He would nivver hurt me."

"He's a Campbell!" The words burst out of Seumas as if he'd tried to contain them but couldn't. Siònaid stared at him with a frown, released his hands, and stood up.

"Seumas, stop 't!" She sighed in frustration. "We've talk't about this sae many times! Why cannae ye understand?"

Seumas stood up too. He stared at Siònaid with a chillingly adult expression, put his hands on his hips, and anchored his feet.

"I'm no afraid o' th' solger. E'en if he is a Campbell. I ken he likes ye, and I dinnae think he means ye harm. But..."

Siònaid sighed. "But what?" she asked wearily.

Seumas sighed in frustration. "But Andrew likes ye too."

There was a time, not too long ago, when Siònaid's heart would have leapt at those words. But that had been then, before Faolán Campbell marched into Glencoe and taught her what love was. Was it only two days? Two days since she had grown up, become a real woman. Two days that made all the difference.

Seumas was wrong about Andrew. He always treated her with fondness, and she had to admit that sometimes she had imagined something more in that blue-eyed gaze. But they'd lived together in the same house for more than a year now. If he felt something besides the affection of a cousin, he would have said something long ago—wouldn't he?

Be caref'll. Seumas' whispered words came back to niggle at her thoughts.

Be caref'll. He likes ye.

A chill began at the base of her spine and clawed its way up to reside as a lump in her stomach.

Seumas was an intelligent child. He was prejudiced about anything not Jacobite, but he didn't miss much. *Ye're nae verra observ'nt*, he had said.

He'd certainly been right about that. Not for a minute had she suspected his presence when she was with Faolán. Then again, she wouldn't have noticed if the whole government army had marched down the street, led by a piper. She gave herself a wry smile, then sobered.

Seumas hadn't been wrong about her feelings for Faolán, so maybe he wasn't wrong about the way Andrew felt. It would go a long way toward explaining his brother's behavior just now. The chill deepened.

"*Ye were talkin' an' laughin' wi' a man, a Campbell,*" Andrew had said. She'd thought the important word was the surname, but now she had the sinking sensation that Seumas might be right.

The problem wasn't that the man was named Campbell—it was that he was a man. A man not named Andrew MacDonald.

The fire was the only light in the cottage. An occasional pop from the burning peat and the soft snores of sleeping men and women were all that broke the silence of another winter night in Glencoe.

They were enough to mask the soft rustling of cloth as a man quietly dressed in black from head to foot, and to muffle his footsteps as he moved to the door and eased it inward just enough to let himself out.

Andrew pulled the door closed and wrapped his cloak closer around him to ward off the cold, before turning to make his way along the Glencoe road. His thoughts were as black as the cloak.

He needed no light to find his way to his destination. Stopping near another cottage, larger than the others, he put his fingers to his lips and produced a low hoot, like that of a night owl. While he waited, his mind went back over the events of the day.

He could feel the rage—the red-hot *need*—that was always there, simmering just beneath the surface. It had been a part of him since that day three years ago when he had rushed down a hillside to meet the enemy and discovered what killing another human being felt like. Sickening, brutal, exhilarating.

He leaned back against the turf wall and let the need spread through him, embracing it as it coursed through his veins. Very soon, he sensed, he would have to let it out, give up his iron control and just *feel*. And now he had a reason.

He smiled to himself. This was going to be interesting.

CHAPTER THIRTY-THREE
INVERNESS, SCOTLAND
- PRESENT DAY

*Darkness... When everything that you know
and love... is taken from you so harshly... all
you can think about is anger, hatred, and
even revenge... and no one can save you.*

"Tell me." Baltair's deep, rolling baritone
filled the small room at Number Twelve
Roseberry Place. His hands were stee-
pled in front of his pale face, and the coal-black
eyes pinned the woman across from him like a bug
on a tray.

He and the girl were alone in the sitting room. A
small black cat wandered in and jumped into Baltair's
lap, curled up, and went to sleep. He stroked its fur
absently with long, supple fingers, never taking his
eyes from the young woman in front of him.

"Tell me what you remember."

Siònaid MacDonald shivered under his gaze,
although she wasn't cold. She tore her eyes away
from his and took a deep, trembling breath.

"I remember 't all," she said, in a voice that seemed to belong to someone else. "Glencoe. Th' massacre... th' blizzard. *Him.*" A shudder ripped through her. "I thought I was dyin'."

"You *were* dying." Baltair said impatiently. "Do you remember what you asked?"

Siònaid's brows drew together as she struggled to recall the exact words.

"I-I asked for revenge."

"Revenge for what?" Baltair's voice was silk.

"For what they'd done. For what *he'd* done." Unbidden, tears rose at the memory of that betrayal and slid down her cheeks to land unnoticed on her clasped hands.

"And what had he done?" Baltair sat back in his chair and crossed one leg over the other, as if he were listening to an amusing story. The black cat raised its head, and then curled tighter and went back to sleep.

"Come, girl. I asked you to tell me. All of it."

"Ye *ken* what he did!" The words burst out in an explosion of breath. "You ken it verra well!"

"Aye, I do know. But do you? Really?" He had lowered his voice to a murmur, so low she had to lean forward to catch the words.

"I will never f'rget—never again." The tears became sobs, and Siònaid let herself give into them, all the heartbreak of that night welling up and pouring forth in a gush of emotion.

"He promised me he'd come back. He said he loved me! He asked me t' wait, and I would hae waited f'rever!" The wail echoed through the house at

Number Twelve Roseberry Place; the words drifted into the air and were gone.

"So how did he betray you?" Baltair lifted one pale hand and studied his fingertips.

"Why are ye makin' me say 't all again?" Siònaid whimpered. "Are ye enjoyin' my pain?"

"How did he betray you?" he asked again.

"He—those solgers—they murder'd them all. They broke th' Highland code; stayed wi' us, drank our whisky, an' ate our food, laughed wi' us—" her breath caught and shadows swirled in her grey eyes.

"Please—dinnae make me tell th' rest!"

Baltair ignored her distress. "Continue. Then what happened?"

"They killed all th' men. Killed e'en th' bairns. Shot them, stabbed them, in their beds. They pullt me out o' my bed, me an' th' other women, an' they drove us out into th' storm."

"And this man you say you loved; did he come?"

"Aye, he came. I saw him there, holdin' the knife he used t' murder my people." Her eyes were directed inward now, seeing the scene again as if it had happened moments ago.

"'Twas drippin' wi' blood, MacDonald blood." Her voice sank. "He look't at me, an' 'twas like th' knife went into me. I could feel my heart rippin' apart."

She raised haunted eyes to Baltair. "I hated him then—s'much as I'd loved him. Cannae ye unnerstand why I wanted revenge?" Her voice was a challenge. "'Twas my right!"

"Do you remember what I told you, when you begged for that revenge?" he asked.

For a long time, she said nothing. Then she raised damp eyes to his.

"Ye-ye said 'twas th' wrong answer," she said, in the barest of whispers. "Ye said I would regret 't."

"I said the outcome might not be worth the cost," said Baltair. "Not quite the same thing."

"But nothin' happened," she said. "I dinnae die. I dinnae get my revenge. An' that's all right."

"Ahh, so that is what you think?" Baltair's lips turned up in amusement. "And why is that all right?"

"'Cause I found love again." A soft smile played about her lips. "I dinnae ken it could happen twice, bit it did. I found it right here, 'n this place, Inverness."

"Ahh." Baltair's exhalation held a tinge of melancholy. "And does he know what you are, this lover?"

"What I am?" She knitted her brows.

"Does he know you're a revenant?"

The words came back, drifting out of the snow and wind of that night. *You will become a revenant.*

"A *rev-enant?*" she had asked him.

"*Cursed to exist...but one purpose...vengeance.*"

Siònaid felt the blood drain from her head. She gripped the arms of the chair in which she sat, hoping to keep from fainting. *Cursed?*

Baltair captured her eyes with those black orbs, and held them fast.

"Isn't it about time you asked me what a revenant is?" he asked softly.

Siònaid was silent, held in thrall to those eyes. Blacker than night, deeper than time. Inhuman eyes.

"Did you not wonder why you do not feel the heat

or the cold? Why, when you touch something, you cannot feel its texture?"

He shook his head. When he spoke again, it was as if he were talking to himself, although he continued to hold Siònaid's gaze.

"It is not easily done, making a revenant. Even I have only attempted it once or twice. Sometimes things can go wrong in the making. Memories can be lost, or functions break down. I expected that."

His tone became thoughtful. "What I did *not* expect—could not have imagined— was that you would forget your entire reason for existence. Forget why I gave you back your life."

Siònaid could not have looked away if her life depended upon it.

Baltair's tone sharpened. "I had to wait; I could not tell you until you found your memories for yourself." He paused.

"Did you not wonder about this place in which you found yourself? Or why you could understand both the old and the new language?"

He snorted, as if taking this much time with someone so stupid was beneath him.

"Did you not wonder what led you to the Highland Players, out of all the people in this city?

He gazed at her in mingled amusement and derision. "Did you not feel that you were *different*?"

"I—" Siònaid stopped. She *had* wondered, of course she had. But who could ever have thought . . .

She wrenched her eyes away from Baltair's and screwed them shut. No. This had to be some sort of jest. Some kind of bizarre initiation ritual led by the

Highland Players. Did they do this to everyone? Had Daniel been subjected to it?

Daniel. He had been stabbed, almost in front of her. How could she be thinking about herself? Self-loathing threatened to swamp her.

Was he even alive? Panic constricted her throat. The Duncans had left for the hospital as soon as Baltair arrived, so Mary should know. Why had she not called?

Her eyes snapped up to Baltair.

"Is he alive?" she demanded. He maintained his blank expression, but she was no longer fooled.

"Is he? Ye ken who I'm talkin' about." She was being rude; she knew it and didn't care. She was tired of people playing with her emotions, of feeding her foolishness about curses and revenants. The only thing that mattered was Daniel.

Baltair ignored her. A long moment passed. The bravado deserted her and she slumped in her chair, drained of energy and will.

"Please? Is he goin' t' be all right?" she whispered.

Baltair turned those black eyes on her, and now his face wore a look of infinite sadness. Her heart stopped at that look and she waited, paralyzed.

He was dead. He had to be. Why had she ever believed she could find a second chance at love? *Cursed*—so that's what it meant. It was her fate.

"He is not dead." Again, Baltair had read her mind. The wash of relief and joy was cut off by his next words.

"What I do not understand," he said softly, "is what you are going to do about that?"

"Wh-what d'ye mean?"

"In the storm that night, you told me you wanted revenge. 'It is all I want,' you said." The words were thrown back to mock her.

"Upon whom did you want revenge, again?" Baltair's tone was patient.

"Him. Faolán...Campbell." It was the first time she'd uttered the name since that night. It hissed and burned in her mouth and left ashes on her tongue.

"Tell me about him, this Faolán. Your lover who betrayed you. What did he look like?"

Against her will, the memory rose to the surface of Siònaid's mind and spilled out.

"He was tall, an' muscular," she recited, as if reading the words from a paper. "He had brown hair helt back in a queue, but bits o' it kept comin' loose in th' wind and blowin' across his eyes. He was verra handsome, bit that wasnae why I loved him." She stopped for breath, and realized she was panting as if she'd run the length of the High Street.

"I loved him. I loved him sae much."

Baltair held her gaze. "And what do you remember most about him?" he asked.

A sad smile played across her lips. "His eyes. He had th' most beautiful brown eyes in th' world. Eyes ye could get lost in."

Baltair stood suddenly. Deprived of her bed, the black cat jumped to the floor, arched her back in disapproval, and stalked from the room.

"And this new love—Daniel MacArthur—what about his eyes?"

Siònaid opened her mouth, and closed it again. She

sat as if carved from stone while her mind dredged up Daniel's image. Handsome when he wasn't sulking or worrying. Brown hair that had a tendency to fall into his eyes.

His beautiful brown eyes. Eyes you could get lost in.

Faolán's eyes.

Siònaid's hands gripped the armrest of the chair so hard her knuckles showed white. She could feel her heart beating in her cold, cursed body. A body remade for one purpose—revenge.

Baltair's soft voice slid into her ears. "Do you understand now? Do you understand why you were brought here to Inverness, to a time far in your future? Do you understand why you were allowed to meet a man named Daniel MacArthur? And did you know that MacArthur is a sept of Clan Campbell?"

"Daniel...is th' reincarnation o' Faolán." Siònaid's voice was flat, emotionless.

"Aye. He carries Faolán Campbell's spirit; the kernel of the man you once loved and came to hate. Daniel MacArthur is Faolán Campbell, for all intents and purposes."

"But it doesnae matter!" She forced herself to sit up straight in the chair. "I was wrong! I dinnae need revenge anymore!"

Baltair shook his head, and the sadness was back.

"That is not how it works, lass. You cannot change fate, and you are no longer the Siònaid MacDonald who lived—and died—in Glencoe. You are a revenant, and you will exist only until you have achieved your purpose." He paused. "You almost did that last night."

Siònaid gaped at him. "I did? But I dinnae stab him!"

"Were you not with him when it happened?"

"Aye, but—"

"The heavens do not require you to destroy him with your own hands, lass." Baltair pinned her gaze again. "When you asked for revenge, things were set in motion—things that cannot be changed. You are a danger to your young man if you are by his side, no matter what you do."

Tears of frustration were running down Siònaid's face. "But I dinnae want Daniel t' die! I love him!"

"That is why, in the blizzard, I asked you if you were sure," Baltair said, with utmost patience. "I warned you that it was not the right path, that if you chose to become a revenant there was no turning back."

"I willnae let him be hurt! I will protect him!" She struggled to her feet and fisted her hands at her sides.

He sighed. "You can try. But there is one thing that I have not told you. Your body—your reanimated body—has a time limit."

"A time limit? What does 'at mean?"

"It means that you were built to accomplish your mission, and for no other purpose. When you do so, you may continue to live in this body—in this time. It is the best I can do."

His voice softened. "If you do *not* do so, if you try to protect him, you will disappear. You can never reincarnate, and you will be erased forever from the annals of time. Do you understand what I am saying, lass?"

He narrowed his eyes.

"You, and your descendants, will live only if Daniel MacArthur dies."

CHAPTER THIRTY-FOUR
MILBURN ROAD, INVERNESS, SCOTLAND - PRESENT DAY

*"You need to spend time crawling alone
through shadows to truly appreciate
what it is to stand in the sun."*
—Shaun Hick

Big Angus Graham stood in the shadow of the nearly finished office building on Millburn Road, watching the activity at the edge of the site. The crew was busy breaking down the scaffolding in order to move it to the next section of the building, supervised closely by Rob Erskine.

Most of the crew, that was. Frank Allan and Gil Dunbar were nowhere to be seen. Angus shoved his bulk off the wall and ambled over to the growing piles of wooden planks and metal scaffold.

He called up to Erskine. "Did Dunbar and Allan come t' work today? I don't see 'em anywhere."

The steward looked up, surprised. "They were here a minute ago. All I know is, wherever one of them is, the other's probably there too. Why, do you need them again?"

Angus waved a hand in dismissal. "No, just wonderin'. No worries."

"Shame about what happened to MacArthur, aye?" Erskine said. "It seems like somebody doesn't like project managers."

Angus grunted.

"Is he gonna be okay?" the steward asked. "He isn't a bad boss, all things considered. Sure gives the job more attention than Chisolm, not to speak ill of the dead."

"Aye, he's comin' along," Big Angus said. "I heerd he'll be fine; prob'ly be back next week."

"You'd better clean the trailer for him, then," Erskine said, and winked. "Least we can do to welcome him back."

"Humph." Angus waved to the steward and started toward the office trailer. When he reached the corner, however, he turned left and continued around the side. His boots squelched in the mud as he made his way to the rear and turned the next corner. Now he was at the back of the huge complex.

He looked down the length of the structure. Most of the outer doors had been installed here; all that was left were the windows. Big Angus headed for the loading dock that would eventually serve the offices assigned to the new complex, and paused to look at the ramp that led inside.

The roll-up door had not yet been installed, but the area beyond was dark as pitch. The foreman reached into the pocket of his parka and pulled out a torch. He clicked it on and moved forward, pausing every few steps to orient himself within the huge storage space.

He reached the fire door that led to the offices, stepped inside, and froze in place, dousing the torch. Voices filtered from one of the offices about midway down the hall. At least two men were standing in the dark, having a conversation in the middle of a busy construction site. An uneasy feeling worked its way up his spine.

He eased himself along the wall of the hallway, inching closer to the room. None of the doors had been installed yet, and all the rooms were shrouded in darkness.

There were three distinct voices, and two of them he recognized.

"It wasn't our fault!" came a whine that could belong to no one but Gil Dunbar. "Chisolm fucked up. Right, Frank?"

"Aye," said Allan. "We done everything you telt us to. We couldn't know he'd change his mind, could we? We took care of it like you said."

A third voice intruded, low and sibilant. "You took care of it? Is that how he ended up in a rubbish bin in the High Street?"

Angus leaned closer, glad that whispers carried in an empty building. *Shoulda paid attention to who else might be missin' from th' crew.* He cursed himself for a fool.

"You two managed to attract more attention than a band of pipers!" the unknown voice seethed. "His body was found the very next morning, in a bin that's emptied *every single morning!*" The speaker exhaled loudly.

"The police aren't fools like you two. Do you think dots won't be connected between that mess and"

"We didn't do MacArthur! You told us t' mind our own business, an' we did," Allan protested. "If we'd a done that, he'd be dead too."

"Shut up!" hissed the third man.

"But that 'un was trouble," Dunbar said. "He was askin' questions! He found out somethin', and he was asking if we was friends with Chisolm. Why would he ask that?"

"Because unlike you two, he's smart! Forget about him; what about Graham?"

Big Angus stiffened. Sweat dribbled down the back of his neck and into his flannel shirt.

"I think he was along for the ride," Allan said. "He wasn't asking any questions. He's jist the foreman; he looked like he didn't wanna be there a'tall."

There was silence, then the unidentified man spoke again. "From what I know of Graham, he doesn't like people who put on airs. Watch him, but I doubt those two interact more than necessary. Now go—get back to the job before you're missed."

Big Angus turned around. He couldn't go back the way he'd come quickly enough to avoid being heard, so he backtracked a few feet and stepped into the empty doorway of an office. He pressed himself against the wall and tried not to breathe.

Almost immediately, he heard footsteps in the hallway. The question was, had they all left together? Impossible to tell. He waited, one minute, two...and then he heard a single set of footsteps going the other way, toward the far end of the hall.

Big Angus let out a long breath. He waited another five minutes, but the building was silent. He worked his way carefully along the hall, trailing his hand against the wall. There was no way in hell he was using the torch, not now.

He heard a small pop and his heart jumped. Angus turned to face the wall next to him, but in the darkness, there was nothing to be seen of a small crack as it crept higher on the bearing wall. Heart racing, he turned away and resumed his slow journey.

It seemed to take forever, but finally he was outside with his face turned up to the wan daylight of a Scottish winter day. After what seemed like a century in darkness, it was the most beautiful thing he'd ever seen.

Big Angus made his way to the trailer and sat down, breathing heavily. It was just as he and Daniel suspected—Dunbar and Allan were involved, and if what he'd heard was true, they'd either murdered their former project manager or had a hand in it.

He cursed under his breath. There was absolutely nothing he could do about it. He had no proof.

What he did have was a warning. They might be watching him, but now he'd be watching them. Sooner or later, they would meet with their co-conspirator, and he'd be waiting.

Angus wished there was somebody he could trust; he'd never signed on to be a detective. Erskine seemed honest, but he couldn't be sure. Trusting the wrong person could get you killed. Look at what had happened to Chisolm, and now MacArthur.

His jaw set. They were wrong about one thing, and

he hoped it would come back to haunt them. He *did* like Daniel MacArthur. His boss didn't put on airs; he came off as a snobby git because he was fussy about cleanliness, that was all. Underneath, he was honest and straightforward.

MacArthur trusted him as Chisolm never had, and he'd be damned if he was going to let the man down. He had no doubts that no matter what they said, the same people who had murdered Kevin Chisolm had tried to do it again. So now he could add another job to his list, bodyguard. Those villains weren't going to get another chance if Big Angus had anything to do with it.

Daniel was sitting up in bed when Big Angus stumped in, looking around warily as if someone might snatch him up and put him in a hospital gown at any minute.

It was the same look Wee Caomhainn had had when the Players visited him. Was the fear of hospitals something elemental to big men?

Daniel's grin faded at the serious expression on his foreman's face.

"What?" he asked.

Angus scowled. "Jist let me gie used t' this place for a minnit, will ye? Gives me the willies." He pulled up the chair and studied his boss.

"Ye don't look too bad," he conceded. "Are they keepin' the place clean enough for ye?"

"Shut it," Daniel said. "Thanks for coming; I haven't

seen your ugly face for a few days, I kinda missed that."

Pleasantries out of the way, the two let the silence grow.

"I was that worrit," Big Angus finally muttered. "Don't do it again."

"Why does everybody think I had a choice in the matter?" Daniel said.

"Well, I have some news for ye. Mebbe it'll help ye keep out o' trouble next time."

Angus filled him in on what he had overheard at the job site. When he finished, Daniel stared across the room at the blank TV for a few moments.

"We suspected those two weren't up to snuff, but I never thought they were mean enough—or smart enough—to kill someone!"

Big Angus' voice was dry. "Well, it doesn't take too many brain cells t' stab somebody." He stopped at Daniel's wince. "Sorry."

Daniel waved him off. "Never mind. It's what happened, isn't it? And it means we were close to something. We scared them."

"We scared somebody," Angus agreed. "That third man's their boss, I'm sure o' that. I doubt those two numpties have the brains t' come up with a plan on their own."

He hesitated. "He sounded like you, boss."

"Like me? What does that mean?"

"Y'know. Educated."

"Did you report this to the police?" Daniel asked.

"Not yet. Wanted t' tell you first."

"Do it as soon as you leave. Even if there's no proof,

they as much as admitted to murder. The detectives who talked to me seemed pretty observant; they won't appreciate us holding back."

"Besides," he grinned at his foreman, "are you going to protect me all by yourself?"

Big Angus puffed himself up. "If I have t'. Only thing I won't do, I'm tellin' ye now, is clean that trailer. "'At's somethin' you'll have t' do yourself."

Daniel repressed a shudder. "Well, it can't be anything like it was when I got there. You're the only slob using it right now, aye?"

Big Angus humphed. "I'll see what I can do to get it back the way it was fer ye," he said. "The site's pretty muddy from all th' rain. I'll track in some fer ye when I have time, since yer so nice."

Daniel knew the banter was a cloak for the real issue at hand. Someone had killed and tried to kill again, and it was only luck that he hadn't succeeded the second time.

A thought struck him. "You were there when I was asking Allan and Dunbar questions about that odd materials order. You're in danger too."

His foreman nodded; all humor was gone. "I know, lad. I'm bein' careful."

Daniel's voice was gruff. "I don't want to lose you. Guess I'll have to get out of here so I can protect *you*."

After Big Angus was gone, he lay for a while staring at the ceiling. *Guess I'll have to get out of here so I can protect you.*

Who was he kidding? How the hell was he going to protect anyone, when the world was made of quicksand and everyone seemed to be lining up to push him in?

Other than Big Angus and his cousin Callum, how many people around him were who they said they were? Allan and Dunbar. The mystery man who called the shots for them. Chisolm. All of them had been slinking around in the shadows, while he was playing Romeo with Eve McDonald.

Or whoever she was. His thoughts slid sideways into an area he'd been trying to avoid for the past week.

Mary's words haunted his waking moments. *Yes, lad. She's somebody else.* Those words were a leaden mass at the bottom of his stomach, more painful than his fading stab wound.

Had she been lying to him all this time, playing him for a fool? Mary had refused to explain; had begged him to wait until she was ready to tell him about it herself.

And she hadn't. In the days since, she'd never even come to see him. She was gone from his life like mist...again. Just like after the wedding faire. Was toying with his emotions a game to her?

No. He closed his eyes and her image rose out of the darkness. Maybe he *was* a fool, but there was no way those moments in the trailer were playacting. She cared about him. That much he was sure of.

So where was she?

Who the hell *was* Eve McDonald?

CHAPTER THIRTY-FIVE

INVERNESS, SCOTLAND
- PRESENT DAY

*Lies and secrets...they are like a cancer
in the soul. They eat away what is good
and leave only destruction behind.*
—Cassandra Clare

The atmosphere in the Highland Players' office was thick with tension. Betty MacBain sat in her customary armchair, a thick volume open on her lap. She hadn't turned a page in ten minutes.

Ailis Brody and Bennet MacGillivray were engaged in a game of chess, heads bent over the board, but neither had moved a piece since Mary and Siònaid had stepped through the doorway. It was as if their arrival had sucked the air out of the room, turning everyone into statues.

Henry Duncan was seated at the table next to Mary, head bent low over his laptop. Every few seconds he would glance up and over the computer and then return quickly to the keys.

Mary was making no pretense of working. She perched on her stool, little bird eyes darting around at the occupants of the room.

The cause of this odd frozen tableau sat in a chair by the door, hands folded, and eyes cast down into her lap.

Mary took out her mobile and entered three words in a group text.

He told her.

One by one the Players checked their devices. Heads lifted and eyes were directed at Eve, no, it was Siònaid now. She didn't notice the attention; her own head remained bowed.

She's been this way since, Mary typed.

Betty's face looked stricken.

What can we do? she typed. Mary shook her head.

"Ach, brilliant!" Henry's gleeful voice broke the strained silence. "We got it!" He turned the laptop around to face the room and pointed to the screen. "It's the one we've been hopin' for. Lads and lassies get ready; we're going to Glencoe!"

"The Visitor Centre?" Mary asked. She pulled the laptop over and studied the photograph of the glen.

"Aye," Henry said. "I've been in talks with them for almost a year now, but when the anniversary of the massacre came and went, I thought they'd forgotten us."

Ailis and Bennet came over to study the screen.

"We're going to re-enact the massacre, then?" asked Bennet. "Can I be a Campbell?" He flourished an imaginary sword and executed some complicated footwork in front of the desk.

Henry laughed. "I'll make a list. Some of us'll have to be MacDonalds, ye ken? And Wee Caomhainn should be Alexander Maclain; he was a big man."

He waggled his finger at them. "This is special—they've never tried something like this before. If we're good, they want to move it to the anniversary of the massacre and make it an annual thing. So, let's be good."

Betty threw her history book onto the side table and heaved herself out of the chair. She went to the bookshelf and ran her fingers along the volumes.

"Mmm, that was 1692. Mary, you'd better check on the differences and tweak our costumes a bit."

"Too bad we can't do it in the glen itself," Bennet said. "I mean, it's right there."

"Aye, but Glencoe village isn't. Have any of you been there?"

"I have," said Ailis. "When I was a kid. It's beautiful, even for the Highlands. But Henry's right; there's nothing left except some foundations. They're excavating for artifacts, I think."

"It's also difficult for tourists to get into the glen, unless they're hikers," said Henry, "and tourists are why we do this, aye? There's a model of one of the crofts at the Visitor's Centre; that's where we'll be. Look; here's a slideshow."

"Oh, look at those three sharp peaks close together!" Ailis said. "I think they're called 'the three sisters.' Wish I'd paid more attention; I remember just gawking at everything."

"C-cannae I see?" came a small voice, and the group around the laptop parted to reveal Siònaid, standing just behind them. Her face was so white it seemed as if she might faint at any second, but her fists were clenched in determination and her lips set.

Mary came around the desk and took her arm. "Are you sure, lass?" she asked. "You don't have to."

"Aye, I do."

Mary eyed her with respect. "Then come around here; you should sit down, aye?" She guided Siònaid behind the desk and deposited her in the chair. She pulled the laptop back around and clicked on one of the pictures, and it enlarged to fill the screen. Sharp peaks pierced the skyline and loomed over wildflowers in the glen below. The River Coe wound through the valley like a ribbon.

"Ohh," breathed Siònaid. She stared at the photograph for a long moment, as the group gathered around her held their breaths. Then Mary leaned forward. "Ready?"

Siònaid nodded, and Mary tapped the next photograph. More mountains appeared, enveloped in mist that swirled around and down and allowed only their dark tops to push free.

Siònaid began to tap the images herself, staring in awe as they came to life before her eyes.

"'Tis th' waterfall," she murmured. Water cascaded down and over huge boulders between the mountains, rushing headlong toward the river far below.

When the slide show was finished, Siònaid pushed each image in turn again, and then repeated the sequence once more. She sat gazing at the screen and its tiny images through eyes that shone with unshed tears.

"You don't have to go, sweetie," Mary said.

Siònaid looked up at her, eyes bleak. "Aye, I do," she said again. "I have t' see 't for myself."

The door banged open to admit Callum MacArthur. "What am I missing?" he asked.

"We got a gig!" said Ailis. "Glencoe. When is it, Henry?"

"Next month, Saturday the ninth. Everybody all right with the date?"

"If not, I'll move things. I'm not missing this one!" Bennet said.

But Callum wasn't listening. His eyes were on Siònaid, sitting in front of the laptop.

He strode to the desk and rounded it to squat beside her chair. "What's wrong, lass?" he asked. "Are you poorly?"

She didn't seem to register his presence, her eyes still fixed on the laptop screen. Callum took her hand gently. Her head jerked and she turned slowly to face him.

"Wha'?" Her voice was dull, as if her thoughts were somewhere else.

"This won't do. Come with me." Callum's voice was rough. He stood and pulled her to her feet.

"We're going to take a walk," he told the Players. Mary nodded.

Callum marched to the door, almost dragging Siònaid behind him. Out on the sidewalk, he put his arm through hers and walked her down Academy Street, past the train station, and up to the High Street. Neither said a word until they reached Cafe Nero and were inside away from the blustery wind.

Callum pushed Siònaid into an overstuffed chair

next to the window fronting the pedestrian street. The silence lengthened as they watched a group of tourists gather around a busker who was playing "Highland Cathedral" on the bagpipes.

The lad was about twelve. His cheeks swelled as he pushed on the blowstick with everything in his small body, but the sound that emerged was strong and sure.

"He's probably practicing for the Europeans," Callum said. "The pipe band championships. They'll be held right here in Inverness come summer."

Siònaid said nothing. She stared out the window as if the busker was the most fascinating thing she'd ever seen.

He tried again. "The Worlds are always in Glasgow; have you ever been?"

Nothing. Callum grimaced and tried again.

"There are bands from all over the world. Amazing sight and sound."

No response.

"I played the pipes in school, but I wasn't very good."

He waited. Nothing.

"Last year the winning band was made up of monkeys wearing rugby jerseys."

There was no indication she'd heard him. He took a deep breath.

"Siònaid!"

She turned and gave him a sweet smile, one that didn't come close to reaching her eyes. "Aye?"

He sighed. "Is it...Daniel? Are you worried about him?"

Siònaid knitted her fingers together in her lap.

"Nae." She lowered her eyes to study her hands. "Mary telt me he's better."

"Aye, he is," Callum said, grateful for any response. "He'll be out of hospital in a day or so; do you want to go with me to visit him?"

"No!" The words burst out with a force that took him aback.

"I mean, I dinnae need t' disturb 'im. I ken he needs 'is rest."

The words were mechanical, as if she were reciting them. A part of Callum was relieved; he'd thought there was something growing between his cousin and the lass, but it seemed the opposite was true. Had the wee dobber insulted her somehow? Treated her like those women he met in the pub? Wouldn't put it past him.

Anyway, Daniel's loss was his gain. "Let's have a coffee, shall we?" Without waiting for an answer that might never come, he leapt up and went to the counter to order two Americanos and a plate of shortbread. He returned to find her engrossed in the view outside the window again.

Over coffee and cookies, Callum conducted a mostly one-sided conversation about anything and everything. By the time the biscuits were gone (he realized he'd eaten them all), he was exhausted.

He'd never met anyone like Siònaid MacDonald. And that name was part of the mystery. Why had she been calling herself Eve, if it wasn't her real name? The Highland Players had always been a weird bunch, almost as if they really did come from the past. When he'd asked about Siònaid, they told him Eve was a nickname.

Ridiculous—did they think he was stupid? How is Eve a nickname for Siònaid? Even if that were true, why wasn't she using it now?

He studied the girl covertly. She was so lovely, in an otherworldly sort of way. That black hair framing a face so pale it was almost white, anchored by those amazing grey eyes. It shouldn't have been a beautiful face, but it had grabbed his attention the first time they'd met. Now he suspected he was falling for her. Just like Daniel had.

There was no doubt at all that his cousin had a thing for Siònaid. Daniel had always worn his emotions on his face. He might be in denial about his weird disorders, but he was honest.

And now Callum was thinking of stealing his cousin's girl while the lad lay helpless in hospital. A part of him felt dirty, soiled by the very idea.

But another part—he looked at Siònaid and she turned and smiled back. Aye, that other part said *every man for himself*.

Callum's phone rang. He looked at the display, and the color leached from his face.

"Wha's wrong?" Siònaid said. "Is't Daniel?" The raw fear on her face told him everything he needed to know about her feelings.

"No, it's nothing. Just an annoying customer." He knew his voice sounded off to his own ears, but she probably wouldn't notice. Sure enough, she relaxed back into the plush coffee shop chair and smiled again. The sheer relief on her face had him clenching his fists.

"I'm sorry; I have to take this. I'll be right back." Callum stood and exited the coffee shop, moving down to stand in the doorway of a vacant storefront.

"What took ye s' long?" snarled the voice on the other end.

"There were people around," said Callum.

"Ye're late," the voice said. "Didn't we have an agreement? Ye're no thinkin' of whelshin', are ye?"

"I told you, there was a setback. I've got your money; chill out."

"Weel, I guess I'm s'posed t' take yer word fer it, aye?" The voice dripped sarcasm.

"I'll get it to you. Funds aren't that easy to move around, and I have to be careful." God, was that a pleading note he heard in his voice? He wanted to reach through the mobile and strangle the man on the other end.

The truth was, this phone call—like all the others—was his own fault. He ended the call before he could say something he'd regret, and stood for a moment staring out at the tourists ambling down the High Street.

Must be nice to have nothing to worry about besides what tour to take or which restaurant to book a reservation in, he thought. Suddenly he wanted to run out and punch one of them. As if that would help.

How had he come to this point? People had already been hurt. Daniel had almost been killed, and now there was one more person to add to his stress. He glanced back toward the window of Cafe Nero. Somehow he was going to get out of this mess, whatever it took.

317

CHAPTER THIRTY-SIX

GLENCOE, SCOTLAND - 8 FEBRUARY, 1692

SIÒNAID

"How much longer?"

Siònaid knew it had to be the third or fourth time the question had been asked. She was disgusted with herself for being so needy, and hated causing his face to cloud over like that.

Every time, he said, "I dinnae ken, *mo gràdh.* Cannae we no just live for th' moment?"

"I'm sorry," she said, through a throat already partially thickened with the grief of losing him.

Faolán gripped her shoulders and forced her to look into his eyes. "Never say ye're sorry, love. I ken how ye feel—it's killin' me too."

Siònaid nodded through eyes swimming in tears. "Aright, I willnae. It's jist that ye said ye're billeted here for nae longer than a fortnight, and th' time is more'n half gone."

Faolán took her face in his hands. He wiped a tear away with his thumb and bent to kiss her. The world went away and it was just the two of them there, hidden in the shadows of the pine forest.

She put her arms around him and returned the kiss with all the love and longing she felt for this man.

He is sae perfect, she thought. *'Tis a'ready a miracle we met a'tall. Maybe 'at has t' be enough.*

"Dinnae forget..." Faolán's deep voice swam to her through the fog in her mind. "When th' army leaves, 'tis no th' end for us."

He was reading her mind again, those velvet brown eyes probing the deepest part of her heart. She could feel herself floating, and clutched him tighter lest she sail off into the grey Highlands sky.

He pulled her back into his arms. "I love ye," he murmured into her hair. "I will come back t' get ye, I promise. Jist as soon as I can."

His eyes crinkled and he ruffled her hair. "Jist wait a little longer, an' we'll be t'gether for always. I'll ask for your hand then."

Her heart plunged at the thought of Faolán facing her uncle. It seemed impossible. Even if Domhnall MacDonald wasn't her real family, he'd promised to care for her in her father's place. Faolán was never going to be his idea of care.

"Why did'ye have t' be a Campbell?" she moaned, and Faolán grinned.

"An' why did I have t' fall in love wi' a rascally MacDonald?" he countered.

"I guess we're like Romeo 'n Juliet," she said, smiling back.

"Who?"

"They're lovers 'n a play by Shakespeare," said Siònaid.

"Ahh, I've heard o' him. English, i'n he? Wasnae he th' dandy that attached himself t' Queen Elizabeth?"

He gestured with his index finger and twisted his lips in a mock frown. "Seems like you Jacobite types shouldnae be readin' political tripe from th' gover'mint, noo."

She tapped his arm with a small fist, and he pretended to flinch.

"How're we like this Romeo an' Juliet?" he asked.

"Their families were sworn enemies, an' allus wanted t' kill each other."

"Well, th' Campbells an' MacDonalds dinnae like each other much," Faolán allowed, "bit I dinnae ken they want t' *kill* each other. Nae most o' th' time, anyway." He smiled. "This Shakespeare lad lived in olden times, dinnae he? Things were much rougher then."

"He died 'n 1616. No that long ago," Siònaid told him.

"So how did th' story end?" Faolán asked. "Did their families gie permission fer them t' wed?"

Her face fell. *Why did I have t' bring up that story?* she thought. A wave of apprehension swept through her, and she took a long breath to dispel it.

"N-nae. They dinnae...they died."

"Oh. Oh well." Faolán hugged her and placed his chin on her head. "Well, that's nae us," he said. "I dinnae think yer uncle'll like it much, bit he'll come around. He'll be happy t' gie ye t' a man who can take care o' ye, an' no matter my name I make guid pay."

Siònaid settled into his embrace and wondered again at the vagaries of fate. What were the chances of a group of government troops finding their way to this isolated glen, and furthermore that one of them would be this man, Faolán Campbell? Never in her wildest imagination could she have dreamed of this.

He was right. He would have to march on when his captain decreed it, and it might be some time before she saw him again. But he would come back. He'd said so.

I love ye. I will come back t' get ye, I promise...Jist wait a little longer.

She would wait forever, if need be. God had arranged their meeting, and she would hold on to Faolán's words like a talisman. He would be back, he would ask for her hand, and Uncle Domhnall would say yes. It was fate.

A crackling sound nearby returned Siònaid to the present, and to the plight the two of them would be in if discovered.

A red deer stepped into the clearing, and for a moment, both were arrested by the beauty of this glorious animal. The huge antlers branched out to at least three feet in breadth, and his russet color stood out against the dark tree trunks as if proclaiming him king of the glen.

Siònaid realized she was holding her breath. The deer stood still for another moment, head held high, and then he was off, moving with impossible grace through the forest without disturbing the foliage around him.

"I ken it's a good omen," Faolán whispered. "Ye see? He approves."

Siònaid laughed. "If ye say so."

Faolán took her hand. "I ken we'd best no trifle wi' our luck, though. Ye leave first. I'll watch ye go and then come round by another path, aye?"

She sighed. "Aye. I'm longin' for th' day we can walk proud doon the road t'gither."

She leaned up to kiss his cheek. "T'morrow?"

He groaned. "That's too long. T'night? I'll throw three pebbles agin' the wall."

Siònaid grinned. "Dinnae ye think 'at might wake ever'body in th' house? Why no try an' animal sound? I've heard a night owl sometimes lately o' an evenin'. Can ye hoot like an owl?"

Faolán rounded his lips and said, "Hoo, hoo."

Siònaid shook her head. "Pebbles'll do."

She pulled her hand from his and started limping back down the trail. Odd, but she felt no fear in the dark forest, knowing his eyes were on her and his love surrounded her like a cloak.

She emerged from the forest near the large croft that belonged to their chief. No one was about, but apprehension crawled up her spine, urging her to move faster.

Maybe I've been sneakin' around tae much, she thought, as she pulled the fold of her arasaid up over her head into a hood. *I'm imaginin' things that isnae real.*

But an image had intruded into her head and wouldn't go away. The image of a man dressed all in black, emerging from the shrubbery and looking toward where she stood on the path, in full sight.

Like now.

Siònaid picked up her pace as best she could with her lame leg working against such effort. The croft was only a short distance away; there was nothing to be afraid of here in the light of day.

Still, she wished Faolán were here. Even if someone saw them together, she knew he would protect her. She brought the image of his face into her mind and focused on it. He would never let anyone—

"Siònaid!"

She jumped and turned around to face the speaker, wrenching her leg and stumbling. She would have fallen, had not a strong arm come around to hold her.

"Steady, lass," said Andrew. He tightened his hold. "What're ye doin' out here? 'Tis colder'n th' top o' Beinn Nibheis!"

Siònaid stood still. "Andrew, ye scairt me t' death!" She waited, but he didn't release his hold. "Ye can let go noo, I'm fine," she said.

He scowled. "Ye're bein' summat unfriendly these past days, cousin." He released his grip and held his hands up in a defensive position. "That better?"

She ignored the jibe and turned to walk the rest of the way toward the croft. Andrew settled into step beside her.

"Where were ye, jist noo?" he asked in a quiet voice.

Siònaid considered her words. Things had been tense between them since he had asked her not to see Faolán again. He hadn't brought it up since, but she couldn't help feeling that his eyes followed her more than before, that he turned up in odd places when she least expected it. Like now. What was *he* doing out here?

"I was out fer a wee walk," she said, keeping her tone light. "Ye ken how crowded th' cottage is, an' I sometimes need t' get away from all those men."

"Alone?" His voice was soft. "Ye used t' take Marsailli wi' ye."

Siònaid laughed, too sharp, too shrill. "Aye, bit Marsailli's seein' Robby all th' time noo, ye ken? I dinnae want to get between."

"Hmm. An' how's your friend? Th' Campbell bastart?"

"Andrew!" She rounded on him in shock. He had never spoken to her like this, ever. Now his face was distorted as though he'd eaten something rotten. She furrowed her brow.

He smiled, and the handsome face of her cousin relaxed into the congenial expression she knew well.

"Sorry, lass. I dinnae mean anythin'. Th' cold must be addlin' my brain. Let's get home an' warm up, aye?"

He fell into step beside her again, as if nothing had happened.

But something had. Siònaid realized for the first time that her feelings for Andrew had indeed changed.

She was afraid of him. But more than that she was afraid for Faolán, *th' Campbell bastart.*

CHAPTER THIRTY-SEVEN
GLENCOE, SCOTLAND –
11 FEBRUARY, 1692

ANDREW

"I promised ye. That was our deal."

Andrew flinched at the words, and a muscle jumped in his cheek. This slimy bastard didn't know the meaning of a promise—he would betray anyone to get what he wanted.

"Aye, 'twas. Bit ye'll pardon me if I dinnae believe ye." He kept his voice calm. "Seein' as how ye've used me more'n once."

"Wasnae my fault, remember?" The other man looked away from the anger in Andrew's eyes. "Wrong place, wrong time. I had need o' ye, and ye had need o' me." He lifted one hand and studied it as if it fascinated him, but his sidelong glance gave him away.

He was nervous. *Why?* Andrew cursed himself for a fool for getting involved with this bastard in the first place, but he'd had no choice and his family's safety came first. As for the rest, hell could take them, and welcome.

He thought back to the day in late November when he'd first laid eyes on Captain Robert Campbell of the Earl of Argyll's Regiment of Foot—pretentious git. Wrong place, wrong time. All because of that damned Coll Maclain...

"Sae many cattle," Coll's whiny voice came back from three months ago as if it were yesterday. "All alone an' needin' an owner. S'been a while, wha' d' ye say?"

Andrew's gaze roved around at the lads gathered in the Maclain croft, looking like stupid cattle themselves, and realized something he should have known all along.

He hated these ignorant gowks. All of them, and Coll Maclain most of all. He eyed the burly youth, practically salivating at the prospect of stealing someone else's property and not caring a whit for the consequences. One of the chief's nephews, Coll was a dull-eyed lout who used his connections to bully anyone smaller than himself. He was a troublemaker, the worst of the lot.

Something welled up inside him, black and rank and fetid, and wrapped its tendrils around his heart. He recognized it for what it was—the longing, that all-encompassing need that had nothing to do with

Coll Maclain and everything to do with himself—and he welcomed it back like a friend.

He heard his own voice saying, "Aye, lads, let's hae some fun!"

The false tone of comradery should have sickened him, but now he brushed it aside. The thing inside him had plans, and who was he to deny it?

They crept through the shrubbery and bracken, leaving the glen behind for the taller trees and mountain passes. Turning north toward Fort William, they paused in the shadow of the great mountain, Beinn Nibheis, and then turned west toward the lands of Clan MacDougall.

Surrounded by MacDonalds, Maclains, and Campbells, the MacDougalls kept to themselves and eked out a living by fishing, farming, and raising cattle. They distrusted their neighboring clans with good reason, and frequently fought them for land and livestock. Like so many others, dislike had become hatred when it came to the MacDonalds of Glencoe, who saw them as fair game.

Coll Maclain raised a leather flask and gulped greedily at it. He'd been drinking since the afternoon, and now as dusk was falling, his voice grew louder and more slurred with each swig.

Andrew swallowed his disgust. He had no argument with the MacDougalls of Argyll; he was along for this venture for reasons he did not fully understand himself. The thing inside had subsided for the moment, but it was never far away.

A war cry split the air. The brush parted suddenly, and they were surrounded by MacDougall clansmen brandishing dirks and short swords. The snarling lips and arrogant posture told Andrew they'd been waiting. So much for surprise.

Howling like ravenous wolves, the MacDougalls were on them. For the next few moments, bedlam reigned in the clearing, shrieks of rage blending with grunts as men lunged, dodged, and parried. In the distance, the bellow of disgruntled cattle could be heard above the clanging of metal and thuds of fists landing on flesh. Caught unaware as they were, the MacDonalds were at a disadvantage and in danger of losing this battle.

Andrew turned at the sound of branches cracking behind him, to see Coll Maclain disappearing into the forest. Rage rose in him at proof of the man's willingness to instigate trouble and then abandon his comrades without a second thought. He brought a fist into the face of the man in front of him, heard a grunt as his adversary went down, and swung around to run after his own clansman.

Maclain was easy to follow. The trail of broken branches and curses suggested no fear of pursuit. Andrew kept his own passage as silent as possible and was able to track the man's retreat easily until at last the sounds of flight were replaced by a heavy wheezing.

Andrew stepped from behind a tree and saw Coll bent over at the waist, hand braced against a tree as he tried to catch his breath.

"An' whit d'ye think ye're doin'?"

Maclain jumped and spun to face him. A momentary look of fright passed over his face and was replaced by the smirk that marked the man's customary expression.

"Whit's it to ye?" he said, his tone belligerent.

"Are ye runnin' awae then, after ye telt all th' men t' come and then made sae much clabber the MacDougall's couldnae help hearin'?"

Coll shuffled his feet and then planted them and faced his clansman, swaying slightly. Had he been sober, he might have seen the shadow crawl across Andrew's blue eyes or heard the menace in his clansman's low tone.

"Ever man f' isself," he slurred. "I dinnae wan them coos nae more. S'no fun, an'—"

Andrew stopped listening. He glanced down and saw that a dirk had found its way into his hand. The black thing took over, and the next seconds were a blur.

When he came back to himself, he was standing over the twitching body of Coll Maclain. A gurgling sound came from the ground, where viscous blood pumped from around the handle of a dirk planted in the man's throat.

Andrew pulled his dirk free and wiped it on the man's shirt. He took a step back and allowed the exhilaration to pour through him. There was nothing in the world like this feeling, nothing. He watched as the twitching and gurgling slowed and stopped, and then turned around to make his way back to his clansmen, only to stop short in surprise.

A man stood in the shadows of the trees. The dimming light reflected off the buttons of a red coat.

"Would ye care to give me yer name?" The voice was polite, as if the two were meeting over a pint in the pub.

"It's none o' your business," Andrew challenged. "Who're ye?"

Slowly, as if he had all the time in the world, the other man dislodged a pistol from his belt and raised it to point directly at Andrew's head.

"I am Captain Robert Campbell, of the Earl of Argyll's Regiment of Foot," he said calmly. "Shall we try that again? Who are ye, an' who's yer quiet friend there?"

The gun never wavered. Far behind them, the sounds of hand-to-hand fighting were dying down.

"Andrew MacDonald." He fisted his hands and prepared to make a run for it.

The captain's hand jerked. "MacDonald? From where?"

Andrew was silent. The barrel of the gun drew a target in the air and settled to point at his heart.

"Glencoe."

An odd look came over the captain's face. "Glencoe?" he asked. He gestured with the gun to the body of Coll Maclain. "And him? Where's he from?"

"Th' same." Andrew braced himself. He'd killed a clansman; the captain had every right to shoot him dead on the spot. But the shot didn't come.

"MacDonald of Glencoe," the soldier mused to himself. "Well, noo." He looked at Andrew with interest. "S'pose he deserved it, then?"

Andrew stared at him. The captain gazed back, expressionless.

"Aye, he did."

The captain brought the gun up and scratched at the stubble on his face with the barrel. "Well, it seems as if ye've been a naughty lad, aye?"

"If ye're gonnae shoot me, jist do it," Andrew told him. He closed his eyes and waited.

After a moment, he opened them again. The captain was watching him, a speculative look in his dark eyes.

"I ken this might be a guid day fer th' both o' us," he said.

Andrew's pulse began to settle back into a normal rhythm, and his hands unclenched. He remained silent, waiting.

"I need a man in Glencoe," the captain said finally. He gestured to the corpse on the ground. "An' ye need t' be quit o' this problem, aye?"

Andrew could feel the bile rising into his throat. He looked at the late Coll Maclain with loathing. *S'all your fault, ye bampot.*

"Ye want me t' be a spy?" he managed after a moment. "I willnae."

Captain Campbell shrugged. "Fine. Let's be gettin' on, then. Fort William's aways frae here. Ye can think on how ye'll explain killin' yer own clansman while we go." He gestured with the gun.

"Wait," Andrew said. "Wha' d'ye need t' ken about Glencoe?"

"We'll get t' that."

"Will ye promise me somethin' if I dae this?" he said. "Will ye protect my fam'ly?"

"O' course," the captain said. "Nothin' will happen t' yer family. Ye hae my word."

Now Andrew studied that hated face and wondered why he hadn't just let the man shoot him three months ago. Three months. Weeks of meeting secretly, passing information about the movements of his clan chief, about the workings of the village.

Three months, and he finally had a sense of the motivation behind this devil pact he'd made with Robert Campbell, captain of the Earl of Argyll's Regiment of Foot. The whoreson was planning something nasty for Alexander Maclain, and Andrew had provided him the information to do it.

He clung to the man's promise, even though he didn't trust the captain an inch. His family would be safe, whatever happened.

But safe from what? Now the captain and his band of Campbell bastards were right here in Glencoe, and the excitement on the soldier's face was palpable. Something bad was going to happen, and he had the sickening certainty that he was going to be responsible.

He could feel the pit of hell yawning at his feet.

CHAPTER THIRTY-EIGHT

GLENCOE, SCOTLAND - PRESENT DAY

*Time steals the years...but I can
still see the story in your eyes,
And your timeless passion that has never died.*
—Crystal Woods

The sun was low in the sky when the van pulled into the Glencoe Visitor Centre's empty car park. Mary hopped out from the front seat. Henry turned off the engine and came around the side of the vehicle to help Siònaid and Betty out. Mary peeked around her husband to peer inside the van.

"Siònaid? We're here. 'Tis time t' get ready." Mary had already gone into character, thickening her brogue in preparation for stepping into the past. She moved past Henry. Betty, seated on the other side of Siònaid, shook her head helplessly.

"We hae t' unload, love, and ye hae t' let Betty oot, ye ken?" Her musical voice was pitched low, like a lullaby.

Siònaid's eyes were round in her white face, dark and unreadable, but her hands shook slightly. She hadn't removed her seatbelt. "Are—are they here?" she asked, in a tremulous voice.

"No yet—nae, here come Ailis and Bennet, and Brian and John close on behind 'em. Oh guid," Mary said, keeping her voice even, "Wee Caomhainn came wi' Brian." Two more cars pulled into the car park and dislodged their occupants.

Siònaid gave Mary a narrow glare. She knew— Mary *knew* she wasn't referring to Brian or Wee Caomhainn. Suddenly, a wave of rage engulfed her. She was sick of it! Sick of being used, manipulated, forced to dissemble and hide.

She was a revenant—so what? It was just a word. She had her memories back, her emotions, the important things that made her Siònaid MacDonald of Islay.

She had made a mistake, calling for revenge. She'd been *dying*, for God's sake. Who wouldn't grasp at anything when life was ebbing away?

You cannot change fate, Baltair had said. *I warned you...if you chose to become a revenant there was no turning back.*

We'll see about 'at, she thought. If Baltair had created her... nausea rose, but she fought it down... if he had given her back her life, surely he was not evil. Surely, despite what he said, such a being *could* change fate. Unless...

Unless he was merely toying with her. Was it fun for him, creating puppets for his own amusement? Is this what mystics did for entertainment when they were world-weary?

No, there had been sadness in his black eyes when he explained what he had done. What *she* had done. Real emotion, as if he had no love for his action. *That is not the right answer*, he had said. Had she imagined the note of disappointment in his voice that night?

He had left her with her memories, damaged as they were. Left her with her conscience, her feelings, her...soul. Surely there was a reason for that. Despite his harsh words, was he hoping she would change things? Was he giving her the chance to change her own destiny?

It didn't matter. If she stayed away from Daniel, he would be safe, but she would dissipate as if she'd never been. Never reincarnate. She would deny the existence of her descendants for all eternity. On the other hand, if she allowed him into her heart again, he would die. But *she* would live on, in this body.

Was that so bad? Now that she had her memories, her mind was intact. This place was exciting and new. There were more books in its libraries than she could read if she had ten lifetimes at her disposal. The Highland Players had taken her in. They would always be there for her.

All she had to do was let Daniel die.

Her racing thoughts stuttered to a stop, and ambient noises filtered into her ears.

"Siònaid?" Betty's voice broke in, bringing her back to the present, to the van in the car park of the Glencoe Visitor Centre. Siònaid blinked and looked into Mary's little bird eyes.

Oh yes, she knew. Maybe they all knew.

Weel, if they can pretend, so c'n I. She squared her shoulders and took Henry's hand. *I'll have t' see him soon as late.* She felt a frisson of guilt slide through her body, and shook it off ruthlessly.

She hardened her heart—who was to say dying young wasn't *his* fate? Why should she be the only one to suffer destiny's whims?

Siònaid forced a smile onto her face and looked around at the Highland Players gathered in the car park. They were humming with excitement, anxious to be in action.

Wee Caomhainn's eyes sparkled with excitement. Brian was unloading boxes from the trunk of his car, and John was striking poses with a sword.

Ailis had one hand on Bennet's arm, and she smiled when he patted it gently. They were a couple, Siònaid realized with surprise.

How many other things had she missed, wrapped up in her own misery and fear? Well, that was about to change. Eve McDonald, that trembling wraith, was no more; she was Siònaid MacDonald, a woman who had lived and died and returned to live again. How many others could say that?

She was a daughter, a sister, a teacher. She had cried over her parents, her brothers, mourned Seumas, and Andrew, and all the others dead now for centuries. It was time to put those memories to rest.

She'd been given a second chance, and she was not about to squander it over a love that could never be. Siònaid straightened her back and gave Mary and Betty a brilliant smile, ignoring the glance that passed between them.

The troupe proceeded into the centre and were led to two rooms that normally served as an office and a staff room. For the next hour, the Players worked to ready themselves for their performance. Under Mary's watchful eye, the women changed from jeans and fleeces to costumes that had been retrofitted as crofters' gowns from the last years of the seventeenth century.

Siònaid's eyes roved over the details of her gown. Mary's expertise was nothing short of astounding; all the details were there, at least on the outside. No matter how she tried, she hadn't been able to convince Mary to reproduce the stays that kept a woman confined and appropriate.

"Ach, lass, nobody'll notice, and it's far better to be comfortable, aye?"

Siònaid grinned to herself. Who was she to quibble? Most days she wore jeans and knitted jumpers, a down jacket, and modern leather boots. Quite proper for both men and women in what she had come to know as the twenty-first century, but a part of her always felt scandalized at showing the curves of her body in such a way.

The idea of men and women wearing the same types of garments was mind-boggling. In her time, the men wore trews of wool, woven by the women for work on the farm. It was only when they went to war or set out on some sort of clandestine mission that they wore the *Feileadh Mòr*, that all-purpose garment that acted as blanket, coat, and camouflage. In English it was called the Great Kilt, Mary had told her. These days it was worn only for formal occasions. *How odd.*

"Everyone ready?" Mary asked, and shepherded them out to meet the men. The Highland Players stood together in the gloom of the back hallway, ready to immerse themselves in the past they loved so much.

Siònaid's heart filled with gratitude at these people who had taken her in and made her one of their own, with no questions asked. Warmth filtered through her cold body and her decision was fortified. Life in this century with these people, even as a revenant, would be worth the sacrifice.

Whose sacrifice? said the voice in her head, and she pushed it back ruthlessly.

Wee Caomhainn executed a courtly bow. Brian and John, dressed for bed in simple woolen pants and long white shirts, grinned at the ladies. Henry and Bennet weren't with the group; perhaps they were getting ready elsewhere. Siònaid smiled at the tableau in front of her, but her throat was tight. Dressed as they were they looked so much like her Glencoe family.

A door opened at the end of the hall, and four men appeared. Henry, Bennet, Callum...Daniel. The dim light reflected off the metal buttons on their red coats and the firearms they carried at their waists, and Siònaid felt the blood drain from her head. The hallway wavered and began to fade, and her knees seemed to have gone to water.

She staggered and would have fallen, had one of the soldiers not rushed to catch her.

"Eve! Are you all right?" a voice asked. She forced herself to focus on the face of her rescuer. Daniel's worried brown eyes gazed back at her.

Those eyes! Faolán's eyes. Sìònaid felt an ageless grief rise inside her, threatening to overwhelm her senses. She fought it, struggled to regain her balance, and slowly the room resolved itself once again into the back hallway of the Glencoe Visitor Centre.

Through the ringing in her ears, Sìònaid heard voices.

"We need a few minutes," Daniel was saying. There was no option for discussion in his voice.

"But—" Callum's voice, sounding annoyed.

Henry cleared his throat in warning.

"You have time," Mary said. "Meet us at the croft cottage in," she consulted her watch, "twenty minutes, aye?" She ignored Callum's protests and tugged the Players away. Silence returned to the hallway.

"In here," Daniel said. He pulled an unresisting Sìònaid into a tiny room that held shelves filled with props and books, and stood facing her, body strung tight as a bowstring. His hands were held behind his back, as though he didn't trust what they might do.

The brown eyes were flat, distant. There was no warmth in them now.

"So," he said, his voice like ice, "would you care to explain what's been going on?"

Sìònaid looked away from the hurt in his eyes, the hurt she had put there. She directed her attention to the floor. "Wh-wha's bin goin' on?"

Daniel raked his hand through his hair in frustration. "I haven't seen or spoken to you in over a month. You never visited me in hospital, never asked how I was doing."

Her head jerked up. "I did ask!" Her voice was a squeak. "I did! Mary said..." She trailed off and looked back at the floor.

Daniel let out an explosion of breath, put his hands up, and backed away from her. He began to pace in circles around the small space, and his voice when it came held both anger and misery.

"I thought we had something, Eve. I thought you felt the same way about me that I feel about you!" He turned away and strode over to stand in front of a shelf. "I guess I was wrong, but you could at least have told me."

Siònaid's will drained away. Everything she had just convinced herself was the way it had to be dissipated into the stale air of the storeroom and was gone.

Without conscious thought, she walked up behind Daniel and put her arms around his waist. He stiffened, but didn't move away. She laid her head against his back.

"Ye werenae wrong." Her voice was muffled in the wool of his red jacket. "Ye werenae."

He swung around and gripped her by the shoulders. "Then talk to me, damn it! Where have you been?" His voice rose. "*Why?*"

Siònaid took a ragged breath, and let it out. She couldn't do it, couldn't let this man die because of her. How had she ever thought she could? For him she would disappear forever, willingly. She sent an apology to her unknown descendants, innocent souls who would never be born because of her selfishness.

She, Siònaid MacDonald, would *not* stay away from Daniel MacArthur. She couldn't. She would protect this man, keep him safe from those who sought him harm. Keep him safe from *her*.

Damn Baltair, damn fate, damn it all. She had made this mess; it was hers to clean up.

She allowed herself to sink into the depths of those eyes she had loved for more than three hundred years, and let it all go. The revenge, the hatred, the grief. A sob rose and choked her, and she clung to Daniel like a drowning person.

His arms went round her, his lips lowered to hers, and he was kissing her with all the pent-up emotion of the last month. Or was it centuries? It didn't matter. She lost herself in the kiss, no longer caring if it was Daniel MacArthur or Faolán Campbell whose arms held her.

"Daniel?" she gasped, when finally, he let her go. She steeled herself, because this would mean everything.

"I hae somethin' t' tell ye."

CHAPTER THIRTY-NINE
GLENCOE, SCOTLAND - PRESENT DAY

There is no present or future—only the past, happening over and over again—now."
—Eugene O'Neil

Daniel sat alone in the storeroom, elbows on his knees. His thoughts whirled, jagged pieces crashing together and flying off in new directions. He grasped for something that made sense, but there was nothing.

How could she think he would believe the nonsense she'd spewed? Her image coalesced out of the mist and became a pale face, grey eyes huge and luminous as she begged him to understand, to believe.

He couldn't. It was impossible.

My name isnae Eve. 'Tis Siònaid. Siònaid MacDonald. I was born in th' year 1672. Th' murders they all be sae canty about? I was there. I lived there, in Glencoe.

As an accomplished liar and prevaricator himself, he thought he was pretty good at putting a new face on the ugly truth. He couldn't hold a candle to Eve—no, Siònaid— MacDonald, though. She had him beat. Was he supposed to believe she was a time traveler, for God's sake?

A rough laugh choked its way from his throat. Wasn't it just like him, though? The first lass he'd dared to have real feelings for turned out to be a pathological liar. It explained so much—the fake name, the ludicrous story about the King of Inverness, the sad litany of memory losses. *I cannae feel anythin'.* She'd played him like a fiddle.

Against his will, her face swam back and refused to go away. Yes, he was good at lying to himself, so he knew when others were lying. He could spot their tells, those little things that gave the game away.

His blood ran cold and he shivered. She had none of those tells. She thought that what she was telling him was the truth. She believed she'd been alive and present at the Glencoe massacre. In 1692. *Jesus.*

She wasn't a liar.

Not a lunatic, either, said the voice in his mind, and he found himself remembering little things.

The chill grew and spread. He'd touched her bare foot on the freezing street. She should have been in agony, but she seemed oblivious. Her memory loss—she remembered nothing, not even the normal day-to-day objects and places in Inverness. Her distress couldn't be faked. No one was that good an actress.

There was that creepy Baltair too. He'd spirited her away at the wedding faire, and when she came back she was different, confused and frightened. He was sure that man had something to do with it.

And what about the rest of the Highland Players? They all seemed a bit spooky, especially that Mary Duncan. None of them acted as though there was anything odd about Eve at all, and surely they would have noticed the gaps in her knowledge, the odd way she dressed.

Another memory crawled into his brain. Eve— Siònaid, standing outside in the rain at the job site. No coat, and yet she seemed impervious to the weather.

Yes! And what about those odd words, uttered in obvious desperation. He'd forgotten all about them, what with the fun of being stabbed.

Do ye, do ye know me? Have ye met me before? He hadn't taken those words in properly that night, lost as he was in the glory of those grey eyes. He'd been too busy deciding it might just be possible he'd fallen in love with her.

And now, she was telling him that she came from this place, Glencoe, with the little added detail that she was 350 years old. Talk about dating an older woman!

He looked up and realized he was still sitting in the storeroom where she'd dropped a bomb on his life.

"I'll jist gie ye some time," she had said softly, and left him alone. *Some time?* No amount of time was ever going to make this all right. And yet...

And yet the part of his brain that was always honest with him, that little voice that swooped in to tell him that yes, he was an arse and no, he wasn't fooling anybody, that part was whispering, *what if it's somehow true?*

He looked at his watch. *Shite!* Mary Duncan was going to kill him! And that might just be scarier than anything else he could think of. He stood, wobbled on his feet for a second, and made his way out of the storeroom.

Siònaid was nowhere in sight. He noted the growing darkness outside and hurried his steps. How the hell he was going to perform his part as an army officer in this reenactment, he had no idea. He wished he'd never told Callum he'd do it, but the fact was he'd needed to see Eve. *Siònaid, damn it.*

Daniel hurried out the side door of the Visitor Centre and took the path that led to the newly constructed replica of a turf and creel croft cottage where the reenactment was to take place. Lights had been erected at the corners of the lot, and a soft glow bathed the heather-thatched roof and earthen walls.

I'm supposed to believe she lived in a house like this? The idea was mind-boggling. The turf structure stood alone against the mountain backdrop, as if alienated from the nearby Visitor Centre by time and culture.

It was an illusion, no matter how artful its construction. Built two years ago using traditional materials from the seventeenth century, the replica was a masterpiece of archaeology and historical research; a crofter's cottage that paid homage to people who had lived and died in the glen more than three hundred years ago.

Henry had told him that normally visitors were encouraged to step into the past and into the cottage itself, where a cleverly designed soundscape provided cries of wildlife that mingled with the chatter of daily life in the glen hundreds of years ago. Atmospheric music greeted visitors as they stepped inside.

Today however, as dusk fell on Glencoe, visitors would be kept behind a rope barrier, and inside the cottage, the Highland Players were preparing to take them back to "the most shameful event in Scottish history, when Highlander turned against Highlander in a horrific and unforgivable night of murder and treachery," as described on posters and social media.

Word had gone out advertising the special reen-actment of the Glencoe Massacre of 1692, and the Centre would reopen after dark tonight in order to lend the performance the necessary ambiance.

"Ye're late!"

Mary grabbed Daniel's arm as he arrived in front of the cottage. In one hand she held a walkie-talkie, which she brandished like a weapon.

"The centre's ready to let people through, and you should see how many cars are in the park!" She was nearly dancing with glee.

Callum strode over. "Where's Siònaid?" he asked, anger evident in his clipped tone.

Daniel stared at them, his eyes glazed. Mary stud-ied his pale face and her eyes narrowed. She put her hands on her hips and spoke in a voice that suggested she would have been a formidable schoolteacher had she chosen that path.

"Callum, there's no time for nonsense. Siònaid's fine. Can you go and ask Henry where he wants Wee Caomhainn to start? Be a love, eh?" Mary pulled Callum away from Daniel and gave him a push toward where Henry was positioning the Players inside the turf and thatch structure and giving them last-minute instructions.

Callum looked mutinous, but he stumped over to the doorway and disappeared inside the cottage. Mary tugged at Daniel's sleeve and pulled him behind the structure.

"She told you, didn't she?"

He stared at her as the words sank in. "Told me? You mean you knew? You believe it?"

"Never mind that!" Her voice was impatient and her brows drew together when she frowned. "This is...unexpected," she muttered to herself.

Daniel looked at Mary as if seeing her for the first time. "Who *are* you people?" he said.

Mary looked at him more closely. His shoulders were slumped, his eyes haunted.

"Why do people always think what they see is all there is?" she murmured. "Never mind, there's no time. Can you do this, lad?" She tugged his arm.

He shook his head, blinked, then looked up, eyes haunted. "I don't know. Is E—Siònaid here?"

Mary nodded her head. "Aye, she is. She's out back with Ailis, getting ready." She captured him with those little wren eyes. "And if that lass can reenact the worst night of her young life, don't you think you can do it too?"

She patted his arm. "We'll talk later. Noo, git ye inside. We dinnae hae th' time!"

Inside the cottage, Henry was giving last-minute instructions.

"Now, lads an' lassies, like we practiced, aye? Of

course, the real massacre happened inside the cottages, all over the glen, but we can't be true to that because the visitors wouldn't be able to see it. So, we'll start with the soldiers appearing from around the side and going inside, and then everybody will pile outside to finish the job. You know your parts; do you soldiers have your weapons?"

Callum brandished a musket in his cousin's direction. Daniel took the dirk Henry was waving at him and tucked it into his belt. He ignored Callum and kept his focus on Henry so his brain wouldn't float away.

"Caomhainn, you're the star of the show, as Chief Maclain. He was shot early on and died instantly, but ham it up all you want. John, Brian, you're the sons. You'll be wounded, but you manage to escape."

He turned to the women. "Lassies, you'll be the last to leave the cottage. Soldiers, you get to drag the women out and throw them into the blizzard."

He looked up at the dark, cloudy sky and laughed. "I guess we can't hope for a blizzard in May, but I'll set the scene for the visitors and they'll have to use their imagination."

A hum of voices could be heard in the distance. Their audience was coming.

The red and grey coated soldiers left the cottage and disappeared around toward the back. Everyone else took their prearranged places inside the cottage and waited.

When their audience was in place, Henry stepped into the light before the cottage. A chorus of *ahhs* went up from the crowd standing behind the rope barrier.

"Welcome t' Glencoe, lads and lasses," he intoned. "I'm Artair MacDonald. "Ach, and th' weather's nae lookin' sae braw." He looked up at the sky. "A blizzard's oan its way, I ken.

"I must tell ye," he went on, "if ye've come t' partake o' the Highland Hospitality, ye should ken we've no much left. We've bin hostin' th' solgers from th' gover'mint army fer twelve days, and ach noo! Them bast—er—fine lads..." He gave the crowd an exaggerated wink, and giggles rose from the visitors.

"Enyway, them solgers can eat. Bit ye're welcome to join us, 'cause th' Code says nae a body will be turnt away. Hold fast, an' we'll git yer beds ready."

Henry turned and entered the cottage to enthusiastic applause from the excited visitors. For a long moment, nothing happened in the clearing.

Then, four soldiers wearing the distinctive red and grey of the seventeenth-century British army came slowly around from the back of the structure and moved with stealth into the cottage.

A low tune rose into the air. Ominous, haunting, it swelled and grew, causing those watching to shiver with anticipation. Every onlooker stood silent, waiting.

Suddenly a piercing scream filled the cottage. A Highlander dressed in his nightclothes stumbled outside. He clutched at his stomach and fell to the ground, writhing in pain. A soldier followed him out and fired a musket into the helpless man, who jerked and went still. Another man fell out the door, a dirk in his back, and collapsed near the first.

The scene became chaos, soldiers herding the helpless clansmen outside and stabbing or shooting them indiscriminately. When the shooting stopped, the women were led out and pushed into the night. They stumbled beyond the lighted area and disappeared.

One of the women stopped at the edge of the circle of light and turned to look back. A soldier stood in the doorway, holding a dagger, and gazed at her for a long moment. The visitors behind the rope held their breath.

The woman stood staring at the man with the dagger as if she were gazing into hell itself, as though the scene was no longer play acting, but real. She took a step forward and reached out a hand. A horrible choking sound came from her throat and she began to sway.

Daniel MacArthur stood paralyzed in the doorway of the replica cottage, watching as Siònaid MacDonald's knees folded and she crumpled to the ground. Then he dropped the dagger and rushed out into the clearing, twisting and dodging bodies until he reached her. He fell to his knees, folded her into his arms, and began to rock her like a baby, oblivious to the crowd only a few feet away, faces frozen in shock.

CHAPTER FORTY
GLENCOE, SCOTLAND - PRESENT DAY

There is the past, and there is the future.
The present is never more than the
single second dividing one from the
other. We live poised on that second as
it's hurtling forward—toward what?
—Laini Taylor

"I've been to a lot of reenactments, but this one was the best,'" Mary read aloud to the Players gathered in the sitting room of their bed and breakfast the next morning. She waved her mobile in the air. "There are so many comments already, and they're all positive."

"Anything about me?" Wee Caomhainn came over to read over her shoulder. "You know, like, 'I never realized Alexander Maclain was so handsome' or some such?"

Henry snorted and put his coffee cup down. "Don't *do* that while I'm drinking!" he said. "But seriously, you were brilliant, Caomhainn. You all were. I

355

think we can count on being asked back again next year, aye?"

Mary was still reading. "You were all wonderful, but the real stars of the show were Siònaid and Daniel. Listen to this, 'I loved the romantic touch at the end, when the MacDonald lass fainted and the Campbell soldier gathered her up, just like Romeo and Juliet!'"

Daniel's face was suffused with red. He ducked his head and made a great show of stirring his cooling coffee while the others enjoyed his obvious discomfiture.

"Aye," Betty said. "I didn't know you had it in you, Daniel. You never seemed so interested before, but you really poured it on for the show. You too, Siònaid." She gave the girl a narrow look. "Nobody would have guessed it wasn't in the script."

Siònaid gave her a weak smile, but said nothing.

"It wasn't in the script because she wasn't acting, were you?" Callum's voice was rough. "You really did faint; we all saw it."

"I—" Siònaid began, and stopped. "I—well, aye, I ken I was feart o' all th' people watchin', an' I..." she trailed off. "I'm fine noo."

Callum let out his breath and stood up.

"I'm taking Siònaid home," he announced. "Daniel, you can ride back in the van." His tone was the one he used at the office when subordinates argued with his directives. The one that said discussion was not an option.

"Wait—what?" Daniel sputtered. "That's not a good idea. She—"

"She's obviously not well," Callum said. "She fainted out there, for God's sake! She needs a comfortable car to ride in, not that bumpy van." He turned to Henry. "Sorry, but it's true, aye? I'm taking her straight to Raigmore, to have her checked out."

"But Siònaid wants..." Daniel tried again. His face was tight and a muscle in his cheek jumped.

Callum blew out a breath. "People don't just faint for no reason, Daniel! She's in no condition..."

"I'm stayin' here."

The voice was soft, but the words clear. Siònaid stood up from the chair she'd been sitting in and faced the two men. "I'm stayin' here 'n Glencoe fer another day wi' Daniel."

She reached out and put a hand on Callum's arm. "Thank ye, Callum, ye're sae braw t' think o' me, but I'm fine. I just dinnae hae enough t' eat b'fore the wee play, 'at's all."

"Why are you staying with Daniel?" Callum sounded like a petulant child.

"I was trying to tell you," Daniel said. "My brother Adam has a place out here, remember? He does mountain tours and sets up races. Anyway, he's been asking me to visit for months, and now seems like the perfect time since we're here."

He kept his tone even. "When Siònaid said she'd like to see more of the glen, I called Adam and asked him to give us a personal tour. He'll be picking us up in a few minutes."

Siònaid watched the byplay between the two men. Callum's face had darkened to an unbecoming shade of red, and Daniel's had gone pale.

"I think that's a good idea," Mary said. There was something in her tone that had both men swiveling their heads to look at her. "Siònaid comes from this area, you know," she said to the room at large. "I'm sure she'd like a wee tour while she's here. Thank you, Daniel."

She put a hand on Henry's arm. "Why don't we use the time to have a visit with your sister Margaret in Invergarry? She's been begging us. Betty can go home with Ailis and Brian."

Callum's face darkened, and without another word, he turned and stomped out of the sitting room.

"Oh dear," Betty murmured. Ailis Brodie reached over and patted her hand.

There was a muffled ring. Daniel reached into his pocket and raised his mobile to his ear.

"Aye? Brilliant. We'll be right out." He clicked off and replaced the mobile in his jacket.

"Adam's ready," he said to Siònaid. He turned to the Highland Players.

"My brother has to go up to Inverness this evening, so he'll take us back with him." He picked up their two overnight bags.

Mary nodded. "Siònaid, you have the key to the house. Make sure you lock the door when you get in, aye?"

At the door, Daniel turned back. "Thank you," he said to no one and everyone.

Mary nodded; her expression solemn. "Aye, lad. Git."

A green Range Rover, mud-spattered and much the worse for wear, sat idling in the car park. While

Adam stowed their bags in the back, Daniel moved to open the passenger door for Siònaid. She waved him off and climbed into the back seat.

"Ye must hae things t' talk about wi' your brother, aye. Ye havenae seen him for a long time, ye said."

"There are reasons for that," mumbled Daniel under his breath. "It doesn't always mean we have things to talk about." But he climbed into the front and allowed his brother a sincere, if distant, smile.

Adam MacArthur gave his brother the once over. "You look better than last time I saw you," he said. "At Ewan's wedding."

"Was it that long ago?" Daniel asked. He sighed. "I was drunk, wasn't I?"

Adam snorted as if the question was absurd. "Well..."

"Daniel doesnae drink anymore," Siònaid piped up from the back seat. "Drinkin' can cause am-neesia."

"Erm," Daniel said.

"An' brain damage."

Adam turned around and Siònaid favored him with a sweet smile. His brows lifted and he looked at his brother.

"Oh," Daniel said. "This is Siònaid MacDonald. She's my g—my friend."

"Ahh," said Adam, and his brows lifted even higher. "Hullo, Siònaid. I'm Adam, Daniel's older brother. Nice to meet you."

He pulled the Jeep away from the kerb and out of the car park.

"So, Daniel tells me you're from these parts, originally," Adam said, meeting Siònaid's eyes in the mirror.

"A long taem ago," she nodded. Her gaze skittered away from those eyes, brown like Daniel's but so different. Adam's eyes didn't compel her, didn't make her feel as if she were drowning in them. He was a very handsome man, but to her, he didn't *shine*, like her Daniel.

Her Daniel. He was hers, to protect and cherish. *To lose.* A heavy feeling stole over her; she felt rooted to the leather seat. She was going to lose him, no matter what happened. If she lived, he would die. If she kept him safe, she would dissipate. There was no future together for them.

Why had she ever called for revenge? Surely she wasn't the first lass to be betrayed by her lover. She'd been such a *bairn*, in no mind to make such a decision. And Baltair, whom she suspected was much, much older than a bairn, why couldn't he have seen that?

Who was he to grant her wish, and then tell her he could not take it back when she no longer wanted it?

"What's wrong, Siònaid?" Daniel had turned around and was regarding her with concern. "Why are you frowning? Do you feel faint again?"

Siònaid saw Adam slant an appraising look at his brother, and then return his eyes to the road. She mustered a smile and tried to relax.

"Nae, I'm fine." She groped for a topic, and found one.

"Daniel, I'm worrit abit Callum."

Daniel stiffened and turned back to look out the windscreen.

"Why?" The word came out on an explosion of breath.

"I—I dinnae ken. There's somethin' about his eyes."

Daniel turned around again, surprised. "What? His eyes?"

Siònaid felt her heart begin to race. "I kent I've seen eyes like his somewhere b'fore. I cannae put my mind aroun' it, but it bothers me."

"Are you two talking about Callum?" said Adam. "Our cousin?" He laughed. "The Golden Child, the Crown Prince, the Perfect One. *That* Callum?"

Daniel snorted. "Tell us how you really feel, brother." It seemed to Siònaid that Daniel wasn't altogether displeased by the words, though. He relaxed in his seat and the shadow of a smile crossed his face.

"I dinnae mean anythin'," she said. "Please dinnae mind me an' my rambles. He's allus been verra nice t' me."

Another snort from Daniel. Adam looked across at his brother and to Siònaid's confusion, burst out laughing. Daniel gave him a sour look.

"Adam's just jealous, Siònaid," he said. "He doesn't like it that Callum actually *is* as wonderful as he seems. He's always been there for me, no matter how much I make a hash of things."

Adam sniffed. "That may be how *you* see it, but I'm not as close to the action as you are. I always thought he secretly enjoyed coming to your rescue, just a few minutes too late of course, when Uncle Ranald used you as a punching bag. Made him feel superior."

"He *is* superior, Adam, and I'll be the first to admit it. Anyway, let's just drop it. Siònaid doesn't want to hear us air our family laundry."

But Siònaid was no longer listening. Her face was pressed up against the car window and her eyes widened as mountains emerged from the morning haze and loomed over the horizon like armored juggernauts. Dark peaks pierced the clouds as if to assert their dominance over the glen below. A ribbon of blue-green water wound its way serenely through the landscape, seeming oblivious to the giants towering over it.

"Glencoe," she breathed. Her breath fogged up the window, and she brushed the steam away with impatient fingers.

They passed through Ballachulish on the A82, and after a short drive, the Jeep bore left onto a smaller road that led to a narrow street lined with small buildings. Halfway up the street, a church spire pierced the clouds that hung low over the village.

The buildings were an odd mixture of traditional cottages and modern houses. The juxtaposition of past with present made Siònaid's head spin, and she felt her stomach slide.

Adam took over as guide. "This is part of the original road that ran through Glen Coe from Ballachulish," he said. He pulled into a small car park next to a sign that read 'Glencoe Cafe' and parked the Jeep next to a battered camper van. He turned to Siònaid.

"Daniel tells me you came from this area originally. I'm not sure what you want to see, the glen or the village, but how do you feel about a wee walk?"

Siònaid smiled at him. "I dinnae ken what I want t'see either," she confessed in a soft voice. "I jist needed t' be here."

Adam nodded. "We'll walk to the end of the street and have a wee look round the Folk Museum, and then out along the old road for a piece. Then we'll turn back and have lunch in the village, aye?"

"The village?" Siònaid said. "It's still here, then?"

Adam looked at her, his brow furrowed. "I'm not sure what you mean."

She regarded him with eagerness and not a little frustration.

"Glencoe. Ye said 'twas here."

"It is. You're standing in the center of it right now." He frowned and then his face cleared and he gave a short laugh. "Ahh, you mean the *old* village, from long ago! The time of the massacre, aye?"

He paused. "The original Glencoe village was at Invercoe," he gestured with one hand, "on the north bank of the river."

He gave her an odd look. "The tourists get confused about it, but I thought, you being from these parts and all, " he glanced over her shoulder and caught a warning headshake from his brother. "Anyway, of course we can walk up there. Not much to see, though." He pointed back the way they'd come, and Siònaid started a determined march in that direction.

Adam fell into step with Daniel. "She's interesting, your girl," he said under his breath.

Daniel sighed. "You have no idea."

The three turned right at the end of the village street onto a narrow, paved road that led toward the river. A short walk brought them into the glen itself and onto a dirt path.

As her feet felt the earth, a feeling of recognition whispered through Siònaid's mind, and she quickened her steps. She knew this place. She had walked this path.

With Faolán. A pang of grief sliced into her heart like a physical attack and she stopped, unable to walk further. Daniel came up and put an arm around her.

"Are you all right, love?" he said.

"Wha's 'at?" she asked, pointing ahead. The morning sunlight bathed the scattered stones of what had once been a foundation. Another pile of blackened stones lay further on.

"That's what's left of the original village," Adam told her, coming to stand beside them.

"'At's all?"

Siònaid felt the breath leave her body. It was gone, all of it. The croft where she'd lived, where she'd taught wee Seumas, where she'd promised her life to a man, and where all of them had been betrayed; it was nothing but a few charred stones lying on a dirt path. She turned to Daniel and buried her face in his jacket.

The memories swarmed up from a past that seemed like yesterday. Arguing with Seumas about politics, listening to Marsailli wax on about her Robby. Uncle Domhnall, Andrew...

Her head snapped up and she clutched at Daniel's jacket.

"I kent it!" Her whisper was almost a hiss. "Daniel, I kent where I saw th' eyes."

Daniel held her at arms' length and captured her worried gaze.

"They're *Andrew*'s eyes." Tears were running down her face and her breathing had become harsh and uneven.

"'At's what I saw. He has th' same eyes!"

"Who, love? Who has the same eyes? Who's Andrew?"

Siònaid ignored him. She turned to stare at the pile of stones.

"Who?" Daniel pressed. She turned to face him again, her face a mask of confusion.

"Callum. He has th' same eyes."

CHAPTER FORTY-ONE

GLENCOE, SCOTLAND – 12 FEBRUARY, 1692

FAOLÁN

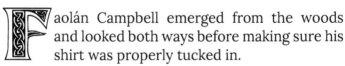aolán Campbell emerged from the woods and looked both ways before making sure his shirt was properly tucked in.

What he had done was wrong, so wrong. He should be drawn and quartered, his body left for the wolves and the wildcats that prowled the glen at night. There was no punishment strong enough for this.

Or maybe there was. Against his will, his mind conjured the face of his mother, staring at him in horror.

A gentleman ne'er takes advantage o' a young lass, laddie. If ye e'er do that, I'll ken it, and I'll skelp yer hide.

Shite! The best way to douse the flame of desire was to have your mother appear in your head.

'Tis nae my fault, Ma! he told the vision. *She had 'er way wi' me!*

It wasn't entirely a lie. Never, ever could he have imagined so much passion in one wee lass. Or so much energy.

He was her first, of course, a knowledge that filled him with equal parts wonder and guilt. Guilt had been eclipsed by wonder at the beginning, but now it had joined hands with shame, and together the two were threatening to take him down.

He and Siònaid both knew what had inspired this morning's activity. The lovemaking had been frenzied, almost desperate, borne of the knowledge that their time together was coming to its inevitable end.

For now. He meant what he'd said. He would come back; they would be married and fill their lives with each other. He'd never believed in fate, but now he embraced it with all his soul.

Faolán paused at the edge of the forest and gazed toward Glencoe village, where his heart's captor had gone only moments before.

What a couple they were. Never allowed to walk hand in hand together, for fear of being seen by others. He was a Campbell and she a MacDonald. He a government soldier and she...a *Glencoe* MacDonald.

His closest comrades knew about them. There was no hope of keeping a secret like this from the lads, not with that wee rattie Eòin around. So, when he told them about Siònaid, about how he felt, they'd exchanged glances and tried to look shocked.

"Ye'd best t' keep canny, aye?" was all Isaac said, but there was no disguising the worry etched on his face.

Damn, it was turning cold. Faolán felt the first flakes of snow on his neck and looked up into the darkening grey sky. He wasn't given to fancy, never had been, but there was something odd about the air tonight. Mist wreathed the mountains and hung low in the glen, ominous in its dark mystery.

He looked back toward the forest, where two lovers had dared to flaunt their happiness such a short time ago. It had been warmer then, or maybe they had simply not noticed. Now the trees were gone, swallowed up in the dusk as if everything that happened there was only in his imagination, and reality was this frozen place of mud and ice where strangers pretended to be friends and called it Highland Hospitality.

Isaac, Archie, and Hector were huddled together in front of the croft where they'd all been billeted these eleven days. Faolán shook his head to dispel the vapors in his mind and strolled over to them.

"Where ye been?" Hector asked. He slanted a glance first at Faolán, then at Isaac. "Looks like the weather's goin' t' turn dreich agin' t'night, and here he is, prancin' abit in th' muck like a chick in spring. How can eny man look sae happy in this shite, I want t' ask?"

"Leave 'im alone," said Isaac. "Ye're jist jealoos." He smacked a hand down on Hector's back, a little harder than necessary.

Rapid footsteps approached along the road, and Eòin emerged from the mist. He continued running until he stood in front of his three mates, panting.

"I jist—I jist—" he bent over and put his hands on his knees, fighting to catch his breath.

"Whad'ye hear now?" Archie demanded. "I swear yer kin t' th' town crier, ye are. Cannae ye gie it a rest, lad?"

Eòin pushed himself erect and stared at the three, his eyes round.

"Somethin's up," he announced. He looked back down the path and lowered his voice. "Cap's oot an' aboot, comin' this way wi' his sergeant. They been stoppin' at all the crofts along the glen from Maclain's, takin' our men ootside an' showin' 'em somethin'. I think it's our orders, an' nobody looks canty."

"Well," said Isaac in a low voice, "we'll fine out soon enough—here's the Cap'n hisself." He gestured down the road and the three men watched as Captain Campbell made his way toward them.

He was walking slowly, as if his mind was weighed down with something too heavy to carry. Gone was the fatuous smile he'd been using the past fortnight; the man seemed to have aged overnight. He drew the men away from the cottage and waited for his sergeant to hand him a document.

"Listen carefully." The captain's voice sounded odd. He cleared his throat. "This here order's been signed by the king and must be followed t' th' letter." His hand shook as he handed the document to Faolán. "Read t' yerself and pass it on."

Faolán took the piece of paper. As he read the words, an iron fist clamped around his heart and dark mist shrouded his vision. He struggled to read it through, each word imprinting on the back of his eyes like a brand. Then he read it again, hoping it would make sense this time.

To: Captain Robert Campbell of Glenlyon.

You are hereby ordered to fall upon the rebels, the MacDonalds of Glencoe on the morning of February 13, and putt all to the sword under seventy....This you are to putt in execution at fyve of the clock precisely...See that this be putt in execution without feud or favour, else you may expect to be dealt with as one not true to King nor Government, nor a man fitt to carry Comissione in the King's service.

The document fell from Faolán's stiff fingers and fluttered to the ground. Isaac glanced at his friend, then bent to pick it up, and began to read. One by one the men of Argyll's regiment read their orders and raised haunted eyes to their captain.

"This is...this is nae real." Hector's voice was strained. "Ye cannae be askin' us t' do such a thing."

Robert Campbell looked through, past, and around his men, unable to make eye contact.

"I didnae ken, not till t'day," he said. "But my name's on th' order. I have nae choice, and nor do ye. It's th' king's order. *Th' king!*"

"Five o' th' clock?" Isaac said in a hoarse whisper. "Tomorrow? He's askin' us t' go agin' the code? T' murder our own?"

Faolán forced his way out of the fog that enveloped his mind.

"It doesnae—it doesnae mean—th' women too? An' children?"

"All t' th' sword under seventy!" The captain's voice was hoarse. "Ye read th' order!"

Faolán saw his own horror reflected on his comrade's faces, shame on that of his captain. They were being ordered to kill fellow Highlanders, in cold blood. God would never forgive this!

"I cannae do it," he said. "I willnae."

"Ye will," said Captain Campbell. "More troops 're being sent o'ernight to finish th' job in th' morning. D'ye think ye're th' first t' find it hard?" He thrust the evil paper at his sergeant. "Enough! We hae more crofts t' see to, an' I'm gettin' tired o' repeatin' myself."

The two soldiers strode off in the direction of the next cottage, leaving shocked silence in their wake.

"What're we goin' t' do?" Eòin's voice sounded like a child's, frightened and helpless.

"We cannae r'fuse outright, ye ken 'at," Isaac said. "'*Dealt with as one not true to King nor Government.*' 'At means treason." He turned haunted eyes to the others. "Bit surely there's somethin'."

"I hae t' go," Faolán broke in. "I hae t' warn her." He turned away and Isaac grabbed his arm.

"Dinnae run, lad. Ye cannae hare off in a panic, noo."

Faolán shook off his friend's arm. His eyes were wild and sweat was beaded on his forehead.

"So wha' d'ye want me t'do? Women an' children too!" A violent shudder gripped his body. "I cannae believe this!"

"Jist git yerself t'gether; we hae till five o' the clock t'morrow an' 'tis only late afternoon noo."

"I hae 'n idea," Eòin said. Everyone turned to look at the small man.

"I bin all round th' village this fortnight," he went on, "so's I ken most th' MacDonalds a bit."

For once no one teased him about his propensity for minding others' business.

"Gie on, lad," said Isaac.

"There be a stone at th' end o' the village, where folk like t' gather an' share news and such."

"Aye, I ken it. Big boulder." Hector said.

"So, whit if I was t' take our host here," he gestured to the cottage behind them, "fer a wee walk by the stone, an' then tell th' *stone* that if it kent whit was t'happen this night, it wouldnae stay there on eny account?"

He shrugged. "I wouldnae be goin' agin our orders, would I, jist talkin' t' a stone? An' if the MacDonald lad wi' me was t' take warning from 'at an' run, tis no my fault, aye?"

Isaac rubbed his chin. "Ye may jist hae somethin' there, ye wee pup," he said slowly. "An' if th' rest o' us was t' sit wi' our hosts an' talk, maybe t' the dog, an' tell it t' gather its things an' run..." He spread his hands out in an innocent gesture.

"Now, Faolán, lad," he added, "ye're diff'rent. If ye was t' visit yer lass when 'tis full on dark, an' if ye two' was t' disappear durin' th' night, I reck'n none o' us here would see it, aye?" He looked around at the others, and they all nodded. Sadness was etched on their faces; none had any doubt what Faolán's decision would be. This was good-bye.

"But be canny, aye?" he cautioned his friend. "Ye hae th' time, an' ye cannae be in a rush, ye ken? Wait fer dark."

Faolán nodded and put a hand on Isaac's shoulder. His career would be over this night, and if it went wrong, he was risking the end of his life as well as Siònaid's. But he had no choice. She *was* his life now.

With a last look, the men turned away and entered the cottage to face those who had fed and sheltered them for the past eleven days. Faolán was left alone on the dark path.

He rounded the cottage to the back, sat down, and leaned against the wall, hugging his coat about him. They were the hardest hours he'd ever spent, every muscle in his body urging him to get up and run to her. The snow began to fall faster. When full dark was upon him, Faolán stood, squared his shoulders, and started the short journey toward Siònaid's cottage, forcing himself to walk.

Intent on his purpose, he failed to notice a dark shadow that detached itself from a cottage and slid up behind him. A hand went over his mouth, and he was swung around to face a man dressed all in black, nearly invisible in the darkness.

"I've been waitin' for this," a voice hissed in his ear. A sharp pain exploded in his stomach, and he was dragged away from the path and hurled against the side of the building.

Faolán's mind struggled to make sense of what was happening. He stared dully at the handle of the dirk protruding from his abdomen and forced his head up to meet the furious blue eyes of Andrew MacDonald.

CHAPTER FORTY-TWO
GLENCOE, SCOTLAND -
12 FEBRUARY, 1692

ANDREW

ndrew pressed his arm across Faolán's throat and held him against the wall. "D' ye think I dinnae ken what ye were up to wi' my cousin?" he hissed. Anger poured from him in waves and his blue eyes had narrowed to slits.

"Consortin' wi a *Campbell.* Thought she was better 'n 'at."

He loosened his grip and watched Faolán slide down the turf wall. Andrew knelt so their eyes were inches apart, and studied the face of his victim.

Sweat beaded on Faolán's brow and his breath came in short, crackling gasps. His eyes were dark with agony. Andrew smiled and moved to sit beside him against the wall. He drew in his legs and wrapped his arms around his knees.

"I dinnae think ye'll last long, what wi' that dirk keepin' ye company." He glanced at the knife buried to its hilt in Faolán's abdomen and shrugged.

"Ye can keep it. A wee gift from th' MacDonalds o' Glencoe."

Faolán said nothing; he seemed to be drifting in and out of consciousness. Andrew leaned over and slapped his face lightly.

"Stay wi' me noo. It's no time t' die just yet." He sat back against the wall and stared at the falling snow.

"It didnae have t' be me she chose, ye ken," he said. "Long as it wasnae you."

Faolán was silent. Andrew jiggled the handle of the dirk until he moaned and opened his eyes.

"Pay attention, lad, dinnae be ruide." He shifted his position against the wall to look into Faolán's face. "Keep your eyes open an' look at me when I'm talkin' t' ye."

Andrew watched the man struggle to focus, and a small smile played about his lips. "A-aat's it. Good lad.

"Now, where were we? Oh, aye. I kent she liked me, an' I'll admit I had some feelin' fer the lass. We would o' got along just fine."

The lips curled into a sneer. "Never kent she was a hoo-er, though."

His nostrils flared.

"I follow'd ye. Thought ye were so clever, hidin' like wee ratties, ruttin' in the woods." Andrew's breath quickened and the next words were a snarl.

"What ye dinnae ken is, th' forest is mine. There isnae a bit o' it I havenae trekked."

"Ye...din-nae understan'..." Faolán's whisper was barely audible. Andrew cupped his hand to his ear and leaned in.

"Wha' dinnae I understan'?" he said, politely. "Th' part where she's a hoo-er, or th' part where a Campbell bastart took 'er?"

Anguish suffused Faolán's face as he struggled to get the words out. "No-o." He took a shallow breath and recoiled against the pain. "Ye hae t'...stop 't...all... die...b'fore...morn'..." He sank back against the wall and closed his eyes again.

"Ahh, sorry, I cannae understand ye. Ye seem t' be havin' some trouble breathin'." Andrew smiled and pushed on the knife handle again.

"Open those bonny brown eyes an' stop tryin' t' talk." He leaned in close. "There's somethin' I wannae say, b'fore ye go." He put a finger to his lips. "'Tis a secret, but ye willnae tell, will ye?" He cackled at his joke and sat back.

"Ye see, I ken your wee captain, Robert Campbell o' Glenlyon. I dinnae think he told ye th' real reason he brought ye here."

His mouth twisted.

"A while ago, your captain was messin' aboot where he dinnae belong." His brows drew together.

"I killed someun, an' th' captain saw." He waved his hand as if to shoo away a pesky insect. "Dinnae fash. 'Twas someun who needed t' die. Like ye."

Andrew leaned close to Faolán's ear and whispered. "I like killin', ye ken? It does somethin', relieves a need, ye could say."

He put a hand over his heart. "Course, I never

killed anybody that dinnae deserve it. Wouldnae be right, aye?" His mouth curved in a mirthless smile.

"The wee rat wasnae th' first. There was another lad back 'n October...wrong place at th' wrong time, an'—" He stopped, seeing that Faolán's eyes had drifted shut again. "Are ye listenin'?"

He shrugged. "Too bad, ye're missin' th' best part o' th' story. He sat back against the wall once more.

"Yer wee captain made a deal wi' me. He wouldnae see me hang if I told him all about th' movements o' one Alexander Maclain, soon t' be th' late chief o' clan MacDonald o' Glencoe."

Andrew gave a harsh laugh. "It's canty, aye? A Campbell an' a MacDonald workin' t'gether t' rid th' world o' one scoondrel?"

He felt a weak tug, and looked down to see a hand clutching his cloak. Faolán's eyes were wide open and he was struggling to speak.

"Ach noo, ye're no dead yet?"

"*All!*" The word came out on an explosive gasp. "N-ae...one...*all*...g-ot or...ord..."

The words trailed off on a sigh, and Faolán's hand fell away. A froth of blood bubbled from the corner of his mouth and he sagged back against the wall. A snowflake landed on one eyelid, melted, and ran away down his cheek like a tear.

Andrew watched, but there was no movement. "Looks like ye're done," he said. "Took ye long enough."

He stood and moved to go, then turned back. "I'll be sure t' take care o' your hoo-er for ye." And he was gone, into the teeth of the howling wind.

As night advanced, the storm escalated into a

blizzard. Snow came faster, piling up in the door-ways and coloring the roof thatch white. The wind howled and pushed against the turf walls, seeking chinks that might allow it entrance.

Sated by another night of revelry, the MacDonalds of Glencoe slept deeply, secure in the knowledge that their cottages could withstand anything nature had in store.

But the danger came not from the storm. At pre-cisely five o'clock in the morning of February 13, Alexander Maclain was roused by a knock on the door. He struggled into his trews and found a group of soldiers waiting. Maclain turned to call for some-one to bring the men a morning draught and was shot dead where he stood.

All over Glencoe, soldiers rose up from their beds and stripped off the nightshirts they had worn over their uniforms. Like silent wraiths, they retrieved their swords and muskets from under their pallets and made their way through the darkness, intent on murder.

In the cottage where Isaac, Archie, Eòin and Faolán had been billeted, all was quiet. The men of the Earl of Argyll's regiment sat up and looked around to find that their hosts had departed during the night, leav-ing them alone in the cottage.

Elsewhere in the glen, soldiers turned their heads and pretended not to see as shadows crept past and away. Swords were mysteriously broken and could not be used, and perfectly good muskets suddenly misfired for no discernable reason.

Andrew MacDonald lay awake in the darkness, watching Siònaid as she slept. He gazed at the long lashes on porcelain skin and knew he had lied to the Campbell bastard. It didn't matter what she had done; he would forgive her. She was so young. She had been seduced, and now that her lover was dead, things could go back to the way they had been.

A noise in the corner caught his attention. He lay still, eyes half closed, and watched as one by one, the family's guests rose from their beds and pulled their night clothes off to reveal the uniform of King William's government. The soldiers reached under their pallets and came up holding muskets and swords.

Incredulity held Andrew rigid. *Not one...all o' ye*, Campbell had said. A chill crawled up his spine. The bastard was dying—why would he lie? The proof was right in front of him. The men who had eaten their food and consumed their whisky these eleven days past were not what they seemed.

Got ord...

He had been betrayed. Captain Robert Campbell never intended to keep his part of their unholy bargain, and Andrew had fallen right into his trap. Nausea spread through him, and he stuffed a fist into his mouth to control the urge to vomit.

He reached for his dirk, then remembered he'd left it planted in the belly of that Campbell bastard. *Damn*. He rolled slowly to the side of his pallet and eased himself onto the floor, never taking his eyes off the shadows that crept through the room. Grateful to still be wearing his black clothing, he slid quietly into the shadows across from the doorway. With luck, no one would see him here.

A shot rang out, then another. The soldiers moved quickly, dispatching the sleeping men where they lay. Andrew watched in horror as his father sat up, rubbing his eyes.

No! his mind screamed. In the next second, Domhnall MacDonald was run through by the sword of a Campbell soldier. He fell back onto his bed and was still.

Marsailli's shriek echoed through the cottage as she was pulled from her bed and herded toward the door. A soldier slapped her hard across the mouth, and she subsided into whimpers.

Andrew watched in helpless fury while Siònaid was pulled in turn from her bed and pushed toward the door to join the other women. He flattened himself against the wall and waited.

Suddenly a small voice rang out. "Leave her alone!"

Wee Seumas was on his feet and running, weaving through the pallets toward Siònaid. A soldier turned his musket and swung it in a lazy arc. The butt met Seumas' skull with a wet thud, and the child flew across the room to land in a heap at Andrew's feet, blood pooling under his head. He stared up at the man in black, and a look of horrified recognition crossed his face. He whimpered once, then his eyes glazed; the small body shuddered once and went still.

"No!" Siònaid screamed, and would have run to the child had the soldier not grasped her arm and held her in place.

The man glanced at the small huddled form, and then his eyes traveled upward and found Andrew, frozen against the wall. He reversed the position of the musket, raised it to his shoulder, and fired.

All fer nothin', a last thought slid through Andrew's mind. His legs folded and he joined his brother on the floor. As his vision faded, he could hear Siònaid screaming, a keening sound that swelled and filled the room.

"Shut her up!" snarled one of the soldiers. "Get 'em out an' fire th' place like Captain said."

The door was swung open and the women thrust out into the storm. Men who had been honored guests the night before stood in the road and cheered as flames rose inside the house.

Siònaid turned and saw a figure stagger out of the darkness to stand swaying in the light cast by the burning cottage. Blood ran down the blade clutched in Faolán Campbell's hand and dripped onto the snow.

CHAPTER FORTY-THREE

INVERNESS, SCOTLAND - PRESENT DAY

*Not everyone who reaches back into
history can survive it. And it is not
only reaching back that endangers us;
sometimes history itself reaches inexorably
forward for us with its shadowy claws.*
—Elizabeth Kostova

hat do you mean, he has the same eyes? Whose eyes? Siònaid, you're not making any sense!"

Daniel raked his hand through his hair for the third or fourth time, wondering why he was surprised. There was nothing about his lass that made sense, and he had chosen to love her anyway.

Perhaps chosen was the wrong word. He'd never really had a choice; ever since his fairy had appeared in front of him on an icy street in Inverness he'd been lost. Funny how he'd called her that in his mind—the reality of Siònaid MacDonald of Glencoe was closer to fantasy than he could ever have imagined.

He believed her. He believed that she had been born over three hundred years ago, in a Scotland he couldn't imagine in his craziest drunken dreams. A savage, untamed time when human life was currency, and a wrong step could mean death. He believed it—and her— because he had to. His sanity depended on it.

There were things she wasn't telling him, he knew that. She said she had been close to death in a blizzard on the night of the Glencoe massacre, that she had found herself on the streets of modern Inverness that night without her memories. That much he could believe; it was the only thing that could even remotely explain the weird patchy amnesia she had.

But there were gaps in her narrative. He held her close to his chest and listened to her heart beat. He felt the odd chill that came from her body. She was so cold, but she didn't *feel* the cold. Did time travel change a person's internal thermometer?

A low chuckle rolled up and he stifled it. Somehow he suspected that Siònaid wouldn't find these ramblings amusing. Besides, none of this was remotely funny; he might well be close to hysteria. He didn't care; he'd never been happier in his life.

His mobile rang, and he let go of her to fish for it in his pocket.

"Hullo?"

"Boss, ye need t' git back here, now." Big Angus' anxious voice rumbled through the air between Inverness and Glencoe.

"What's up?"

"Allan and Dunbar are missing."

"Missing? You mean they quit?"

"Nobody kens. Erskine's beside hisself; they was arses, but good workers all th' same, an' now we're short. But 'at's not all."

Daniel could hear the tension in his foreman's voice. He waited; he was sure this wasn't going to be anything he wanted to hear.

"Those detectives was at th' job yesterday, askin' fer ye. Said they had more questions."

A phantom pain knifed through Daniel's back where he'd been stabbed on a rainy night. The culprit hadn't been caught, and there were no leads. The police would have deemed it random violence and moved on, were it not for the connection to Kevin Chisolm.

He needed time to sit down and put the pieces together. His mind had been on other things all this time, other things and other centuries. For the past month, his work brain had been on auto-pilot, and now karma was coming back to bite him in the arse.

"Be there in two hours," he told Angus, and heard the sigh of relief whisper through the airspace. He clicked off and turned to Adam.

"I need to get back to Inverness right away. Do you mind?"

"Whatever you need," his brother said. "Is something wrong?"

Daniel looked at Siònaid, saw his own anxiety reflected in her eyes.

"No, just something at work." He forced a laugh, saw the disbelief in Adam's expression, and decided not to look at Siònaid again. He and Adam hadn't been close for years, yet his brother could tell he was lying. Siònaid was nobody's fool; she would read him too easily.

Adam glanced between the two and gave a short nod. "No worries. Let's get on then."

This time Daniel insisted on Siònaid taking the front seat. He was grateful to his brother for the constant litany about the sites they were passing because it freed him to work on the puzzle.

What did he have? He closed his eyes and let his mind go still.

It had started with Kevin Chisolm's murder, still unsolved.

Chisolm had signed a materials order for the wrong rebar. There was no current or recent job that called for rebar of that size, and yet the order had been made.

Frank Allan and Gil Dunbar knew about it. Those two were in it up to their necks. They'd lied when questioned, but they were rotten liars.

Big Angus had heard them talking to an unknown man who seemed to be their boss—*sounded like you, boss*, which meant Angus thought he was a toff.

Daniel allowed himself a wry grin. They'd come a long way, he and Angus. A *big dumb bear*, he'd thought when he first met him. The truth was vastly different where Angus was concerned. He was canny and intuitive, and his size gave him the courage to venture where more timid men might not.

Size wouldn't stop a knife, though; he felt the phantom pain again and grimaced. Especially when you didn't know it was coming.

Kevin Chisolm probably hadn't known it was coming. Angus said that Allan and Dunbar had as good as admitted they'd killed Chisolm, but there was no proof. Daniel had been in hospital and Angus had nothing to go on.

They'd reported it to the police, who promised to look into it, and now the two suspects were missing. Gone to ground? Killed by someone who was cleaning up? And what more did the detectives want to talk to him about?

His mind kept going back to that materials order. Rebar of a size and strength much too small for a job like Millburn Road. A tensile strength that was used in small, one-story buildings, not huge office complexes like the one that was nearly finished.

A worm of worry slithered through his veins and took up residence in the middle of his chest. He tried to remember the amount of rebar on that requisition. Big Angus had the order, hidden safely away in his own flat in Inverness. The squirming creature in his chest was telling him it was important.

Daniel pulled up Big Angus' number on his mobile and listened to the ring on the other end until it went to voice mail. The worm flipped and wriggled. He tried again and listened to a robotic female voice telling him that the person he was trying to reach was "unable to come to the phone right now. Leave your name and number, and I'll return your call as soon as I'm free. Thank you."

It was a company mobile, and Big Angus hadn't bothered to set a greeting. The impersonal, non-existent person on the line made Daniel feel worse, as if the robot-woman knew that Angus was not going to be free and would never be returning his call.

Daniel shook himself out of the black mood that threatened to overwhelm him. He glanced at Siònaid, her lovely face turned to face Adam as she gestured and asked eager questions. Whatever happened, he had to keep her out of it.

The person who'd stabbed him had to be connected, a random attack was far beyond the realm of coincidence. Which meant that Big Angus was in danger too, and Erskine. And maybe even Callum and Uncle Ranald.

He decided not to waste time going home.

"Adam, can you drop me at Millburn Road? Siònaid, you have a key to the Roseberry house, Mary said?"

"Aye," she said with pride.

"Good. Go in, lock the door, and don't open it for anybody but the Duncans or me, aye?" He pinned her with the most serious gaze he could muster, and it must have worked. She opened her mouth, and then closed it again.

"Aye."

"I'll come by later."

The Range Rover pulled into the Millburn site, bumped through the puddles, and parked near the office trailer. Daniel got out, retrieved his bag from the boot, and came around to the passenger side.

Siònaid fumbled with the buttons until Adam reached over and lowered the window for her. Daniel reached in and took the hand that had automatically come up to meet his.

He smiled at her serious face, then pulled her closer and kissed the palm of her small hand. I *love you,* he mouthed, and two pinpoints of color appeared in her pale cheeks. A smile broke out on her face. *I love ye,* she mouthed back.

Daniel stood and watched as the battered vehicle carrying his brother and his woman disappeared toward the city center. He turned toward the trailer, but something held him in place. He tilted his head up and gazed into a menacing grey sky, leaden with the promise of rain.

Siònaid's eyes were grey like the clouds, but their promise was different. They pulled him in, calmed his heart, and whispered that everything would be all right as long as she was with him. Curious, it was almost as if he could hear the words in his mind.

He shrugged. Getting more fanciful by the moment. He needed to get on with it—track down Big Angus, find out what had happened to Allan and Dunbar.

Those two were killers, that much was obvious. One of them had very possibly stuck a knife in his back on a rainy night last month. It was exactly the kind of cowardly thing those wee sleekit bastards would do.

Had the police interviewed them? They must have, but they weren't about to share their findings with civilians, like the person who'd gotten stabbed, for instance.

Another thought floated up out of the mud and damp at his feet. If the police *had* spoken with Allan and Dunbar, those two now knew someone had spied on them. They knew someone might have recognized their boss. And that took the element of surprise out of the picture.

Had the eejits told the boss, and had he decided they were too much of a liability to keep around? Were they languishing in the canal, or stuffed into a rubbish bin like Chisolm?

Daniel stared for another minute at the rolling grey clouds. It seemed as if they were reaching for him, trying to get inside his head. Thunder rolled away off the loch, and the wind was picking up.

It whistled through the empty windows of the office building, past the hallways and dark rooms that would soon house busy offices. It whispered past the crack in the bearing wall, which had now been joined by others all working their way up the wall of the structure like tiny snakes.

Daniel shivered where he stood in the deserted work site. He looked once more toward Millburn Road, and wondered if Siònaid was home now, locked safely inside with her guard cat.

He pulled out his mobile and texted Adam. *Is she home?*

Mission accomplished, came the return text, and Daniel relaxed. Adam was a good man. So were his other brothers, Ewan and Jonah. Sophie, his little sister. and Iseabail. When was the last time he'd talked—really talked—with Izzy?

When this was all over, he was going to get in touch with all of them, reconnect. Be a human. He'd spent too much time in the shadows, nursing his self-pity and feeding a condition that wasn't even his fault. It was time he went to see a doctor, got the therapy he needed, and stopped letting alcohol do his thinking for him.

He realized all this introspection for what it was. He was stalling. Every moment he stood out here was a moment he wasn't closed up in that stale trailer. Damn thing was like a coffin. A dirty, coffee-stained, mud-splattered coffin.

Daniel sighed, shouldered his bag, and slogged through the puddles to the trailer and up the wooden steps. One hand on the metal handle, he stopped to summon the image of Roseberry Place and its current occupant, before carefully closing her away in a special compartment in his mind. *Later.*

He opened the door and found himself staring down the barrel of an ugly, black handgun.

CHAPTER FORTY-FOUR
INVERNESS, SCOTLAND
- PRESENT DAY

Only those you trust can betray you.
—Terry Goodkind

iscuit the black cat sat at the end of the couch with her head cocked. Her green eyes were fixed on the girl who was staring at a blank television screen. Neither had moved for a long time.

Siònaid turned away from the screen. "Somethin's wrong," she whispered to the cat. "Mebbe 'tis jist my imagination, bit still..."

Biscuit said nothing. She lifted a paw and extended her pink tongue to clean herself, making it look like the most important task in the world.

"I ken he said he would come, an' I could see he was worrit about work, so I shouldnae fash him—" Siònaid looked at the cat. "I'm nae stupid, ye ken."

Biscuit yawned.

Siònaid's eyes darted to the shiny black mobile that sat on the side table. It was hers, a gift from

Mary, but she'd never used it. Mary and Henry had shown her how to touch the numbers on its face in order to speak with the people she knew, and she'd nodded obediently and filed the lesson away under, *things I dinnae need t' ken.*

She knew now that the voices inside were not those of trapped souls. She was no longer afraid of the thing, but a residual anxiety lingered. Still, this was the time to conquer her fear. If she could just hear his voice, just make sure he was all right...

She looked at the mobile and thought about her lesson.

Number one was Mary, two was Henry, and so on through the list of Highland Players. Daniel was number four. She dragged her eyes away from the mobile and back to the cat.

"Ye see, I'm afeard that if I'm nae wi' him, somethin' bad could happen," she said, knitting her fingers together on her lap. "But I'm afeard if I *am* wi' him, somethin' bad *will* happen." Her voice trembled. "I dinnae ken what t' do!"

The cat opened her mouth. "You don't have to be with him any longer," Baltair's voice said. "You set it all in motion in Glencoe. You're going to get your revenge today. Congratulations."

"No!" Siònaid moaned. "'At's nae what I want!"

The cat yawned again, stood up, and stretched her length along the couch. "It doesn't matter what you want. It's too late." The animal jumped gracefully to the floor and turned her back on the distraught girl. She sauntered off, swishing her tail in mockery. "It's too late, it's too late..."

Siònaid jerked and opened her eyes. Biscuit was nowhere in sight, but the words in her dream seemed to hang in the room. *It's too late.*

No! It couldn't be. She reached for the mobile on the side table. When she touched its face, little boxes with strange pictures appeared on the screen as if summoned.

What had Mary said? It was the green button with a white image that looked like a tipping boat. Her trembling finger hovered over the strange picture for a second, and then she steeled herself and tapped it lightly. Immediately the screen changed, and there were the numbers. She touched the four, put it up to her ear, and listened.

A strange buzzing sounded and she dropped the mobile. Daniel's voice sounded from her lap, and she grabbed the black box up again with a sigh of relief. He was safe.

Hullo, this is Daniel MacArthur of MacArthur Construction. I can't come to the phone right now; please leave a message and I'll get back to you as soon as possible.

"Daniel, is everythin' aright?" Siònaid said, hoping that her words were getting into the mobile somehow.

There was no answer, just a click before the thing went silent. Siònaid stared at it in frustration. Hadn't he heard her? She pressed the four again, listened.

Hullo, this is Daniel MacArthur of MacArthur Construction. I can't come to the phone right now; please leave a message and I'll get back to you as soon as possible.

Siònaid threw the mobile down onto the couch and put her hands up to cover her face. Why did he keep saying the same thing?

She could feel her racing heartbeat, and forced herself to calm down. *Mary.* Mary would help. She pressed the one.

Mary's delighted voice came over the air. "You're using the mobile! Good for you, lass!"

"Mary, I jist tried t' call Daniel, bit he cannae hear me! He jist keeps sayin' th' same thing. Somethin's wrong!"

"Calm down, lass. What is he saying?"

Siònaid repeated what she could remember, and Mary's musical laugh came through the mobile.

"That's not him, lass. It's his voicemail message. Didn't you say he's at work? He's probably just away from his mobile at the moment." There was a pause. "Try Callum if you're worried. He's six."

Siònaid clicked the red button that meant *stop*, and Mary's voice disappeared. She stood up and paced in a circle in front of the hearth, unable to get Baltair out of her head. *It's too late. Congratulations.*

Pearls of sweat beaded on her forehead, and the mobile slipped in her damp hand. Mary was wrong; something had happened to Daniel. She could *feel* it.

Try Callum. Aye, they worked together; he would know how to reach Daniel. She pressed the six.

Callum's voice came out of the mobile. "Siònaid. What's up?"

Relief coursed through her. "Callum? D' ye ken where Daniel is?"

There was a long silence, then Callum's voice came back. "Why? Did you lose him?"

His voice was flat. Was he angry because she had stayed with Daniel this morning? Impatience flooded her. None of that was important right now.

"I-I jist needed t' speak wi' him. He went t' th' job, he said, but I cannae reach him."

"The job?" Callum said. "Wasn't he having a holiday with you?" He sounded annoyed, as if she were wasting his time.

There was a long silence in which Siònaid thought he had ended the conversation.

"Why would he go to the job site?" His voice was low, as if he were talking to himself. Another long silence, seeming somehow heavy. Siònaid shivered.

"I'm sure he's all right, Siònaid. I'll give him a call; just stay where you are. I have to go now."

Siònaid sat staring at the blank black screen for a long time. There had been something about Callum's words—no, something about his tone. They hadn't matched. Her heartbeat quickened again. He *knew* there was something wrong, and he didn't want her to know.

She got up and ran to the kitchen, where there was a larger telephone box hanging on the wall. Next to the telephone was a handwritten list of local phone numbers.

What had Mary said? 'If you ever need to go somewhere and we're not here, call the taxi service, number's right here.'" Well, that time had come. She was going to find Daniel.

It's too late.

"Nae, 'tis not," she announced to the empty room. "I willnae let it be too late." She picked up the handle of the telephone as she'd seen Mary do, and tapped in the numbers for the Inverness taxi service.

"Welcome, Mr. MacArthur," said Gil Dunbar.

He gestured with the gun. "How about ye come over here and sit down? Sorry, ye'll have t' use th' floor; all th' seats is taken."

Daniel's eyes darted around the room. Frank Allen sat in the leather chair with his feet propped up on the desk, a sneer on his ruddy face. Next to the desk, tied to the metal chair, was Big Angus Graham. His head lolled forward and his eyes were closed. Bruises covered his face and his nose was swollen to twice its size.

Dunbar led Daniel to a spot adjacent to the desk and pointed the gun at the floor. "I guess this'll do. Have a sit. Sir."

Daniel sat down, pulled up his legs and crossed his feet at the ankles to take up as little space as necessary. Why that seemed important he couldn't guess, but making himself as small as possible seemed a good idea.

It suddenly occurred to him that this would be a great time for a panic attack, and yet nothing was happening. Sure, his heart was racing, but the breathlessness, the sweating, and the nausea were curiously absent. Maybe it was a lesson to him—when the threat was real, there was no time for all that nonsense.

His mind was crystal clear. He'd been an eejit, let himself walk into this like a sheep to the slaughterhouse.

Frank Allan stood up and stretched his arms over

his head, flexing his meaty hands. Then he took a length of rope from the desk, strolled over to Daniel, and knelt in front of him.

"I'm pretty sure a high-up snob like you isnae goin' t' be rude like yer foreman, so it willnae be necessary t' rough ye up. Even though it'd be fun." He grinned, showing a mouth full of decaying teeth. Daniel shuddered at the breath that came from that mouth and closed his eyes.

He kept them closed while his hands were tied behind his back and the rest of the rope wrapped around his chest. Too late he remembered a television show where the clever detective had taken a deep breath and held it so the rope wouldn't be so tight; probably was all TV magic anyway. The rope bit into his arms and constricted his chest.

His mobile rang in his jacket pocket.

"Oh dear," said Gil. "I dinnae think ye can answer that, tied up as ye are. Here, let me help ye." He reached into the pocket and pulled out the mobile, holding it up. "Who's Evie? Yer girlfriend?" He shook his head in mock concern and dropped the mobile onto the desktop. "I guess yer not home."

The mobile rang again. Daniel watched it light up, listened as it went to voicemail, and prayed that Sìonaid stayed put. She couldn't drive and didn't understand addresses, but she'd worry. The thought hurt, but better that than the alternative.

He'd get out of this somehow—and then he remembered Kevin Chisolm, and the sharp bite of a knife in his own back, and for a minute his vision clouded and he thought he might pass out.

Another mobile rang. Frank Allan put his device to his ear.

"Aye, boss? He's here, an' so's the big foreman. Had t' rough that one up some, but he willnae be 'n pain much longer anyway."

Allan paused while the person on the other end of the call spoke, and Daniel watched his face turn red, then white.

"Well, he walked right in...no, we didn't hurt him... bit we thought..." Allan stopped talking and listened.

"Aye, sir," he said finally. "We'll take 'em there an' wait. No, sir. Yes, sir." He ended the call and turned to look at Dunbar, then at Daniel. He glared at the mobile screen and a look of disgust crossed his face. "Toffs," he said.

"Boss says take 'em t' the room." He walked over to Daniel and yanked him up by the arm. "Up ye go. Ye'll have t' walk by yerself." He looked at Big Angus. "Might have t' carry this big lug."

"Fuck that." Gil Dunbar walked over to Angus and slapped his cheek hard twice. Graham's eyes opened as far as the swelling would allow, and he lifted his head. He spotted Daniel, and a look of apology passed over his battered face.

Daniel shook his head and mustered a smile. Angus lowered his head again.

They were herded out the door and down the wooden steps. To Daniel's surprise, instead of taking them to a vehicle, the two crewmen marched them toward the office building itself and around the corner to the back.

A loading dock stood at the corner of the building.

Allan and Dunbar pushed their prisoners up the ramp and into the darkness of the building itself.

Even in daylight, the light inside was dim, making progress difficult. Dunbar pulled out a torch and flicked it on, and the stumbling parade proceeded down the hallway and past doorways until they arrived at a newly installed door about halfway along the main hall.

Dunbar and Allan opened the door and pushed their helpless prisoners into a small windowless room, shoving them onto the floor next to each other. Daniel inched his fingers toward Big Angus until their hands touched. The foreman's hand jerked, and then he relaxed. *Human touch*, Daniel thought, *the great healer*.

Time passed. With the door closed, the room was dark as pitch. Their captors said nothing; the call from their boss seemed to have robbed them of speech.

After a while Daniel realized his eyes were beginning to adjust to the darkness. Now he could make out the shapes of Allan and Dunbar against the opposite wall, near the door. He turned to his right and saw that Angus was watching him. The big man nodded and squeezed his hand.

Another half hour or so passed before footsteps were heard in the hallway outside. Dunbar and Allan stiffened and moved further away from the door.

It opened and a figure stood silhouetted in the dim light from the hallway. A man, by the height, but the darkness in the room made it impossible to see more. So, Daniel thought, *this must be the boss*.

Suddenly Big Angus gripped his hand with such force that he gasped, despite his resolve to remain silent. The figure in the doorway stepped closer, and Daniel felt his heart clench before it made a long plunge to the region of his stomach.

"I'm sorry, cousin," said Callum MacArthur. "I never wanted it to come to this."

CHAPTER FORTY-FIVE
INVERNESS, SCOTLAND
- PRESENT DAY

But the world is strange and endings are not
truly endings no matter how the stars might
wish it so. Occasionally Fate can pull itself
together again. And Time is always waiting.
—Erin Morgenstern

Daniel stared at his cousin, the man who'd had his back for so many years, and realized he was looking into the face of a stranger. Callum's blue eyes were rimmed with red, and something dark swam in their depths.

"Why?" Daniel whispered. "What's happened to you?"

The eyes shuttered. Callum's mouth became a taut, bitter line.

"It has nothing to do with you." The words were ground out, harsh with hidden emotion.

Daniel felt something shift inside. Fear gave way to anger, sweeping away the lethargy that had been

403

holding him in its grasp since he'd entered the trailer and walked into the barrel of a gun.

"That's ridiculous," he said. He shifted his body and pushed against the ropes. "It obviously has quite a lot to do with me." Sarcasm welled. "Do you think I put these ropes on myself? He gestured to Big Angus. "Or were you under the impression that I beat up my own man, for fun?"

"Shut up," Callum bit out the words. "I tried to keep you out of it, tried to keep you safe, but you just wouldn't stop. Why did you have to start caring about your job now, of all times?"

A rustle near the door caught Callum's attention. He turned to look over his shoulder. "Get out."

Daniel watched as the erstwhile cocky Allan and Dunbar scrambled to be first out the door. In their wake, silence descended once more on the dark room.

Callum began to pace back and forth, his movements jerky, almost robotic. Daniel watched this new manifestation of his elegant cousin with fascination.

"I have a reputation to uphold," Callum said. "I'm a perfectionist, you know that." He swung around and pinned Daniel with those piercing blue eyes. "Of course, I knew you all called me the Golden Boy; you were making fun of me, but I never minded. Because it was true. I worked hard for that."

Daniel said nothing.

"But being the best takes its toll. It can sap your energy if you let it."

Callum started pacing again. "I didn't take the easy way out, like you did. Languishing in the pubs and feeling sorry for myself. I'm better than that.

"A man needs relief, though. I'm not a machine." Now his tone had taken a turn toward the aggrieved. It was becoming almost whiny, something Daniel had never imagined hearing from Callum.

That may be how you see it, but I'm not as close to the action as you are, Adam had said. Was that true? Had he been so in awe of Callum MacArthur, heir apparent to MacArthur Construction, that he'd missed the cracks in the facade? So blinded by gratitude that he'd failed to see the flaws?

No, not flaws. It was much, much worse than that. Callum stopped pacing and knelt with his face close to his cousin's. Daniel leaned back from the madness in those blue eyes.

"It started out small," Callum said. "That's how they get you. Just a little bet, and you win, so it's so easy to bet again, and you win again. I didn't even need the money! But I kept playing, just as they knew I would. They *know* when it's time, and then you lose. So you bet again, and lose again, and before you know it you're in too deep to get out."

Some sense of preservation kept Daniel silent. He glanced over to see a look of horror in Big Angus' eyes, evident even through the bruising. He gave an almost imperceptible shake of his head as a warning, but it wasn't necessary. Callum was lost in his narrative.

"The debts began to pile up, and naturally I couldn't go to Father. Can you just picture that?" His laugh was harsh. "I had to make money somehow; even you can understand that much, can't you? They would have taken MacArthur Construction away from me!"

Callum sat back and wrapped his arms around his body. His head was lowered and the words uttered into his lap, but they were as clear as if he was giving a report at a board meeting.

There was a long silence. It was time to say something. Anything.

"So, what did you do?" Daniel kept his voice even, hoping his cousin would not hear the tremor in his words.

"What else could I do?" Callum looked up. "I began to make some changes in the orders, just little ones, things that would make no difference. I was able to pocket the difference and no one knew."

He stood up suddenly and began to pace again. "I couldn't do it alone, of course. There are always men who will stay quiet and do what is needed, men who have dirty secrets of their own, and I found Allan and Dunbar." He looked toward the door and his lip curled. "They're not too bright, but they don't mind doing what needs to be done."

"They killed Kevin Chisolm, didn't they?" Daniel could have bitten his tongue, but the words were out so he went on. "Why? Was he in on it?"

Callum jerked his head up. "That arse! He didn't mind signing the orders for me, did he? But then he started dating one of the secretaries in the office and had a change of heart." Callum's voice dripped with mockery. "Was going to be a new man, get married, start a family, who'd marry a slob like that, I ask you?"

Daniel sat back against the wall and let the wheels turn in his head. It was hard to feel sorry for Chisolm; he'd sold his soul and then wanted it back.

There were no take-backs, not in this new upside-down world.

Things were not going to end well here, that much was obvious. Callum would never have confessed all this if he meant to leave witnesses.

"Who stabbed me?" he asked. "Were you behind that too?"

"Sorry about that," Callum said. His voice held real regret. "But you found the materials order that eejit forgot to destroy. You and this big gowk here," he sent a derisive glance toward Big Angus, "started asking questions." He shrugged. "It was only a warning; you didn't die, did you?"

Something cold slithered into Daniel's mind. *The materials order.* For cheaper, lighter rebar than this job demanded.

"Where did that rebar go?" he asked, his voice barely above a whisper. "Don't tell me—"

"Aye, then, I won't." Callum shrugged again. "But I think you've figured it out. You may be weak, but you're not stupid."

He rounded on Daniel. "Do you have any idea how much money I got out of that simple switch? And no one will ever know."

Daniel stared at him, astonished at his cousin's inability to see what he'd done. Cheaper materials, suitable for a one-story structure, had been put into this one, a sprawling, three-story building where hundreds of people would be working every day, never knowing how much danger they could be in.

"This isn't you, Callum." Daniel hated the pleading note in his voice, but desperation drove him on. "You were the best! What happened to your pride, your drive? What about Uncle Ranald?"

"Survival happened!" Callum snarled. "Pride doesn't do much good when you're dead, and that's what I'd be if I didn't pay up. I didn't have a choice!"

"You always have a choice," Daniel said, his voice breaking. "Please, Callum. You can't let this building be finished! Turn yourself in. I'll help you. Tell the police about those people, about why you did this. Please!"

Callum stopped pacing and looked at his cousin squarely for the first time. "You've always been annoying, you know that?" His hands flexed and curled into fists. "You couldn't even face your own problems; you had to hide in a bottle, and now you want to be all righteous? What a joke."

He pulled out his mobile and checked the display. He gave his cousin a long look. "I know it doesn't mean much now, but I am sorry."

He walked to the door and opened it. "Finish up," he said to the two men waiting outside.

Allan and Dunbar sidled back into the room, and the four listened to the sound of Callum MacArthur's footsteps as they dwindled away down the dark hall.

Gil Dunbar pulled the gun out of his jacket pocket and advanced to stand in front of the two bound men.

"We weren't allowed to stick ye afore," he said, all the arrogance back in the absence of his boss. "This time it'll be different."

Dunbar pulled the weapon up and waved it between Daniel and Angus. "Who wants t' be first?" Then he stopped and cocked his head. "Wha's 'at?"

A low rumble, like thunder before a storm, sounded somewhere deep in the darkness of the building. Allan moved to the open doorway and stuck his head into the hallway. The rumbling increased in volume, sounding now more like an approaching train than thunder.

The floor beneath Daniel began to vibrate. He looked at Angus in shock, all fear of the gun forgotten in an instant. Allan turned around; his face drained of color.

"Th' buildin's comin' down!" he yelled. "Git out!"

Dunbar gave a last look at the helpless men on the floor and then turned to sprint out the door after his partner. In their wake, cracks appeared along the floor and dust filtered down from the ceiling.

There was nothing in the room and nowhere to hide. Daniel and Angus watched in horror as the concrete walls began to shake. The rumbling swelled.

A figure appeared in the doorway, holding on to the edges to stay erect. A girl, long black hair coated with dust, face white as the painted walls. She paused and then raced into the room.

"Siònaid?" Daniel managed. Then, "Siònaid, get out! The building is collapsing!" He struggled to his knees. "Go!"

She ignored him. Pushing away bits of the ceiling that had fallen into the center of the room, she moved behind Daniel and began working at the knots binding his arms and hands.

"Ye're nae goin' t' die! I willnae let ye!" Her words were almost indistinguishable over the rumbling around and above them.

She managed to free Daniel, and together they went to work on the ropes binding Big Angus.

Bits of the ceiling and walls were showering down around them. Daniel pulled Siònaid into his arms in a futile effort to shelter her from the debris, knowing that they were all going to die here. And yet, all he could think was how wonderful it was that this brave, stupid, wonderful woman was with him at the end.

"It's nae too late! He's wrong, it's nae too late!" she was saying, over and over. She pushed herself away and hauled him to his feet. Angus was already standing, swaying with the rocking of the dying building.

Arms around each other, the three staggered into the hall. On the western end a plume of grey dust was growing, filling the space and racing toward them in a suffocating cloud. They turned east and headed for the stairwell at the end. Siònaid's limp was no longer an issue; the two men could barely walk themselves. She was the strong one now, her determination larger than the encroaching cloud.

They almost made it. Only feet from the end of the hall, the cloud caught up and enveloped them in its ferocity. Dust swirled and filled their eyes and noses, and Daniel felt himself dragged away from the others. A large piece of concrete detached from the outer wall and tilted toward him, and everything went black.

The light picked at his eyelids. He opened them just a little, and shut them against the relentless brightness. Sleep was impossible, though, so after a while he tried again, and this time forced himself to keep his eyes open.

He was back in Raighmore Hospital; he recognized the incessant beeping from his last visit, but this time the pain was mostly in his head. He looked at the people ranged around his bed and groaned. Uncle Ranald, Big Angus, and those two detectives again. He closed his eyes, too late.

"You're awake." Ranald MacArthur's rough voice grated on his ear and pounded his head. Daniel winced and squinted up at his uncle.

The man looked awful. His skin was grey and pasty, his eyes bloodshot, and his hands shook. Still, he didn't look as bad as Angus. The big man's arm was in a sling and a plaster covered his nose under green splotches.

"You look better than usual," said Daniel.

Angus gaped at him. "Ye just woke up and ye're tellin' jokes?"

Daniel grinned. "We nearly died. Life is funny."

His thoughts came together and the grin slid off his face.

"Where's Siònaid?" Panic rose in a hot wave.

Angus gave him a blank look. "Who?"

"Siònaid, the girl who saved us! Is she all right?"

The two detectives sat up in their chairs, eyes narrowing.

411

Uncle Ranald cleared his throat irritably. "What are you talking about? What girl?"

Sergeant Murray stared at Daniel with an off-putting intensity. "We found you two under a piece of the outside wall, lad.

"Just the two of you."

FEBRUARY 13, 1692

GLENCOE

The snow came faster, pelting everything in its path with a raging fury. Icy flakes clung to Siònaid's eyelashes, melted, and froze again. The cold was a living thing, reaching into her soul and sucking each breath away.

She was staring at death; she knew it. No one could survive this hell of wind and snow. She had already lost sensation in her hands and feet, and her memory was leading her to places she wanted to forget.

She had closed off the terrors of this night, but now they were returning, battering her mind and clutching at her heart like a raptor's talons. How quickly time twisted joy into horror.

Seumas, lying bloodied on the rush floor. Uncle Domhnall, half-asleep and unable to understand the musket ball that took his life. Andrew, a mask of anger and hatred on his face as he fell.

Her thoughts wavered, blew apart in the howling wind, and returned to gentler times. She had once thought she loved Andrew, knew now that it was the simple affection of a young girl for a handsome man who paid her attention. Now she knew better. She had discovered the wonder of real love in the person of Faolán Campbell.

Faolán. His beloved face appeared before her, and she allowed the vision to fill her soul. Memories of their lovemaking, so sweet and gentle, danced and swirled in her head. Was it only hours ago?

Siònaid wrenched her tattered mind away from the image, knowing it for the lie it was. She turned back to face the blizzard's wrath.

She was alone now. The chief's wife had succumbed first to the vicious elements. Blue lips without even the strength to speak, limbs that refused to hold a once-sturdy body, Lady Maclain folded into the snow and was just...gone. Another woman sat down against a rock and crossed her arms in defiance, refusing to walk further.

She and Marsailli had struggled along together, until a backward look told her she was the only one left in this alien landscape of snow and ice. She turned back to search, but the girl was lost, melted into the white landscape as if she had never been.

She limped on alone. Snow fell from frozen hair and covered the shoulders of her thin gown. The wind battered her numb body, forcing her to her knees. Siònaid rolled onto her back and stared into the abyss of white that swirled above and around her. Her eyes closed.

Words found their way into her mind.

"What is your desire?"

She knew that voice! She had heard it before. She had argued with it, defied its wishes.

"What is your desire?" the voice said again. She reached for the words she needed, and found them. Buried in the frozen depths of her mind, cold like the snow that blanketed her with a white coverlet.

She forced her lips open, pushed the words out into the storm. "Re-venge?" Why did it seem as if she had said this before? Why was she hesitating now?

"That is not the right answer," the voice said. "Have you learned nothing?"

"I—"

"I worked so hard to show you. Think."

Siònaid grasped for a memory, and a name swam out of the fierce winds.

"Daniel."

"Aye, lass." The voice sounded pleased.

"Daniel is...Faolán?"

"Aye. Daniel is Faolán. And Daniel loves you. Do you understand now?"

"No." She could feel death hovering, but she held tight to her hatred. "Faolán betrayed me."

"Did he? Think."

"He was there. He was holdin' a dirk wi' blood on it."

"Whose blood?"

"My clan's blood, o' course."

"Are you certain?"

"Aye, I saw 't." But she wondered. What had she seen? A man with a dirk dripping blood. Swaying in the doorway.

Swaying. His other hand clutching his abdomen where a darker stain spread.

"'Twas his own blood? Another emotion rose up to wrap itself around her frozen heart. It felt like hope.

"He...didnae...he didnae come to hurt me," she whispered. Her voice floated into the frigid air "He...he came t' save me, e'en though he was hurt himself."

"Good lass," said the voice.

"He didnae betray me..." Her words were feather-soft, imbued with wonder.

"So, what is your desire?" the voice asked.

There was a long pause, while the storm raged and howled its fury. Then...

"Him. I want him."

"That is the right answer," said Baltair.

Through the fog of churning snow, a shadow wavered, took form, and staggered toward her. A new voice called out, the words almost lost in the wind.

"Siònaid!"

He was here, beautiful and real. His face was etched with pain, drawn and white as the snow, but he was here. He fell to his knees and his lips parted in the smile she adored as he gathered her into his arms, brushing snow from her face with a trembling hand.

"Rest now, mo ghràdh," Faolán whispered. "I'll never leave ye."

When the blizzard finally blew itself out, the morning sun glistened on a sea of white that covered the sleeping lovers with its frigid beauty. Nothing moved; nothing disturbed the silence in the glen.

PRESENT DAY

GLENCOE

Daniel MacArthur boarded the bus from Inverness to Fort William at Stance Four, fighting an odd feeling of loss. Of course, he was contemplating leaving the city where he'd been born and lived all his life, but that wasn't it. Something danced on the edge of his memory, just out of reach.

As the bus wound through town toward the A82, he thought back for the hundredth time over the last six months, trying to capture the feeling.

It was as if he were the only person in the world who knew something, yet he had no memory of what it was. It was a lump in the middle of his stomach that occasionally traveled upward to grab onto his heart and then subside again, leaving emptiness and sorrow in its wake.

He supposed having a three-story building fall on you could be considered a trauma, and the doctors were certain that experience was at the root of his problems.

They told him he'd awakened in the hospital raving about a girl, saying she had saved him. But everyone else insisted there had been no such person. The only bodies found had been those of Frank Allan and Gil Dunbar, who had sold their souls and paid with their lives.

In the old days, he might have shared the odd feeling with his cousin. But Callum MacArthur, tucked securely into Porterfield Prison and awaiting sentencing, was silent. He had refused visitors and no one talked about him, that shining star that had fallen from the sky and crushed the MacArthur empire.

The company was finished. Every project completed in the last ten years was being checked for structural inadequacy. The legal battles loomed, waiting eagerly to consume what had once been the pride of Ranald MacArthur.

Uncle Ranald himself was a broken man. Daniel found himself visiting his uncle frequently, talking about anything but construction. Circumstance had gentled his uncle's personality, removed the barbs, and smoothed the edges. Now his attitude was deferential, even grateful.

Daniel hadn't seen Big Angus Graham since they'd both left the hospital. They'd shared the most harrowing experience of their lives, but the reality was they had nothing else in common. Angus had moved on to another job, eager to put the horror behind him, and their occasional texts had dwindled and eventually stopped.

The bus passed a small building with a red door. A poster outside advertised homes for sale and rent, but Daniel's heart lurched as it always did when he passed that particular building. He felt a longing for something he couldn't name.

A real estate office didn't seem right for that building. What had it been before? He imagined a kilt shop, or maybe a bagpipes store. Maybe a tour office? Something to do with history would be perfect.

Once, he'd passed two women on this street. One was tiny, like a little brown wren, while the other was buxom and red-cheeked. He stopped and looked back, sure that they would turn in at the building with the red door, but they'd continued on without stopping. The sadness he'd felt was as real as the glass window on the bus he was riding now.

It was as ludicrous as the feeling he got when he walked past the McDonalds on High Street. He'd never been inside, never eaten that bilge in his life, but now when he saw those golden arches, he felt tears filling his eyes. Ridiculous. He gave up thinking and let his eyes drift closed until the bus pulled into the station at Fort William.

Adam met him in the car park. He took Daniel's backpack and stowed it in the back of the Range Rover. When he had pulled back onto the road, he glanced sideways at his passenger.

"Are ye ready?" he asked, concern etched on his features. "It's a big change."

"I'll know soon enough, aye? I'll decide after this visit," Daniel said.

"Well, I for one welcome the addition to my wee

workforce," Adam laughed. "I understand why you want a change after what happened, but coming all the way to a tiny place like Glencoe seems a bit of a stretch." A question hung in the air.

Daniel shrugged. "I don't know why it had to be Glencoe, either." He said, tentatively, "You're going to think I'm crazy, but—"

"Don't worry," Adam waved a hand in the air. "You can't be any crazier than you were before. I mean, you were a certified drunk, and there wasn't a female tourist for miles who was safe."

He dodged a fist. "Don't hit the driver, ye numpty. But seriously, Daniel, you've changed."

Daniel was quiet, thinking. It was true; he had changed. He'd confided in the neurologist who saw him after the accident, and in doing so, he realized he hadn't had a panic episode for a long time.

"Was there anything new in your life in the last few months?" the doctor had asked.

"I don't know," Daniel said. Something teased his brain, but it was as elusive as the Highland mist. In the end, he decided to stop worrying about it. If there was something, it would come to him in time.

"Well, whatever the reason," Adam was saying, "I like the new you. Especially since I need help with the tours, and you seem to know quite a bit about the history around Glencoe. Plus, it's good to spend more time with my brother." Adam's eyes were warm.

"Welcome back to the family," he said, and Daniel felt a lump grow in his throat.

They drove through Ballachulish in comfortable silence, and turned left into Glencoe Village.

"How about a coffee before we get you settled at your guesthouse?" Adam asked. Without waiting for an answer, he pulled into the carpark of the Glencoe Cafe and parked near the entrance.

A bell above the door jingled as they walked into the tiny cafe. Daniel pulled the menu over and scanned the luncheon items, suddenly realizing he was starving.

"Hullo," a voice said.

He looked over the top of the menu and saw a petite girl holding a notepad and pen. She had shoulder-length black hair worn in a sleek bob and very pale skin, and she was wearing jeans and a worn tee shirt that said "Manchester United" on the front. But that wasn't what held him immobile.

It was her eyes. They were huge, long-lashed, and the most luminous shade of grey he'd ever seen.

He had seen those eyes before, somewhere.

"Hey. You okay?" Adam asked.

Daniel ignored him. His universe had narrowed to a tiny corridor where he and the girl simply stared at each other.

"I'm Daniel," he said.

"I-I know," she said softly. "I don't know how, but I know." She smiled.

"My name is Eve. Eve MacDonald."

AUTHOR'S NOTES

THE HENDERSON STONE

Truth can indeed be stranger than fiction, a case in point being the Henderson Stone of Glencoe. In fact, the massacre was considered a failure, as only thirty-eight men and women died that night rather than the intended wholesale extermination of a clan, and the reason for that lay with the perpetrators themselves.

Most of the men of the Earl of Argyll's Regiment did not know what they had been sent to do until the last minute. Many accounts told of efforts by the soldiers to warn their hosts.

They were Highlanders like the MacDonalds. They had eaten their food, drunk their wine, and played cards with them for eleven days, and they were horrified at the orders they were given.

One such story is that of a boulder now known as the Henderson Stone. The day before the massacre, a villager was standing with an Argyll soldier, who suddenly spoke directly to the stone, saying "Great stone of the glen, great is your right to be here! But if you knew what will happen this night, you would be up and away."

Please visit the website below for more about the strange vagaries around the Glencoe Massacre on February 13, 1692.

https://discoverglencoe.scot/key-information/
history/about-glencoe/glencoe-massacre/

ACKNOWLEDGMENTS

arl Dannenberger - My amazing husband. His tireless work to publicize, market, and promote the books allows me to live my dream. Because of him, I can just write. For GLENCOE, he was my go-to expert on building construction and job sites.

àiri MacKinnon – Kinswoman and friend. My expert on Invernese – always there even for the ridiculous questions.

enny Tomasso – Minister of Mayhem. Helps me to understand exactly where to stab someone in the most dramatic way, how to blow things up spectacularly, and where to hide the bodies.

athy Kiel – Unflinching beta reader, that greatest of friends who will be honest without worrying about the consequences.

teve and Mary Maclennan – Highlanders for Hire and the inspiration for my Highland Players. Check them out here if you want to set up an ambush or watch a reenactment of Scottish history: https://www.facebook.com/highlanders4hireltd/

ictor Cameron – The first friend I met in Scotland, who introduced a stranger to Rait Castle. He is always ready and willing to take me on another journey into the heart of the Highlands, and infuses his love for his country's history into everything he does.

rian Sharp – He runs, he photographs, he flies a drone. Owner of Mountain Wave Running: https://www.facebook.com/mountainwaverunning2, Brian took me on a tour of Glen Coe that I'll never forget, and in the process became the inspiration for Adam MacArthur in the book.

aomhìn MacFhionghuin (Kevin MacKinnon) – another kinsman I was lucky to meet in Inverness, he is a walking Highlands history book, always willing to share his huge knowledge base and love of his country's past

ABOUT THE AUTHOR

MacKinnon has always been a writer. When she was eight, she began her career with a story called "Princess Zelda", a heavily plagiarized mixture of Moses and Cinderella. It was so good (in the author's humble opinion) that she begged her mother to take it to the local library and get them to publish it. A gentle refusal to do so, while seen as a betrayal of the highest order, did not stop MacKinnon from continuing her writing,

427

although she has since learned that there are a few more steps between pencil copy and library.

MacKinnon writes emotions: love, hate, fear, redemption, second chances. Her writing is primarily historical paranormal romance with modern mystery thrown in for spice, and a little horror to stir the senses. And humor. Always humor.

MacKinnon lives in New Jersey with her husband. Two months each year are spent in the Scottish Highlands, her happy place and the source of her inspiration.

Learn more about M MacKinnon by visiting her website: www.mmackinnonwriter.com.

Or connect with her on social media:

Facebook: https://www.facebook.com/M-MacKinnon-539689769771150

Twitter: @MMacKinnon8

Instagram: www.instagram.com/mmackinnon_author

If you've enjoyed *Glencoe*, please consider giving the novel some visibility by sharing it on social media, or leaving a review on the sales platform of your choice. A review doesn't have to be a long, critical essay—just a few words expressing your thoughts, which could help potential readers decide whether they would enjoy it, too. *Tapadh leat!* (Thank you!)

Made in the USA
Middletown, DE
01 June 2023

31901797R00260